Lyn Andrews was born in Liverpool in September 1943. Her father was killed on D-Day when Lyn was just nine months old. When Lyn was three her mother Monica married Frank Moore, who became 'Dad' to the little girl. Lyn was brought up in Liverpool and became a secretary before marrying policeman Bob Andrews. In 1970 Lyn gave birth to triplets – two sons and a daughter – who kept her busy for the next few years. Once they'd gone to school Lyn began writing, and her first novel was quickly accepted for publication.

Lyn lived for eleven years in Ireland and is now resident on the Isle of Man, but spends as much time as possible back on Merseyside, seeing her children and four grandchildren.

Praise for Lyn Andrews' dramatic Merseyside novels:

'A vivid portrayal of life' *Best*

'Lyn Andrews tackles her subject with the panache of an indisputably gifted storyteller' *Historical Novels Review*

'She has a realism that is almost palpable' *Liverpool Echo*

'Gutsy . . . A vivid picture of a hard-up, hard-working community . . . will keep the pages turning' *Daily Express*

'An outstanding storyteller' *Woman's Weekly*

'The Catherine Cookson of Liverpool' *Northern Echo*

'A true page-turner for those who love a heart-warming saga' *Lancashire Evening Post*

'Plenty of realism and if you enjoy wartime sagas this one will please' *Nottingham Evening Post*

Lyn Andrews

Liverpool Songbird

HEADLINE

First published in Great Britain in 1996 by
HEADLINE PUBLISHING GROUP

This edition published in 2020 by
HEADLINE PUBLISHING GROUP

2

Cataloguing in Publication Data is available from the British Library

ISBN 9781472267399

Typeset in Palimpsest Book Production Limited,
Polmont, Stirlingshire

Printed and bound in Great Britain by Clays Ltd, Elcograf S.p.A.

Headline's policy is to use papers that are natural, renewable and recyclable
products and made from wood grown in well-managed forests and other
controlled sources. The logging and manufacturing processes are expected
to conform to the environmental regulations of the country of origin.

HEADLINE PUBLISHING GROUP
An Hachette UK Company
Carmelite House
50 Victoria Embankment
London EC4Y 0DZ

www.headline.co.uk
www.hachette.co.uk

For Ruth Gladwin of Stephens Innocent and Mark le Fanu of the Society of Authors, without whose support and advice this book would never have been published. And for Anne Williams, my editor, whose faith in me has never wavered.

AUTHOR'S NOTE

My sincere thanks go to Eric Sauder, co-author of *R.M.S. Lusitania*, for allowing me to use descriptions from his excellent and informative book, which for dedicated nautical readers is a 'must'.

I would like to point out that although *Lusitania* and *Aquitania* were built only seven years apart, there were few similarities between them. *Lusitania* being by far the most luxurious and opulent of the two, I thought it would add to the enjoyment of my readers to use the interior descriptions of the *Lucy*, as she was fondly known on Merseyside.

All the songs I have used are in the public domain.

Lyn Andrews
Southport 1995

PART ONE

Chapter One

1925

'I don't want to go, Mam! I'm tired, I want something to eat and then I just want to go to sleep.'

'Alice, luv, if you don't go, there won't *be* anything to eat. Please, luv, go for yer mam.'

Seventeen-year-old Alice O'Connor looked pleadingly at her mother. 'Can't our Lizzie go instead of me?'

'Our Lizzie can't sing, you know that. You can, so they'll cough up a few more pennies.'

Alice sighed heavily. That was true at least, but she was so tired. She was bone weary from working from morning till night in Tate and Lyle's sugar refinery at the bottom of Burlington Street. It wasn't much of a job; all she did all day was brush up, but the floor space was enormous. It was tiring, she was on the go all day and the foreman never seemed to take his eyes off her. She knew he regarded her as the dregs of society which his superiors, with misguided benevolence, saw fit to employ in the most menial capacity and pay accordingly.

Every time she looked up she caught him glaring at her.

'Use some elbow grease, Alice O'Connor, you idle little slut! Put your back into it, girl!' was what he'd bawled at her this afternoon. She wasn't idle, she was just tired. All she'd had to eat all day was a dry bun and a cup of very weak and watery tea. And she wasn't a slut either. She

3

couldn't help the way she looked because her family had nothing. The O'Connors were the poorest of the poor in Benledi Street and existed permanently in the terrifying shadow of the workhouse. It was only because of the few shillings she and her elder sister Lizzie brought home, and the generosity of the neighbours, that they still had a roof over their heads at all.

Da sometimes found work as a casual labourer down at the docks but he didn't try very hard and what he did earn was spent in one of the seventy pubs in the area, usually The Widows on Scotland Road. Sometimes Mam met him at the dock gate and tried to cajole him into parting with a shilling or two, but the price she paid was high. A black eye, cuts and bruises, or worse. Sometimes she sent Mary, who at seven was the youngest, into the pub after him. Then he was shamed into parting with some money but Mam still didn't come off lightly. He'd belt her when he got home for showing him up in front of his mates.

'Isn't there anything to eat, Mam? I'm starving.'

Nelly O'Connor shook her head. 'No, luv. I managed to cadge a couple of stale loaves from Skillicorns but the kids 'ad them when they got in from school. I've 'ad nothin' meself, Alice.'

Alice looked around the dismal kitchen despairingly. Her sisters Agnes and Mary and her brothers Eddy and Jimmy were huddled silently around the pathetic little fire that burned in the dirty, rusted cast-iron range. Their faces were pinched and white and they all wore stiff, ugly, bottle-green corduroy clothes, stamped with the letters L.C.P. so they couldn't be pawned. At least they were warm and serviceable, she thought, even though to have to wear them was in itself a stigma. They were provided by the Liverpool City Police – the scuffers, as they were known.

'Where's me da?'

4

'Where do yer think, Alice?' Nelly said sharply. It was a stupid question to ask on a Friday night when Tip had had an afternoon's work down at the Princes Half Tide dock. He would now be drinking his wages away in the pub.

Every penny he got his hands on was soon spent – on the drink. That was the cause of all their problems. Nelly didn't tell him exactly how much Lizzie or Alice earned because something had to be kept for the rent, but there was never much left for other things – the basics like food and clothes, light and heat. Every day was a struggle just to exist, to keep body and soul together. Ever since Lizzie and Alice had been babies he'd been like this. He'd become disillusioned with life and the grinding poverty they all lived in and strived hard to overcome. But there was no escape from worry and misery for Nelly. Oh, she too could have drowned her multitude of sorrows in a bottle of cheap gin, but then what would happen to her kids? Sometimes people asked her why she put up with him. Why didn't she leave? Well, where could she go with six kids? she'd answer. The workhouse, that's where.

Alice had deliberately walked along Vauxhall Road on her way home from the refinery to avoid passing the pub in case Tip saw her and demanded her wages. She knew from experience that it wasn't much use trying to hang onto them, he'd just knock her flying and take them.

'Where's our Lizzie?' she asked.

'Still on her way home, as far as I know. She said she was going to hang around Holden's shop to see if she could beg a few bits.'

'And if she does she'll eat them,' Alice said bitterly although she really didn't blame Lizzie, her sister had been working all day too. It was everyone for themselves in this family and had been for as long as she could remember, except for Mam. Mam often went without to give them whatever food there was.

The front door banged shut and then Lizzie appeared in the doorway, clutching a brown paper bag. Like Alice, she was thin and pasty-looking. Her faded flannel dress hung loosely on her and was covered by a voluminous old black shawl. Even though she was a good bit older than Alice, her stunted frame and gaunt features made her look younger.

'What did yer get, Lizzie?'

'Not much. A bit of tea, a twist of sugar an' a small tin of condensed milk.'

Nelly relieved her of the small parcel. 'Well, it's better than nowt. We can have a cup of tea at least.'

Alice looked questioningly at her mother. 'How? There's not enough fire to boil the kettle up.'

'I'll go an' get those few bits of wood from the stairs. Where's that old iron bar? Eddy, I saw you with it last.'

'I left it in the yard, Mam, yisterday.'

'Mam, if we pull any more boards off the stairs they'll fall in,' Alice added.

Nelly ignored her and went out to the yard. Downstairs all the floorboards and doors had long since been used for firewood. A fire not only gave them some warmth, it was also necessary for cooking. The younger kids scoured the streets after school, picking up rubbish from the gutters, begging old boxes, newspapers, bits of wood, rags, anything that would burn.

Lizzie sat down wearily in the old bentwood chair. 'I'm worn out an' I'm hungry an' I'm cold.'

Alice had little sympathy. 'So am I but I've got to go out again.'

'Where to?'

'Well, I'm not going far. I'll go up to the Rotunda, there's usually a good crowd on a Friday night. I wish I had some stockings and a good warm coat though.' She regarded the battered pair of men's boots she wore with thankful resignation. At least she had boots; often in the

6

past she'd gone barefoot in the depths of winter. They all had. As for a good warm coat, that was a luxury she'd never had.

Tears had misted Lizzie's grey eyes. 'I did once. Remember all those things Tommy bought me?'

Alice nodded. Once Lizzie had been 'walking out' with Tommy MacNamara from William Moult Street. The whole family were villains of the first order but he'd bought Lizzie some decent clothes and shoes and stockings. He'd also sworn to break Da's neck if he tried to pawn them and Da had been afraid of him. Lizzie had looked like a real lady then, walking arm in arm down the street with Tommy. So grown up, so smartly dressed. Lizzie had been quite attractive too. After an outing with Tommy, she would sit and tell Alice all about the places Tommy had taken her to and the people they'd met. Alice had promised Lizzie that when she was old enough to 'walk out' she'd tell her sister all the great things she'd done and seen too. But poor Tommy had been killed in the Great War and everything had gone to Solly Indigo's pawnshop in Burlington Street. A smile played around the corners of Alice's mouth. Lizzie had let her wear some of those clothes and it had felt great being warm and decently dressed.

Nelly came back with an armful of splintered stair boards which she carefully fed, piece by piece, into the range where they burned and crackled with a cheerful glow. It wouldn't last long and it did nothing to improve the room, Alice thought, looking around dejectedly. The walls were stained with brown patches of damp, as was the ceiling. The window panes were so dirty it was impossible to see out of them, not that there was anything pleasant to see other than the back yard. A piece of cotton lace curtain, grey with age and smuts from the fire, was tacked across it and two of the panes were broken, the holes stuffed with rags.

7

There was a gas jet on the wall beside the door but there was no money for a luxury such as gas light. They made do with bits of candles. There wasn't much furniture either. A table with a broken leg had been inexpertly mended with a bit of thin hemp rope twisted round and round the broken joint. A battered old armchair, from which the stuffing was protruding in several places, was pushed into the corner by the range, beside an old scarred chest of drawers. The bentwood chair, now occupied by Lizzie, four old paint tins that served as seats for the kids, and two misshapen cushions from a sofa constituted the rest of the furnishings. There were no ornaments, pictures or bric-a-brac such as other people had and they'd never owned a tablecloth or rugs for the floor.

Upstairs there were two bedrooms and neither had any furniture, just some straw-stuffed mattresses covered with stained and grubby ticking. There were no sheets, no blankets and no quilts, just a pile of old clothes, little more than rags. They all slept head to tail, Nelly in with the girls in one room, the lads in the other and they fared better because there were only two of them. Tip usually never made it upstairs but sprawled in the armchair in the kitchen.

Nelly put the kettle on the fire and when it was nearing boiling point she emptied the tea and the sugar into it. Alice went into the small, dark, airless scullery and came back with three chipped mugs. Nelly used a large iron nail to pierce the tin that contained the condensed milk, and when the soupy liquid had been transferred from the kettle to the mugs, she handed one to Alice, one to Lizzie and cupped her cold, chapped hands round the third.

'There now, get that down yer, luv, an' then get going,' she urged.

The tea was making Alice feel a bit better. 'I'm going to the chippy on the way home, Mam, but I'm going to eat my portion. I'm not havin' him pinch it off me.'

'Oh, he'll be too drunk. He'll probably have passed out long before you get back, Alice. See what you can get, luv, we're all starving and perished and that fire's dying back already.'

As she pulled the front door closed behind her, Alice shivered. It was freezing cold. The wind was from the east and it was bitter. It seemed to come down Benledi Street straight from the river as though there were no warehouses or factories in between. There was sleet mixed with it too. She pulled her shawl closely round her body, wishing again that she had a pair of thick woollen stockings and mitts for her rapidly numbing fingers.

She walked up the street and onto Scotland Road, avoiding as many of the pubs as she could, just in case one of the figures that came stumbling out was her father. It wasn't far to the Rotunda Theatre at the junction of Scotland Road and Stanley Road, but it seemed like miles when you were half starved, half frozen, and tired out. Still, if she didn't manage to get a few coppers she'd be going to bed even hungrier than she was now.

She passed a few people she knew; some spoke to her, some didn't. No one in this neighbourhood was well off but at least they all seemed to have more than she did. She was looked on with either scorn or pity at work, mainly because of her appearance. They didn't have money for coal to heat up water for such luxuries as a bath. It was hard enough for Nelly to try to keep their clothes clean, using water boiled in the kettle and carbolic soap. Once a week they did have their hair washed but the rest of the time they had to make do with cold water, a bit of rag and half a bar of Fairy soap which Nelly usually managed to buy or beg from either Mrs Holden's shop in Silvester Street or Burgess's in Burlington Street.

Alice passed Daly's Tobacconists, Stanley's Pawnshop, the Maypole Grocery, W. Costain Provision Merchants, Bentley's Cabinet Makers, and Reiglers. The smell issuing from the Pork Shop brought tears to her eyes but she trudged on until she reached Stanley Road and crossed over, threading her way between the traffic. She hoped there were no scuffers around or she'd be chased away for begging. You could actually be arrested, it depended on the mood the scuffer was in, but most of them turned a blind eye. No one would willingly go begging if they had a choice and the police seemed to understand that.

The theatre was an impressive building, built on and round the corner. It belonged to Bent's Brewery. It was four storeys high with ornate windows and stonework and topped with a dome that bore its name in large letters. On both sides were awnings over small shops, giving it the appearance of an arcade. It was brightly lit and crowds were milling around the main entrance at the front. There were Mary Ellens selling fruit and nuts and she knew she would have to compete with their bellicose cries. There were also two lads juggling with coloured balls and an old man playing a mouth organ. She sighed. It wasn't going to be easy.

She folded her shawl back from her head and ran her fingers through the mass of tangled, tawny coloured curls, unaware that despite her drab clothes, the pallor of malnutrition and exhaustion, she was a pretty girl. Her large, soft brown eyes, fringed with thick lashes, were her most attractive and appealing feature. The mass of unruly curls framed an oval face with a slightly upturned nose, high cheekbones and well-defined eyebrows.

'Well, this ain't earning money, Alice O'Connor,' she said firmly to herself, so she took a deep breath and began to sing.

> Just a song at twilight,
> When the lights are low
> Where the flickering shadows,
> Softly come and go.

Her clear, strong, soprano voice rose above the discordant notes of the harmonica and people began to take notice of her.

She progressed slowly along the arcade on the right of the building to the arcade on the left and back again, her hand held out appealingly. She was truly grateful for the pennies and halfpennies that were pressed into it but she realised she should have got here earlier. She'd noticed the time on a clock in Stanley's window. It was after seven and the show started at half past. People wanted to be in their seats by then. She began 'Beautiful Dreamer' but the crowd was thinning and the doorman was eyeing her menacingly. The jugglers and the old man had gone but she put her heart and soul into the last verse, knowing that in a few minutes everyone would have gone inside and further effort would be a waste of breath.

As the last notes died away, a well-dressed lady dropped a silver threepenny bit into her hand.

'You have a lovely voice, child. Such a pity it will be wasted. With training and grooming you could be inside on the stage, instead of out here begging.' She smiled kindly before turning and hurrying inside.

Alice stood alone on the pavement. The commissionaire had closed the doors, shutting out the biting wind, but he continued to regard her with hostility through the glass panels. For a few seconds she stared malevolently back, then turned away. The lady had said she could be in there singing, if she had the right training and grooming, whatever that meant. It was something that had never occurred to her. People did earn their living singing, and a good living it was too. You only had to see the number of punters who crowded into the 'Roundy' to realise that. She'd only ever sung in the streets of Liverpool and she'd done that from the time Mam had realised she had a voice people would listen to and had taught her a couple of songs. They were old-fashioned now but no one seemed to mind. It was a form of begging but they'd all been very glad of the coppers she'd managed to earn.

What was it like in there? she wondered. Where did they all sit, or did they stand, and what kind of people performed? She peered closely at a large, brightly coloured poster pasted to the sooty bricks of the wall. There was Leo Barnes, the world-famous ventriloquist, whatever that was. Sidney Romano, a virtuoso on no less than five instruments, and Miss Letty Lewis, the Cockney Songbird. She read the words slowly, hesitating over the unfamiliar ones. She had gone to school, spasmodically, and could read and write and add up in her head. What exactly was a Cockney Songbird, though? Maybe it was a stuffed bird in a cage that sang when you turned the handle. She'd seen one of those in Solly's shop once. Did this Letty Lewis have one of those?

Hunger put a stop to her deliberations and she walked quickly back to Reigler's shop.

'A whole meat and tattie pie, please, mister.'

'Have you got the money, girl?' Fred Reigler asked suspiciously. He'd been caught out like that before. There were so many hungry kids in this area, aye, and they were crafty too.

'Yes, I have. Here.' Alice indignantly handed over the coins.

A hot pie the size of a man's fist, with a thick pastry crust, was passed over to her. She walked out, breaking pieces off and stuffing them into her mouth. Oh, nothing had ever tasted so good and she still had sixpence left for Mam.

She finished the pie and found herself standing at the top of the entry, or jigger, that ran behind the theatre and out into Boundary Street. Now that her belly was reasonably full her curiosity was aroused. She decided to see if there was another way into the building, a back door maybe.

There was, but there was also an old man, reading a newspaper, sitting in a little box-like room. Flattening herself against the wall she sneaked past and walked cautiously down the dark, narrow passageway. The sound of people clapping became louder, which intensified her curiosity. She wanted to see what it was like inside and who everyone was applauding.

Halfway along the jigger there was a trap door, like the doors leading into the cellars many of the houses in the surrounding streets had. It opened quite easily and she realised that it must be the entrance for deliveries. She slid neatly down the slight incline and found herself in a gloomy, narrow corridor lit by a single gas jet. The clapping was louder now and nearer. Two doors faced her. She bit her lip wondering what was on the other side of them. Tentatively she reached out and pushed the larger of the two gently. It opened a crack and she peered through, her eyes widening in amazement. The theatre was huge and there were hundreds of seats. Like armchairs, they were, and covered in a soft red material. The stage was brilliantly lit and heavy red curtains edged with gold fringe were looped back across it, revealing a backcloth depicting a sunny flower garden. She'd never seen anything like it in her life. It was like something from a dream.

Her eyes grew wider and her astonishment increased as she heard the orchestra play the opening bars of 'Beautiful Dreamer'. Her gaze fell on the tall, slender figure of Letty Lewis. She had masses of golden curls piled high on her head, held up with a silver ribbon. She wore an evening gown of pale pink satin that sparkled with beads and silver fringe. But what fascinated Alice was the song she was singing. She could sing *that* song just as well as Letty Lewis, if not better. Hadn't the lady who'd given her the threepenny bit told her so? She watched, totally enthralled, until Miss Lewis had finished, taken two bows and

13

left the stage, then she closed the door on that enchanted world.

She looked down at her creased and grubby skirt, black shawl and heavy boots, at her red, work-roughened hands with their broken, dirty nails. No one would ever pay a lot of money to listen to her sing, like they had for Miss Letty Lewis, the Cockney Songbird.

The few coins she'd earned were clutched tightly in her hand and she remembered that Mam would be waiting for them. No, there would be no stage in a fancy theatre for little Alice O'Connor, just the cold, harsh streets of Liverpool.

Chapter Two

Alice trudged home with as much energy as she could muster. It was easy to pick out their house, she thought; it was the only one in Benledi Street that was in darkness. The bits of candle stubs didn't give out much light. She peeped enviously in through the windows of those houses where the curtains hadn't been drawn. Inside them there was light and warmth and people she was sure had easier, more comfortable lives than her own.

Only Mam and Lizzie were in the kitchen. Lizzie was curled up in the armchair with her feet tucked under her, her shawl swathed tightly round her. It was the best way to try to keep warm. Mam was sitting in the bentwood chair, her eyes screwed up in concentration as she poked pieces of cardboard into the boots of Eddy, Jimmy and Mary who were all obviously in bed.

'I got sixpence, Mam, and I've had a pie so there's no need to fetch me anything else. I was a bit late getting started but a lady gave me a threepenny bit.'

Nelly got to her feet. 'Here, Lizzie, you finish this. I'm going up to Daly's for chips and I'll stop off on the way and see what I can get from Burgess's.'

Lizzie reluctantly uncurled herself and picked up Jimmy's boots while Alice sat in the chair her mother had vacated.

'Don't be too long, Mam, or *he'll* be in.'

Nelly didn't need Lizzie to remind her of that, and worn

out though she was, she managed to hurry down the hall.

'Give me a pair, Lizzie, I'll help you,' Alice offered, picking up Mary's boots. They were at least two sizes too big for their younger sister and had to be kept on with bits of rope passed under the instep and tied across the top. They rubbed, and Mary always had blisters.

Lizzie handed Alice a piece of thick cardboard and Alice sighed. It wasn't an easy task because they had no scissors or even a sharp knife. In the dim light she began to tear off a piece.

'Do you think we'll ever have decent boots or be able to pay to have them cobbled when they get holes in them?'

Lizzie shrugged carelessly. 'I suppose the kids will all grow up and get jobs an' maybe our Agnes and Mary will get married.'

Alice paused. 'Wouldn't it be great if we could get married, Lizzie? Just think, to get away from here and *him*!'

Lizzie was scornful. 'What feller would want you or me? Look at the pair of us. Walkin' rag bags, we are, and with not a pick on us.'

'Tommy Mac wanted you, Lizzie.'

'Aye, that's when I was a bit of a kid. Besides, there's not many around here like Tommy. He understood. He was brought up – dragged up – like us, Alice.'

'We've not been dragged up. Mam takes care of us the best way she can. How many hidings has she had so we can eat? Ma Mac never gave a hoot for any of her kids.'

Alice poked her fingers into the body of the boot, squashing the cardboard down as flat as she could, knowing from experience how lumpy cardboard chafed. 'I went and had a look inside the Roundy. I went down the back jigger. Oh, Lizzie, you should have seen it! It was dead posh! And there was a lady singing, Miss Letty Lewis, the Cockney Songbird. I'll always remember that name. She looked like an angel, Lizzie, I swear to God she did.'

Lizzie knew what the inside of the theatre was like. Tommy had taken her, a lifetime ago. When she thought about it, it brought tears to her eyes. 'It's a waste of time lookin' in places like that, Alice. It only makes you more miserable in the end.'

'It doesn't. Do you know what she was singing, Lizzie? One of *my* songs. I could have sung it better too. The lady who gave me the threepenny joey told me I could.'

'Oh, stop tellin' fibs, Alice!'

'I'm not! She did say it. Training and grooming she said I needed, and then I could sing on the stage.'

Any further argument was curtailed as the front door was thrown inward with a crash that made the window panes rattle. The two girls looked at each other with dread.

'It's Da!' Lizzie whispered fearfully.

'An' before Mam's back! Get a move on, Lizzie! Go out the back way an' warn her. He'll scoff her chips and poor Mam must be faint with hunger by now.'

Lizzie sprang to her feet, panic giving her strength, and darted into the scullery just as Tip O'Connor staggered into the kitchen from the hall.

Alice forced herself to smile and be pleasant.

'Hello, Da. Sit down here.'

Tip ignored her, glaring through small bloodshot eyes at the dreary, dimly lit room. 'Where's your mam?'

'Out, lookin' for firewood. She won't be long,' Alice lied stoutly, praying that Lizzie would be able to waylay Nelly at the top of the street. 'Why don't yer go up to bed? I'll give yer a hand. There's a few holes in the stairs.' She wished malevolently that he'd fall through the stairs from top to bottom.

Again he ignored her but lurched over to the chest of drawers and wrenched open the top one where Nelly kept what few bits of spare clothing they had.

'Where's she hid it?' he bellowed.

17

'Hid what, Da?'

'Me dinner! Where's me bloody dinner?'

'Da, you know there's nothing in there but bits an' bobs of clothes.'

He rounded on her. 'Then where's she put me bloody dinner?'

'There ain't none. We've had nothin' either, Da. Mam was waiting for you, for your wages, like.' She didn't dare look at him. She fixed her eyes on the floor.

'Bloody leeches, the lot of yer! Always wantin' money. Where can I get money? Who's going ter give me any bleedin' money?'

'I know, Da,' Alice coaxed, 'times is bad. Sit down an' get a bit of sleep.' If she could get him off to sleep, not even the house falling down around him would wake him, but he was being belligerent and obstinate. He staggered into the scullery and she heard the three mugs and two plates being smashed and thanked God that the kettle and the stew pan were made of stronger stuff, although they were acquiring a few more dents by the sounds of it.

'Alice O'Connor, were you born in a barn? Leavin' the door open like that!'

Alice froze as she heard Nelly's voice. Lizzie hadn't managed to warn her. She darted to the doorway waving her arms and mouthing the words 'Me da! Me da!' but she was too late. Nelly walked into the room, a greasy parcel and a paper bag hugged against her, just as Tip emerged from the scullery.

Nelly's eyes narrowed and she pursed her lips. She wasn't going to part with the chips readily. She was no match for him, she never had been, but as she thought of the kids shivering upstairs, Lizzie out God knows where and seeing Alice with fear in her eyes, a hard glitter came into Nelly O'Connor's tired eyes.

'Giz me dinner!' Tip demanded.

'Our Alice went out tramping the streets – singing –

for the money for this, an' we're all hungry. You could have bought your own dinner, you had wages.' She knew what the result of this defiance would be and braced herself.

The blow sent her reeling against the wall but she hung grimly onto the parcel of food even though her ears were ringing and lights danced sickeningly before her eyes.

He lunged towards her again but Alice stepped in front of him. 'Leave me mam alone!' she yelled.

'Shut yer bleedin' gob!' Tip yelled back, catching her by her hair, shaking her as though she was a rag doll and then throwing her in the direction of Nelly's cowed form.

Alice bit back the tears of pain. He must have pulled out a handful of her hair.

'Get to bed, luv! Get up the stairs and leave him ter me,' Nelly hissed.

Tip's attention was caught and held for a second by the figure of Lizzie standing transfixed with terror in the doorway.

'Get hold of our Lizzie an' the pair of you get to bed!' Nelly urged.

Lizzie needed no telling. She ran. But Alice didn't follow her. Stubbornly she stood in front of her mother although Nelly tried to push her away.

Tip made another attempt to grab the food, brushing Alice to one side. Nelly turned her back on him and then with a groan fell to her knees as his clenched fist hit her squarely in the middle of the back.

'Mam! Mam!' Alice screamed although all this was nothing new. She'd been brought up with his drunken violence. 'Give him the flaming chips, Mam!'

Nelly didn't answer and Tip sent her sprawling with a kick.

It was too much for Alice. The unfairness, the injustice, the sheer brutality shot through her like a flame. Looking round she seized the wooden chair and with all the

19

strength she could muster lifted it above her head and smashed it down hard across her father's head and shoulders. It broke into pieces and uttering a roar like a wounded bull, Tip turned on her.

She managed to shield herself with her arms from the first couple of blows, but then he kicked out at her knees and her legs buckled. She lay on the floor curled up in a ball trying to protect her head and her stomach. Each burst of pain was worse than the last and faintly she could hear both her mam and Lizzie screaming. Then there were other voices, the pain became unbearable, and she felt herself sinking into a black abyss.

When she came to, Alice was lying on the mattress in the bedroom. Her whole body felt as though it was on fire and as she tried to move, a groan of agony escaped her.

'Lie still, Alice, luv. He's probably cracked your ribs.'

'Mam? Mam, are you all right? Where is . . . he?'

Nelly smoothed the straggling wisps of hair from her daughter's face. 'He's downstairs, out cold, Alice. Lizzie ran up the road for Alf an' Bernie Maguire. She said he was killing you. Bernie laid into him with his docker's hook. I thought he'd killed him, but he's just unconscious.'

Tears of pain, relief and exhaustion slid down Alice's thin cheeks. 'Oh, Mam. I'm hurtin'.'

'Hush, luv. It's all right, yer mam's here. Get some sleep now, you'll feel better in the morning.' Nelly doubted she would but there was no money for doctors and she wouldn't let them take Alice to hospital. No one ever came out alive from hospitals.

Alice closed her eyes. She felt that bad she wished she was dead. She wished Da had killed her, then she'd be out of her misery and the scuffers would come for him and he'd hang at the end of a rope in Walton Jail. It would have been better for everyone. Tomorrow, well, tomorrow she'd have to try and drag herself to work, or failing that she'd have to go singing in the streets, they *had* to have money. And it would all go on and on, forever. Her sobs increased although it hurt her to cry. She couldn't face any more, she just couldn't. She'd run away. She'd manage on her own and it would be one less mouth to feed, one less for Mam to worry about. But what about Mam? Oh, she was too tired, too shaken up and sore to think any more. But she had to get away. If Da started again, she'd kill him. She didn't know how, but she would, and then she'd be the one they would hang.

She couldn't move the next morning. Waves of pain washed over her and every joint ached. Nelly brought her a cup of weak tea and a slice of bread and dripping, but she couldn't eat it. She begged her mam to have it but Nelly shook her head firmly and said she'd give it to Lizzie. She also said that Bernie Maguire had been back. He'd come up and looked at her and then gone downstairs, hauled her da into the back yard and belted him hard, swearing it would be nothing compared to what he'd do if he ever laid a hand on Alice again.

'So, that should keep him quiet for a bit, any road,' Nelly finished with grim satisfaction.

Alice turned her head away. For how long though? Her da had a short memory. Bernie had belted Da before when he'd thrown little Mary bodily out of the front door into the street. It hadn't stopped him starting on them when his bruises had gone down, and the Maguires would only step in when they felt like it. No one would dream of sending for the scuffers if they thought things could be sorted out among themselves.

Alice drifted in and out of sleep all day and all night, and when she woke again properly she knew what she was going to do. She wasn't going to stay here. She'd find herself a room – just a cubbyhole would do – and she'd work all day and sing all night. She'd bring money home to Mam but she wasn't going to live in Benledi Street any

21

longer. She couldn't. She just couldn't stand the sight of Da any more, whether drunk or sober. She didn't trust herself. She'd be gripped by that terrible rage again and she'd kill him, even if she had to wait until he was asleep to do it. She *had* to get out.

Three days later she left the house. She'd told no one of her intentions – Lizzie would have tried to stop her and then would have told Mam. It hurt her to think about the worry she would cause her mother but she knew Nelly would have begged and pleaded with her and she couldn't have stood that.

As she walked slowly and still painfully up the street, she didn't turn round. When she reached Scotland Road she noticed the shops being decorated and realised it must be nearly Christmas time. That meant that a Cooper's van would come round and a parcel would soon be delivered to number ten Benledi Street, from the Goodfellows Society. It meant food, exotic and luxurious food like oranges, apples, fruitcake and capon. Food they never saw at any other time of the year. Da would lay claim to most of it but it comforted her a little to think that her share would go to Lizzie, the kids or Mam.

She had no money so it was useless to try to find a room yet. Instead she made her way down Burlington Street, across the bridge over the canal and to the gates of the sugar refinery. They were locked and she called to the keeper who came out of his little hut and glared at her.

'What do yer want?'

'I work here. I'm the brusher-up.'

'Not any more, you ain't. Mr Roscoe said he ain't seen hide nor hair of yer since Monday, so they've got someone else. Now, clear off an' stop wastin' me time.'

She turned away, stunned. It was something she hadn't thought about. She had been too preoccupied with other things, but she should have known. Jobs weren't kept open, there were always a dozen people waiting to fill your shoes if you didn't turn up. She sat down on the step of the Golden Fleece, near to tears. Now what could she do? She hadn't reckoned on losing her job. She watched a couple of barefoot urchins poking at something in the gutter, something that moved. They squealed with laughter and jabbed at it again with a sharp piece of wood. She caught the faint distressed mewing and picking up a stone she hurled it at them.

'Gerroff! Leave the poor thing alone, you cruel little sods!'

One of them rubbed his arm where the stone had caught it and they both thumbed their noses at her before running off across the road. She got up and went over to the edge of the kerb. A tiny, scrawny black and white kitten was lying on its side. She bent down and scooped it up, tucking it into the crook of her arm and covering it tenderly with her shawl. The poor little thing was half dead but she couldn't leave it here. It looked too young to have been taken from its mother; how it had escaped being drowned in the canal she didn't know.

'We're a bit alike, you and me, cat. Half starved, beaten up, an' with nowhere to go,' she said aloud. Well, standing in the middle of Burlington Street feeling miserable wasn't solving anything for herself or this poor scrap. It was a long walk into town so she'd better get going.

Church Street and Lord Street were her best bets. There were always plenty of shoppers around. She'd stop and have a rest and a drink of water from the Steble Fountain at the top of William Brown Street, then maybe she'd head to Castle Street and Water Street where all the offices were. People would come streaming out onto the street at lunch time. After that, if her voice and her strength held out, she'd go to the Pier Head; that, too, was always crowded. If she was lucky, by the end of the day she might well have earned enough to pay for a bed for the night, a hot meal at the Sally Army place and some milk for the poor creature who lay shivering under her shawl. Tomorrow she'd really try and get herself sorted out.

Just the thought of not having to go back to Benledi Street made her feel much better, much brighter and more optimistic, so she quickened her steps as she headed for Byrom Street.

Chapter Three

She hadn't done too badly, she thought, as she sat on the steps of the Trafalgar Memorial in the middle of Exchange Flags, the open space at the back of the Town Hall. It was surrounded by fine buildings, including the Cotton Exchange, the centre of trade in the commodity on which the wealth of the city had been founded. These days the business was done inside and not out on the Flags, but there were always people hurrying about, mainly messenger boys.

The kitten was still lying in the crook of her arm. She'd earned a shilling and she'd reckoned the kitten had helped. People had caught sight of it and their expression had softened. Maybe it was a lucky charm, or maybe it was because people felt more generous, it being nearly Christmas.

The afternoon was bleak. Grey clouds went scudding across the sky, driven by a strong north-easterly wind. It would be colder and more blustery down at the Pier Head where the wind gusted in from the Mersey estuary, but it couldn't be helped. If she was to be able to afford a hot meal and a bed, she'd have to earn at least another sixpence.

She got to her feet and walked towards the back of the Town Hall and out into Castle Street where the wind cut through her thin clothes, making her shiver. A lazy wind, Mam called it. It went through you instead of round you.

She turned right down Water Street which led to the George's Dock Gate, the Pier Head and the landing stage. She'd start at the entrance to the Riverside Station, keeping out of the way of the scuffer. Posh folk arrived there on the boat trains, to board the big liners that went all over the world. She wished she knew more than two songs. She was getting sick to death of her small repertoire.

She took up her position on the corner of Prince's Parade at the head of the line of waiting cabs, both horse-drawn and motorised. The kitten was now lying on her breast with its head poking out from the folds of her shawl and the first passengers from the Euston to Liverpool boat train were emerging. There was the usual cluster of porters and half a dozen or so street urchins darted in and out between them, pleading to be allowed to carry bags and cases for a penny. They continued to tout for business until they were chased off by the porters, for they often ran off with the luggage. She was heartened to see a good many well-dressed people emerging into the cold winter's afternoon, pulling fur collars closer round their ears. Gloved hands held small, smart hats more securely against the gusts of wind. She took a rather painful breath, attempted to square her shoulders and began.

> Beautiful dreamer
> Wake unto me,
> Starlight and moonlight
> Are waiting for thee ...

A couple of coins were dropped into her hand but then she caught sight of the burly figure of a policeman, accompanied by a railway official, bearing down on her and she quickly turned and melted into the crowd, following the throng along the Prince's Landing Stage, out of sight of the officers of the law and the London and North-Western Railway Company.

On the landing stage itself there were carriages and horse-drawn wagons and a good many people going about their business. The mountainous black hull of the biggest liner in the world, Cunard's *Aquitania*, towered above everything. Its four red and black funnels disgorged black smoke, a sign of its imminent departure.

Well, this was as good a place as any, she thought, taking up her stance by the small wooden Post Office. It was noisy, very noisy and she knew she would have to put more effort into her performance just to be heard above the shouts of news vendors, carters and the repeated blasts of the steam whistle of the *Duchess of York*, the signal warning those crew members still inside the Style House that it was time to drink up and get aboard.

With a lot of difficulty she had started into the second verse of 'Just A Song At Twilight' when a motorcar coming along tooted its horn loudly and repeatedly and the kitten leaped from her arms.

She uttered a shriek, her song forgotten, as the little animal tottered over the cobbles and beneath the hooves of a shire horse that had also been startled by the din.

'No! No, Mog, come back!' she screamed, darting out after it.

'Hey! Hey, you! Look out! *Look out!*'

She heard the cry and turned her head in time to see the gleaming metal of the car's radiator at close range. She opened her mouth to scream but the breath was knocked out of her as the bonnet of the car caught her squarely and tossed her onto the road.

She was oblivious of the commotion around her as the two young men in the car jumped out.

'Oh, God, she's not dead, is she?' the younger of the two cried, looking down anxiously.

David Williamson bent over her, holding her wrist, feeling for the pulse. 'No, she's breathing but how badly she's hurt I can't tell. I don't think we should move her.'

Charles Williamson gnawed his bottom lip. 'She just ran out in front of me! She never even looked!'

'No one's blaming you, Charlie,' David said curtly. 'But what the hell are we going to do?' He looked around. The small crowd was dispersing, losing interest once they'd seen it was only a slum girl who'd been knocked down, no one of any importance.

'Isn't there a policeman anywhere?' Charlie asked.

His brother looked up at the *Aquitania*, his expression harassed. 'I haven't got time for questions, statements or form filling. I'm supposed to be aboard now.'

'Well, I can't hang about either. I promised I'd be back with the car and Father will be furious if I'm late. You know how keen he is to be off early to Southport, to this reception at the Prince of Wales.'

David Williamson made a decision. He'd told Charlie to get a move on, hence their unusual speed. Then he'd seen something leap from the girl's arms and she'd screamed and run after it. So, in his opinion he was partly to blame for what had happened. 'We can't just leave her here,' he said. 'I'll have to take her aboard. I'll carry her, you bring my case.'

His brother was appalled. 'You can't do that! They'll have a fit! Just look at the state of her.'

'I don't intend to keep her for the voyage, Charlie. There's a doctor on board. I'll get him to have a look at her then give her some money and fetch a cab to take her to hospital if she needs to go.'

'Mister! 'Ere, mister, this is 'er cat.'

David Williamson's attention was diverted by a small and very scruffy boy who with one hand tugged at his uniform jacket and with the other held out a tiny, mud-spattered kitten, dangling it by the scruff of its neck.

'It's that damned cat! The one that caused all this!' Charlie glared at the animal.

'It's 'ers, honest it is, sir.' The lad looked hopefully up

at David. As soon as he'd seen the men jump from the car and the crowd start to gather he'd darted over to where the carter was hanging on hard to the bridle of the horse, pushed quickly and fearlessly between the huge, iron-shod hooves and yanked the tiny bundle of fur up from the cobbles and out of danger.

'Charlie, give him a couple of pence and bring the cat too.'

Charlie Williamson cast his eyes towards the grey sky before handing over the money and relieving the lad of the kitten. With his thumb and forefinger he held it up and looked at it with disdain. It was a sorry creature.

As David picked Alice up gently, she moaned; her eyelids flickered open and then closed again. He explained the position briefly to the Third Electrical Officer who was stationed at the crew gangway.

The man looked askance at Alice's limp form and the kitten that Charlie was holding. 'I'm not taking responsibility for anything. Not her or the livestock!' he grunted.

'Oh, for God's sake, Robinson, I'm not asking you to! She'll be off the ship before we sail and so will the cat.'

'On your own head be it then. If the old man hears about it there'll be hell to pay.'

'If no one tells him, he won't know about it, will he?' David snapped. 'Come on, Charlie, bring the flaming cat, and then go for Dr Kendrick. Anyone will direct you to the surgery.'

As he carried Alice for'ard to the officers' quarters, along the narrow companionways that hummed with the vibration of the huge engines that would turn the four massive screws when she sailed out of the Mersey in an hour's time, the few crew members he encountered just stared or raised their eyes to the ceiling and passed on their way to perform their allotted duties. That all junior officers were mad was the general consensus of the lower ranks.

The junior engineers' quarters were far from spacious or luxurious. A small cabin, seven foot by seven foot, was fitted out with a bunk, a small washbasin and stand, and a set of drawers and wardrobe combined. There was hardly room for one person, let alone more. David laid Alice down on the bunk and removed her dirty, battered boots.

Beneath his brusque exterior, David Williamson was a compassionate young man. He had two younger sisters and he had been brought up to show sympathy for the plight of the poor. Admittedly, living as he did in Crosby, he didn't come into contact with many of the sad wretches, but he'd seen enough of their lives in the squalid dock areas that seemed to characterise all the ports he'd ever visited to realise how desperate their existences must be.

Taking a towel from the washbasin he soaked it with cold water, wrung it out and wiped some of the dust and grime away from the girl's face, and suddenly realised that she was quite lovely. Thin, too thin, but with some flesh on her bones and decent clothes on her back she would be quite a beauty. He looked anxiously at his watch. He had to report for duty in ten minutes, they were sailing in an hour's time.

Charlie and the doctor arrived simultaneously and crowded into the tiny cabin.

'What's all this about, Williamson? Oh, I see.' Kendrick nodded his understanding as he caught sight of Alice on the bunk. She was beginning to show signs of movement but his attention was diverted by the kitten which, deposited by Charlie, had curled up beside Alice and gone to sleep. 'What the hell is that?'

'It's hers. She ran after it, straight out in front of the car. There wasn't anything we could do,' David informed him.

'Then why the hell didn't you take her and it to the Royal Infirmary or the Northern Hospital?'

'Er, no time, really. Got to get back with the car, you see,' Charlie explained hurriedly.

'Well, it was a bloody stupid decision to bring her on board, that's all I can say. I should report you.' He scowled. 'Well, let's have a look at her then.'

Alice was still stunned. The small, crowded unfamiliar room kept closing in on her and then retreating and there was a strange humming noise and a warm, oily sort of smell. She struggled to get up.

'Hold on, young lady. Lie still for a few more minutes.'

She stared up at him apprehensively; no one had ever called her young lady. 'Who are you?'

'I'm a doctor who should be checking his drugs, dressings, surgical appliances and nursing staff, that's who.'

Alice lay still, barely taking in his words, but reassured by the quiet authority in his voice. The humming noise was soothing and she relaxed as gentle hands examined her.

'A bit bruised. Maybe a cracked rib or two, I can't really tell, and probably concussed. We can't keep her but she really should go to hospital for observation.'

The word 'hospital' galvanised Alice and she struggled to sit up. 'I'm not going to no hospital! It's . . . it's like the workhouse. You never come out of no hospital alive, me mam says so!'

'Don't be ridiculous, girl, this is nineteen twenty-five! You need rest and nourishing food and,' he added under his breath, 'a bath.' He turned to David. 'There's no serious damage. Nothing that a few days' rest won't cure.' Squeezing past Charlie, he opened the door with some difficulty.

'Thanks.'

'No trouble, but get her and it ashore before you ruin your career entirely.'

Alice stared around her timidly. 'Where . . . where is this?'

31

David smiled reassuringly. 'A cabin on board the *Aquitania*.'

Her eyes widened. 'What?'

'Don't get alarmed. You ran out after your kitten in front of the car and I brought you here. And the kitten's not hurt. That was the ship's doctor. How do you feel now?'

'Sore. It hurts when I breathe and if I can't breathe properly, I can't sing.'

'Sing?'

'That's how I earn me living . . . now. Street singing.'

'Don't you have a family?'

'Yes, but . . . but I don't live with them any more. Me da . . . well, it was him that cracked me ribs, not your car. So I left.'

He looked at her pityingly. 'What's your name?'

'Alice. Alice O'Connor.'

'Well, Alice O'Connor, I'm sorry but you can't stay here, we sail soon.'

'Where to?'

'New York. America,' he added in case she didn't know where the city of New York was.

She looked up at him wistfully. He was really handsome. He had thick, dark, curly hair, his face was tanned and his brown eyes were full of concern. He'd been kind to her and it was warm and comfortable in here. She wished she could stay. She was sure she'd like America.

'Are you sure you feel all right?'

She nodded but the movement caused her to close her eyes and clasp her head.

'No, you're not!'

'I'm just hungry. I haven't had nothing to eat all day.'

'Nothing? Nothing at all?'

'No.'

He glanced at Charlie appalled. 'Good God Almighty! Why didn't you say so?' It had never occurred to him that she might be starving.

32

She didn't reply.

He dug into his pocket and handed her a coin. 'Here, my brother will take you ashore. Go and get something to eat and then take a hackney cab up to the hospital. Tell them what happened and what Kendrick said about concussion.'

She stared in utter disbelief at the coin in the grubby palm of her hand. It was a guinea, a golden guinea! She'd never even seen one before but she had heard about them. 'All this . . . is for me?'

'It won't go far,' he said, thinking that he spent more on a suit than she had probably seen in her entire life. As the eldest son of a solicitor he'd never known hardship. Quite the opposite. He experienced a strong pang of guilt. Time was pressing and Charlie was fidgeting. 'Here, seeing as we've managed to deprive you of your livelihood for a while, you'd better have this too.' A ten-shilling note was thrust at her and she snatched it from him before he changed his mind. This was certainly worth getting knocked over for. She picked up the kitten and gently folded her shawl round it. It mewed weakly at being disturbed. It *had* brought her luck, she thought. She'd been right to keep it.

Gently David helped her off the bunk, gave her her boots and guided her to the door. 'You will go to the hospital when you've eaten?' he asked firmly.

She smiled up at him. 'Yes.'

The smile was one of pure joy and it completely transformed her face. She was truly beautiful when she smiled, despite the dirt, he thought. 'Promise me?'

'I said I'll go, didn't I?' she answered him. But not when, she added to herself.

'Goodbye then, Alice O'Connor, and good luck with your singing.'

'Who knows, one day we might be paying to come and listen to you,' Charlie interrupted heartily, attempting to

33

cover his embarrassment and his eagerness to get away and be rid of her. She looked a fright.

David saw the look of wonderment that filled her eyes. He frowned at his brother and shook his head. Trust Charlie! Why the hell had he said such a fatuous thing? Why go putting fantastic and utterly unattainable notions in her head?

When they'd gone he looked down at the bunk and sighed. He'd have to get it stripped – the cat would have had fleas and she was probably alive with bugs. Poor girl, a verminous state was something she obviously couldn't help, part and parcel no doubt, of being poor.

He dismissed her from his mind as, reaching for his cap and glancing at his watch, he turned his thoughts to his duties and the impending dressing-down that was almost certainly waiting for him.

Chapter Four

Robinson acknowledged Charlie and Alice with a nod as they went ashore but Alice was too preoccupied to notice. Get a meal, her rescuer had said, but that in itself presented a serious problem. Who would believe that she had been given a sovereign and a ten-shilling note? She'd get arrested for stealing, sure as eggs were eggs. She clutched Charlie's arm.

'What's the matter now?' he asked apprehensively, hoping she wasn't going to faint or cause him to lose more precious time. He should have been on his way back now. Nor was he very happy about leaving his father's brand new Minerva down on the waterfront. It was locked but there would be a tremendous row if the paintwork was marked. He sighed, thinking of the sporty little Jowett two-seater he'd set his heart on. He didn't want to get into his parents' bad books.

'Will you come with me, like?'

'Where to?'

'Over there. That eating house.'

'I haven't got time to be escorting you into eating houses.'

Alice stared at him hard. He'd been driving the car so it was his fault and he wasn't going to deprive her of a slap-up meal.

'Well, I'll get arrested if you don't. No one's going to believe that someone like me, in this state, has come by all this money honestly, like, now are they?'

She had a point, he admitted to himself reluctantly. He was embarrassed by the odd glances they were attracting, the fresh-faced, well-dressed young man and this dirty, scruffy, undernourished ragamuffin. He just hoped people weren't thinking he'd picked her up. Paid for her 'services'.

'An' if I get nicked then what will you tell him?' She jerked her head in the direction of the landing stage and the *Aquitania*.

'Oh, all right. I'll come with you and tell them you didn't steal it, but that's all. I'm late. Very late.'

Alice nodded with satisfaction. It was getting dark and as soon as she'd eaten she'd have to think things over. She'd have to make new plans, for she'd never imagined she'd have such wealth. 'Where do you live?' she asked conversationally.

'Crosby.'

She'd heard of it. 'Is that far?'

He shrugged. 'It depends on how you look at it. It's not far by car or train, but it is if you have to walk.'

They had reached their objective and Charlie pushed open the half-glazed door for her then followed her in.

It was warm and fuggy inside, thick with odours of food, stale fat and unwashed bodies. Alice sat down at a bare wooden table in the window and he went to the counter to explain the situation to the burly harridan who appeared to be in charge of things.

'That ... that girl over there,' he pointed to Alice who nodded. 'She's got money but it's not stolen. My brother gave it to her.'

The woman stared at him unblinkingly.

'Yes, well, I ... I just wanted you to know that she didn't steal it.'

The woman looked him up and down and Charlie began to blush.

'Right. Fine,' he muttered, turning away. He needed a drink but he wasn't going to get one until he got home. If they hadn't stopped at the George on the way to the ship, all this would never have happened. He went back to Alice.

'Right, that's settled,' he announced with relief. 'Goodbye and good luck.'

She smiled at him and he turned and walked to the door.

'Hey!' she called.

Charlie turned. 'Now what?' His tone was sharp.

'You never told me your name, or his.'

'Mine's Charlie Williamson and my brother's name is David. Now goodbye, Alice O'Connor.'

She watched him disappear into the winter gloom, and then turned her mind to important things. Like food and a saucer of bread and milk for Mog.

She ordered soup, mutton chops with peas and boiled potatoes, jam sponge pudding with custard and extra bread and butter and a pot of tea.

''Ave everything that's on offer, why don't yer! Save time an' me bloody legs!' the blowsy waitress remarked sarcastically.

'I might just do that an' all,' Alice shot back. 'An' anyway, it's yer job.' It must be last Christmas since she'd had as much food to eat and the whole lot only came to two shillings! She could more than afford it. There were still eight whole shillings left from the ten-bob note. The guinea was pushed inside the pocket of her skirt and she'd tied a knot in the pocket to keep it safe. She clasped the thought of her riches to her in astonished delight.

When the edge had been taken off her hunger her headache started to recede and she began to take more notice of what was going on around her and beyond the window. She jumped nervously as the *Aquitania*'s steam whistle blasted out repeatedly, using the same signal as that of the *Duchess of York* to summon lingering crew members from the pub. She'd be leaving soon and then he'd be gone too. He'd been so good to her and she would really have liked to stay. It had been a warm, cosy little room. She wouldn't have taken up much extra space.

She'd heard tales about America. Dinny Kavanagh from up the street went to sea and he always seemed to have plenty of money. She'd heard him say you could make a fortune in America without even breaking your back. It was known as a place where the poor got on in life. New York, David Williamson had said they were sailing to. Would it be like Liverpool? she wondered. Would it be bigger or smaller? Oh, he had been so nice, so kind, even bringing the doctor to see her. She'd never met anyone like him before. He was obviously well off, his clothes were good and she'd noticed the watch on his wrist and the gold signet ring on his finger. And yet he'd bothered with the likes of her and he'd laid her on his bed, taken off her boots, wiped her face with that cool towel. He'd really seemed to care about her, he'd even saved Mog. Lots of people she knew had been knocked down, sometimes by cars but mainly by runaway horses. No one made a fuss about them, except maybe the scuffers – if they died.

As she finished the last slice of bread, she felt drowsy. She didn't need to go singing tonight. She'd go to the Sally Army hostel and get a bed and then sleep. Oh, wouldn't it be great to have a bed to herself, a clean bed. She looked down at her clothes and then turned her hands over. The bed might be clean but she certainly wasn't. She'd have a bath, that's what she would do. Now that was a real luxury. She'd never had a bath in her life. When they'd been little her mother used to stand them in the sink in the scullery and wash them. Nelly would be getting worried about her now and she had enough on her plate. Alice really didn't want to upset her. She'd just have to think of a way of getting word to her that she was doing just fine. But she didn't want to think of her Mam.

Reluctantly she left the warmth of the eating house and went into the sharp, frosty dusk, but instead of turning towards the city she made again for the Prince's Landing Stage, quite why she didn't know. When she reached it, the *Aquitania*'s gangways were being hauled up and the tugs had taken up the hawsers. High above her on the boat deck, so high she got a crick in her neck looking up, people were waving down to friends and relatives. The whole ship was ablaze with lights. By, it was a magnificent sight and he was on there – somewhere.

She stood watching as the ship moved slowly away from the stage and out into the river escorted by the tugs. The customary three long blasts on the steam whistle echoed around the waterfront and were answered by some of the many ships out in the river, including the ferries. It was their way of saying 'God speed' and 'Safe journey'. Soon she had passed the New Brighton lighthouse and was just a blur of light fading into the cold winter darkness.

Alice sighed and turned away. David. David William-son, she said to herself. She'd remember that, the way she would remember Letty Lewis, the Cockney Songbird. That called to mind the night she'd stood outside the Rotunda. Training and grooming, the lady had said. Would she ever be able to get them both? Would she find them in America? The thought held her spellbound for a few seconds. Well, why not? Now she had money. That Charlie had said maybe one day they'd be paying to hear her sing and if she was singing on the stage, in a dress like Letty Lewis had worn, he'd certainly sit up and take notice of her. Suddenly it became of paramount importance that she see David Williamson again and not dressed as she had been this time, in tatty, dirty rags.

Other people had gone to America – thousands of them. She'd seen them waiting for the ships and they'd been hard up too. There had been no pennies to give to her for entertaining them. Even the biggest ships took poor people, if they could pay. Her fingers closed round the coin in her pocket. Surely a golden guinea would be enough for her fare. And she had eight shillings. When she got there she could sing, in the streets to start with, while she sorted out the training and grooming and maybe . . . maybe she'd see him again.

These astonishing new ideas hurtled through her mind, making her head spin. Oh, what she wouldn't give to get away from here. Away from everything and everyone – except Mam. She'd write to Mam. A proper letter explaining that she wasn't to worry. She'd be all right. Alice resolved to take it to the house later on. No sense in wasting money on stamps. You could buy a single sheet of paper and an envelope in a newsagents. She'd shove the letter through the letter box. She knew Nelly wouldn't mind her going to America, not if she was to have a chance in life, a better life. That's all Mam had ever wanted for them all and she wanted to make Mam proud of her. It would make all the hardships and beatings worthwhile – well, in a small way, but there was just a chance that if she went in, Mam might try and talk her out of it.

Alice walked up James Street not noticing anything that was going on around her, too absorbed in her thoughts. Only when she got to the bottom of Lord Street did she realise where she was. Bunny's department store was on the corner, its windows lit up, but she passed it without a glance and walked along Church Street, still deliberating what to do.

She at last stopped outside Marks and Spencer. In the window they had stockings marked 6d. a pair. Good, thick, warm black ones. She darted inside and found her way to the appropriate counter and when she emerged sixpence lighter, it was with a pair nicely wrapped up. There was no point in wasting money on new clothes when there were plenty of second-hand shops around. She could probably rig herself out for three or four shillings and that would include boots. But she hadn't been able to resist a pair of stockings.

Her new-found wealth amazed her when she thought of all the luxuries it afforded. She could get a tram to anywhere in the city for twopence. She could go across the river on the ferry for the same price. She could buy more food, lots of food. She could have a bath, complete with soap and towel, for sixpence, at Burrough's Gardens Baths. Yes, that's what she'd do. She'd buy some clothes and get the tram from Byrom Street. She didn't want to walk along Scotland Road in case she bumped into Lizzie or the kids or, worst of all, Da. She'd write the letter, sneak down the jiggers, shove it through the door and then get a tram back into town. Then she'd get a bed and in the morning – well, who knew what the morning would bring? She had had so many novel experiences today that she felt as though hundreds of mice were darting around in her stomach. She liked being rich, she decided, it suited her very well indeed.

Had David Williamson or his brother Charlie seen her when she emerged from the public baths in Burrough's Gardens they would hardly have recognised her. She'd been very apprehensive at first about the big cast-iron bath into which the hot water had gushed, filling the small cubicle with clouds of steam. She'd paid her money and had been handed a towel, a piece of soap and a long-handled scrubbing brush stamped with the words 'Liverpool Corporation'. The attendant, a thickset woman swathed in a white cotton overall, had shown her into the cubicle and with a sort of spanner thing had turned on the taps. When the bath was three-quarters full, she turned off the water.

41

'Bring the towel an' brush back ter me when you're done. The soap yer can keep, what's left of it,' she said flatly, shutting the door and leaving Alice alone.

She gingerly put her right foot into the water. It felt wonderful but she'd make sure she hung on tightly to the side of the bath just the same. She lost no time in stripping off her clothes and wrapping the kitten in her shawl. Then she lowered herself in. As the warm water covered her body, she relaxed so much that she nearly dozed off, but pushing aside her lethargy she worked up a lather with the soap and began to scrub away the dirt and grime.

At a second-hand shop at the bottom of Great Crosshall Street she'd bought a heavy flannel skirt, a paisley print blouse, a new shawl, a petticoat, a pair of drawers and boots. The shopkeeper had thrown in a bit of velvet ribbon to tie up her hair. She looked with distaste at her old clothes lying in a pile on the floor. She wasn't even going to take them away with her, she was going to ask the attendant to get rid of them. That was what having money meant, she thought with satisfaction.

There was a tiny mirror on the wall and when she'd finished she was amazed at the image of the girl who stared back. It was a new Alice O'Connor. Her skin glowed pink from the brisk rubbing and she'd towelled her hair vigorously and tied it up with the ribbon. Was this what the lady had meant by grooming? If it was, then all she needed now was the training.

She tucked the kitten into her new shawl. 'Right, Mog, all I've got to do is get a letter to Mam and then it's a new life for you and me. You'll grow into a big fat cat, you see if you don't.'

She got a single piece of writing paper and an envelope from Daly's on the corner of the street. Josie Daly had been in her class at school but Alice didn't like her. Now she'd have to be nice and ask her to lend her a pencil.

'Who're you writing to, Alice O'Connor? I didn't think

42

you knew anyone important enough to write to.'

Alice just stared at Josie who was eyeing her up and down. The retort 'Mind your own business' sprang to her lips but she couldn't afford to alienate Josie who was holding the pencil.

'It's to me mam, if you must know, Josie.'

Josie rolled her eyes expressively. 'Oh, aye, an' I came over on the last boat with a cargo of Irish confetti! It's a feller! It's got to be, you're all dressed up. Where did you get those things?'

Alice decided it would be easier to play along. 'I bought them. Me feller gave me the money, but don't let on,' she hissed, jerking her head in Mr Daly's direction.

Josie smirked and tapped the side of her nose before handing over the pencil and turning away to serve someone else.

Alice sucked the pencil, trying to formulate words and sentences in her head. It took her a while but at last she was satisfied with her efforts.

In a short while, Alice was picking her way through the pitch-dark maze of back entries that she knew like the back of her hand. Soon she emerged into Benledi Street. Keeping in the shadows, away from the circles of yellow light cast by the street lamps, she reached number eight but then she gasped, shrinking into the doorway as Nelly emerged from number ten.

'Alice? Alice, is that you, luv?' Nelly peered into the darkness. 'I've been out of me mind, girl! Are yer all right?'

Alice knew it was useless to remain silent. She stepped forward and pushed the letter into Nelly's hand. 'I'm fine, Mam, honest.'

'What's this? Where did you get this letter from?'

'It's for you, Mam, from me. I . . . I'm going away.'

'Going away? Going where, Alice?' Nelly noticed her daughter's changed appearance. 'Where did you get those clothes? You look . . . different.'

'Oh, never mind the clothes, Mam. I *am* different. It . . . it's all in the letter. Everything. I wrote it all down. I'm going to America, it's my big chance. You always said we should have a fair chance. Well, I've got it.'

Nelly stood shaking her head in disbelief, unable to comprehend what Alice was saying. 'Alice, in the name of God, what have you done?'

'Nothing, Mam! I got knocked over but I'm fine, it was the best thing that ever happened to me.'

'Come on in, luv,' her mother coaxed.

'No! I . . . I can't. I won't. I hate him! If I come in he'll take all me things to Solly Indigo and then he'll get drunk and start belting me again. I'm going, Mam. It's my only chance!' She couldn't bear to see the look that was creeping into her mother's eyes.

'You can't, Alice! Come on inside, yer da's out.'

'No, Mam. It's all in the letter. You're not to worry. I'll send you money and I'll . . . I'll come back when I'm famous from singing in the theatre. I promise I will, Mam. I swear to God I will!' Before Nelly could say a word, Alice hugged her quickly and then turned and ran up the street, the tears coursing down her cheeks.

Nelly leaned against the door of the house, her hand to her mouth, her eyes fixed on the disappearing figure of her daughter. 'Oh, Holy Mother of God, look after her!' she prayed, then she looked down at the now crumpled envelope. Would she ever see Alice again? A great weariness came over her and she brushed away her tears. She couldn't blame Alice. What was there here in Benledi Street to stay for?

For the first time in her entire life Alice O'Connor slept in a bed that was clean, comfortable and not shared with anyone else apart from her good luck charm, the cat. There were no sheets but she hadn't expected any. There were plenty of blankets though and a pillow, and the room was warm, heated by a stove in the centre. She lay staring drowsily at the regimented line of beds. Oh, this was sheer luxury and with no drunken arguments or fights to interrupt her sleep and tomorrow . . . tomorrow was going to be even better than today, she just knew it was. It had upset her to leave Mam but at least she had been able to talk to her, to give her a quick hug. She hadn't left Mam to fret, not knowing where she was at all.

She left the hostel at eight o'clock the next morning, after having had a wash and tidied her hair in the communal and very basic bathroom. Today she felt a different person entirely, as if she'd washed the old Alice away last night in the bath.

She made her way again to the eating house at Mann Island and her appearance was so changed that the waitress didn't recognise her at first. She ordered a bacon butty, a mug of tea and a bowl of bread and milk for Mog.

When they arrived, the woman looked at her suspiciously. 'You done all right fer yerself, girl. Why did that feller give yer all that money yesterday?'

'Mind yer own business!' Alice shot back at her knowing what she was implying.

'We don't have tarts in 'ere. This is a respectable caf.'

Alice got to her feet. 'I'm not a flaming tart! An' I'm not coming in here again to be insulted.' She gulped down the tea and clutching the sandwich and her cat, stormed out. She'd eat her breakfast on her way to the shipping offices. 'Never mind, Mog,' she said when they got outside, 'I'll give yer some of me bacon. And we've still got half a crown left and the guinea. That's twenty-three shillings and sixpence altogether. I don't suppose they'll charge for you, but in case they do you'd better keep still and quiet under me shawl.'

There was a line of people waiting outside the Cunard Building, all dressed much as she was, so she joined them and waited patiently until the doors were opened and the crowd moved forward. It seemed an age before it was her turn.

'Yes, miss?' The clerk behind the polished wood counter eyed her with a look of resigned boredom.

'I want to go to America. To New York, on one of those.' She pointed to a large poster pinned to the wall above the counter. It depicted the three black hulls and seven red and black funnels of the *Mauretania, Berengaria* and *Aquitania* against a dark, smoky sky and was topped with the words 'CUNARD – THE FASTEST OCEAN SERVICE IN THE WORLD'.

'Well, you've missed the *Aquitania*, she sailed yesterday. The *Mauretania* is due in today, she'll sail again in two days – to New York,' he added.

'Then I'll go on that one.'

'Right. I assume it's a single ticket? You won't be coming back?'

Put into words, someone else's words, it sounded very final, rather frightening and yet exciting. She nodded.

'Name?'

'Alice O'Connor. Miss.'

'Five guineas, please, miss.'

Her mouth fell open and her eyes widened with shock. '*Five guineas!*'

'That's the price of a single ticket steerage class. For that you get bed and board, simple food but wholesome, on a fast, safe ship. You'll be there in less than five days.'

'But . . . but I've only got one guinea. It's a golden one though,' she added hopefully.

'You'll need another four, miss.'

'Another four? Isn't there a cheaper ticket?'

'No, and you'll find that prices are pretty much the same at other shipping lines and they all take far longer to get there.'

'They all charge the same?'

The clerk tapped his pen impatiently on the edge of the inkwell. It was a situation he often came up against. Couldn't any of them read? The prices were displayed prominently enough on the walls. 'Well, you might get a tramp that's going across the Atlantic, that would be cheaper, but how long it would take I don't know.'

The people behind were getting impatient. He dismissed Alice with a nod and called, 'Next!'

She turned away, devastated. To acquire one golden guinea had been a miracle; four more were an impossibility.

She wandered disconsolately along the Strand towards the Albert Dock, then along Wapping to the Salthouse and finally the King's Dock. He'd said a tramp and she knew he meant one of those small, creaking, rusty ships you often saw in the docks or chugging out to the Mersey – slowly. They didn't look very safe. Well, beggars can't be choosers, Alice O'Connor, she told herself, trying to revive her drooping spirits and banish her disappointment. It was vitally important that she get to America. Over the last two days it had become her sole ambition. It was her destiny – she just knew her luck would change when she got there. Maybe she'd better take his advice.

It was past lunch time when she finally found the captain of a tramp steamer who would even listen to her. Everywhere else she'd met with cold, firm rebuttal or open disdain and hostility.

The *Castlemaine* wasn't very big. It only had one funnel. A dirty tattered flag hung limply from its short mast, from which the paint was peeling, and there was a lot of rust on the hull. In fact, there were more red patches than black ones.

'What do you want, girl?' the tall man standing on the deck beneath the bridge barked as she walked gingerly across the plank of wood that spanned the dirty, oily strip

47

of water between the ship and the dock wall.

'I want to go to New York. I can pay.'

'Oh, aye. Why haven't you gone to the big companies?'

'I tried. They're too expensive. Oh, please, mister, are you going to America?'

He looked her up and down. A fine looking girl and no mistake. 'I am and it's Captain Burrows to you, not mister.'

'Then will you take me, Captain? Please?' trying desperately to look appealing. She didn't like the look of him much, he reminded her of her da, but he had said he was going to America.

'How much have you got?'

'A guinea. A golden one.'

He laughed. 'Gold or not makes no difference, it's not enough. I charge at least two. You've got to be fed.'

She was becoming desperate. 'I won't eat anything, I'm used to going hungry. Will that help?'

'No, it won't. You'd be taking up a berth that I could get maybe three guineas for.'

The tears started in her eyes. Her money wouldn't last long and she just couldn't go back. She never wanted to go back to that life. If she didn't get to New York she'd never ever see David Williamson again and that now mattered a great deal to her.

'We could come to some arrangement though. You're not a bad looking judy.'

Alice's cheeks flushed as his meaning dawned on her and she shuddered. 'I'm not a girl . . . like . . . that.'

He shrugged. 'Suit yourself. If you change your mind, come back tonight. We're leaving on the midnight tide.'

She walked slowly back along Wapping and sank down on the top step of a bonded tea warehouse, her gaze wandering to the river and the ships that were plying to and fro, and those that were far out along the Crosby Channel heading towards the Bar Light and the open sea.

Ever since she'd made her decision to leave Benledi Street she'd had good luck. She'd earned a few shillings, she'd met David Williamson and been on board the *Aquitania*. She'd had good food, a bed, a bath and new clothes. Surely luck wasn't going to desert her now. Oh, she knew that a better life awaited her across the ocean, it *did*. She'd never been so certain of anything before. But what would David Williamson think of her, if she ever saw him again, if she'd made a whore of herself just to pay her fare? If she stayed though, her money would be spent and she'd be back where she started, dressed in dirty rags, singing in the street to keep food in her belly and a roof over her head. She might even be forced in the end to go back to Benledi Street.

'It looks like we've run out of your bit of luck, Mog,' she said despondently to the ball of fur in the crook of her arm. Mog gazed up at her, as if she understood, and Alice stared blankly into the distance.

How long she sat there she didn't know. All the memories of a deprived, cruel and violent childhood pressed in on her. There had been nothing good in her past, except her ability to sing, and she'd only ever done that to earn money, never really for pleasure.

When she finally got to her feet, she was cold and stiff. Her mind was made up and although she didn't know it, some of the softness had gone from her eyes. She was going. She didn't care what it cost. It might not be so bad, she told herself. After all, Mam had put up with it at least six times as she, Lizzie, her brothers and Agnes and Mary proved. But what would Mam think of her? Her heart plummeted but she pushed the thought of Nelly firmly to the back of her mind. Mam would never know and life was cruel and hard. She had no intention of ... of ... well, carrying on with *it* once she got to New York. She squared her shoulders, settled the kitten, wrapped her shawl tightly round her and raised her chin determinedly.

I'm not really being a whore. I'm just paying me way, she told herself firmly as she retraced her steps back along Wapping towards the King's Dock.

Chapter Five

The cabin she was given, which was to become her home, her refuge, and her prison for the next three weeks, was dark, cramped and dirty. She wrinkled her nose as the odours of bilge water, coal dust and stale food assailed her nostrils.

'It's worse than our flaming scullery!' she exclaimed acidly. She thought of the only other cabin she'd ever seen and wondered what kind of room she'd have got on the *Mauretania*, had she been able to afford the fare.

'What do you expect for the pittance you're paying?' James Burrows snapped back. He was already regretting his decision. To take the *Castlemaine* across the Atlantic in the depths of winter was no easy task, without burdening himself with a passenger. One that looked like trouble, too.

He'd left her with the promise that he'd be back later when they'd cleared the Bar Lightship, and she sat down on the edge of the narrow bunk, feeling desolate.

'We've got nothing to unpack, have we, Mog?' she said flatly. She hung her shawl on a hook behind the door. At least the room was warm, she thought. Like a coal hole but warm. There was that faint oily smell she'd noticed on the *Aquitania*. Perhaps all ships smelled the same.

She'd given Captain Burrows the sovereign and now she looked for somewhere to hide the half-crown which

51

was all the money she had in the world. The bulkheads were bare, there was no porthole. A small hurricane lamp hanging from a hook was the only source of light. Lifting up the thin flock mattress she managed to prise up one of the boards that formed the base of the bunk. She ignored the scattering of insect life this caused, for she'd lived with bugs for too long to be concerned or squeamish about them.

With her money hidden and her eyes accustomed to the gloom, she pondered James Burrows' departing words and a feeling of dread replaced the desolation. The worst was yet to come. She wondered how long it would be before they were clear of the estuary and the Bar Light. An hour, two, hopefully much longer. They didn't appear to be moving very quickly.

After half an hour she had managed to allay some of her fear, but sitting down here with nothing to see or do to distract her wasn't helping. There was also the stench, the noise and the vibrations to contend with. Everything creaked and rattled and it was disconcerting. She could also hear the sea and it alarmed her to think that only a thin wall of rusty old metal separated her from it. She decided to go up on deck.

At the end of the narrow passageway was a steep ladder. It was pitch dark. She climbed up on deck and stared around, holding tightly to the rail. It was cold. A stiff wind had sprung up and it whipped her hair across her face. The smell of the river was strong but she took deep breaths of comparatively fresh air. She could see the lights strung out along the coastline like a necklace. Turning back, she could see in the distance the lights of the trio of buildings at the Pier Head and it suddenly hit her that she was leaving Liverpool. She was leaving behind everything she had known, everything that was familiar, and a sob rose and caught in her throat. 'Oh, Mam! Will I ever see you again?' she whispered.

'He says you're to get below. You're not supposed to be up on deck.'

She turned sharply at the sound of the voice. A tall thin lad of about her own age, with a shock of unkempt dark hair that fell into his eyes, was regarding her with open curiosity.

'Who are you?'

'Georgie Tate. I'm the cabin boy.'

'Well, it's not much of a flaming cabin!'

He shrugged. 'That's nothing to do with me. Cabin boy's only a name, a bloody stupid one an' all.'

'What do you do then if you don't see to cabins?'

'General dogsbody, that's what I am. I do everything, everything that's rotten. Swab the decks. Clean the heads, help in the galley, give the donkey man a hand.'

Most of the list she didn't understand. 'What's a donkey man?'

'The feller who looks after the donkey boiler. How much is he charging you?'

'A guinea and . . .'

He suddenly grinned. 'And what?'

She turned away. 'Never you mind what!'

'Well, yer luck's in.'

She still couldn't look at him. Was this a regular thing? she wondered. Besides the cargo, did the *Castlemaine* always carry a whore? 'I'm not a whore!' she snapped. 'I . . . I've got reasons why I *had* to come on this floating rust bucket.'

'All right, don't get airyated with me, girl! What's yer name, anyway?'

'Alice. Alice O'Connor.' She looked at him more carefully. He wasn't laughing at her, his dark eyes were regarding her with concern. 'What did you mean, me luck's in?' she asked cautiously.

'He won't be down for hours yet. There's a storm brewing up out there.'

'How do you know?' Relief was mingled with alarm.

'I just do an' I heard Timms, the mate, saying so. Have you ever been to sea before?'

'No.'

'Not even on the ferry?'

She shook her head, thinking she was seventeen years old and she'd never even crossed the river in her life.

'Then I hope yer a good sailor. But,' he finished cheerfully, 'it doesn't last.'

'What doesn't?'

'Seasickness.'

'Oh.'

'Don't worry, I'll look after yer, Alice.'

He seemed pleasant enough and she was grateful for his concern. 'How long have you worked here, on this . . . lump of scrap?'

'Two years. I ran away from home.'

'What for?'

'Me mam died and the owld feller married again. A real bitch, she was. I hated her an' she hated me, so I ran away to sea.' He paused. 'Why are *you* running away, Alice?'

'Because of me da and . . . other things.'

Before he could question her further, James Burrows bellowed at him from the bridge. 'Get that bloody woman below!'

Georgie hastily pushed her towards the stairway. 'I'll come and see yer when I can. I promise.'

'Thanks,' she replied, descending again into that suffocating darkness, but feeling that she'd at least met someone she could talk to.

She had no idea of the time but she was tired. She stripped down to her petticoat and drawers and pulled the blanket up over her and, clutching Mog to her, tried to sleep. Exhausted, for a moment she sank into oblivion but what seemed like minutes later, started awake. Everything was creaking and groaning and she wondered fearfully if the ship would spring a leak. The movement seemed to increase and the engines thudded and the single screw vibrated noisily. She clung tightly to the edge of the bunk. She had no idea where the kitten was. Her alarm increased as she watched the hurricane lamp swing to and fro like the pendulum of a clock and the sound of the waves hitting the hull became frighteningly loud. She felt queasy, claustrophobic and ... trapped.

As the hours passed, it got worse. The ship pitched and rolled and she was flung bodily from the bunk onto the floor where she lay whimpering in terror until nausea swamped her. Oh, she wished she was dead. In fact she knew she must be dying for she'd never felt so bad in all her life. She felt so ill that all the terror receded. Even if the ship was torn apart by the waves or swamped and sent plunging to the bottom of the Irish Sea, she couldn't have cared less.

Some time during the night she heard Georgie Tate's voice and felt someone lift her and put her back on the bunk. A damp cloth was passed over her face.

'Oh, I want me mam! I want to go home! I'm dying,' she moaned.

'You'll be all right, Alice. It'll get better, honest it will.'

'It won't. I want to die! Oh, let me die, please!'

'I'll come back and see you later,' he promised.

She was past caring.

He did come back, three times, and so did James Burrows. He glared at Alice's prostrate form and that of the black and white kitten which was clinging to her skirt with its claws.

'Get that bloody stinking mess cleaned up, Tate, and get rid of that bloody cat!'

'It's doin' no 'arm, Captain. It'll keep the vermin down.'

James Burrows nodded his agreement. 'Bloody women, more trouble than they're worth! I'm too soft-hearted, that's my trouble,' he muttered as he slammed out.

Ten hours passed but Alice didn't know or care. Georgie had cleaned her up and had tried to get some thin gruel down her but it had come straight back up again. The cat had greedily lapped up the rest of the gruel from the chipped enamel dish Georgie had put on the floor.

'It's dying down now, Alice. You'll feel better soon, honest you will.'

He hadn't lied; by midday the sea was calmer, the swell only moderate and the wind had dropped, but they'd lost time. If they met more bad weather, and at this time of year it was almost guaranteed, then it would be a long time before the voyage was over, Georgie knew. But he'd look after her. Once she'd got over this she'd be all right. She'd have her sea legs. He'd decided he liked her. She wasn't a whore, she was just running away but it was different for girls. If they had no money and no job then it was usually what they turned to. But he wondered just what the circumstances were that had driven her to make such a bargain with Captain Burrows.

It was two days later when Alice woke from a deep sleep and looked around her, amazed that she was still alive. She certainly hadn't died, unless heaven was a dark, poky, smelly room. She sat up, pulling the stained blanket up to cover her nakedness. She blushed, wondering just who had seen her in this state. She vaguely remembered hearing voices, men's voices. Then she heard someone singing, not very tunefully, and realised she was hungry. She found her skirt and blouse, her stockings and her boots, put them on and opened the cabin door cautiously.

Georgie Tate was in the companionway, sloshing a wet and dirty mop up and down it.

He grinned as he caught sight of her. 'I told yer you'd be all right, didn't I?'

She blushed. 'Was it you who ... well, I remember

56

hearing someone talking to me.'

'It was me, oh, an' the skipper came down once to look at yer. Are yer hungry?'

'I'm starving. I never thought I'd ever say that again.'

'It doesn't last – well, not usually. Come on, I'll get you something.'

'Where's me cat?'

He grinned. 'It's around somewhere, probably earning its keep.'

'It's too little!'

'Oh, stop goin' on about the bloody cat! They 'as nine lives and they like ships. Nearly every ship 'as a cat to keep the mice an' rats down. Our last one died of old age an' I give it a proper burial an' all. At sea. Its name was Salty. 'As yours got a name?'

'I just call it Mog.'

She followed him to the galley, yet another small, cramped space and another that was not very clean either.

'Yer can have bacon or bacon an' bread.'

'I'll have a bacon butty, please.' She suddenly remembered that that was the last thing she'd had to eat before she'd left Liverpool. 'How . . . how long was I sick?'

'Best part of three days.'

'Three days! Where are we now?'

'In the Atlantic. We've just passed the old Head of Kinsale. Where the *Lucy* went down,' he teased.

She'd heard of the sinking of the *Lusitania* and her eyes grew wide with fear. If a ship like that could sink, what chance had something as small as this?

'I was only teasing yer. She was sunk by a torpedo, in the war.'

'Then just stop it, Georgie Tate! I'm not used to boats an' you know it.'

'Ships,' he corrected her. 'Anything bigger than the ferries is a ship.'

'This isn't much bigger than the ferries,' she replied with spirit.

She ate the thick sandwich and washed it down with the mug of tea he gave her. 'Was that you singing?' she asked when she'd finished.

'Yeah.'

'What were you singing?'

' "Show Me The Way To Go Home".'

She'd thought she'd heard it. 'I sing. Do you know any more songs?'

'Oh, aye, plenty. "Always", "It Had To Be You", "Lime-house Blues".'

She'd never heard of any of them. 'That's what I do, for a job, like. Sing.'

He regarded her with incredulity. 'Honest? On the stage, like?'

'No. I . . . I was a street singer.'

He looked disappointed but she was the first girl who'd taken any interest in him and she was pretty.

For the first time in three days she remembered that she hadn't 'paid' her full fare and a shadow crossed her face. 'What's he like?' She jerked her head in the direction of the deck above.

'Better than some. He's hard, but when yer make yer living tramping around the world in an owld tub like this, yer got to be hard.'

'Is he . . . is he married? He looks old.'

'I think he was, once, an' he's not that old. He's not bad, Alice, really. He's fair, I'll say that for him. He pays up on time, too.'

She pursed her lips. She'd made a bargain with him and he'd expect to be paid up on time too. That time would probably be soon. 'Is there anywhere I can get a wash?'

He nodded, suddenly uncommunicative, seeming to sense what was in her mind.

'Where?'

'I'll fetch yer some water an' yer can borrow me comb.'

She nodded her thanks and made her way back to her cabin.

He didn't speak when he brought her a metal bowl half full of water, a bit of lye soap and an old towel. He handed her a cheap comb and she smiled nervously at him, disconcerted by his silence, sensing his disapproval.

She felt better when she'd washed herself all over. There was no mirror but she combed out the tangled curls, tied them up and hoped they looked tidy. The piece of ribbon now bore more resemblance to a piece of string. She wondered how long it was going to take to get to New York and if there was any chance of washing her clothes. She also began to wonder what she would do with herself all day. The waiting for Captain Burrows was almost more than she could bear.

She'd straightened the bunk, after checking that her precious half-crown was still under the boards, and she was wondering whether to ask Georgie Tate for some more water to scrub the place out when the door opened and she looked up, her heart sinking. The moment she'd been dreading had arrived. The tall angular figure of Captain Burrows filled the doorway.

'You've recovered then?'

She nodded, looking down at her boots.

'So when we hit the next squall or storm I don't want to see Georgie Tate running round after you like a wet-nurse and neglecting his duties.'

'The next one?'

'It's New Year's Day and we're heading across the Atlantic Ocean, girl! It's not a bloody day trip to New Brighton or Llandudno.'

'I missed Christmas?'

'We all did. So what?'

'Is it really New Year's Day?' she pressed, stalling for time.

'Aye, the first of January, nineteen twenty-six.'

In other circumstances she would have been glad, wondering what this year would bring. Instead she sat on the edge of the bunk, biting her lip.

Captain Burrows gazed at her. She was still pale, there were dark shadows under her eyes and he wondered how old she was. Sixteen? Seventeen? Eighteen at most.

'Haven't you got any family, girl?'

'Yes, but me da is always drunk. He was always belting . . . me.' She was going to say Mam, but she didn't want to think of Nelly now. 'We never had nothing,' she finished. She took a deep breath. She'd better get this over with. 'Ain't you . . . don't you want to . . . be paid, like?' she stammered.

He didn't answer but she couldn't look at him. She was too ashamed, too afraid.

'I don't know.'

'Why?'

'Because I haven't made my mind up yet. There's plenty of time.'

She stood up. All she wanted to do now was get it over and done with. She certainly didn't want to have to go on day after day, night after night, sick with apprehension. 'I always pay me way.'

He looked down at her, at the determined jut of her chin, the pursed lips, the huge soft brown eyes that challenged him, yet in whose depths fear lurked. She wasn't a whore, he'd known that as soon as he'd spoken to her. Probably no man had ever had her, and she looked so like Maggie that his heart turned over. Maggie when she'd been young. When she'd loved him, when she'd been uncomplaining, waiting eagerly for her husband to come home from sea. Then she'd grown peevish, sullen and unresponsive and finally had run off with a bloody soldier. It was Maggie he was seeing now, not Alice. 'Oh, what the hell,' he muttered to himself.

'All right, girl, it's pay day!' He snapped, starting to unbutton his shirt.

Alice turned away from him, fiddling with the buttons of her blouse. Oh, God, let it be over soon! she prayed. And please don't let me think of Mam or ... David. David Williamson.

Chapter Six

She lay staring up at the bulkhead, the tears slowly sliding down her cheeks. It had been terrible. It had hurt her and she'd bitten right through her lip, drawing blood, to stop herself from screaming. She felt bruised and battered and . . . dirty. It was no use asking Georgie Tate for more water and soap. This dirt couldn't be washed away, it was inside her. She never wanted to have to go through it again and when he'd finished, he hadn't spoken to her. He seemed angry. He'd dressed and left, slamming the door shut behind him. Maybe he wouldn't bother her again. Maybe she'd paid in full now, but she couldn't be sure.

At last she fell asleep, a fretful, dream-filled sleep where she saw Mam standing pointing accusingly at her, Lizzie calling her a whore, Da picking little Mary up and throwing her out through the door. And then she saw David and Charlie Williamson driving that big shiny car, laughing together, but they didn't see her and she had to run and keep running so they wouldn't catch up and knock her down.

She woke, shaking, sweating and sobbing, and realised that Georgie Tate was sitting on the end of the bunk, staring at her. She didn't care what he thought. He was a friend, the only friend she had in the world, and she had to talk to someone.

'Oh, Georgie! It was awful! It was awful!' she sobbed.

He patted her arm ineffectually. 'Never mind, Alice, it's over now.'

'No, it's not! What if—'

'He won't,' he interrupted. 'He's not like that. Oh, 'e goes to the whorehouses, like everyone else, but he's . . . he's never brought one on board.'

James Burrows was a baffling enigma to his crew. A man who got drunk and visited the brothels the way they all did when they reached port. But a man who read books and listened to good music on the gramophone he had in his cabin. 'He's in a terrible temper,' Georgie added.

'Is that . . . bad?'

He shrugged. 'He never usually gets that mad over something . . . like . . . that.' He didn't say that there had been speculation among the crew that he'd finally gone insane.

'It's all them books, an' all that howling music,' had been Georgie's contribution to the debate. He'd got a clip round the ear from Tibbs for his pains.

She began to relax. If Georgie said he wouldn't come to her again, she could face the rest of the voyage. After all, Georgie knew him better than she did.

'Will I get you something to eat or a mug of tea?'

'Tea, please. I . . . I'll feel better then.'

'Will I teach you them songs now?'

She managed a smile and nodded.

She was stunned by the sheer vastness of the heaving grey-green ocean. As the days passed, there was nothing for miles and miles, as far as the eye could see, but that mass of water. Not a ship, not a bird, not even a fish. Whenever he had a spare few minutes, Georgie would sit with her on deck. Gradually, day by day, they exchanged confidences and life stories. He became increasingly fond of her but knew nothing could ever come of it, this love, this admiration. He never reached out for her, he avoided

64

all physical contact. He knew what she looked like semi-naked and she was beautiful. He could never think of her . . . like that, nor of what Captain Burrows had done to her, without feeling ashamed. Ashamed of his own masculinity.

'And that's all you know about this David Williamson?' he asked when she'd finished relating the events that had led up to her leaving Liverpool.

'Yes, but it made me want more, a better life, and I know I can have it in America. I know I can earn my living on the stage. So, will you teach me all the songs you know?'

'I said I would.'

'How do you know so many?'

He grinned. 'It's a secret.'

'Stop teasing me, Georgie Tate.'

'I go to the theatre, well, vaudeville, but I don't tell this lot. They'd think I was cracked, like the skipper. That's where I hear them, an' I remember them. Not all the words but most of them. You should go, Alice. Times Square is the place for it. It's great.'

'I will. That's where I'll go to sing.'

So they sat on deck in the shelter of the squat funnel and they sang. He began by teaching her a song that had been his mam's favourite, 'If You Were The Only Girl In The World'.

He was truly amazed when she first sang 'Beautiful Dreamer'.

'Alice, that was great! I know yer said you could sing but I never realised yer 'ad a voice like that! Yer really should be on the stage!'

She grinned ruefully. 'Aye, the landing stage.'

It became a ritual. Every evening as the half-light that passed for afternoon gave way to enveloping darkness, her clear sweet voice would ring out across the *Castlemaine*'s deck and over the cold grey waters of the great

65

Western Ocean. The rest of the crew, a surly, taciturn and mainly ignorant collection of misfits, grew to look forward to evening, to hear her increasing repertoire. When she sang 'Just A Song At Twilight', strong, hard men felt stirrings of gentler emotions few knew they even possessed.

On the bridge, James Burrows would sigh heavily, wondering if it was merely the effect of the immensity of the ocean or the isolation of his command that made the sweetness and clarity of that voice tear at his heart and stir up an aching loneliness. At times he would seethe with a rage he didn't understand and curse himself for a fool for ever having agreed to take her on this trip. Sometimes he thought her voice was like that of an angel, sometimes like that of a siren that would surely lure them to their doom.

The storm put an end to the singing. Burrows had noted the signs. The rising wind that drove the ragged clouds across the face of the moon. The broken white tops of the waves and the ominous increase in the force of the swell. The barometer was falling fast; a storm of quite violent proportions was imminent. Burrows ordered Tibbs to lash everything down.

When the storm caught them, Alice was frightened, but not sick. She spent most of her time in her cabin, lying on the floor, praying, gabbling the same words over and over again as she was thrown from bulkhead to bulkhead. 'Oh, please, God, don't let us sink! Don't let us drown!'

The ship shuddered and groaned as it struggled to rise from each trough, metal plates straining and timbers protesting as hundreds of gallons of water streamed from its decks. Sometimes it seemed to James Burrows as he saw the next mountainous wall of water bearing down on them that they'd be breached, completely swamped. He was freezing cold, soaking wet and at times mortally afraid.

66

'Come on, old girl, you can't let it beat you now! You can't give up!' he coaxed, no thought in his mind other than just surviving the next wave.

As though in response to his urging, the *Castlemaine* would rise steeply and then hang suspended for a couple of seconds, everything calm and deathly still, and then with a shudder she'd plunge down again into the depths.

Water seeped in everywhere and added to Alice's terror. She saw no one, for the entire crew worked ceaselessly just to keep the ship afloat. This isolation had more than once induced her to struggle to the door and scream for Georgie Tate or Captain Burrows, but no one had even heard her cries. After two nights and two days she was exhausted.

The following night she slept heavily and the next morning she struggled up on deck and was shocked to see the havoc the sea had caused. The mast and rigging were reduced to little more than broken, splintered spars. The lifeboat had been torn from its davits, its remains – a pile of matchwood – lay in the apex of the funnel. Hatch and ventilation covers had been ripped away and the weight of water had crushed and twisted the wheelhouse. Georgie and two other men, eyes dark-rimmed, faces haggard with lack of sleep, were clearing up and lashing planks of wood over open hatches.

'Are yer hurt, Alice?' Georgie called.

'No. Just a bit bruised. I was . . . I was terrified though,' she shouted.

He managed a grin. 'So was I,' he yelled.

'Any man who wasn't is a bloody fool! You learn to respect the sea but never to trust it.'

She looked up to the bridge from where James Burrows was watching the crew and Georgie went back to work.

Burrows saw the fleeting look of fear in Alice's eyes. 'You needn't worry your head any more, girl. I've enough to do without wasting time on you.'

Her shoulders slumped with relief. 'Will it get like that again?'

'I damned well hope not, we've lost enough time. These storms can be a thousand miles wide so there's no skirting them.'

She shuddered and he turned away.

'Will yer give us a song ternight, Alice?' Georgie called. 'We could do with a bit of cheerin' up.'

' "Show Me The Way To Go Home" would be bloody appropriate,' Tibbs growled. His shoulder hurt like hell. He'd been thrown from top to bottom of the stairway.

She nodded. Things were beginning to look brighter. The weather wasn't too bad now but best of all Burrows had said he wasn't going to be bothering her again.

'I'll sing like . . . like a Cockney Songbird.'

'You're not a Cockney. You have to be born in London, in the sound of Bow Bells, to lay claim to that title, Alice,' Tibbs informed her.

'Well, a Liverpool Songbird then.' She liked the sound of it so she said it again. If Letty Lewis could be the Cockney Songbird, why couldn't Alice O'Connor be the Liverpool Songbird? She laughed. 'I'll sing to you all the way to New York if you like. I'll take requests.'

No one answered. Surprised and furtive looks were exchanged and they all seemed to move together in a conspiratorial group.

'What's the matter? What did I say?'

Tibbs looked at Georgie. 'You'd better tell her, lad. I thought she knew.'

'Tell me what?' Alice demanded.

'We're not going to New York.'

'What! Why?'

'We're going to Charleston, that's why.'

'South Carolina,' Tibbs added.

Alice looked from one to the other, shaking her head. 'But . . . but he said he was going to America!'

'We are. Just a different part of it, that's all.'

Alice turned and stared up at the bridge, then before anyone could stop her she was up the ladder like a flash. She flung the door open and it crashed back on its twisted hinges.

James Burrows glared at her. 'No one comes up here unless I ask them to! Get off my bridge!'

She was too furious to care. She'd been through hell. The loss of her virginity, sickness, stark terror and for what? 'You lied to me! You cheated me! You said you were going to New York! You know I would never have come if you hadn't said that!' she screamed.

'I said I was going to America. You never mentioned New York. You never mentioned a specific place. America, you said. That's where you wanted to go!' he shouted back.

'I didn't! I want to go to New York and you cheated me! You took ... everything! I want me money back!'

'I'll give you your bloody money; it'll be worth a guinea to be rid of you! We're going to Charleston, now get off my bridge before I throw you off!' he roared. He caught her by the shoulders and thrust her out into the arms of Georgie Tate who had followed her up. 'Get her out of my sight!' he bellowed, seething with anger and guilt – she had looked so like his wife on the day she had stood screaming abuse at him, the day she'd left, fifteen years ago.

Georgie helped her down.

Alice's fury drowned in the welter of emotions that now swamped her. Hate, disappointment, disgust and bitter shame. 'I hate him! I hate him! The dirty ... lying ... cheat!' she sobbed.

Georgie helped her to her cabin, scooped up her cat and dumped it in her lap, trying to console her. 'It's still America, Alice.'

'But it's not New York and I have to get to New York, you know that!'

'Alice, he won't be there, not now, an' it's just a dream! You're just chasing after a dream. You can sing anywhere.'

'I want to sing in New York. I want to be rich and famous so he'll come and see me. Is it far, Georgie? Is this place, Charleston, far from New York?'

He nodded. 'It's a long way. A very long way. America is a big country.'

She lay down on the bunk, her face turned away from him. She'd finally put her dreams into words. She *did want* to be rich and famous so Mam would be proud of her and David Williamson would come and listen to her. Then she could forget everything that had happened on this ship – when she *was* the Liverpool Songbird.

'Will yer still sing for us, Alice?' Georgie asked timidly.

'No! I'll never sing on this ship again! Oh, go to hell, Georgie Tate!' she cried unfairly.

'It's not my fault, Alice,' he said miserably, closing the door and leaving her with her shattered hopes.

Chapter Seven

It was three days before she would speak to Georgie again. She didn't stir outside her cabin and she left most of the meals he brought her untouched or half eaten.

It upset him to see her so miserable. He had persuaded Tibbs to retrieve her fare from Burrows, the monetary part of it. She'd just nodded her thanks when he'd handed it to her.

'Alice, yer going ter have ter eat! Yer going ter get sick,' he pleaded.

'I am sick. I'm sick to death of this flaming ship and *him* and . . . everything! What am I going to do now? You tell me that, Georgie Tate?'

'You could go back to Liverpool. We're picking up cotton an' going back,' he suggested timorously, fully aware how this suggestion would be received.

'No! I'm never going back! I told you that, not until . . .'

'Oh, Alice, use yer sense! It's a dream. The likes of us never get what we want.'

'I will! I'll do it! I'll be rich and famous!'

'Yer can sing, Alice, but yer can't talk properly. You . . . we don't know about manners an' things like that.'

She stared at him sullenly. He was right. 'I can learn,' she said stubbornly.

He gave up. 'So, what will yer do when we get there?'

'I don't know. I've got my guinea, I'll get somewhere to stay.'

'I could let you have a pound, when I get paid off, like.'

She softened. 'I couldn't take your money. You work too flaming hard for it. They've got you for a flaming skivvy.'

'I want yer to have it, Alice,' he urged, desperate to let her have the only tangible proof of his affection he could give her.

'We'll see.' She kicked her heels idly against the side of the bunk. The only place she'd ever known was Liverpool. She had no idea what any other city or town was like. She'd gone over and over things in her mind, cursing James Burrows, Tibbs, the entire crew, but most of all herself. Basically she was an optimist and finally she'd become pragmatic about her position. She was heading for a strange country where everything and everyone would be alien, but it had to be better than Liverpool. And now her curiosity had been stirred. 'What's it like, this place?' she asked finally.

'It's all right, I suppose. I've only ever been once before. It's hot, there's lots of strange plants and things and lots of blacks too. They all used to be slaves, so Tibbs said. He knows heaps of things about the places we go to.'

She'd seen black people before; being a cosmopolitan port, Liverpool had its share of all nationalities.

'Do you think I'll be able to earn anything, Georgie, street singing? Enough to live on until I get on the stage?'

He shrugged. 'Last time I was there I saw a lot of blacks singing. They were good, too.'

'Oh, well, I've got a bit of money to tide me over.'

'They have different money, Alice. Dollars.'

She looked confused. 'So?'

'You'll have to get your money changed.'

'How do I do that?'

'Captain Burrows will change it for you.' Instantly he knew he'd said the wrong thing.

'I'm never going to speak to him again. I'll starve first!'

72

'Well, maybe if I asked Mr Tibbs, he'd do it. He might know where there's some cheap rooms too. Will I ask him?'

'If you like,' she said ungraciously.

'Won't you come up on deck ternight? It's gettin' warmer now. You don't have ter sing,' he added, seeing the look of chagrin that crossed her face.

'No! I hate that lot!'

'Well, we all miss yer.'

She turned away, her lips set in a tight line, and he left her, filled with determination to help her in any way he could.

Next day she was surprised when Tibbs came to see her.

'Georgie Tate said you'll need your money changed and you'll be wanting somewhere to stay.'

She nodded.

'Don't be so bloody bad-tempered, girl. It doesn't suit you. You should have made sure of our destination before you sailed with us. How much money have you got?' he asked before she had time to snap at him.

'Twenty-three shillings and sixpence.'

'It's not much.'

'I know but it will have to do until I can earn some more.'

'You could earn some here. We'd have a bit of a whip round if you came up and sang us a few songs.'

'No! I'm not singing for you, for anyone on here again!'

'Suit yourself. Well, give me the money and I'll bring you the dollars, at the going rate.'

'How do I know you won't rob me?'

'God damn and blast you for a suspicious little tart!'

She was about to yell back at him but bit back the words. It was true. She'd acted like a tart and she was suspicious. She unearthed her money and handed it to him.

'When we dock I'll come and fetch you and I'll take

73

you to a rooming house I know. It's nothing fancy, but it's cheap, clean and decent.'

She nodded her thanks.

'I'd wipe that look off your face if you want to get a job. No one will want to employ you if you keep scowling and glowering like that.'

She pulled a face at his retreating back and thought about what Georgie had said about manners and the way she spoke. She'd have to try to improve herself.

The following day when Georgie brought her meal he handed her some small, green coloured banknotes.

'What's this?'

'Your dollars. Mr Tibbs sent them.'

'They don't look worth much.' She thought they looked very insignificant and insubstantial compared to the gold sovereign and silver half-crown.

'Well, they buy just as much. Why don't you come up top? It's like an oven down 'ere.'

'I might, later,' she replied, but she'd already decided she'd sulked down here long enough. It *was* like an oven and her thick clothes were uncomfortably hot. 'How long will it be now, before we get there?'

'Another two days.'

'How long is it since we left?'

'Nearly three weeks. We lost time with the weather.'

She seemed to have been cooped up for a lifetime, she thought, and even though she would hardly admit it to herself, she was becoming more interested in the place they were heading for.

When she finally went up on deck she was amazed by the change in the weather. The sky was a clear azure blue and the sunlight danced on the calm blue-green water. The tops of the waves sparkled with silver spangles and the wind was warm. It even smelled different. She unbuttoned the front of her blouse as far as was decent and rolled up her sleeves.

'So, you've emerged then?'

She managed a smile at Tibbs. 'It's hot.'

'When you get to Charleston, buy some lighter clothes. Cotton is best and it's cheap.'

She looked down at her stained, creased clothes and wrinkled her nose. 'I need a bath. I had one before I left.'

'This isn't a fancy passenger liner, but ask Georgie Tate for some water and he might wash your clothes – if you ask him nicely.'

'I can wash me own things! My own things,' she amended. 'Anyway, I haven't got any others to change into.'

'Wrap a blanket round you, they'll dry quickly.'

She regarded him thoughtfully. 'Will you really find me a place to stay?'

'I said I would.' He had two daughters of his own, one the same age as her. He didn't like the thought of Alice being left to fend for herself on the streets of a strange city in a foreign country. She looked so young, so vulnerable, although he knew she was a sharp little minx and she had guts. Many women would have died – literally – of fright during that storm. 'You'll have to look fairly presentable or they won't give you a room, so get yourself cleaned up.'

Georgie brought her soap, a towel, a bowl and two buckets of sea water. She washed herself all over, then washed her hair. She spent a happy half-hour rubbing and rinsing her clothes. Georgie took them away while, wrapped in her bunk blanket, Alice sat and waited for him to bring them back. They were a bit stiff and retained a slight smell of salt but they were clean and she felt and looked much better when she was dressed again. It was dusk, a warm, heavy, purple-coloured dusk when she went up on deck.

'That's an improvement,' Tibbs, who was standing watch, commented.

'Will we be there soon?'

'The day after tomorrow, early in the morning. The best part of the day.'

'Georgie said it's not too bad a place.'

'It's a damned sight better than New York. A dirty, stinking, violent place that is. God knows why you were so set on going there. Charleston's a beautiful city, once you get away from the docks. There's a fort in the harbour, Fort Sumpter, where the war between the states started.'

'The Great War?'

'No, you little ignoramus, long before that. In eighteen sixty-one it started. The war that freed the slaves, although to listen to a lot of people in Charleston it might have been yesterday. One song you'd better not learn is "Dixie".'

'Why?'

'Because you'll be lynched, although there's some who would applaud you!'

'I don't know that one anyway.'

'I'll teach you a song, if you like.'

'What song?'

'One you might come to look on as your own one day, if you stay in America.'

'Mine?'

'Not literally. It's called the "Star Spangled Banner".'

'What's that?'

'A flag. The American flag. The Stars and Stripes. "Old Glory" as it's sometimes called.'

'Why would I want to sing about flags?'

'Alice O'Connor, you're impossible, do you know that?'

She grinned up at him. 'Go on then, teach me it. I might want to sing it one day.'

He had quite a fine baritone, so he'd been told. 'Right, listen closely.' He began the first lines of the American national anthem.

He was cut short by a shout from the bridge. 'Mr Tibbs, this is a British ship! If you want to sing a national anthem, sing your own!' James Burrows yelled.

'I hate him!' Alice said venomously as the mate fell silent. 'Mr Tibbs, can you learn me to speak properly?'

He was surprised. 'Why?'

'Because I'm sick of being . . . common an' ignorant.'

'It's teach, not learn.'

'Will you teach me?'

'I can't teach you everything.'

'I've got two days and I'll try to learn as much as I possibly can.'

He grinned at her. Somehow she'd managed to worm her way into everyone's affections. 'You're the strangest little minx I've ever known, Alice O'Connor.'

He was right, Charleston was a beautiful city, Alice thought as two days later the *Castlemaine* nosed her way into the harbour, past the fort that Tibbs had told her about. Fancy such a little place like that starting a war, she thought.

She was fascinated by the colour of the sea. It was a sun-spangled ultramarine. The funnels, masts and rigging of the ships in the harbour presented a familiar sight and as they drew closer she could see more of the city and eagerness began to bubble up inside her. The buildings were white or pale grey and they gleamed in the morning sunlight. Palm trees and tropical plants grew in profusion between them and carts, lorries, cars and carriages lined the waterfront. The whole atmosphere seemed different from that of Liverpool, she thought. Despite the hustle and bustle on the waterfront, the city beyond seemed tranquil, as though sleeping in the sun.

When the engines were shut down and she heard the clanking of the anchor chain, she went back down to her cabin to collect her shawl. She wouldn't need it but she was loath to leave it behind; it had cost her money. Georgie had persuaded her to leave Mog behind. She was a

77

bit bigger now and had the run of the ship. Georgie saw that she was fed and soon she would be able to catch her own meals.

'Cats aren't like dogs, Alice. They don't *need* us, not really. They're . . . independent. Mr Tibbs taught me that word,' he finished proudly. 'Besides, we need a cat more than you do.' So she'd agreed in the end. After all, she'd have enough trouble looking out for her-self in this new country.

She looked around the little room that had become so familiar and felt a tremor of apprehension. She'd come all this way, to the other side of the world. What lay ahead?

Georgie appeared in the doorway.

'Are yer ready, Alice?'

'Will you be coming with me and Mr Tibbs?'

'No.'

She was a little disappointed. 'Oh, I thought you would be. Well, thanks, Georgie, for everything. You've been a real friend. I wish . . . I wish I had something to give you.'

Georgie looked embarrassed. 'I've got this for you, Alice. Go on, take it. I . . . I want you to 'ave it.' He held out a dollar bill.

'But you'll need it. You earned it.'

'I'd only waste it on drink.'

'You could use it to go to a vaudeville show.'

'No. It's yours.'

She added it to the others. 'Thanks, Georgie, I . . . I'll always remember you.'

'Alice, when yer get famous, will yer . . . will yer sing the song I taught yer?'

She smiled at him. A dazzling, confident smile. 'I will, I promise. You believe in me, don't you, Georgie?'

He could only nod. His throat seemed to have closed over.

She put her arms round him and kissed him on the

78

cheek. 'You've been good to me and I'll always remember you, Georgie Tate.'

Tibbs was waiting for her at the gangway and as she left she turned and waved to Georgie who was standing gazing after her, a look of mute misery on his face.

'Where are we going now?' she asked, unable to believe that she was once again on land, that there was solid unmoving ground beneath her feet. She had arrived. She was in America. Not in the place she really wanted to be – she was as far away from David Williamson as she'd ever been – but it was a start.

'Away from the docks,' Tibbs answered. 'Stay by my side and don't dawdle.'

At close quarters there was nothing tranquil about this part of the city, she thought. Bales of cotton were piled mountainously high on the dockside. The streets thronged with people and traffic, and were lined with telegraph poles and warehouses. 'The Lloyd Shirt Manufactury and Laundry. Established 1887' she read over one building they passed.

'Where are we now?'

'On Meeting Street. We're heading towards the Old Market end.'

She twisted her head from side to side, exclaiming at the new sights, sounds and smells. 'Are all those places banks?'

'No, the banks and insurance offices are on King Street.'

'What's that?' She pointed to a three-storey building which sported striped awnings over its windows and an imposing entrance, above which fluttered a large red, white and blue flag.

'The post office and court house, and that's the Star Spangled Banner.'

Her gaze alighted on a large white house that stood behind tall iron railings. 'Oh,.look at that! It's so beautiful!' she cried, her eyes going rapidly over the gardens, where flowers the like of which she'd never seen bloomed in myriad profusion, to the tall, white, pillared balconies linked with open verandas.

'There are some fine houses here. Some of them are over a hundred years old and have been in the same families for as long, too. There are more on the East Battery and Rutledge Street and there's the Grove – a mansion – built just before the War of Independence. A very long time ago,' he added, forestalling the question he could see forming.

She was warm, sticky and thirsty when they finally arrived at the Old Charleston Market and he led the way to a small, faded pink stucco building.

'Is this it?'

'It is. The Park Rooming House it's called.'

'Where's the park?'

'Do you have to take things so literally? Just shut up, let me do the talking and mind your manners.'

She followed him inside. The hall was dark and cool, the floor tiled and devoid of any carpet or rugs. Beside the small old-fashioned desk stood a large plant in a ceramic pot, covered with brilliant pink flowers. She'd never seen anything like it before and reached out gingerly to touch it.

'It's called a bougainvillaea.'

'You don't half know a lot of things.'

'I read. If you want to improve yourself, you should find time to read. Can you read?'

'Of course I can! I went to St Anthony's.'

Any further conversation was curtailed as a small woman, dressed entirely in black, appeared.

'Good morning, Miss Shelton, ma'am. Do you remember me? Mr Tibbs, Mate of the *Castlemaine.*'

'Why indeed I do, sir.'

'Do you have a room for this young person? She came over with us from Liverpool.'

The woman eyed Alice up and down. 'For how long?'

'I don't know. How much is it, please, ma'am?' Alice replied carefully.

'A dollar a week. Fresh linen and towels are provided, but no meals. There's a bathroom down the hall.'

'Well, for two weeks then, please.' She handed over two of her precious dollars and gave her name which was entered in a large book.

'Right then, you'll be fine here. Miss Shelton will be able to answer all your questions.'

Alice smiled at Tibbs. 'Thanks for helping me.'

'Well, we can't have you saying we all let you down, can we? Goodbye and good luck, Alice O'Connor.'

When he'd gone, Alice followed Miss Shelton down the hallway to the room she'd been allocated. It was quite small but after the cabin it seemed spacious. The walls were painted white and slatted wooden shutters were closed over the open windows. The sunlight that filtered in fell across the tiled floor in a pattern of oblique lines. There was a narrow bed covered with a clean blue and white cotton counterpane and drapes of muslin were looped back against the wall. A chest of drawers, a cane chair, a bleached oak towel rail over which was draped a pristine towel completed the furnishings.

Alice pointed to the muslin drapes. 'What's that for, please?'

'It's mosquito netting. They're insects, a sort of fly that bites. There's no need to use it now, not at this time of year.'

Alice suddenly remembered it was January. 'Is it winter here?'

Miss Shelton smiled. 'It is. It can be chilly and wet but we never get snow or frost. Now we do have regulations, you'll find them on that card, and you must abide by them otherwise you'll have to vacate the room.' She indicated a small printed piece of cardboard tacked to the back of the door. 'There are numerous places to eat in the vicinity but decent girls don't go near Beresford Alley, or Myzack and Princess Streets. You *are* a decent girl?'

'Oh, yes, Miss Shelton, I am!'

'Will you be looking for work, Miss O'Connor?'

'Yes.'

'Doing what?'

Although pleasant enough, Miss Shelton didn't look like the kind of woman you could say street singing to. 'Er, waiting on or cleaning, a maid, I suppose.'

'You'll find that jobs like that are done by the blacks,' Miss Shelton said sternly.

'Oh, well, maybe shop work.'

'Then you will need to go to the authorities first, since you're an immigrant.'

Alice had a deep mistrust of anything to do with authority. 'Do I have to?'

'Yes.'

'When?'

'As soon as possible. How long have you been travelling?'

'Three weeks and it was awful. There was a terrible storm, it went on for days. I was sick.'

Cecile Shelton softened. Her new lodger was a very pretty girl and she'd obviously had a long and terrifying voyage.

'Well, maybe tomorrow then. I can take you myself, I have to go downtown.'

'Oh, would you, ma'am? I'd be really grateful. I don't know anyone. It was New York I really wanted to go to, but . . . here I am.'

'Well then, I'll leave you to freshen up. Is your luggage still on the ship? Is someone going to bring it down?'

'No. I . . . I haven't got any. It . . . it got lost . . . in the storm,' she lied, seeing Cecile Shelton's eyebrows rise. 'Is there anywhere I can buy some things – cheaply?'

82

'Oh, yes. There are some thrift stores. I'll give you directions. When you're ready, just ring the bell on the desk in the hall.'

When she'd gone, Alice looked around. This was real luxury, she thought, fingering the bedspread and towel and looking more closely at the muslin netting. Fancy them even going to all that trouble so as not to have people getting bitten by flies, and there were certainly no bugs here either. She'd find the bathroom, have a bath and then she'd go out and do some exploring. She'd get something to eat, go to one of those thrift stores and then find the areas where she could earn money singing – she knew a lot of songs now. She'd start outside the theatres, like she'd done in Liverpool.

She sat down on the bed and stroked the crisp cotton counterpane. Her spirits rose. She had a roof over her head, some money for food and a couple of second-hand dresses. It never really got cold and Miss Shelton seemed kind and friendly in a stiff sort of way. From her experiences so far she decided she liked America. It was certainly better than Liverpool and Benledi Street. She'd got this far and was confident that all she needed was her voice and her looks to rise to fame and fortune. Little did she realise that youth, beauty and a golden voice were attributes that were plentiful in Charleston.

Chapter Eight

The thrift stores Miss Shelton directed her to were not second-hand shops as she'd imagined they would be. Everything was new. The clothing was of an inferior quality and badly finished off but though it was cheap and didn't compare with the garments sold in the stores in the prosperous parts of town, it was beyond Alice's slender means. In the end she asked a store assistant if there were any second-hand shops. The answer was negative but the girl told her that market stalls by the harbour sold cheaper goods. Alice thanked her and walked back down Meeting Street.

She bought two cotton dresses, some cotton underwear, a pair of stockings and a new straw hat from a black woman who had set up her stall in the shadow of a mountain of cotton bales.

'Can you tell me where I can get shoes?'

'Lige has the boots an' shoes. Keep on walking down there.' She pointed with a stubby finger towards the Harbour Master's offices.

Alice threaded her way between the dockside traffic and bought a pair of flat leather shoes that looked as though they hadn't had much wear.

The following day she set out looking clean and neat in the striped green and white dress and the wide-brimmed hat. She asked directions to the theatres and noted the time of the performances and the street names. She wandered from the harbour front and then through Beresford Alley, Princess and Myzack Streets where the brothels abounded. Then she retraced her steps up Meeting Street and out to the East Battery and Rutledge Street, where the houses were magnificent mansions set in gardens shaded by palms and filled with flowers.

On her wanderings she became acutely aware that what Georgie Tate had told her was true. She saw many black singers and musicians. Competition was going to be tough.

In the days that followed she tried all the theatres and moving picture palaces. She sang her heart out outside stores and hotels until she was moved on by irate doormen and managers. She earned a very small amount. Only coins were handed to her, dimes, quarters and cents, never a dollar bill, and she encountered open hostility from both black and white Charlestonians.

Now she was beginning to cut down on her meals to save her precious dollars. At first she'd found the food in the many small food shops and cafes in the less salubrious parts of town very different to what she was used to. There were vegetables and fruit she'd never seen before so she sampled them all – and put on weight. Her shoulder blades no longer stuck out, nor did her collar bone protrude and emphasise the hollow at the base of her throat; her breasts became fuller, her cheeks plumper and her appearance provoked many an admiring glance and comments and invitations of the baser kind. These she was used to and she dealt with them with scathing sarcasm. But now she was eating less she realised how quickly she'd become used to regular meals, as well as clean lodgings and clothes, and the opportunity to wash properly. She was also acutely aware how fast her money was running out.

By the end of her second week, after she'd reluctantly handed over another dollar, she was becoming more and more worried. She had to find a job. She'd gone to all the theatres and asked for work but had been told that there was nothing, nor were they holding auditions in the foreseeable future. She hadn't even known what the word meant, until they'd explained it to her.

After her third week, her bright dream of success was growing increasingly dim and she decided she'd have to try for something else, anything at all, but again she had no luck. The stores had no vacancies and when she finally took her courage in both hands and started to call at private houses, asking for a job as a cleaner or maid or laundry girl, she found Cecile Shelton's prediction to be true. There were very few white menials in this town.

In desperation she stopped outside a house in the East Battery and gazed at it longingly. It was a mixture of square columns and oval verandahs. A gleaming motorcar stood outside the door. What must it be like to live in a house like that, to have all the comforts and security that money brought, she wondered. It was obviously no' use going to ask for work – there was a black gardener carefully trimming the profusion of bougainvillaea and jasmine that cascaded over the perimeter wall and a black maid was shaking a duster from one of the large open windows upstairs. She'd have to try singing. She'd give them Georgie Tate's favourite; it might bring her luck.

She began 'If You Were The Only Girl In The World'. She had hardly got into her stride when the front door opened and a woman emerged dressed in a pale grey crepe dress that seemed to float around her shapely calves. Her hat was a small silver-grey confection with a white satin rosette on the side, her shoes were a soft dove-grey leather, as were her gloves, and she carried a white clutch purse. She was preceded by a dignified elderly black man dressed in a formal suit, who opened the car door for her.

Alice carried on singing as the woman handed something to the butler, but the notes faltered and died away as the car moved off. The butler crossed over and held out fifty cents.

'Mrs Phillips would be glad if you'd go away, girl, and don't come bothering folk again and lowerin' the tone of the neighbourhood.'

Alice took the money and began to walk slowly away. There couldn't have been more contrast between herself and Mrs Phillips. She had everything, Alice thought bitterly, while she herself had nothing. The gracious old houses depressed her; they were a reminder that so far she'd got nowhere in this land of opportunity. She was hungry but all she had was a dollar and fifty cents. It was enough for lodgings for another week but it left just fifty cents for food and that would only last two days. Miserably she turned her steps towards the Park Rooming House.

She'd hoped Miss Shelton wouldn't be in the hall, but her hopes were dashed.

'Quite a pleasant afternoon, isn't it, Miss O'Connor?'

'I suppose so,' she replied listlessly.

'Is there something wrong? Haven't you been able to find employment?'

'No. I've tried everywhere.'

Cecile Shelton tidied the papers on the desk into a neat pile. 'I see.'

'I'm not trained for anything, you see. I've only got a dollar fifty to last me all week. I . . . I was wondering if you'd let me stay on, give me a week's credit just until I get some work.'

'But you've been here three weeks and have found nothing.'

'I know, but I'm bound to get *something* soon!'

The older woman sighed heavily. 'I'm very sorry, Miss O'Connor, but I can't do that. I can let that room three times over. Cheap, clean, decent rooming places are hard to come by and this isn't a charitable institution.'

Alice hung her head and her shoulders slumped. By the weekend she'd be on the street. She felt she couldn't go to her room now, it wouldn't be hers for much longer. Instead she left the building and made her way to White Point Gardens.

It was late afternoon and she stood staring out over the expanse of blue water, feeling utterly desolate. All her hopes and dreams had turned to dust. She'd made a mistake, a terrible mistake in coming here, trusting in tales of wealth and unlimited opportunities. Oh, why had she let herself become infatuated with stupid dreams? She'd never sing on a stage in a theatre. She'd never be rich and famous and she'd never see David Williamson again. She was bitterly aware that that brief meeting with him had fanned the flame of her ambition. He was a stranger who had picked her up from the gutter and shown her kindness, and because of that she'd travelled three thousand miles across the world, and for what? To end up homeless, that's what. She was homesick. She missed Mam terribly and Lizzie and all the kids. She'd never see them ever again. She was stranded high and dry in a foreign land, with no money, no job and no prospects of one either. She really should have written to Mam, at least to let her know she had got there safely, but letters cost money.

She noticed that the sun was sinking, long shadows were creeping over the flower beds, dulling their riotous colours. The trees looked ghostly with their long trailing fingers of grey moss and the figure on top of the Jasper Monument was deep in shadow. Twilight descended rapidly here.

She left the confines of the gardens and walked quickly back down the East Battery, trying to ignore the beautiful houses with their brightly lit windows. There were a few cars and carriages on the streets but she ignored them until one stopped beside her. She quickened her steps in alarm.

'Miss! Miss, don't be frightened, Miss India only wants to know can she give you a ride home?'

Alice stopped, turned and looked up at the black driver of an old-fashioned closed carriage. She couldn't see the occupant.

'What do you think I am, flaming stupid? How do I know who's in there?'

'Miss, I'm just carrying out instructions.'

'Then let me talk to whoever's in there.'

He got down and opened the carriage door.

'Where are you going? It's not safe for a young girl to be out alone at night.'

It was a woman's voice but Alice was still wary. 'Is there just you in there?'

A woman's head and shoulders appeared from the gloom. 'Of course there is.' She alighted with the help of the driver and Alice could see she was small, plump and middle-aged. Her clothes were ostentatious but expensive and her large flower-bedecked hat partially hid her face.

'I'm Miss India Osbourne. You're very wise to be so suspicious. Caution is a good quality. Now where are you going?'

'The Park Rooming House off Meeting Street.'

'You see, you have to cross town and there's white trash and black trash hanging around on street corners. Get in, I'll drop you off.'

Alice got in. She was curious. 'Don't you live along here, ma'am?' she asked as with a jolt the carriage moved off.

'No, I live on West Street. You're not American, are you?'

The carriage lurched and Alice caught hold of the leather strap that hung by the door. 'No, I come from Liverpool, England.'

'Have you been in Charleston long?'

'Three weeks.'

'You've no family here then?'

'No, ma'am.'

'No friends or acquaintances?'

Alice shook her head. 'The only person I know is Miss Shelton at the Park.'

'What's your name?'

'Alice. Alice O'Connor.'

'And do you have a job, Alice?'

'No, ma'am. I've tried. I've tried hard but there's nothing and I'm not trained for anything.'

'Then what have you been doing for money?' India Osbourne had quickly taken in Alice's cheap clothes.

'I've been singing in the street. I used to do it in Liverpool, but there's too many other people here doing the same thing. I'd hoped I could get a job singing on the stage.'

'Your voice is that good?'

'Well, so people have told me, but no one will even listen to me. I couldn't even get an ... audition.'

India Osbourne sighed. 'I'm sorry things are so bad, Alice. If you get very lonely perhaps you would come to visit me or maybe we could meet next Sunday. I often drive along the Battery; sometimes I like to take the air in the gardens.'

Alice felt so miserable and homesick that she warmed to the older woman. 'That's very kind of you, ma'am. I'll come to the gardens, if you don't mind.'

They had reached the Park and Alice prepared to get out.

'Well, I'll see you next Sunday, Alice.'

'I'm dead grateful ... very glad. I'll look forward to it.'

'I hope you have some luck this week.'

'So do I or I don't know what I'll do.'

By Friday, she'd managed to earn a dollar. A dollar for the entire week, she thought. There'd been days when she was so hungry that she'd felt faint. You should be used to it, she told herself, but she hardly had the strength to walk the streets. She'd made up her mind that if Miss Osbourne turned up on Sunday, she would ask her if she could help. Well, she was rich and she must know plenty of people – rich people; maybe one of them would give her a job. She didn't mind how menial it was. If she could just earn enough to pay her lodgings and have one meal a day she'd manage until something better turned up. But that's what she'd told herself before, that some lucky chance would present itself, and it hadn't. Very probably Miss India Osbourne wouldn't present herself either next Sunday.

White Point Gardens were almost deserted when Alice arrived, just as dusk was falling. Only a few people strolled along the pathways or were seated on the benches. She sat down beneath a live oak from which the trailing fingers of grey moss drifted gently in the evening breeze. This will be a waste of time, a flaming wild goose chase, she thought, but only minutes had passed when she saw the small, ample figure of India Osbourne threading her way between the trees and shrubs. She was wearing a dress and jacket of a particularly bright peacock blue. It was trimmed round the neck and on the jacket facings with pale lemon crepe. The colour matched the large hat trimmed with blue ribbon. She looked like a small fat parrot, Alice thought.

'Ah, you're already here, Alice.' She was puffing and wheezing as she sat down and eased her feet slightly out of the elegant shoes that were a size too small. 'Ah, vanity, vanity! How do we suffer for it,' she sighed as the pressure was relieved. 'How have things been this week?'

'Oh, I'm so glad you turned up . . . er . . . came. Things are terrible. I've had no luck. I've no money for another week's lodgings – well, I do if I don't eat. I can't get a job and I just don't know where to turn, honestly I don't.' Her voice cracked with emotion. It was all true.

India Osbourne looked at her in concern. 'Alice, why did you come to Charleston?'

'Because I couldn't stand my da belting Mam and me. We had nothing and it was the middle of winter and it was freezing cold. I lost my job because Da battered me so badly I had to stay off. I'd heard tales about America, how you could get on, get good jobs. I really wanted to go to New York.'

'New York? Whatever for?'

She felt so miserable that she didn't care how stupid and feeble her motives for coming sounded. 'I was singing at the Pier Head in Liverpool where all the big ships leave from and I got knocked down by a car. He ... the man ... he was so good and kind to me. He took me on board the *Aquitania*, got the doctor to see me and gave me money, more money than I'd ever seen in my whole life. I ... I'd never met anyone like him before.'

India clasped her plump hands together and shook her head. 'So, you fell in love with a stranger?'

Alice was startled. She hadn't looked at it like that. But she did love him, she must do, to have come all this way. 'I suppose I did. I told him I sang and his brother said something about one day they might pay to hear me and ... and I ... that's what I want most in the world. For him to see me, dressed like a real lady, singing on the stage.'

India impatiently brushed away a tiny silver-coloured moth. 'Does he live in New York?'

'No, he lives near Liverpool.'

'But how will he hear you sing? Even if you'd gone to New York, if he doesn't live there what is the point?'

'I don't know. Oh, I don't suppose I really thought about it properly. I wanted to follow him. I thought that with him being in and out of New York with the ship, I might see him again. I had to get away. I had to have a chance in life and I'd never have got it in Liverpool – you don't know what it's like there if you're poor.'

'So you used the money he gave you for your fare?'

'Yes, only . . . only it wasn't enough.'

India shot her a knowing glance from beneath her lashes. She didn't need to be told how the girl had made up the difference.

'They . . . they cheated me. I thought they were going to New York.'

'I see, and now you're stuck here with no money, no job and no fare to go home, even if you wanted to go?'

Alice nodded miserably.

India sat up and smoothed out an imaginary crease in her skirt. 'Alice, let me hear you sing.'

'Sing?'

'Yes, sing. I might be able to help you.'

Hope surged through Alice. 'Really?'

'I said might. Let me hear you sing first.'

Alice thought of her repertoire. It would be better to sing something modern. 'I'll sing "Always".'

India Osbourne nodded and settled herself more comfortably on the bench. As Alice's voice broke the twilight stillness with sweet clarity, she nodded to herself. Yes, she'd do well. Very well indeed. She did have a good voice. In fact, an exceptionally fine voice. She was young, talented, beautiful and still innocent. A rare combination. A very rare combination.

Chapter Nine

All the way to West Street, Alice couldn't believe her luck. She'd been at her wits' end. She'd given up her dreams but she must have a guardian angel somewhere who was looking after her.

'I've a big house on West Street,' India had informed her. 'Part of it I use as a club. I have girls who sing to entertain my customers and they stay with me. I give them a home, a very good home with all the comforts, and in return they give me whatever tips – gifts of money – people pass to them as an extra thank you for their performance. I charge an entrance fee, quite a substantial one. It keeps all the undesirables out and my girls are all well worth it, they're very professional singers. Because of the Prohibition Law, no alcoholic beverages are supposed to be served but people come to enjoy themselves and we're all very discreet.'

'And you'll take me? You'll give me a home and I can sing in your club?'

India nodded, smiling. 'But I had to hear you sing first, Alice. You'd be no use to me as just a pretty face.'

'Oh, Miss Osbourne, it's . . . it's like a fairy story come true! I'll go and get my things from the Park now.' She felt like throwing her arms round India Osbourne's plump shoulders and hugging her.

'How much stuff have you got there?'

'Only another dress and the clothes I came over in and

they're all a bit tatty looking now. They weren't new when I bought them.'

'Well, leave them there. I can't have you looking like the rag picker's child. You'll need some elegant clothes for my establishment.'

'You mean you'll buy me clothes as well?'

India nodded and suspicion began to creep into Alice's mind.

'What for? Where's the catch?'

'There isn't a catch. I run a nightclub, a select one. My girls are all singers and wear evening gowns. You haven't got any decent clothes, let alone an evening gown, so I'll buy them and take the money from your tips. Is that fair?'

Alice nodded. It sounded all above board.

The house was a large one on the corner of West Street. It was of red brick and was built in the Colonial style with long sash windows. Plush blinds were now lowered over these windows but a soft light filtered through.

'We don't open on Sundays. It's not at all the thing to do. I do have standards,' India said sanctimoniously as Alice followed her up the steps.

Inside the hall, Alice's eyes widened and her mouth dropped open at the sheer opulence of the place. The walls were covered with a deep cyclamen-coloured paper that sported an ivy leaf design in an even deeper pink. The light was electric and the shades were of frosted glass. There were potted plants and gold-framed pictures in profusion and the rich plum carpet was so thick her feet sank into it.

'This part of the house is where we live; through that door there is the club.' India's manner was brisk and businesslike.

'Can I see the club, please? I've never even heard of one before.'

India opened the door with a theatrical flourish and Alice gasped. The room was decorated in shades of blue, from dark navy through sapphire to pale aquamarine. There was a sort of small low stage at one end with midnight-blue velvet curtains fringed with silver draped tastefully behind it. Numerous small delicate tables were dotted around the room, as were chairs, their seats upholstered in blue velvet. But it was the stage that held Alice's rapturous gaze. A stage! A real stage! She was going to sing here, in a nightclub with an audience who would pay to listen and might even give her money, tips as India had called them. Oh, why had she ever doubted herself? Many times over the last weeks she'd regretted leaving Mog on the ship. She had been a lucky mascot but now it seemed that luck hadn't deserted her after all; in fact it was smiling on her. This was far more than she'd ever hoped for.

India took her arm firmly and drew her back into the hall.

'Like I said, we don't open on Sundays and you must be hungry and thirsty and would probably like a bath. There are three bathrooms, one on each landing.'

Alice followed her up the staircase still in a state of bemused incredulity. Her mind couldn't take in all the palatial rooms or the fact that this was to be her home. The room India now showed her was beyond her wildest dreams and quite the most magnificent bedroom she'd ever seen. The carpet was cream but covered with a design of roses in brilliant hues. The curtains were crocus yellow and heavily fringed, as was the bedspread. The headboard and footboard, the dressing table, wardrobe and writing desk were of polished mahogany. There was a white porcelain washbasin with gilt taps and cakes of scented pink soap. Large thick white towels hung from the rail on the adjacent wall. A long low rosewood table stood at the foot of the bed and held a bowl of fresh flowers, a bowl of fruit and an array of ornaments. A low, buttoned-back chair covered in gold damask was set by the window which was open slightly, the breeze lifting the net curtain gently.

'I ... I must have died and gone to heaven! This ... this is for ... me?' Alice at last managed to stammer.

India laughed, an affected, brittle laugh. 'Well, what on earth is the point of having money if you can't spend it on beautiful things? Why keep it in a bank? There are no pockets in shrouds, I always say. Everything you will need you'll find in the dressing-table drawers. I'll send some food up and then you can have a good night's sleep and we'll talk about your job in the morning.'

'What do I call you, to thank you, like?'

Again there was that affected little laugh. 'Miss India. Everyone else does.'

Alice was sitting on the bed still dazed when a young mulatto girl brought up a tray laden with food. She didn't speak so Alice just smiled her thanks. She was glad she was alone for she knew as she attacked the bowl of thick soup that her manners left a lot to be desired, but she was starving. There was a plate of ham and sweet potatoes. There was corn, dripping with butter, crusty bread, a large slice of sticky chocolate cake and there was wine too. She'd never tasted wine so she sipped it cautiously. It was light and dry and full of bubbles. Oh, this was heaven!

When she'd eaten everything, she stripped off her clothes and filled the basin with water. She felt too nervous to go along to the bathroom. She might come back and find all this gone, find that it had all been a dream after all. She'd leave exploring the wonders of the bathroom until tomorrow; she'd had more than enough luxury for one day.

The soap was perfumed and the towels were soft. She took the tortoiseshell-backed hairbrush and brushed out her long mass of tawny curls, then she opened the dressing-table drawer and gasped as she drew out a nightdress and robe of alabaster silk, so flimsy it was as light as thistledown. She held it against her and looked at the reflection in the long cheval mirror. Then she rubbed it gently against her cheek, savouring its cool, perfumed fragility. She pulled it over her head and then turned slowly to observe the effect in the mirror. This was to sleep in? It was far too good for that; it was like a stage dress and a better one than Letty Lewis had worn at the Rotunda. It billowed around her like rippling waves, the layers of snowy lace like the foaming tops of the Atlantic waves.

She turned down the bed covers and stroked the soft, lavender-scented sheets and pillowcases. She'd thought that luxury was the bed in the hostel, then she'd been overwhelmed by the bed at the Park, but they were nothing compared to this. This was fit for royalty.

She was still marvelling at her good fortune when the door opened and a small, pretty girl appeared. She had large, lustrous dark eyes fringed with luxuriant lashes and a cloud of short blue-black curly hair. She wore a robe of pale blue satin edged with rows and rows of matching lace.

'Hi, I'm Marietta.' The tone was friendly, the voice low and soft, the vowels drawn out.

'I'm Alice. Alice O'Connor. I . . . I can't believe this place.'

'Not many people can!' came the amused reply. 'Isn't it awful? Her taste's terrible. Still, I suppose it's apt.'

'I think it's like a palace.' Alice defended her benefactress in a curt tone. Besides, she thought it was very tasteful.

Marietta sat down in the chair. 'Where did she find you? You're from England, aren't you?'

'In White Point Gardens. I was starving, broke, not a hope of a job and about to be chucked out of my lodgings. And now I've got all this and I'm going to sing on a stage, a real stage, and for a proper audience.'

Marietta raised her dark eyebrows. 'Is that what she told you?'

'I saw it. I saw the nightclub. Oh, it's been my dream! It's all I ever wanted to do, sing on a stage. I just can't believe this.'

Marietta studied her fingernails. 'Neither can the Charleston Sheriff's Department or the South Carolina State Police. She's as sly as a fox, is Miss India Osbourne. They never find any liquor on the premises and they can't charge her with anything else either. No evidence.'

Some of Alice's euphoria disappeared and was replaced by suspicion. 'She said it was against the law to serve drink.'

'It is. It's a crazy law, but . . .' Marietta shrugged her plump white shoulders.

'But what?' Alice demanded.

'Honey, the place is a speakeasy.'

'A what?'

'A club where illegal booze is sold, amongst other things.'

'What other things?' Alice's suspicion was rapidly deepening.

'Alice, just what did she tell you, for Christ's sake?'

'That she'd give me a home and that I'd sing for the paying customers and any money, tips, she called them, I'm to give to her, for my keep, I suppose. That's fair, isn't it? I've never seen a house like this. I've never been anywhere so grand.'

'Jesus! I didn't think there were any innocents left in the world. You think that's *fair*? You think she's a soft, kind-hearted woman who has picked you up off the streets and given you a home?'

'Yes.'

Marietta laughed pityingly.

'Don't we sing?' Alice was feeling very uneasy.

'Oh, sure, honey, we sing but it's not all we do.'

100

Understanding was dawning on Alice. How could she have been so blind, so stupid? She'd been desperate but she should have known. She'd been too trusting, too dazzled by India's 'kindness', all this luxury, the promise of ambition fulfilled. It all had a price. 'What is this place?'

Marietta got to her feet. 'This place is The Star of India. It's a speakeasy and a whorehouse. We sing and she sells cola, fruit juice and lemonade as a legitimate cover. She charges an entrance fee. A big fat one. That pays for us, for *all* our talents. We have some high an' mighty customers, all solid respectable "gentlemen". That's how come no liquor's ever found. She gets ample warning of a raid and it's all gone by the time the police arrive. She runs this place well; it's all very discreet, she has rules.' Marietta laughed cuttingly. 'The biggest bloody hypocrite in town, that's Miss India Osbourne!'

Alice sagged as though she'd been punched in the stomach. She felt sick and winded with the shock. 'A wh-whore . . .' she stammered.

'A whorehouse,' Marietta said flatly. 'I suppose she made sure you've no kin and no friends?'

Alice nodded. The feeling of nausea was being replaced with a fury akin to that which had overtaken her when she'd smashed the chair on her father's head.

'And you didn't go back to wherever you were staying for your things?'

Alice jumped to her feet. Her eyes were blazing in a face drained of all its colour.

'Where are you going?' Marietta asked.

'To find her! To find Miss India flaming Osbourne!'

Before Marietta could stop her, Alice had run down the stairs. Her bare feet and the thick carpet made her descent silent. There was a slight noise coming from a door on her left, the one opposite the club, and she flung it open.

'Alice!' India cried in surprise.

101

'You sly old bitch! You bloody liar! This is a flaming whorehouse! It's a speak . . . speak . . . something! I'm not staying here! I'm not a whore!' she yelled.

India's smile vanished and her eyes became hard. 'Oh, don't come that Miss Prissy Purity with me! How else did you pay your passage? Did you expect me to believe those lies about a stranger giving you money? You have to pay for everything in this life, one way or another, and you sure as hell know that's the truth!'

Alice did know but she plunged on, 'I won't stay here! I won't and you can't make me! You can go to hell, *Miss* Osbourne!'

India shut the door but not before she'd glimpsed Marietta standing at the bottom of the staircase. 'It's not me who'll go to hell, Alice O'Connor, it's you if you quit! You've got a choice. Stay here with me and have the comforts of life or go out on the streets and starve. You'll be forced to sell yourself in the end, so why not get well paid for it and live in luxury? Go back out there and you'll be raped sooner or later, maybe even killed. It's your choice. You said you wanted to sing on the stage and that's what I'm offering you. A chance. It's only right that I get some remuneration for my pains. I'm a businesswoman. I had nothing when I started out, not even a good voice! There was no one to look out for India Osbourne!'

The door opened and Marietta came into the room.

'Oh, take her back upstairs, Marietta. Talk some damned sense into her.'

Alice was still shaking but she let the other girl lead her back upstairs. She sat down heavily in the dainty chair. 'I don't care what she says. I'm not a whore. I won't do it. I won't!'

'You mean you've never . . . you're still a virgin?'

'No. I had to do it to pay my fare, but only once! I won't do it again. I won't be turned into a whore. I won't!

I can't let Mam down by doing . . . that.'

Marietta sat down on the bed. 'I said that once myself, honey, and so did all the others. I came here from Louisiana. I ran away from home, if you can call a stinking shack in a bayou home. I was full of plans and dreams, like you. Plans but no money and no training, just a singing voice. Not a bad one but nothing startling. I was singing outside a place down near the harbour. I'd been raped, beaten up, and I was starving when she found me. Some men just take without paying up. It's easy being here, honey, believe me. We've all got hard-luck stories to tell and no one damned well cares whether we live or die. Not even the police.'

'Oh, leave me alone!' Alice yelled at her.

'Sure, but I just wanted you to know that what she said is true. Go back out there and you may well end up in the harbour – dead.'

Alice covered her face with her hands. Oh, God, now what? She knew from bitter experience that she would starve back on the streets, and she didn't think India or Marietta were just trying to scare her. Marietta wouldn't lie about being raped and beaten up.

Oh, it had been different at home in Liverpool. Mam was there, she'd watched over her. The house in Benledi Street hadn't been much but it had been a roof over her head. A home of sorts. Here, if she left India's house there was nothing. No place to call home, no future and no hope of one. And no Mam. The anger left her and the tears welled up in her eyes. She couldn't even go back to Liverpool, she had no money. She'd let herself be hypnotised by dreams and ambitions. By the hope of a dazzling future. Georgie Tate had been right. She was chasing an impossible dream and it had suddenly turned into a nightmare.

She caught sight of herself in the long mirror. A beautiful girl with a wild tangled mane of hair and the eyes and expression of a hunted animal. She couldn't bear to look at herself. With a malicious swipe she swept the ornaments from the top of the dressing table and her fingers closed over the handle of the hairbrush. One hefty throw shattered the glass in the mirror and the image disappeared but it didn't help. She knew she was trapped. There was no way out.

Marietta uttered a scream when the mirror smashed but Alice didn't even notice. Her gaze alighted now on the bowl of flowers on the low table. She picked it up and with all her strength she hurled it at the window. The sound of breaking glass was deafening; the whole lower half of the window shattered and the floor was strewn with glass.

Marietta grabbed hold of her. 'For Christ's sake, Alice, are you crazy? She'll kill you!'

'I don't care! I don't care!' Alice screamed.

'You will. You'll have to pay for this.'

The door was flung open and India was confronted by the devastation and a seething, unrepentant Alice.

'You goddamn little slut! Look at the mess! You ungrateful, vicious . . .' India struggled for words and breath. Her stout body, encased in a tight corset, wasn't used to moving quickly up flights of stairs.

'You trapped me, you sly, evil old bag!' Alice yelled back.

'If you speak to me like that again, Alice O'Connor, you'll be out of here so fast it will make your head spin!'

Angry, vituperative words bubbled up in Alice's head but before she could speak, Marietta caught her arm.

'For God's sake, Alice, that's enough. Keep your mouth shut or she'll kick you out,' she hissed.

India was quivering with rage. 'You just listen to Marietta and be thankful I'm a charitable woman.'

Alice laughed, a harsh, derisive sound, but Marietta squeezed her arm warningly.

Chapter Ten

The window was reglazed and the mirror and ornaments replaced but Alice's acceptance of her situation was far from complete. She met the other girls. They came to see her, to introduce themselves in ones and twos, and they all had heartrending stories to tell and backgrounds like her own. And they all said that life in this house in West Street wasn't really bad.

'Miss India has rules and the clientele are at least gentlemen compared to the houses on Beresford and Myzack,' Laura, a pretty blonde from Atlanta, Georgia, assured her.

'Sure, but at least they don't pretend to be anything other than brothels.' Marietta was sarcastic. She was the most outspoken but Alice learned that Marietta had been with India the shortest time, apart from herself.

'Is it every night? Do we have to sing and ... well ... you know?' She wasn't able to say it. She swallowed hard, trying not to think about it.

Laura laughed. 'Oh, Lordy no! We have quiet nights and we have a "rest" on Sundays. We have to be available but it's not party time every night. Sometimes I don't have any clients and I get so bored I count the flowers on the wallpaper, but some of us have our regulars.'

It all depressed Alice terribly. She'd lived all her life cheek by jowl with poverty and there had been times when she'd been desperately ashamed of being dirty and dressed in rags, but it wasn't like this shame. This was so seedy. Everything was false. It was all a great pretence.

At first she was determined to take no interest at all in the clothes that were brought and hung up in the wardrobe and placed in the drawers of the dresser. She fought hard to suppress her natural curiosity, but when Marietta took the dresses out, one by one, and laid them across the bed, she just wasn't able to help herself. She'd glimpsed clothes like these in the posh shops in Liverpool's Bold Street but she'd never stood with her nose pressed against the window of Cripps or De Jong et Cie and longed for such gorgeous creations. There hadn't been any point. All she'd longed for then had been one good meal a day.

Almost reverently she smoothed out the folds of the evening dresses. The pale lilac georgette with its floating panelled skirt. The turquoise satin, the bodice of which was covered with tiny silver bugle beads and pearls. The shell-pink crepe de Chine, cut in the new short fashion with a huge bow of pink and silver ribbon at the hip. There were underclothes of pure silk. Low-heeled leather pumps and silk stockings. Day dresses of printed cotton and muslin and a smart suit of pale blue linen. There was a hat, a clutch bag and gloves to match.

Marietta smiled sardonically, holding out the cloche hat of fine white straw edged with blue ribbon. 'For Sundays. She insists we all look smart and ladylike on Sundays, the hypocritical old cow! Oh, and she's arranged for someone to come in and see to your hair.'

'What's wrong with my hair?'

'It's too long. Too old-fashioned. You're to have it cut.'

Instinctively Alice's hand went to her thick sun-streaked curls. 'No!'

'Honey, why do you keep arguing? It's easier in the end just to fall in. Besides, it will suit you short. There'll be no need for you to have it marcel-waved or have to suffer agonies wearing curling pins.'

The hairdresser was a small dapper man with black hair that was oiled and smoothly plastered down. He sported a small moustache and spoke with a slight accent.

'This will be a joy to cut!' he exclaimed as he began to brush out Alice's mane of hair.

As she watched the last of her long thick curls fall to the floor, the tears sprang to her eyes and brimmed over. The transformation was complete. Mam wouldn't recognise her now. In fact, no one would. She even had a new name, for India had decided that Alice was too plain, too ordinary. She was now to be called Alicia. Alicia O'Connor. Gone was the dirty, skinny little slummy. The girl who looked back at her from the mirror had a softly waving bob that ended just beneath her ears, making her look older than seventeen. Next week she would be eighteen but birthdays had always been irrelevant. She'd never had a birthday present or any kind of celebration, so why worry about it now? The collar of the raspberry-pink cotton day dress, trimmed with navy piping and a large floppy bow, added to the illusion of maturity. Only the large brown eyes, misty with tears, remained the same.

'Alicia, you look good. Real good.'

'Oh, I hate that name, Marietta. I really *hate* it!' She pointed to her reflection. 'That's not me. Not the *real* me. It's someone different, the real me has gone.' She was glad Mam couldn't see her. Yes, she looked very elegant, some would say even beautiful, but she knew Nelly would have preferred the daughter she knew, the girl dressed in rags with the mass of tangled hair. The girl who had been ignorant and half-starved but who had earned every penny decently. Even the way she'd begged in the street had been honest. She'd given something in return for the coins she'd received. A song. A bit of entertainment to relieve the boredom of waiting for the theatre to open.

'What will you wear tonight? It's your debut.'

Alice shrugged. 'I don't care.' At any other time she'd have been as excited as a child with the array of finery that hung in the wardrobe. She'd have fingered each outfit and agonised over her final choice.

'Honey, try and look on the bright side of it,' Marietta pleaded.

'What for? There is no bright side.'

'Yes, there is. You'll get to sing on a stage before a real audience. Isn't that what you've always wanted to do?'

'That doesn't matter now. I don't care if I never sing again. I don't want to sing in this place.'

'You wait until you hear the applause, it's marvellous! It's like a drug. You'll want more and more, you'll get hooked.'

'I don't want any applause. My singing's not what they want me for. It's not,' she struggled to find the right word, 'it's not real, not genuine.'

'You'll change your mind.'

'I won't.'

But she did.

Her final, reluctant choice as to what to wear settled on the turquoise beaded satin, the skirt of which only came to mid-calf, showing the white silk stockings and white leather pumps with a Louis heel and a strap over the instep. The camiknickers she wore beneath the dress were of cream silk edged with imported lace. Marietta fastened a band that sparkled with beads round her short hair and clipped long diamanté earrings to the lobes of her ears. 'Have you decided to go ahead with Miss India's choice of song?' she asked.

Alice had been thinking about that all the time Marietta had been fussing with her hair. She hadn't wanted to sing the old familiar songs, she doubted she'd ever sing them again. Nor would she sing 'If You Were The Only Girl In

The World,' poor Georgie Tate's favourite, or 'Always'. She remembered how she'd sung that for India Osborne only a few days ago. How she wished she'd never opened her mouth.

'Yes. It's different.'

'Oh, it's that all right! It's like a dirge. Not the type of song for this place.'

Alice didn't have any sense of what fitted any more. Everything looked and felt alien. She was shaking with nervous apprehension as she went downstairs to the night-club, and beads of perspiration sprang out on her brow.

Resplendent in a crimson and black evening gown, India stepped onto the small stage and made shushing gestures with her plump hands.

'That dress makes her look like a goddamn slice of watermelon,' Marietta whispered spitefully.

'Oh, Marietta, I'm scared! I'm scared stiff and I'll forget the words, it's all new!' Alice gripped the other girl's arm tightly as India announced her as 'a young lady from England with the voice of a nightingale'.

The group of three black musicians played the opening bars of 'The Londonderry Air', a traditional Irish piece, and Marietta pushed her gently forward to face her first audience comprised entirely of men in evening dress.

Alice swallowed hard and took a deep breath. Her opening notes were faltering but as her voice filled the room, she found her nervousness slipping away. If she could forget everything that had happened to her just these few minutes she'd be happy. Now, she told herself, she was the equal of Letty Lewis, the Cockney Songbird, but she knew she sounded far, far better. The Liverpool Songbird's voice was stronger, clearer, sweeter and the thunderous applause that broke out as the last notes died away confirmed the knowledge. No one was applauding dutifully. This *was* genuine. She couldn't help herself. A dazzling smile transformed her face and seemed to lighten

111

the entire room. Her eyes sparkled and she tapped her foot as she began the popular, lively "Bye 'Bye Blackbird'. She forgot everything and everyone. The drunken violence of her da. The *Castlemaine*, Georgie Tate, Mr Tibbs and Captain Burrows. She forgot Mam and Lizzie and India and Marietta. She was singing for just herself, because she really enjoyed it. She was singing on a stage. A real stage, not the streets of Liverpool or Charleston.

Again the applause was deafening and she stepped from the podium as though she was walking on a cloud.

'Oh, Alicia, you were fantastic!'

Marietta's praise was sincere. Alice smiled back but the feeling of elation began to evaporate and her heart sank as she saw India approaching. To Alice's horror she was accompanied by a tall, well-built man she judged to be in his thirties. The euphoria was replaced by a cold, hollow feeling in the pit of her stomach; the beat of her heart slowed and the palms of her hands were clammy.

India was all smiles. 'Alicia, dear, that was wonderful. A truly wonderful performance. Mr O'Farrell is absolutely delighted with you and so eager to meet you.'

Alice looked up at the man. He was old, though not as old as most of the clientele, and he was quite handsome. His thick, dark brown hair was cut short. He was clean-shaven, his skin lightly tanned. His eyes were a startling blue and admiration and curiosity were discernible in them.

'Miss Alicia, I'm charmed to meet you.'

He took her hand and his skin felt warm and dry. She was surprised by the lilt in his voice. 'You're Irish.'

'It's not a sin. I can't help it.' There was amusement in the blue eyes and in his voice.

She looked away, confused and apprehensive.

'Alicia, this is Mr Michael Eugene O'Farrell, President of O'Farrell Enterprises.'

She couldn't look at him. She felt sick.

'Would you like a drink?' he asked quietly. She was very young, little more than a child, he mused. Yet she was truly beautiful and her voice as she'd sung the plaintive words of a song he'd always loved had been so sweet and pure that it would tear the heart out of you, as his mother would say. 'I don't mean the moonshine India sells at inflated prices.'

Alice shook her head, and looked up. Thankfully India had gone. 'I . . . No, thank you.' She swallowed hard. Oh, best to get it over and done with. 'Shall we?' She made a half-hearted gesture towards the doorway in the hall. He nodded so she turned away from him and made for the door and the staircase beyond.

As she showed him into her room, he strode in as if he knew the place well. She closed the door behind him, momentarily leaning her forehead against the cool wood, desperation rising up in a great tide within her.

Faster than she'd thought he would, he spun round and, reaching out, gently turned her towards him. Her eyes tight shut, she tilted her face obediently up toward his. Gently he kissed her cheek then her lips and he felt her flinch.

'I won't hurt you, Alicia.'

She opened her eyes and he saw the naked fear and revulsion in their depths.

She couldn't help herself. 'My name's not Alicia, it's Alice. Alice O'Connor and I . . . I'm not a whore.'

He drew away from her. 'You mean you've never . . .?'

She shook her head. 'Only once and I was really, really desperate. I couldn't afford my fare.'

He took her hand and drew her towards the chair, indicating that she should sit down. He took a cigarette case from his pocket and proffered it to her. She shook her head, so he lit one for himself and sat on the edge of the bed. He had no intention of forcing himself on her. He didn't frequent places like this very often. He'd been

113

restless tonight, bored and unable to put his mind to anything serious, so he'd come out looking for a diversion.

'You're a long way from home, Alice O'Connor. You're from Liverpool, aren't you?'

His actions had surprised her. She hadn't expected him to consider her feelings, let alone be aware of her origins. 'How did you know?'

'The accent. It's one you don't forget. I was born in Dublin and I sailed from Liverpool.'

She shrugged. She'd thought she'd lost her Liverpudlian twang.

'So, how did you end up here? You've a voice like an angel and "The Derry Air" is one I've always liked. It's not exactly a modern song nor one you'd expect to hear in a place like this. Is it another of India's attempts to be cultural?'

Again she shrugged but she looked up into his face. She didn't want to talk, to explain, she just wanted to get it over and done with.

He saw the flash of fear. 'Alice, I'm not going to rape you. I've never forced myself on a woman and I don't intend to start now.'

Her chin jerked up and she looked at him with relief and some amazement. 'But you've paid!'

'So, I paid my entrance fee. Sure, it won't break the bank.'

'Then . . . what?' she stammered, still unsure of him.

'Tell me about yourself. How you got here. Where you learned to sing.'

She eyed him warily. 'Why? Why do you want to be bothered with me?'

'I like to study human nature. I'm interested to know how a little bit of a girl like you ended up here, over three thousand miles away from home.'

Simply and often haltingly she told him her story, sometimes wiping away a tear.

114

His expression changed. A frown creased his forehead and the blue eyes became cold and hard as she spoke of her da and then Captain Burrows. She didn't tell him about her feelings for David Williamson. She'd told India and somehow it had seemed to increase the hold the woman had on her, and when she'd put it into words it sounded so vain, so stupid.

When she'd finished, there was a silence between them and she wondered what he was thinking.

To Mike O'Farrell it was an all too familiar story. He'd seen many girls like her in Dublin in the area he'd lived in. He'd known girls whose fathers had beaten them black and blue week after week, some in the street where he'd lived. But for the fact that she had the face of an angel and a voice to match, God alone knew what would have happened to her.

'Do you think we ... we should go down soon?' She wanted to remind him of his promise.

'Do you have to sing again?'

'No, but ...'

'But there may be other customers?' He stood up. 'Get your coat.'

'What?'

'I said get your coat or wrap or whatever you wear to go out in.'

'I don't understand. Are you going to take me out?'

'I am. There will be no other customers tonight. I'm going to take you to a place I know where you'll enjoy yourself and, Holy Mother of God, don't you deserve a bit of pleasure out of life?'

She was incredulous but then her eyes narrowed. 'Why are you doing all this for me? Is there a catch in it?'

'No, there bloody isn't! Let's just say you sang a song that reminded me of home and I want to show you a bit of gratitude for that, nothing else. Nothing sinister in it at all.'

Suddenly all Alice's fears fell away and she grinned at him. 'You're mad!'

Mike threw back his head and laughed. 'All Irishmen are mad, didn't you know that, Alice O'Connor?'

She laughed with him but suddenly the laughter died in his eyes and he became serious.

'Of course we're mad. Why the hell do you think we take the emigrant ship in droves and leave behind the most beautiful country on God's good earth? Oh, we've a free state now, all the years of fighting are over, but there's still no work, very few opportunities.' Then, quick as it had gone, the gaiety reappeared. 'Ah, go on and get your coat, you bewitching little rossi!' he laughed, shooing her across the room.

'India won't like it.'

Mike crossed his arms over his chest and his brow furrowed in a frown. 'India can go to hell and if she complains, I'll blow her little business wide open.'

Alice laughed and snatched up a short velvet jacket from the wardrobe. India would be furious but she didn't care. Mike O'Farrell wasn't going to force himself on her and he was making sure no one else did either, at least not tonight. She refused to think about tomorrow. He was taking her out to enjoy herself and she trusted him and that's all that mattered for now.

India did protest, strongly, but Mike silenced her with a few well-chosen questions.

The plump little woman was seething. 'I've spent a fortune on her and you've no idea of the damage she's done. Smashed up her room in a fit of temper!'

'Is that so? She's a girl of rare spirit then. Ah, you'll be suitably recompensed – in time.'

India tried a different tack. She looked up at him coyly. 'Then we'll be seeing you more frequently?'

Mike wanted to hit her. 'Oh, very definitely, Miss Osbourne. Probably every night.'

'Did you mean that?' Alice asked as he hailed a cab.

'I never say things I don't mean,' he replied as he handed her into it.

She'd never been in a motorcar. She would have bubbled over with excitement if it hadn't reminded her of David Williamson and the car that had knocked her down. She wondered where he was now. Halfway across the Atlantic, or at home in Liverpool? If she closed her eyes she could see his face. It was something she often did. She could remember the way he'd looked down at her, his eyes full of concern.

'Don't you want to know where we're going?' Mike O'Farrell's question put an end to her musings.

'Where?'

'The Plantation Club. Oh, it's nothing like The Star of India,' he added reassuringly, seeing the fear return to her brown eyes.

'Then what's it like?'

'It's small and dark and smoky. I want you to hear a different kind of music. I want you to enjoy yourself.'

'Where is it?'

'In Beresford Street.'

'But . . .'

'I know. It's not a very refined area but you'll be safe with me.'

She wished she understood him. He *must* have some kind of motive. Was all this concern just to calm her suspicions? But he'd paid for her. He could have taken her at India's. No one she'd ever known had really considered her feelings except Mam and David Williamson, and she didn't want to think of either of them now. She tried to focus on the present and keep her wits about her. Who knew what she'd let herself in for with this strange Irishman. . .

117

Chapter Eleven

Mike O'Farrell was right. The club *was* dark, small and so fuggy with cigar and cigarette smoke that it caught the back of her throat. When they'd alighted from the cab she'd followed him down some steps to the basement of a warehouse but she hadn't felt at all uneasy. The atmosphere in the club was something she'd never experienced before. As her eyes became accustomed to the gloom, she could see that most of the patrons of the Plantation were black. The few other white people were, like themselves, in evening dress. The music was being provided by a group of five black musicians. But what music! It made her tingle all over.

'It's great! I've never heard anything like this. What is it and what are all those people doing?' Already her feet were tapping and she watched the couples on the dance floor with amazement.

'They're dancing, believe it or not. The dance is called after this city – Charleston. The music is jazz, ragtime, and it's going to sweep the world.' He ushered her to a small table on the fringe of the dance floor but she didn't take her eyes off the exuberant dancers until two tall glasses filled with a light amber-coloured liquid were placed in front of them. She looked at the drinks suspiciously.

'Take that look off your face, sure it's only tea. Iced tea. That's all they serve here. The city fathers have already tried to close them down for playing this "Devil" music and corrupting people's morals, so no risks are taken with liquor.'

Alice tasted hers. It was tea.

He laughed at her expression. 'You don't have to drink it.'

'It doesn't taste right like this. Cold and with no milk.' She sipped it again, pulled a face and then turned her attention back to the dance floor.

Mike watched her. Her eyes were sparkling; her body, even seated, was moving in time with the rhythm and her fingers tapped the table top. The music had obviously captivated her. Joy and vivacity radiated from her like the rays of the sun. He'd never before experienced any of the emotions that were now coursing through him. He smiled to himself sardonically. Was he falling in love, and at first sight, with this chit of a girl? It was the only explanation for how he felt. He hadn't even had a drink, she was intoxication enough. He wanted her, any man would, she was young and beautiful, but he also wanted to protect her, cherish her, keep her away from anything and anyone rough, demanding or cruel. Such beauty and talent should be nurtured not crushed by lust and greed. But he was almost old enough to be her father. Was it possible to love someone you'd only known for an hour? Would she tell him that? Would she laugh cruelly and reject his love, if it was love?

'Oh, I wish I could dance.' Alice's wistful cry cut through his thoughts.

'I'll get someone to teach you. I'm too old to be throwing myself all over the place like that,' he laughed. He enjoyed dancing, the old-fashioned kind of dancing, but he liked to listen to the music, watch other people doing the Charleston and the Black Bottom. Privately he thought that anyone over twenty-five executing those abandoned frenetic steps looked a fool, and Michael

120

Eugene O'Farrell had no intention of making himself a laughing stock.

Alice's reply was cut short as a tall, slim black man approached the table.

Mike got to his feet and stretched out his hand. 'King! How are you in yourself? I've brought a friend. Alice O'Connor. Alice, meet "King" Oliver. This is his place.'

Alice smiled and shook his hand.

'We haven't seen you much lately, Mike.'

'Import and export. Business and travel. You know how it is.'

'Travel to Europe?'

Mike nodded. 'I caught Paul Whiteman's show at the Grafton Galleries in London. It sure was really something to hear.'

'I'll bet. Don't you dance, Miss O'Connor?' Oliver asked, seeing Alice's gaze fixed once more on the dancers.

'No. I never had any time, before I came here, to America.'

'But she can sing.'

'Really?' There was a genuine interest in Oliver's voice.

'Oh, I can't sing anything like this,' Alice said hastily, looking from her host to Mike.

'Ah, go on. Don't keep putting yourself down. You sang "'Bye 'Bye Blackbird" tonight and it was great altogether.'

'But that was different.' Alice was becoming nervous under the intense but friendly gaze of King Oliver.

'I thought it was your ambition in life to be able to sing on stage and become famous?' Mike chided. 'Isn't that what you told me not an hour ago?'

'It is! But . . .'

'Will you sing for me, Alice?' Oliver asked.

'Now? Here?'

He nodded.

Before she could protest, Mike pulled her to her feet. 'Sure she will. She's got a voice that with training wouldn't

121

disgrace the Charleston Grand Opera House.'

'But I haven't got any training! I only know a few old-fashioned songs,' Alice protested as both men propelled her gently but firmly towards the stage.

'OK, boys, "'Bye 'Bye Blackbird", follow her,' Oliver instructed the band while Alice turned to face her audience. It had all happened so fast she didn't feel nervous. There wasn't time. She smiled down and over what looked like a sea of eager, expectant faces and her heart began to beat faster. This was a real audience, a proper audience. Men and women, black and white, who wanted nothing more than to enjoy themselves. To be entertained by her, Alice O'Connor.

She'd never enjoyed herself so much! She felt glowing, tingling, alive! Oh, it had been wonderful. If she never sang another note publicly it wouldn't matter now. She'd had this magical, glorious night. She'd completely lost track of the time and she'd forgotten about India Osbourne but eventually Mike had led her back to the table and placed her jacket round her shoulders.

'Time to go.'

'Oh, I don't want to. I want to stay here for ever.'

He took her hand. 'Out of the question.'

'Mike, I don't want to go back to India.'

King Oliver had appeared beside them. 'Is that where you found her?'

'Tonight was my first night. I had no money, no job. I had no choice.'

'I'll offer you a job, Alice. Here, but I can't pay you much.'

She was astounded. So astounded she couldn't reply.

Mike grinned. 'So? Answer the man.'

Alice found her voice. 'Oh, please! Yes, yes, please!' Tears of joy and pure relief filled her eyes and she grasped Mike's arm to steady herself. She felt dizzy.

'Then see you tomorrow, Alice. About eight o'clock?'

'Pinch me! Pinch my arm so I'll know I'm awake.'

Mike laughed and gently nipped the soft skin above her elbow but she was still in a daze as he led her up the steps and out into the street. She looked up at the sky. A soft, heavy, midnight-blue sky with thousands of stars all looking brighter than she'd ever seen them look before. 'Oh, I can't believe it! I've got a job! I just can't believe that someone's going to pay me money to sing! I won't have to sweep floors, beg or . . . do anything else for it.'

Mike refused the offer of a cab. They'd walk towards town and the Battery. He wanted time to work things out. To think, to try to get his thoughts and ideas into some kind of order. Alice almost skipped along beside him like a child, humming to herself and singing aloud snatches of the songs she'd rapidly picked up from Andy, the pianist, who'd told her she had a good ear for music, that she was a 'natural'. She hadn't really understood what he meant but she was thrilled just the same. This was what she'd come to America for. It was for this that she'd endured seasickness, the storms and the attention of James Burrows. It was coming true, all of it. It really was happening.

As he looked down into her face, glowing with sheer happiness, Mike made up his mind. She wasn't going back to the house on West Street. It might not work out, he had no idea how she would behave or even react to his suggestion, but he was willing to try.

Alice suddenly stopped, realising they had turned into Rutledge Street. 'Where are we going now?'

'We're nearly there.'

'Where?'

'Home.'

Her jaw dropped and she stared at him. 'You *live* here on Rutledge?'

He nodded. 'And from now on, so do you.'

'Me?' she gasped.

123

'You're not going back to India. You've got a job now. You need somewhere to live, I've got plenty of room.'

The suspicions swooped back into her mind. Was this what he'd been planning all night? Were he and King Oliver in cahoots, as Americans said?

'No. I ... I can't. You'll want a big rent and ... and what will people say?'

'Goddamn you, Alice O'Connor! You're the most suspicious woman I've ever met! I'm offering you a decent home, a more than decent home. A life of bloody luxury compared to what you're used to, and you think it's some plot to sell you into white slavery or something else as desperate!'

Instantly she was contrite. 'I'm sorry. It's just that no one's ever been good to me, not without a price.'

He opened the ornate gate set in the white stuccoed wall and led her into a garden bathed in moonlight. A garden filled with palmettoes, magnolias, jasmine, bougainvillaea and tropical plants Alice had never seen before. The moonlight seemed to make the stuccoed walls of the house shimmer against the midnight-blue sky. She caught her breath in disbelief. Her gaze wandered to the shuttered windows on the upper storey, then down to the windows on the ground floor, which were open and blazed with light. A balcony ran along the entire front of the house, supported by four white pillars with latticework in a strange Eastern design connecting each column.

'This is your house?' she breathed in awe.

'All mine. Legally left to me by my father.'

His voice was bitter, Alice thought, as he led her up the wide front steps and onto the porch. Gently he pushed her down onto a swinging, white-painted rattan seat covered with soft, upholstered cushions.

She'd passed houses like this many times on her wanderings around the city. She suddenly remembered the lady in grey, Mrs Phillips, who had given her fifty cents to go away and not lower the tone of the neighbourhood. This neighbourhood.

'Why are you doing all this for me? You only met me tonight and you thought ... you thought I was a whore. You even paid for me. You know what I am and where I come from.'

He looked out over his well-tended gardens and it was as if the years had rolled back and he was seeing them for the first time, as he'd done nearly twenty years ago. A lad of seventeen he'd been then, filled with anger and the raging fire for revenge.

'Because I know what it's like to be poor. To be cold and hungry. Ragged and despised. I know what it's like to have to beg.'

She was astounded. 'You?'

'Yes, me. Michael Eugene O'Farrell from the Coombe in Dublin.'

She looked at him in silent mystification.

'Where did you live in Liverpool, Alice? The exact area.'

'Benledi Street, off Scotland Road.'

'A slum? Rotten, falling down, bug-infested houses? Streets of them. Back to back with a filthy alleyway between them?'

She nodded.

'Just like the street where I was born and where I lived until I was seventeen. The houses were beautiful Georgian buildings originally, but when they dissolved Grattan's Parliament, the high and mighty up and left. Now they're just derelict, with a family in every room, including the cellar. There were eight families in our house and things were desperate for everyone. Oh, Dublin's changing but there's still terrible poverty. The treaty and the civil war have changed some things but before that even if you were rich you had no rights. Catholics couldn't vote. Oh no. No Catholic was even allowed to go to Trinity College

– the university.' He took out his cigarette case, lit one and drew deeply on it as old memories stirred in him. 'There were three of us – that lived. Me, Kitty and Deidre, and Da and Mammy. When I was eight, didn't Da leave us. He emigrated. Took the ferry from Kingstown to Liverpool and then the ship to America. Oh, the plan was all worked out. He promised faithfully he'd send for us. There was only enough for one fare, you see, and Mammy had begged, borrowed and starved to get that together!' He ground the cigarette out viciously beneath his heel. His face was in shadow so Alice couldn't see the hatred in his eyes but she could hear it in his voice.

'He didn't send for you.'

'No, he bloody well didn't! Not a word. Not a letter or a bloody note.'

'How did she manage?' Alice's thoughts were of Nelly and how she'd begged and borrowed, and she'd had some wages to help, occasionally, after she'd prised them out of Da.

'She begged in the streets, like you. I got what bit of work I could. I'd turn my hand to anything and when I didn't get anything I stole. She always said God didn't put a mouth on this earth that He doesn't feed but that's a bloody lie! Typical, empty, useless platitudes the Father used to spout on Sundays at Mass. Well, my father turned me into a thief but I swore that one day I'd find him and make him pay for every goddamn lie I had to tell my mother. Aye, and for every single one of her tears!'

'And did you?'

'I did so. I worked my passage from Liverpool. I knew he'd come south, to Charleston. The only bit of information Father Maguire managed to get for us. So I followed him, riding freight trains, cadging lifts where I could until I got here. It wasn't hard to find him then. He'd had the luck of the Irish all right, he'd made a bloody fortune. Mainly by gambling and then by buying up property.

126

Renting it for a while then selling it on. Houses that were falling down like the one he'd left us all in, but could still be rented to two or even three families. Mainly poor black families.'

He paused to light another cigarette.

'What did he say?' she asked.

Mike laughed and there was a lifetime of bitterness in the sound. 'When I arrived here at this house? When I saw all the magnificent rooms and furniture? I was seventeen and all I could think about was my mammy and my sisters going barefoot in the snow along the quays or up Sackville Street, as it was then, begging, while he had been living like a bloody king. I beat him half to death.' Feeling her shrink back, he smiled. 'There's no need to be afraid of me, Alice. I've never raised a hand to any man since that day. I never needed to.'

'And then?'

'Then I went back to Dublin. I took his conscience money and bought a house. A grand, well-appointed house in Donnybrook and moved them all in there. He had a stroke while I was home, so I came back to oversee his "investments" and make some of my own. He died a year later. He couldn't stand being crippled. He couldn't stand seeing me taking over.'

'Didn't you . . . didn't you . . .'

'Feel guilty? No. Not once. What kind of a man is it that lives in the lap of luxury, knowing his family are starving in a hovel?'

'Is your Mam . . .'

'Alive?' He laughed but this time there was no bitterness or pain in the sound. 'Yes, she'll live to be a hundred. Both Kitty and Dee are married with families of their own. She won't live with either of them nor will she come to live here. She still insists it's *his* house. The one he denied her. The girls keep an eye on her, she wants for nothing. She has a woman who comes in to do the housework and don't they have a fight every week over something, then she sacks poor Molly but takes her back on the next day. Oh, she's a desperate stubborn woman, but she values her independence.'

'Will you ever leave here? Go back to Dublin for good?'

He shrugged. 'I might. One day. Maybe when they repeal this bloody stupid prohibition law and there's no more money to be made selling bootleg whiskey.'

'Is that what you do?'

'Among other things. Import and export. Oh, I'm very careful and I'm not greedy. He left me a rich man, my father. I don't want to make a vast fortune like some do and I don't tread on anyone's toes either. I intend to die in my bed of old age, not with a bullet in my back.' He got to his feet and held out his hand. 'So, that's why I'm offering you a home, Alice O'Connor. Lodgings, nothing else, no strings attached.'

'Then I'll pay my way.'

'There's no need.'

'I won't be a kept woman!' she flashed at him.

He threw up his hands in mock horror. 'All right! All right! You can pay me a token rent which I will bank in your name. Come and I'll show you inside and you can meet Alexander.'

'Who's he?'

'My butler. He'll put some manners on you, Alice O'Connor, and between us we'll make a lady of you.'

He led her from room to room and her eyes grew wider and wider. When he'd said his father had lived like a king, he'd meant it. The reception rooms were large and airy and filled with expensive furniture, most of it imported, which had been lovingly cared for over many years. The dining room was decorated in pale yellow and green silk, the rosewood table and chairs and buffet gleaming in dark contrast. The electric lights were covered with shades shaped like Oriental lanterns. Prints of Chinese and

128

Japanese rural scenes decorated the walls. A magnificent Chinese carpet covered most of the floor but the exposed boards had a mirror-like polish on them. In contrast, his study was a sombre room, dark woods, dark green carpet and drapes. Then he led her up the wide staircase and she gripped the delicate wrought-iron scrolls of the banister, feeling once more that everything was a dream.

There were numerous bedrooms and bathrooms decorated in pale pastel shades, but the room he led her into and informed Alice was hers made her gasp aloud. The walls and ceiling were covered in silk which, when viewed in one light looked pale lilac and in another, pale blue. The material was draped and pleated across the ceiling and gathered into a rosette in the centre, from which hung a crystal chandelier. The carpet was pale blue, like the walls, and the ivory damask curtains at the deep sash windows matched the bedspread. The headboard and footboard of the bed were ornate, inlaid with mother-of-pearl in an intricate Oriental pattern, the mosquito netting elegantly tied back with pale blue cord. The tables beside the bed and beneath the window were small, carved and gilded. In the name of God, how much money did he have? He must be as rich as the King of England! She stared up at him, her thoughts quite clear in her eyes.

He smiled. 'I'd give it all away if I could have spared my poor mother one minute of hardship, one hour of heartache and worry over that bastard!'

She sat down on the edge of a chair. 'I don't know what to say, or do. How can I pay you back?'

'Write to your mother, Alice. Tell her you're safe and well, that you've got a job and a home and send her this.' He placed a fifty-dollar bill on the table beside her.

She gazed at him. 'I'll pay you back,' she said stoutly. 'If you won't take any rent, then the money you put in the bank can go towards paying you for this. Please. I'd feel better about it all.'

He nodded. 'And tomorrow Alexander will take you shopping.'

'But what will people think about me moving in here? I mean your friends, like?'

'I don't care. I don't move in the exalted circles of Charleston society. I'm "new" money, not quite respectable. If your relations haven't been here for over a hundred years or fought in the War of Independence, all the best homes are closed to you.' He could see she didn't understand him, so he smiled. 'Ah, don't worry your head about it. Good night, Alice O'Connor.'

She smiled at him, a smile of such radiance that his heart lurched. He turned away. He must be the biggest eejit in the entire bloody world, he thought. But he was sure now of his feelings. He loved her.

When Alexander brought him his usual nightcap of bourbon, Mike could see the man had something on his mind.

'Come on, out with it now. You've a face like thunder.'

Alexander drew himself up. 'Who is the young person upstairs? Is she staying the night? Will she require Ruth's services?'

'She's my good deed for the day. I rescued her from The Star of India. She's far too young and naive to be in a place like that and she's only been in Charleston a few weeks.'

Alexander's eyebrows rose and he inhaled deeply. He'd only caught sight of her for a few minutes, but long enough for him to see she was a pretty girl and as his employer had just said, young and naive. The look of innocent wonderment on her face had been clear for all to see and he'd warmed to her, though of course he'd make it clear to Mr O'Farrell that he didn't appreciate her being introduced into the house without his being fully informed. But now it appeared she was a prostitute. He struggled for words and with his composure. 'You've brought a . . .

whore home, here, to this house?'

The amusement died in Mike's eyes. 'She is *not* a whore! Hard up, uneducated, living by her wits but not a whore. She's going to live here and work, sing at the Plantation.'

The light of battle flooded into Alexander's dark eyes. 'And how's that going to look in this part of town? Folk will talk and the Hendersons' butler is sure to ask me straight out and then gloat 'cos we've a . . . a nightclub singer living here.'

Mike stared at Alexander. He liked the man. He was efficient, honest and tactful. He was also a snob but Mike didn't hold that against him. All the butlers he knew were the same. He certainly didn't want to lose him. 'I don't care what anyone thinks but obviously you do. So, what do you suggest? Apart from throwing her out which I won't do.'

Alexander began to ponder the matter, his dignity restored, his feelings and opinion considered. What he wanted to say was that he considered it high time Mike O'Farrell was married. He'd dropped enough hints over the past two years about there never being any 'company' calling. No ladies brought home for dinner or escorted to the opera, balls or soirees. Lately the hints had not been very subtle. All to no avail. But maybe, just maybe, this one could be the one. Not one he'd have chosen, of course, but she was young and she could learn.

'We could say she's your niece. Your dead sister's child?'

'Jaysus! Alexander, can't you do better than that? Besides, both my sisters are alive and well, thank God and God bless the mark!' Mike spoke part in seriousness, for although he denied it, he was superstitious.

'Well, the daughter of some old friend in Dublin who's died then.'

'She's from Liverpool but I grasp your meaning. He begged and pleaded with me, in his will of course, that she should become my ward. I'd be her legal guardian.'

131

Alexander nodded but there was no relaxation of the disapproval in his stance. 'What about her singing at that place?'

Mike refilled his glass. 'It's a perfectly respectable club, unlike most, and I won't stop her singing. You can tell people she sang on the stage in England or Ireland or anywhere you choose. Tell them what you bloody well like, but I'm not going to stop her. Anyway, I can't. I've no claim on her at all and she's been kicked in the teeth by fate often enough already. Most of all by her own father. She's come from the slums of Liverpool, the way I came from the slums of Dublin.' Years ago he'd told Alexander his life story one night when he'd been very drunk, morbid and moribund. In return Alexander had told him that his grandfather had been a slave on a plantation in Georgia, and not a house servant but a field hand, before Mr Lincoln and the war had freed them all.

Alexander nodded slowly. 'You're her legal guardian until she's twenty-one and she had a very promising stage career until her pa died.'

'And stated, in his will of course, that I had promised to be her guardian and further her career over here,' Mike added.

Alexander still didn't look totally convinced.

'What's the matter with that story?'

Alexander looked down at his highly polished shoes. 'If, well, if she were to be your fiancée . . .' That was as far as he got.

Mike flung open the door. 'Out! Don't push your luck any further!'

Chapter Twelve

Lizzie walked wearily down Titchfield Street having managed to beg a few potatoes from Burgess's on the corner of Burlington Street. It was a long walk to Silvester Street and Holden's shop. She'd have to walk the length of Titchfield Street and then turn into Blenheim Street. She had sixpence, the last of her wages, and it would have to last until next week. She had to try and see what she could get from Ivy Holden and still have change over.

The wind was fierce and blustery. It lifted the straw and bits of paper from the road and blew them into a swirling, eddying sort of dance. The smell of horse manure was strong; although motor lorries were becoming increasingly numerous, many commodities were still transported by horse and cart. A few spots of rain touched her face but she was too tired, hungry and dispirited to notice. Christmas was approaching but it only made her feel more miserable. You didn't automatically get a Goodfellows parcel. You had to be recommended, but then nearly every family in Benledi Street deserved strong recommendations. The fact that her family were the poorest of the poor and needed a parcel most didn't count for much. A few families, like the Garrettys and the O'Hanlons, did share a bit of their parcels, but the rest didn't. She had no interest in the red and yellow crepe paper streamers or the holly and tinsel that were being put up in most shops. She didn't even notice the words 'Happy Christmas' that were painted in whitewash on the shop windows nor that the more adventurous and artistic proprietors added sprigs of holly too. Christmas was the same as any other time of the year for them. It could be worse, in fact, if Da had no money for drink to celebrate with his mates.

She walked slowly; exhaustion made it hard to find any energy at all. Morosely she thought about other Christmases. Last year had been the second without Alice. Mam had surreptitiously wiped away her silent tears all that day and Lizzie had heard her crying when she thought everyone was finally asleep.

Lizzie often wondered what kind of a Christmas Alice had had last year. In fact she often wondered what kind of a life Alice had now. She had a job singing and a place to stay, that much they knew, but they didn't know anything else. Da collected the letters from the main post office. Mam had tried, and she had tried, to sneak off to the post office, telling them that Da couldn't come down himself because he wasn't well enough, and were there any more letter from America? They'd both been turned away by officious clerks demanding proof of identity and letters of permission from Da. They'd only ever seen that first one but Lizzie knew Alice sent money. She didn't know the exact amount and they never saw a penny of it. Da could barely read so he probably just threw the letters away. But at least Mam could console herself that Alice was safe and well and happy.

There had been a couple of good Christmases, or what passed for good in their house, Lizzie reflected, but they'd been during the war years. She held the paper bag tightly to her under her shawl. Those four years had been terrible years for everyone they knew. She knew Mam had felt guilty that she had no son old enough to go and fight for King and Country. Many's the night she had prayed they'd come and take Da off to go and fight, but being a docker was a reserved occupation. He'd had plenty of work, about which he had complained constantly, and money too, but they saw very little of that.

'How can I go and sit with Mary O'Hanlon and Jinny Thomas and all the rest when I don't know what they're going through?' Nelly had said time and again. But it had broken her heart to see the telegrams arrive, day after day, week after week, month after month. The neighbourhood had been decimated. Nearly all the lads she'd grown up with were dead or crippled. Tommy had been killed too. Lizzie's eyes misted with tears. Poor big-hearted, loud-mouthed, generous Tommy MacNamara. People had said he was daft but he wasn't. A bit slow, that's all, and that was because he'd had to bring himself up. All Ma Mac cared about was her gin and stout, certainly not her kids. She was in the pub morning, noon and night and Tommy's da was inside Walton Jail more often than he was out of it.

Tommy had volunteered, unlike his older brothers. She'd heard Ivy Holden telling Mam that Ma Mac had enough white feathers to stuff a pillow. Tommy's brothers had been carted off by the military police in the end. Big Kevin Mac had been killed too and as for the rest of them, as far as she knew they'd just disappeared off the face of the earth. People said the army was still looking for them.

The whole family were villains of the worst kind. Even Tommy fenced stolen goods and was in on almost every crime they'd committed. Except for anything violent. He had no stomach for beating people up, he'd said. Of course war was different, he'd explained.

He'd been kind and gentle and loving to her. He'd bought her lovely clothes and shoes and even underwear. Mam had gone mad about that. Fellers only bought you things like that after they'd married you. She'd retorted that Tommy was going to marry her, he'd told her so. He'd bought her perfume and little trinkets and bits of cheap jewellery. He'd taken her to music halls and they'd gone on day trips to New Brighton and even Llandudno. And best of all, Da had been terrified of the whole MacNamara family so she'd been able to give Mam all her wages. Even after Tommy had gone off to war she'd been able to earn a good wage in munitions and they'd also managed to hang onto it by threatening Da with the terrible things Tommy or his brothers would do if they found out he'd taken it off them. Even though they were in Flanders they had mates at home who would do them favours, like giving Da a good hiding. Lizzie had never been sure about that threat but it worked. Da had believed it. Things had been better then, they had had money for coal and a bit more food and some second-hand clothes for the kids. And then on the terrible day they heard that Tommy and Big Kev had been killed, Da had taken all her clothes and shoes, the cheap trinkets and bits of jewellery to the pawnshop. He'd not let her keep a single thing. Now she had nothing tangible to remember Tommy MacNamara by, only memories and images.

She was unaware that tears were mingling with the raindrops on her cheeks. Now she was old and drab. Any chance, any small claim to attractiveness had gone. She'd be a 'spinster of this parish' for the rest of her life. Or until Da went too far and killed one of them. He was becoming more and more violent. Poor Mam hadn't been able to get up for days after he'd found out that Alice had gone. He'd blamed that on Mam, but she'd been given a hefty clout too.

The rain had become heavier and Lizzie tried to hasten her steps. It was dark, one of the street lamps had gone out, and as she turned into Blenheim Street she collided with someone. She slipped on the wet cobbles and fell awkwardly, sprawling in the road. The potatoes escaped from the bag and rolled into the gutter, followed by the silver sixpence. She wasn't really hurt, physically, but as she saw the sixpence roll down a grid, she just sat in the road and burst into tears.

'Come on, girl, up you get. Are you hurt? I didn't see you, the lamp's out. Have you broken anything, do you think?'

She looked up and through her tears she saw the concerned face of a policeman. His helmet was pulled well down and the collar of his cape was turned up against the weather. Instinctively she shied away from him. Scuffers meant trouble.

'Come on now, luv. I'm not going to hurt you. I promise.' He held out a large hand encased in thick cream-coloured woollen gloves.

Tentatively Lizzie took it and was drawn gently to her feet. He towered over her. All the scuffers were tall but he was one of the biggest she'd ever seen.

'No damage done.' He was still looking concerned.

'No, but I've lost me spuds an' me sixpence. It rolled down the grid. It's all I . . . we had.'

Jack Phillips looked at her closely. He was a kind man and he considered himself to be fair in his dealings with the people on his beat. Every working day of his life he was confronted with the wretched poverty they lived in. He knew all the real hard cases, the villains, the drunkards.

'You're Tip O'Connor's girl, aren't you?'

Lizzie shrank away from him, terrified now that she might be tarred with the same brush as her da.

'Then I know you've a lot to put up with, luv. He's not the best father in the world, is he?'

She slowly shook her head.

'Pull your shawl over your head, you're getting soaked. I'll rescue the spuds but the sixpenny joey will have gone into the main drain by now, especially with all this rain.'

Lizzie did as she was told and stood in silence watching as he poked around in the gutter with his truncheon for

137

the potatoes. One by one he put them in the large pocket inside his cape.

'Come on, I'll see you home.'

'No!' The word was uttered in a terrified voice.

He sighed deeply. He understood. He was respected in this area but he certainly wasn't liked, but then it wasn't his job to be liked. He wasn't paid to be popular. 'What if you slip again? There's that much soggy litter around here it's a fair bet you will.'

Lizzie knew what Mam's reaction would be but she was too weary, too shaken and too distressed to argue. The rain had become torrential. It was swept almost horizontally along the streets by the increasing gale. She bent her head against the force but was completely taken aback when the scuffer put his cape round her thin shoulders. It reached down to her feet.

'It's not too far to walk and besides, this tunic is good thick worsted,' Jack said, seeing the astonishment in her eyes.

No one had ever done anything like this for her before – well, not since Tommy had been killed. The tears welled up again.

'What number is it?' he enquired.

'Ten, but I'll be all right when we get round the corner.'

'I said I'll see you safely home, luv, and I never break a promise.' His smile was wry. God help her, she looked as though she was about to drop of starvation and exhaustion any minute and she must be soaked through. God alone knew how long she'd been out in this weather.

'Have you got a job?' he asked in an attempt to lessen her fear of him.

She nodded. 'It's not much an' Mam or me don't see much of the money. He takes it.'

He didn't need to be told that. He'd arrested Tip O'Connor for drunken brawling too many times to remember. His name was at the top of the list of habitual drunkards in the station house.

'How do you manage then?'

She shrugged. 'Mam always manages to pay the rent, she's only ever got behind once. People are good, too. You ... well ... the police help with clothes an' boots for the kids.'

'Where does your sister work now? The one who I used to see singing outside the Rotunda?' He'd seen and listened to the girl many times, turning a blind eye to this form of begging. She had a wonderful voice and one of the pleasures in his austere life was music. He was a bachelor and lived with his mother in Media Street, off Kirkdale Road. She refused to move to a better area, even though her husband had been dead for over ten years. 'This is my home and I've good neighbours. I'm too old to be pulling up my roots and moving to God knows where' was the answer he always got when the subject was broached.

'Our Alice went to America, nearly a year ago. Just before Christmas. We had a letter from,' Lizzie thought hard, 'a place called Charleston. She's got a job and a decent place to live. I wish ... I wish I could have gone with her.' She'd never said those words aloud before. She missed Alice terribly and so did Mam. But if she, too, had gone, then there would be no one to go out and earn a wage. The rest of the kids were too young although Jimmy did sell newspapers and bootlaces, whenever he could. But he was like Da. It was like trying to get blood out of a stone getting money out of Jimmy.

They had arrived at her front door which despite the weather was slightly ajar. Jack could see the flaking plaster, the patches of rising damp, the missing floorboards. The whole damned street needed demolishing and the houses rebuilt, but that was too much to ask of the landlords. They'd never put their hands in their well-lined pockets so people like the O'Connors could at least have a decent roof over their heads, not one that leaked like a sieve.

Awkwardly Lizzie took off his cape and handed it back to him. It was so heavy, the rain soaking into the wool, that she struggled with it.

He took it from her and removed the potatoes from the pocket. 'Here, wrap them in your shawl or you'll go dropping them again.'

She did as she was bid then looked up at him again. 'Thanks for seeing me home.'

'What's your name? You never told me.'

'Lizzie.'

'Short for Elizabeth? It's my mam's name too, but she gets called Bessie.'

Nelly had heard their voices and had come to the door. Her eyes widened in fear when she saw Lizzie with a policeman.

'Oh, Holy Mother of God! What's she done?' she cried. 'She's a good girl, honest she is, sir. I won't believe anything you tell me she's done!'

'She hasn't done anything wrong, Mrs O'Connor. There's a lamp out in Blenheim Street and in the dark I bumped into her. Sent her flying would be more truthful. She's not hurt and we salvaged the spuds, but I'm afraid the sixpenny joey's gone. Straight down the drain, it went. She's soaked, so I'd advise you to get a hot cup of tea down her and a few blankets round her before she gets pneumonia.' At the sight of Nelly's face he could have bitten his tongue. How bloody stupid! How bloody tactless! There would be no fire and therefore no hot water and probably no tea either. Just a few potatoes and maybe a bit of stale bread.

'Would you mind if I just stepped in for a second, Mrs O'Connor? Just while I get this cape on again?'

Nelly nodded silently. What else could she do?

140

It was colder and damper inside than it was out in the street, he thought as he shrugged the heavy garment over his broad shoulders and fastened the metal clasp, stamped with the Liver bird. He earned four pounds and ten shillings a week, with two shillings and sixpence extra for boot allowance. This entire family had only sixpence and that had now gone. He looked at the pinched, pallid faces of the two women and silently cursed a society that did very little for its poor, its sick, its elderly, its war heroes. Most of them were decent people. These women battled daily to overcome dirt, disease and hunger while their priests urged them to go on having kids they couldn't feed, for the glory of God and their reward in the next life. He wasn't a deeply religious man but the plight of the O'Connors stirred a flame of anger in him. He dug into his trouser pocket and brought out a ten-shilling note. Charity such as this was deeply frowned upon by his superiors and he had to admit they did have a point when it was argued that any money would only end up in the pubs in the area.

'Mrs O'Connor, is there any way you can hide this from him – your husband?'

Nelly's eyes were riveted on the note. It would keep them for weeks if she was careful. 'I'll find a way, so help me God I will, sir.'

He thrust the note into her hand, confident she wouldn't go up and down the street announcing the fact that a scuffer had given her ten shillings.

Suddenly Lizzie smiled up at him and he realised that she was younger than she looked.

'Thanks for everything,' she said, feeling suddenly shy.

'Well, it's nearly Christmas. I'll be off now but you get a fire going and take those wet things off you, Lizzie.'

They stood in the doorway and watched him walk back up the street, shoulders straight, head unbent before the rain driving into his face. 'Well, I've never known a scuffer do that before, but God bless him just the same,' Nelly said as he turned the corner out of their sight.

As he walked down the road Jack Phillips couldn't get the image of Lizzie O'Connor sitting sobbing in the road out of his mind. He'd put them forward for a Christmas parcel and also for police issue clothes and a small donation from the Police Benevolent Fund, and what's more he'd keep his eye on them all, particularly Tip O'Connor. Maybe they'd get lucky. Maybe Tip would become involved in another drunken fight. He'd have no money for a fine, so a couple of days in jail would give the family a better Christmas . . .

'I'll go out and get some coal and some chips,' Nelly said as she shut the door.

'But Mam, he'll know we've got money then.' Lizzie stared at her mother anxiously.

'I won't light the fire until he's gone to sleep – passed out more like. I'll put the chips in the scullery under the sink so he won't smell them. Later you can go over to Mrs O'Hanlon and ask to warm them up in her range. It'll be late but at least we'll eat. I'll wake the kids up for it.'

Lizzie smiled. 'Mam, you're dead crafty.'

'I have to be and I've had plenty of practice,' Nelly replied, grimly snatching her shawl from a nail on the wall.

'He was dead kind to me, Mam. He took his cape off and put it round me and it was so thick and warm.'

'If only they were all like that. Half of them think that it's our own fault we're poor, the other half – well, at least they're fair-minded and charitable. If it wasn't for them, half the kids along Scottie Road would be barefoot and naked. Oh, I know they get poked fun at wearing that horrible green stuff with its stamp, but I'm not too proud to take what's given.'

'You'd best go, Mam, or you won't get back before me

da comes home and then it will be like the time he battered our Alice.'

Nelly's expression changed. 'I'll never forgive him for driving her away. Never!'

'Go on, Mam,' Lizzie urged.

As she closed the door behind her mother, Lizzie leaned against it and pushed the wet strands of hair away from her face. He'd been good to them, that scuffer. He'd treated her gently and with respect, as if she was really someone worthy of note. And she didn't even know his name.

PART TWO

Chapter Thirteen

1927

Alice straightened her hat as Ruth turned down the bed and picked Alice's discarded nightdress and wrap from the floor.

It was Tuesday and on Tuesdays Alice went down to West Street, the opposite end from India's house, where a modicum of respectability remained. She went to the home of Alfredo Bransini, the Italian tenor, now retired, for what he called 'voice training' and she called a singing lesson. She'd been going for a year now, ever since the Plantation had been closed down. Mike always swore that the illicit liquor that had caused its demise had been deliberately planted and the police informed. There had never been any kind of trouble there before.

When the police rushed in, there had been pandemonium but Mike had managed to get Alice out the back way and home, so she wasn't carted off downtown. Still, she missed the place terribly. In the end, King Oliver had moved north with his musicians but she'd had to stay behind. The singing lessons had been by way of a consolation but it wasn't the same as singing to an audience where you didn't have to worry about things like breathing properly or whether the whole lesson would degenerate into a shouting match. Signor Bransini lost his temper at the drop of a hat and yelled at her, usually gesticulating wildly with his arms. After a while she'd learned that the best way to deal with this was to shout back and gesticulate just as wildly. It was all very wearying.

'Alexander says Mr Mike is waiting,' the black girl announced after having gone to the door of the room in response to the butler's summons.

'I'm ready.' Alice glanced around her, making sure she'd forgotten nothing and sighed. She'd been here for two years now and she'd become accustomed to the splendid rooms and the luxuries of life. She didn't need to tidy away or wash her own clothes, Ruth saw to that. Alexander supervised the small staff that comprised Ella the cook, Jimmy who did the garden and any small jobs around the place, Ruth who doubled as parlour maid and ladies' maid, and Florence who was a maid of all work. Alice had been very wary of them all for the first few weeks. But she'd been even more wary of Mike O'Farrell. And although her suspicions had gradually faded, she still found his treatment of her puzzling. He was an enigma. He didn't seem to want anything from her. Oh, he kissed her, usually on the cheek or forehead, but it was a brotherly kiss. Officially she had been his ward, and then three months ago a sudden mad, crazy notion had made her ask him if he loved her.

Mike had been completely taken aback but soon recovered. 'I'm very fond of you, Alice, but God help the man who falls for you,' he answered.

She was stung. 'Why?'

'Because you are a hard-hearted, crafty little madam.'

'I'm not!' she cried. 'Have I ever been stubborn or conniving?' Once she wouldn't have known what a word like 'conniving' meant. 'How can you say that?'

He laughed. 'You must be to have got this far. We're alike, Alice. Maybe that's why we get on so well.'

'We do get on, don't we? But . . .'

'But what?'

'Well, it doesn't *look* right.'

148

He sighed. He'd thought she was happy with the explanation he'd concocted for her living beneath his roof. She had recently been included in the occasional dinner parties that he'd given for his business associates – all men. Alexander had taught her how things were done and not done, and she'd struggled to suppress her accent. She'd done well but she'd been quick to note the glances of curiosity and speculation shown – and just as rapidly hidden – by these men, all of them 'new' money like Mike himself.

Understanding dawned on Mike. 'I can see Alexander's hand in this. If it's announced that we're married it will look better, be more socially acceptable, more respectable.'

'I've always been respectable! Mam brought us up decent. Decently,' she corrected herself.

He leaned back in his chair and scrutinised her face. 'Setting aside Alexander's meddling, just what *do* you want, Alice?'

She shrugged. 'I don't know. Alexander says guardians often marry their wards.'

'In fairy stories and usually to get their hands on the poor girls' money.'

'Mike, be serious. Maybe if people thought I was your wife we'd get invited to places.'

The laughter left his eyes. 'I'm a Catholic Irishman, Alice. Marriage will be for ever for me, even if divorce is becoming easier in this rip-roaring age. It's " 'til death do us part" for me and when I say those words I'll mean them.'

'You're a bloody hypocrite, Mike O'Farrell! You've never set foot in a church for years. If you did, it would probably fall down around you and the priest would keel over with the shock. I didn't say I *wanted* to be your wife, just . . . just . . .'

'Now who's the hypocrite? You want me to present you as my wife?'

149

'Well, why not? We could say it was a very quiet wedding, no fuss. Just a small announcement in the newspaper.'

'You've got it all worked out pat, the pair of you. You see, I was right. You *are* a conniving little madam.' He got up and walked to the mirror over the mantel shelf and adjusted his tie.

'There won't be any . . . any sharing the same bedroom or anything like that.'

He looked at her in the mirror. She was asking a great deal. To everyone they would be man and wife and yet they must sleep apart. Kisses would be without passion. Embraces, except those in public, would be nonexistent.

'And what about the rest of the staff?' he asked. 'It will seem to them to be a very odd marriage.'

'Alexander has told them all that they shouldn't tell *anyone* at all. This arrangement, as he calls it, will increase their status, but I don't think they care about that. It's only Alexander who's a snob. Besides, if anyone says a word, he's promised to have them dismissed and with no reference.'

'That man has too much bloody power in this house,' Mike muttered to himself.

'But if they keep quiet they'll get a bonus.'

'He's very generous with *my* money,' Mike sniffed, gazing thoughtfully at his highly polished shoes. 'All right I'll humour you,' he pronounced finally. 'Have it your way. I don't want a domestic war to start over it. I value my peace and sanity.' If only she *did* love him, he thought. He'd willingly marry her now, this minute. But there was always his pride standing between them. She'd never accept him and he wasn't prepared to make a fool of himself. This 'arrangement' would probably be the nearest he'd ever come to actually marrying her. It also meant that in public he could show affection for her and that was better than nothing at all. Perhaps in time she'd learn to love him. Or was that just wishful thinking or something you read in books?

She hadn't replied. She was stunned by his acceptance of what was in fact Alexander's idea.

And so to the outside world she was now Mrs Alice O'Farrell. At least it had pleased Alexander who wore a smug expression for days. Now all the innuendos would cease; the fact that the story was a sham didn't seem to bother him at all. The 'proprieties' were being seen to be observed and his own dignity therefore was protected.

It was Alexander who interrupted her thoughts. 'Mr O'Farrell says Signor Bransini will be angry if you're late again. If you don't go down now he's going without you. Ma'am,' he added, almost as an afterthought.

Alice frowned. This sardonic tacking on of her formal but fictitious title was Alexander's way of reminding her of her real place in the household. But it also told her there was to be no more chatting idly with Ruth and certainly no more giggling with young Florrie.

'Oh, all right, I'm coming,' she called. Mike watched her trip lightly down the stairs and his heart beat faster as it always did when he looked at her. In the two bitter-sweet years she had been with him, there had been many times when he'd physically ached to hold her, kiss her, love her, and it had taken superhuman strength and a bottle of bourbon to keep his desires in check. There had been other times when he'd wanted to pour out his feelings like a moonstruck boy. His fear of rejection and ridicule increased after one night when she'd had too much wine at dinner and talked in greater detail of the incident that had led her to be taken aboard the *Aquitania*. She'd mentioned a man's name, the name she hadn't revealed when she'd first told him her story that night in India's. He should have known there was a man in her life somewhere, the root of her ambition.

He'd felt a jealous rage sweep over him but he'd fought

it down. He had no right to be jealous, he had no claim on her. She wasn't his wife. Maybe in time she'd forget this man. It seemed to have been a very brief encounter. What could she really know about this David Williamson? She'd not even spent a full hour in his company.

He handed her down the last few stairs. 'Mrs O'Farrell, have you any idea of the time at all? I've bought you two watches, or is it three?'

It was true. He'd bought her quite a lot of jewellery, expensive jewellery. He'd often told her, when she forgot all decorum and shrieked like a delighted fishwife when he presented her with another magnificent bauble, that if she was going to be his wife, albeit in name only, then she had to look the part.

'I'm not late. My mantel clock said it was only two minutes to ten.'

'And Signor Bransini is expecting you at ten fifteen and the traffic down there will be all snarled up.'

She didn't reply as Alexander opened the front door. Mike handed her into the car and closed the door. She smoothed down the pleats in the skirt of her peach-coloured crepe dress and patted the matching cloche hat. No vestige remained now of the girl who had arrived in Charleston on the *Castlemaine*, at least not outwardly. She always told herself that she'd never change, not inside where it mattered. She'd always be little Alice O'Connor from Benledi Street, no matter where she went, what she did or how she was dressed. She wrote regularly to Nelly, always enclosing money, but she'd only ever had one letter in reply. More of a note it had been, written on cheap paper in a spidery hand and with poor spelling. Nelly had said how glad she was that Alice now had a great life, but there was no mention of the money. Still, maybe Nelly had asked someone to write it for her, she was virtually illiterate. If she had, then she certainly wouldn't want half the street knowing her business. The letter was the only tangible thing she had from her life in Liverpool, the only thing to remind her where she'd come from. The gutter.

As they pulled away down the street she turned and looked at Mike at the wheel beside her. She was fond of him and very, very grateful to him for taking her away from The Star of India and giving her a chance in life, but lately she'd become bored. She wanted to sing on a stage, and since the Plantation had closed down, she hadn't been able to do that. All the other clubs were so seedy and often violent that Mike had flatly refused to take her anywhere near them.

'I've been to rough places before,' she'd countered.

'Not as Mrs Michael Eugene O'Farrell,' he'd replied in a tone that told her the subject was closed.

'What *is* going on in that devious mind now, Alice?' he enquired, breaking into her thoughts.

'I want to sing again.'

Mike sighed. 'We've been through all this before, Alice. You're not going to sing in those desperate places downtown. Alexander would take a meat axe to the pair of us!'

'No, not in those.'

'Then where?'

She bit her lip. She couldn't tell him she was bored stiff. Not after he'd given her so much and asked nothing in return. 'Here. At home. Couldn't we have a soirée? Ruth told me the Hendersons next door often have them.'

He turned and looked at her in astonishment, narrowly missing hitting an omnibus. 'In the name of all that's holy! Who the hell would we invite?'

'You must know some refined people. Let's ask the Hendersons.'

'They'd sooner walk barefoot to Savannah and back than cross our doorstep. They're "old" money and Episcopalian too.'

'Oh, please, Mike. You must know someone. All those

153

friends of yours must have wives and daughters.'

He looked thoughtful. She had a point. His associates couldn't care less about respectability or social position, but their wives did. Nearly all of them were trying to claw their way onto the fringe of society, new money trying to become old money in a single generation, but with little success. They kept on trying, though, and gave their own dinners and parties and soirées, or so he gathered from the complaints he heard from their spouses. He'd been invited of course, but so far he'd been spared having to attend, never mind host, these 'entertainments', by keeping Alice in ignorance of their invitations; he knew Alexander had been meddling again. 'I'll think about it. Ask around, test the water, so to speak.'

Her eyes danced with excitement and she leaned over and kissed his cheek. 'Oh, you're really good to me. I honestly believe in guardian angels! Someone's been looking out for me ever since I left Liverpool.'

'Would a guardian angel come in the guise of a scruffy cat, do you think?' he laughed.

She laughed with him. 'It wasn't a scruffy cat!'

'Maybe cats have guardian angels too. That cat's life certainly changed for the better when you found it, Alice.'

'Sometimes I wish I'd kept her. I know being a ship's cat is all right, but sometimes . . .'

'Oh, Jaysus! I couldn't have stuck the cat as well!'

She laughed again and then turned her mind to planning her soirée.

The increasingly elaborate plans formulated mainly by a self-satisfied Alexander had to be shelved as, before she could write out invitations, Alice received one herself. It was printed on stiff white card and was accompanied by a letter, both delivered to her on a silver tray by Alexander. Mrs Maura O'Hare, wife of Gerry whose great-grandfather had been hanged in Cork for stealing and

154

butchering a calf to feed his family, had had the same idea. She had also heard that Mrs O'Farrell had a wonderful voice and begged Alice to agree to sing for her guests.

'Did it come in the post, Alexander?'

'No, by hand, ma'am.'

'Do I use a card to reply?'

'A single sheet of notepaper will do. It's not the St Cecilia Society Ball.'

'What shall I sing? She won't want any of the ragtime numbers, will she?'

'Indeed not. I hear Mrs O'Hare is becoming quite well known for her "improving" entertainments.' There was a faintly sarcastic emphasis on the word 'improving'.

Alice panicked. 'Oh, God, she won't want me to sing anything from an opera, will she?'

'Maybe an operetta.'

'But I don't know anything like that!'

'There's a lovely song called "Lorena". It's an old one but still a favourite for soirées. I heard it was sung next door recently.'

'Can you teach it to me?'

Alexander nodded; he'd known the mention of the Hendersons next door would settle the matter. 'Another old favourite in this town is "Jeannie With The Light Brown Hair". I heard tell Confederate soldiers used to sing it.' There was a note of cold resentment in his voice but she didn't notice it.

'It's that old? Well, that's two. Will they be enough?'

'Are you the sole artiste, ma'am?'

'No. She says Miss Euganie Walton will play two sonatas, whatever they are.'

'Miss Walton?' Alexander's eyebrows rose a fraction as he wondered how someone as nouveau riche as Mrs Maura O'Hare had managed to get the niece of a senator even to cross her threshold let alone play the piano. 'Then two will be enough.'

'What do I wear? Full evening dress? Long gloves, short gloves, no gloves?'

'Full evening dress and long gloves,' Alexander replied. 'And not too much jewellery. It's not done to flaunt money,' he added patronisingly.

'I haven't got any money, it's Mr Mike's and well you know it!' Alice shot back with spirit. 'And he pays you good wages, so get off your high horse!'

Alexander ignored her. Beneath the aloof exterior was a kind heart and he liked Alice. She'd learned quickly and eagerly but despite all the clothes and jewels, she'd never be a lady. It was a true saying that you can't make a silk purse from a sow's ear, but she did have her own pert charm.

Alice spent hours learning the words of 'Lorena' and just as many hours choosing what to wear. In the end she settled for the jade-coloured chiffon that shaded to a deeper green at the hemline. Tiny pearls and silvery beads were sewn across the loose bodice in a sunburst pattern and edged the hem of the hip-hugging sash.

'You look like an angel, Miss Alice,' Ruth enthused, after helping Alice with her toilette.

Alice smiled back and then a wide grin split her face as she caught sight of Mike standing in the doorway. 'Do I really look all right? I mean I've worn everything Alexander told me to wear, but not too much jewellery.'

'Alice, you look grand. You'll have the men and boys for miles around thinking up excuses to beat their way to the door after tonight.'

'Oh, I don't want anything like that. I just want to sing again. For people, an audience.'

He took the black velvet cape that lay across the bed and draped it over her shoulders. 'I have a feeling that after tonight you will be doing just that. I think you'll be in great demand and that I will have to attend God knows how many of these polite but deathly boring evenings.

And before you attack me, I'm not saying *you* are boring. But give me a good old-fashioned hooley any day of the week.'

The O'Hares lived in a large house on the East Battery and as they arrived, in the midst of cars that were disgorging people Alice had never seen before, Maura O'Hare came forward to greet her. She was rather a plain woman, Alice thought, in her early thirties, and the magenta evening dress with its black fringe did absolutely nothing to enhance her looks.

'Mrs O'Farrell! I'm so glad you could come. I thought he kept you locked up. We see so little of you in town.'

Alice smiled.

'Alice is rather shy, Maura. Not really used to high society yet.'

Maura O'Hare shot Mike a penetrating glance to see if he was mocking her with his reference to high society. It didn't appear so.

'Then I'm even more pleased that you've agreed to sing for us.' She'd heard rumours that Alice O'Farrell had sung nearly every night in Oliver's club until it had been raided and shut down. Nor did she look at all shy, Maura thought as she led Alice into the salon.

The dove-grey walls, drapes and carpet of the room could have made it appear cold, flat and uninteresting, but cushions and huge flower arrangements of deep pink cyclamen, tearoses and the fragrant pink and cream Stargazer lilies lifted it, making it very elegant. Obviously Maura O'Hare had had a designer in, Alice thought, because judging by the clashing colours of her dress and hair she had very little taste.

She recognised some of the men but none of their wives, who in the main were over-dressed, obviously vying with each other in the size of the precious stones they wore. 'Like flaming Christmas trees,' she muttered to herself. Aye, and you'd have looked like one too, Alice O'Connor, left to your own devices, she chided herself.

Mike had said the soirée was for a charity. Mrs O'Hare had charged an entrance fee. The fact that the proceeds from the evening would go to a good cause was the only reason Miss Euganie Walton had agreed to attend. Miss Walton stood apart, literally and metaphorically. It was obvious that she was a lady in the true sense of the word.

Mike jerked his head in Miss Walton's direction. 'She comes from one of Charleston's best known families.'

'She looks – oh, what's that saying of Alexander's?'

'A pearl amongst swine?' Mike suggested, grinning. 'Ah, maybe that's a bit too strong. Come on, let's introduce ourselves. I don't care whether it's etiquette or not. Besides, most of this crowd wouldn't know etiquette if it jumped up and hit them in the face.' He took Alice's elbow and steered her across the room. 'Miss Walton, may I present your fellow artiste and my wife, Mrs Alicia O'Farrell.'

Alice shot him a malevolent look before smiling at the girl, the only woman in the room close to her own age. 'It's not Alicia, it's Alice. He's teasing me.' She looked round the room. 'What a lot of people and I don't know anyone.'

'Neither do I, Mrs O'Farrell. I believe I'm to accompany you. It's "Lorena" and . . .'

' "Jeannie",' Alice supplied. 'The one with the light brown hair. It's a bit old.'

'It's so old it should be given a decent burial,' Euganie Walton replied, her eyes full of laughter.

Alice smiled back conspiratorially. 'Shall we bury it tonight?'

'What would you really like to sing?'

Alice thought. ' "Alexander's Ragtime Band" would be a bit too racy, I suppose.' She laughed then grimaced, thinking of Alexander's reaction and the wrath she'd bring down on her head for spoiling the 'improving' and charitable evening. She'd probably never be let out again.

'I'm afraid it would shock these, er, ladies to the core.'

Alice raised her eyes to the ceiling. 'I know and I'd be banned from most of the parlours in town. What about "Whispering"?'

'Fine. "Whispering" it is.'

'Now just what are you two ladies whispering about?' Maura O'Hare joined them, totally at a loss to understand why both her young artistes went into fits of laughter. It was very unsettling.

'Just what the hell are you up to?' Mike asked, leading Alice to her seat as the O'Hares' butler repeatedly struck a small gong to indicate that his mistress wished to make an announcement. Alice's eyes were full of mischief.

'Nothing.'

'Don't be lying to me, Alice. I can see the divilment in your eyes.'

'Just a bit of a change in the programme.'

Mike looked stern. 'Alice, don't wreck the party. Remember, people have paid. It's for charity and Maura O'Hare has gone to a lot of trouble over it all. Besides, any ragtime and you'll never be asked to sing again.'

'It's nothing like that. It's just a bit more modern than that owld dirge.'

'Be careful, your accent is slipping,' Mike grinned.

'Oh, shut up. Euganie is going to start,' she hissed back.

She watched Euganie Walton closely and realised that she was a talented pianist. The applause for her showed genuine appreciation, she thought, when Euganie finished her pieces and stood up, though quite a few men had to be nudged into awareness and even wakefulness by their wives. Well, no one was going to sleep through *her* performance, even if she had to say so straight out.

Alice's smile for Euganie Walton was warm and sincere as she approached the piano. 'I've a mind to sing "Alexander's Ragtime Band",' she hissed indignantly. 'That would keep them awake all right. Some people are *so* rude.'

'It's very warm in here and you know that saying about music and the savage breast,' Euganie smiled, as the applause died down.

'You're too polite and kind. I tell you the savage in here will be me if I see one pair of closed eyes or hear a single snore.'

She felt a little nervous, she always did at first, but she knew it wouldn't last.

'Are you ready, Mrs O'Farrell?' Euganie asked in a louder tone and nodded to the butler who again beat a tattoo on the gong.

Alice nodded. Her voice was clear and filled with emotion as she sang the opening lines, 'The years creep slowly by, Lorena, the snow is on the grass again ...'

Mike watched Alice with increasing pride. When she sang, whether it was around the house or in public, be it ragtime or traditional ballads and love songs, she never failed to charm him. He glanced around and saw that everyone was awake and taking notice. His lovely Alice was possessed of great beauty and talent and all these women thought she belonged to him, one way or another.

He supposed that from Alice's point of view their 'marriage' was working well. At home she treated him with a sort of offhand affection. Not quite as a father figure but as an older brother. At least that's what he told himself, and maybe time would change things for the better. There were instances of affection. The little gifts, inexpensive trinkets she'd found for him on her wanderings around the city. The small and very battered book of *Moore's Melodies*. The way she'd sit on a footstool at his feet, reading. Often she'd look up at him and ask him the meaning of a word, and how he'd longed to stroke the shining, softly waving hair. He had done so, once. She'd been struggling with *Morte d'Arthur* and he'd explained the love of Arthur for his Queen Guinevere and her love for the young knight Lancelot.

'Oh, Mike, wasn't that sad?' she'd said when he'd finished, and her eyes had misted with tears.

'It's just a story, Alice,' he'd replied and had let his fingers caress the fine, tawny-coloured hair.

He didn't know what Alexander had bribed, coaxed or threatened the staff with, apart from the 'monthly bonus' he paid, but they were very discreet. No word of the unusual nature of their 'marriage' was heard outside the house – he'd have been one of the first to hear it. As for the circle they moved in, to outsiders they appeared to be the perfect couple.

It was so ironic that he'd never laid a finger on her. He wished with all his heart that she did belong to him. Would it be such a great mistake to tell her so? Was he deluding himself, thinking she'd spurn him? Would she? Would she use his love as a weapon against him, if he ever failed to grant her wishes? Or was he needlessly depriving himself of her love? He wasn't getting any younger. Nearly every other man in the room was married. Properly married. Maybe he'd give it some more thought.

Chapter Fourteen

The week before Christmas, after dinner, Alice was sitting on a footstool at Mike's feet, staring into the fire. 'I love Christmas now. I used to hate it. We—'

'I know. No presents, no happy family sitting round a table full of food in a kitchen that was warm, with the fire roaring away up the chimney.'

He understood. He knew what it felt like.

'And creeping in at the back of the church for Mass, hoping no one would notice that you hadn't a decent rag to your back. And then, on the way home, having the other lads making a mock and a jeer of you. Lads who had good tweed jackets and fine strong boots. Lads and girls who had toys.'

'Sometimes we were lucky, we had a parcel of food.' She told him about the charitable Goodfellows organisation.

'With us it was the Quakers. If you ignored the Father giving out about them from the high altar. "Blessed are the poor." He almost used to shout the bloody words. What the hell would he know about being poor? Him with the belly on him from three square meals a day and a housekeeper to see to him. Even a drop of Jameson's or Powers to keep out the cold. I had seventeen Christmases like that, Alice.'

'So did I,' she replied quietly.

'Well, all that's in the past now. There'll always be food and a fire and gifts.'

She nodded thankfully.

'Will we go out and get the greenery?' He smiled, trying to banish the memories and lift the mood.

Holly, ivy and the fir tree filled the house, all brought down from the northern states where these evergreens flourished in the colder climate. Like the previous year, Alice had been on countless shopping sprees, taking Ruth with her and, once, Alexander. Mike knew that that occasion was to choose a present for him. He'd sighed heavily as he'd watched her go. The only perfect gift she could give him would be herself. For a man who made snap decisions in business he was unable to come easily to this one. He'd found himself looking at rings when he'd gone to purchase a necklace for her.

For Alice, though, life regained some of its old spark. She threw herself wholeheartedly into the preparations for the festivities. She'd had three more invitations, three more requests to sing, all from friends of Maura O'Hare. But her own soirée caused an argument.

'Why don't you want me to have it on Christmas Eve?' she demanded when Mike vetoed the date. 'You said Christmas will always be something special from now on and Christmas Eve is just the right time.'

He regarded her thoughtfully as he lit a cigar. 'Because I like a bit of peace and quiet then. Christmas is a family time and, strange as it may seem, we *are* a sort of family. You, me, Ruth, Alexander, Jimmy, Ella and young Florence. I thought you'd understand, Alice. All those other Christmases, remember? And I don't want my house full of drunks and women screeching with laughter like demented banshees.'

Alice bit her lip. 'They're not *proper* family.'

'Well, they're as near to one as either of us is likely to get. My mother, Kitty and Dee won't make the Atlantic crossing and neither will your mother.'

'Mam couldn't. She's got the kids to see to and anyway,

164

what's wrong with the people I'm inviting? They're your friends.'

'They're not friends, they're business associates. It's different entirely.'

She lost her temper. 'You're a flaming hypocrite! You really are! You have them here to dinner, you go laughing and joking with their wives at parties but you won't call them friends and you won't let them come here to my party!'

'*Our* party, and I can choose who I want or don't want to entertain in my home.'

'You keep telling me it's *our* home! Now all of a sudden it's *yours*. You promised me I could have a party.'

He sighed. He'd caught the tremor, the pleading note in her voice. 'I'm not going back on that, Alice. I just don't want you to have it on Christmas Eve.'

'Well, the day before then?'

'The day before it is,' he replied resignedly.

She flung her arms round him and kissed him but sadly he realised that she was like a spoilt child; she was using endearments and gestures of affection as weapons to get her own way. The kiss was exactly that – a gesture.

Alice was very disappointed that Euganie Walton was unable to come to her party. She received a note saying Euganie was really sorry but she had another invitation which she'd already accepted. But all her other guests turned up and she judged it to be a success even though she knew Alexander was looking down his nose at the behaviour of some of the guests and only looked happy when the last of them had departed, unsteadily. He was a terrible snob sometimes, she thought.

They had their quiet family Christmas, like the previous year. She'd bought gifts for everyone. Mike gave the staff money, knowing it was always appreciated more than trinkets. The two of them had lunch in the dining room but

165

later they went and had tea in the kitchen which was the only room in the house where she felt really comfortable. She *was* still the same person, inside, she often told herself.

She wore the gold collar set with seed pearls that Mike had given her and he sported the gold cufflinks, small replicas of the Tara Brooch, set with emeralds, that she had had specially made. She'd seen a picture of the brooch in one of his many books about Ireland. He ignored the fact that they'd been paid for with his money, touched that she'd gone to so much effort, put so much thought into the choice.

That evening they sat in the drawing room as darkness was falling, neither of them making any move to switch on the lights.

She sighed deeply. 'It's been the best Christmas ever. I mean that. Better even than last year. You spoil me.'

'You just ate too much last year,' he laughed. Then he smiled at her more seriously. 'It's been one of the best Christmases for me too, Alice, and you deserve to be spoilt – just a bit.'

She grinned. 'Just a bit, mind. You spoil me something rotten all the time and I don't deserve it. I don't give you anything back in return.'

He smiled again. 'Ah, but you do, Alice. You give me company, friendship, amusement, laughter and the joy, the sheer joy of listening to you sing.' It was all true. Oh, he supposed that what she gave him couldn't be assessed in monetary terms. It was all beyond price, in a different league from just dollars and cents.

Alice sat down on the rug at his feet and began to pluck at the lace edge of her handkerchief. She was suddenly shy.

'You . . . you know, if I could have chosen from all the men in the world to have as a da, I'd have picked you.'

His smile vanished and he managed to suppress the groan. The light in his eyes died. So, at last. This was

166

really how she viewed him, what she really thought of him. It hurt. It hurt like hell but he was so glad, so relieved now that he'd said nothing about his love for her. It didn't make the pain of rejection any easier to bear though. His expression was bland. The mask was back in place. The one he wore whenever he didn't want to disclose his true feelings, the mask of the slightly amused, benign Irishman at ease with the world.

'Will you indulge me? Sing for me. Sing the Christmas carols. It wouldn't be Christmas without carols and then we'll have a drink for the day that's in it.'

Perched on the arm of the long sofa she started with 'O Little Town of Bethlehem' but when she began 'Silent Night' she noticed the little group standing by the door, just in the hallway. Ruth, Jimmy, Florrie, Ella and Alexander gazed back at her. She smiled to herself. She supposed they were her family now. Maybe one day she'd go back to Liverpool, like she'd promised Mam she would. She'd sung on a stage, of sorts, and of course at the soirées, but she wasn't famous. She probably wouldn't ever be but she'd got far more from life than she'd ever dreamed of. To ask for more would seem like a sin.

As her silvery, dulcet voice filled the room, Alexander thought he saw tears on his master's cheek, caught for a brief second in the light of the tiny candles that adorned the Christmas tree.

After the Christmas and New Year celebrations were fully over, Charleston began to prepare for the great balls and events held by the Cotillion and the St Cecilia Societies, a social whirl that would go on until Lent. Alice read the notices for them in the *News and Chronicle* with hungry interest, knowing she wouldn't be invited. She was 'new' money and this was a circle of society quite different from the one she'd got used to.

'Oh well, I suppose Euganie Walton will be in demand,'

she said wistfully when she'd finished. Mike didn't reply. He'd been very quiet, she mused, sort of distant, since Christmas. He'd been out a lot and even when he was in he secluded himself in his study. The Cotillion Society Ball was on Saturday, to be held at the South Carolina Society's Hall, she read once again, and there would be a musical interlude when Miss Sofia Scarlatti, the highly acclaimed diva from New York, would sing two arias, one from *Tosca* and one from *La Bohème*.

'What's a diva?' she asked Mike.

'I've no idea.' He was busy reading the business section of the newspaper. 'Go and look it up in that dictionary I bought you.'

'It's not that important.'

'Every new word should be important, Alice. That's the way you learn.'

'You sound like a school teacher and an old dragon of a father,' she grumbled.

'Well, isn't that the way you see me?' he questioned with a dry, brittle laugh.

She went for the dictionary. ' "A prima donna. A great woman singer. From the Latin goddess",' she read aloud. 'She must be very grand.'

The following day Alexander brought in a calling card from Euganie Walton.

'She's here?'

'In the small salon, ma'am.'

'Why didn't you bring her in here?'

'It's not done,' he answered flatly.

'Oh, well, bring her in now.'

As soon as she walked through the door, Alice could tell Euganie was bothered about something. She looked agitated and uneasy.

'Mrs O'Farrell. Forgive me for calling at such short notice.' Euganie belonged to a generation that clung tenaciously to correct etiquette.

'Oh, call me Alice. Mrs O'Farrell makes me feel a hundred.'

'Then you must call me Euganie.'

'Sit down, please, Euganie. Did you have a nice Christmas?'

'Yes. I was really sorry I couldn't come to your soirée.'

'Well, it's nice of you to come and see me now. You must be very busy; I was reading about all the balls and parties in the paper.'

Euganie looked uncomfortable. 'Well, that's really why I'm here. Oh, I hate to ask! It looks . . . so bad, as though we're using you.'

'What for? I don't understand.' Alice was confused.

'Miss Scarlatti has gone down with a head cold and a sore throat. There's not enough time to . . . to, well, get anyone else of importance. Oh, this is really embarrassing, Alice. I begged my mother not to send me.' Euganie twisted her hands in her lap and looked at the floor.

'What? What's so embarrassing, Euganie?'

'Could you possibly stand in for her?'

'*Me?*' She almost shrieked the word.

Euganie nodded.

'I can't sing opera! I don't know anything about it! You've heard me, Euganie, I can only sing popular ballads or jazz.'

'I've heard you and with a voice like that you can sing anything. I know you go for voice training. Oh, Alice, please, it would make such a difference to the evening.'

Alice pressed her hands against her flushed cheeks. To sing at one of Charleston's most prestigious events, in front of everyone who was anyone in this town. To replace Miss Scarlatti! It was too much.

Euganie was watching her closely. 'Please, Alice. They won't expect you to sing grand opera, really they won't.'

They both looked towards the hall from where they

could hear Mike talking to Alexander. Alice called to him to come and join them.

He was surprised to see Euganie Walton. 'Miss Walton. Now isn't this a pleasure. How are you in yourself?' He bowed slightly.

'Mike, Euganie says Miss Scarlatti can't sing for them. She's got a cold or influenza or something. They want me.'

'We want her very much, Mr O'Farrell. I know it looks awful, just asking on the spur of the moment, but—'

'I can't do it, Mike!' Alice interrupted.

Euganie looked at him pleadingly. 'I'm sure she'll be a great success.'

'Of course you can do it, Alice. You can do anything you put your mind to. You've a great gift.' Although outwardly agreeing with Euganie, privately he was annoyed. They were all so damned high and mighty with their society balls, their opera singers. They would cut Alice dead in the street and himself too, given the chance. Just like the snotty bloody Hendersons who lived next door. But he wanted Alice to have her moment of glory. To show them all that this slip of a 'slummy' had a voice to equal all their prima donnas. To show them that a voice like Alice's was a gift, a talent, not something that could be made or bought with any kind of money, 'new' or 'old'.

Euganie sensed Alice's resolve weakening and she looked gratefully at Mike. 'You do have a great gift, Alice. I'll help you as much as I can. We'll sort out pieces, I'll teach you them. Signor Bransini will be only too glad to help, too, I'm sure.'

'No, he won't. He'll just yell at me and wave his arms like a windmill and make me worse!' Alice wailed.

'But you'll do it, won't you?' Euganie again looked to Mike for support.

'Of course she will. It's what she was born to do – sing.'

Alice looked at them both and then nodded slowly,

wondering just what she had let herself in for now.

Euganie returned home with the good news and then came back with an armful of sheet music.

Alice asked Alexander for coffee and instructed that the coffee pot be kept filled.

She sang 'The Londonderry Air' but Euganie said it wasn't really a 'strong' enough piece. The 'Rose of Tralee', Mike's favourite, was definitely out of the question.

Eventually she agreed to 'The Last Rose of Summer', quite a difficult piece to execute really well, according to Euganie. She also agreed to the Brahms 'Cradle Song' and finally she passed Alice the score of the Easter Hymn from *Cavalleria Rusticana*. 'It's beautiful, Alice. So moving.'

Alice was aghast. 'I can't do this, it's all in a foreign language.' The notes and words of Mascagni's Intermezzo danced before her eyes. 'Euganie, I can't even read it!'

'I'll teach you. I'll translate and you can learn.'

'Oh, God Almighty, I'll make a terrible fool of myself. I will.'

'You won't!'

Alice paused. 'Euganie, you really don't know about me.'

'I know you have a voice that is the equal of any prima donna I've ever heard.'

Alice twisted her hands together. 'I ... I was born in Liverpool. We were poor. Very poor. I used to sing to people waiting to go into the theatres. How can I stand up in the South Carolina Society's Hall and sing to all those people? I'm nothing.' She was on the point of saying she wasn't even Mrs O'Farrell, but decided against it.

Euganie dismissed her fears. 'Oh, Alice. None of that matters. No one knows or needs to know. You have something special. Something no one else in this town, maybe even this state, has. And you have such potential. Do you want to go on just singing at soirées for ever?'

171

'No, but I don't know if I can sing classical stuff.'

'Just try, Alice, please?' Euganie begged.

It was a long day and by mid-afternoon Mike swore he could stand no more. He said he knew that by Saturday she would sing like an angel – like the cherubim and seraphim put together – but right now his head couldn't take any more of what sounded like the banshee on a bad night. Alice threw a cushion at his departing back. Her own head was aching and in her heart she agreed with him. It *did* sound awful and she'd never, ever learn these words. All three pieces were new to her and she *had* to get them all perfect. Word, note and pitch perfect. Otherwise she'd die of embarrassment.

'Oh, he's right, Euganie. I sound terrible. I keep missing those very high notes.'

'It's just the C, Alice, and it will get easier with practice.' But it was to get worse. When Euganie finally left, Alice was exhausted. Her head ached and her throat felt dry.

Next morning Alice agreed with Euganie's suggestion that Signor Bransini must be called in. Mike hastily left the house muttering excuses and Alexander, with Ruth and Ella in tow, decided it was time to go on a household shopping expedition, leaving young Florrie to provide coffee and sandwiches and suffer the sounds coming from the small salon.

On Friday afternoon everyone was utterly exhausted and Euganie said the best thing would be for everyone to have a rest now. Both she and Signor Bransini would call, briefly, on Saturday afternoon for a final rehearsal.

But there wasn't much rest for Alice. Now she had to turn her attention to what she would wear. There was no time to go shopping or to have something made. By the time she had been through her entire wardrobe, most of which had ended up on the floor, she was nearly in tears. There was nothing suitable. Nothing. But what in God's name *would* be suitable? How was she to know? She buried her face in the folds of the skirt of her favourite duchess satin dress when Alexander arrived back with a large box.

She looked up at him. 'What's that?'

'Mr Mike asked me to go into town and choose something for you, ma'am.' From the layers of tissue paper he drew out the most beautiful dress she'd ever seen. It was white chiffon over white silk and was floor length. Around the hipline was a wide sash finished on the left side with a bow. The entire thing was encrusted with silver bugle beads, as was the bodice. Its back was cut very low with floating panels of chiffon coming from the shoulder. There were white satin pumps decorated with diamanté stones, long white gloves and a headband of white satin adorned with two ostrich plumes.

'Oh, Alexander! It's perfect!'

'Well, this one had to be special.'

She held it against her. 'You don't have to tell me that! Oh, what would I do without you, Alexander?'

What passed for a smile crossed his face and for the first time Alice felt he approved of her. 'I won't let you down,' she said.

'Just don't you let Mr Mike down, never mind about me. Why don't you go out for some air? You've been cooped up in the house too long. It will clear your head. I'll send Ruth up here to hang this up – and everything else!' he added.

She nodded; it was a good idea. If she stayed in she'd drive herself mad with worry. She'd go to White Point Gardens. Despite the association with India Osbourne, it was one of her favourite places.

It was almost half past four by the time she got there. The wintry sun was sinking low in the sky, its rays shining over the blue waters of the harbour. The trailing grey strands of tree moss wafted gently in the breeze. She had so much to be grateful for, she mused. When she'd arrived on the *Castlemaine*, down there at the harbour wall, she'd had no idea how much her life would change and in so short a time. She'd been full of hopes and dreams but she'd been so ignorant, so naive. She hadn't even known a word like 'naive'! She hadn't known how to dress, how to hold a conversation. She'd been poor little Alice O'Connor from Benledi Street and now, now she was someone of note. Tomorrow night she would be feted as Mrs Alice O'Farrell, Charleston's own diva.

'I *can* do it. I *can*. Euganie says I can!' She spoke the words aloud. She had a voice every bit as good as that Miss Scarlatti. She'd look every inch a lady, too, in the white chiffon dress, wearing the jewels Mike had bought her, She felt far more relaxed now, she told herself as she wandered between the beds of formal flowers and short avenues lined with shrubs. She was confident that she would look just as beautiful as any society woman listen-ing to her. Mike had taught her that if you had guts and determination you could do anything, go anywhere. That's what this country was all about.

She had reached the last grove of palmettoes, their fronds rustling in the freshening wind. At the end of the pathway stood the tall white column surmounted by its statue that faced out across the bay. She looked up at it without curiosity. The face of Sergeant William Jasper beneath the martial helmet bore a determined, defiant look. One hand was pointed seaward, the other held a large flag. From portraits she'd seen she knew that the flag was blue and the small crescent in one corner was silver. Mike had told her it had been erected in memory of the Second South Carolina Regiment, which under Colonel Moultrie had defended Fort Sullivan in the War of Independence against the British in June 1776. The inscription bore Jasper's rallying cry: 'Let us not fight without a flag.'

She turned away from it. It was getting chilly. She'd go

174

home now, have some tea and a rest. She glanced carelessly towards the harbour then her eyes widened, her hands flew to her cheeks and she gasped. Tied up down there was a ship she would never forget. A ship whose black hull and four red and black funnels she'd never thought to see again. A ship she'd often dreamed about. The *Aquitania*! The *Aquitania* was here in Charleston and he ... he'd be here too! She forgot about everyone and everything. Mike, Euganie, Alexander, the Cotillion Ball and her debut into society and semi-classical music. Clutching her hat she began to run, along the pathway, through the gates and down the road that led to the harbour, the ship and a very special member of her crew.

Chapter Fifteen

She was flushed and out of breath by the time she reached the gangway and the ship's officer who was standing at the bottom of it looking bored. Her heart was thumping against her ribs.

'Oh, can you help me, please?'

He grinned. 'I hope so, miss.'

What a difference clothes made, Alice thought as she smiled back at him. 'Could you get a message to someone on board?'

'Most of the passengers are ashore, doing a tour of the city, but they'll all be back for dinner at about eight.'

'No, it's not a passenger. He's crew, David Williamson, but I don't know exactly what he does. What his job or his rank are.' She gazed earnestly up at the man.

'He's an engineering officer, miss.'

'Could you tell him Alice O'Connor from Liverpool is here and wants... would like to see him, please? If it's possible.'

He looked up the gangway and caught sight of a steward who had come on deck for a smoke. 'Morrison, come here, I've a job for you,' he called.

Reluctantly the man came down to them. 'I was just 'avin' a spello, like, sir. A quick fag while the bloods are ashore.'

'Take this young lady up to the First-Class Smoking Room and then go and find Mr Williamson and tell him he's got a visitor. If he's not on duty he'll be in the Pig.'

Morrison nodded. He wished he could find time to spend in the Pig and Whistle, as the crew bars on all ships were called. He hadn't even finished his cigarette and in half an hour or so the passengers would start arriving back, asking for tea or something stronger as they dressed for dinner. There was no time for poor bloody stewards to be knocking back drinks in the Pig.

Alice followed him, her heart beating now in an odd jerky way, her stomach churning with apprehension. There was that faint oily smell she remembered so well, and the humming noise emitted by the ship's generators. She was really here, on board the *Aquitania* again! In a few minutes she would see him again too.

'Here yer are, miss, rest yer feet while I go and dig 'im out.'

Oh, it was so good to hear that familiar accent again. 'Thanks. Look, I'm really sorry you've had to go without your smoke.'

Morrison gaped at her. 'You're a Scouser! A posh one though.'

She laughed. 'I'm not posh but I'm proud of coming from Liverpool.'

His face split in a wide grin. 'Oh, yeah, the 'Pool is great. Put yer feet up an' 'ave a blow,' he urged before he went to find David Williamson.

Alice looked around, thinking that last time she was on this ship she would have been astounded by the elegance of it all. Now she was used to luxury. Even so she had to admit the room was very elegant. All the chairs and sofas were covered in deep crimson brocade and were anchored to the floor. The small tables with their crystal ashtrays were mahogany. At either end of the room were magnificent marble fireplaces with gilt-framed mirrors above them. Above her the deckhead was adorned with intricate

178

plaster work. In fact it really didn't look like a room on a ship at all.

She stood up and went to check her appearance in one of the mirrors. She was still standing there, wishing she had worn her new outfit, when she heard him come in. She turned, her eyes dancing with excitement, her face alight with joy. He was just as she'd remembered him. No, he looked even more handsome in the white tropical uniform, the high, brass-buttoned collar contrasting with his tanned face.

'My God! It *is* you! I'm afraid I was ... well, I couldn't recall you. I asked Morrison to describe you and I was still mystified.' He smiled a little lopsidedly. 'I don't know any "real lookers", to use Morrison's expression. Well, not here in Charleston.' He took her outstretched hand. It was only Morrison's description of her that had made him come up here, for he was tired, having only just finished his watch. Now he couldn't believe his eyes. This stunningly beautiful girl dressed in the height of fashion, whose eyes were full of laughter and zest for life, was the same dirty, scruffy bag of bones he'd carried on board two years ago. 'I remember your eyes, but not this.' He spread his hands palm upwards in a gesture that enveloped her appearance.

'I look a bit different to the last time, don't I? I couldn't even speak properly then.' He still held her hand and the physical contact made her blood sing.

He smiled to put her at ease. 'I don't seem to remember that there was anything wrong with the way you spoke. You'd just had an accident, remember?'

She remembered very well and withdrew her hand. God, but she'd been crawling with bugs that day. Her cheeks began to redden.

'What happened? How did you get here? What happened to the cat? Sit down and tell me, please,' he laughed. Alice laughed with him, nervously, overcome with the

179

momentousness of her impetuous action.

'Would you like a drink? Soda, tea, coffee, something stronger?'

She sat down a little unsteadily. 'No. No thanks.'

'Maybe later.'

She smiled but strange feelings were welling up inside her and she was glad she'd sat down. 'I live here now. I've been here two years.' She smiled again before embarking on an edited version of the events that had led to this day and this meeting.

By a quarter to seven Mike was getting worried. The heavy dusk was deepening into darkness. She'd only gone out for an hour, a breath of fresh air, so Alexander had informed him.

'Do you think she's really panicked over this performance tomorrow night?' he asked.

'She didn't seem too jumpy. Well, no more than she's been for the last couple of days.' Alexander pursed his lips. 'She liked the dress and seemed in lighter spirits when she went out.'

'Then where the hell is she?'

'Maybe she's gone over to Miss Euganie's house.'

'Without a calling card?'

Alexander shrugged. 'You know Miss Alice.'

'Maybe I should telephone.'

'Or she might be with that Mr Bransini.' Alexander always refused to call him Signor.

'I'll phone him as well.'

'He doesn't have a telephone.'

'Then I'll send Jimmy down or maybe even you.'

Alexander looked affronted. 'I'll send Ruth. She's got more sense than Jimmy or little Florrie.'

Alice wasn't at the Waltons' house and fifteen minutes later Ruth arrived back from West Street with the same information.

180

Mike wasn't too worried – yet. Alice knew how to take care of herself and she knew the city. She would more than likely have had money in her purse too. Enough for a cab home. She'd probably had some hare-brained idea, met someone, forgotten the time. Punctuality was not her strong point. 'I'll give her another half-hour and then I'll go out looking for her. We'll all go out looking for her.'

At half past seven Alice walked up the front steps and into the hall. She still felt as though she was walking in a dream. Oh, he was so nice. He'd been genuinely interested in her story. He'd laughed at the amusing parts, looked sympathetic at the intense and upsetting ones, and she'd finally taken her courage in both hands and invited him to the ball – Mrs Walton had been so relieved that she had agreed to sing that she'd told Euganie to tell her she could bring anyone she liked as guests.

The minute she walked into the drawing room Mike flung down the *News and Chronicle*. 'Jesus, Mary and Joseph! Where the hell have you been?' he demanded. 'You've had everyone worried about you. Why didn't you telephone? Now I'll have to let the Waltons and Bransini know you've arrived home safe and sound. And hasn't the worthy Mrs Augusta Walton been having ten blue fits thinking you'd run out on her!'

She looked contrite. 'I'm sorry. I really am sorry. I didn't even think about the time. Oh, Mike, the *Aquitania*'s in! Here, in Charleston! She's on a cruise. It's a new idea they're trying out and there's some sort of union trouble at home. She's here until early Sunday morning and I . . .' She faltered. She'd have to tell him she'd seen David. 'I met someone I know. A friend. He . . . he helped me once. I asked him to the ball tomorrow night – Euganie said I could ask anyone.' Her cheeks were flushed and her eyes danced with happiness. Her dream had come true. It was fate. The union trouble, the *Aquitania*'s cruise, Sofia Scarlatti's indisposition, the Cotillion Ball. He'd hear her sing

181

at the most elegant of all Charleston's social functions and she'd be dressed like a princess.

Mike felt a pool of ice form in the pit of his stomach. His eyes lacklustre, he picked up the newspaper. He couldn't look at her. 'I see. Does he have a name, this friend?'

'David. David Williamson.'

He drew in his breath. She'd confirmed his fear. By some malign chance she'd found *him* again. For a single mad moment he'd prayed it wouldn't be him. He could tell by her eyes and the joy she positively radiated that she was besotted by this man. 'And what does he do? I hope to God he's not a stoker.' He managed a twisted, sardonic smile. 'Wouldn't that upset the high and mighty of the land tomorrow night.'

'He's an officer. An engineering officer. You have to sort of work your way up. Take things called "tickets", so he told me. He wants to be a captain one day. He . . . he's very nice. He comes from a good home. His father is a lawyer or something like that.' She'd only just found all this out.

'At least he won't disgrace you tomorrow night then. And tell me, Alice, just how did you describe yourself and all this?' He threw out his arm in a wide sweeping gesture.

'I . . . I told him you were my guardian.'

'Oh, that was really clever of you, Alice!' He was openly sarcastic now. 'Sometimes you are a complete eejit! What happens when you're announced tomorrow as Mrs Alice O'Farrell?'

'I had to think of something quickly! I'll ask Euganie to announce me as just Alice O'Farrell. I told him . . . I told him I've changed my surname to yours, to make things easier, less complicated, like. Because you're my guardian.'

He shrugged. 'O'Connor, O'Farrell, I don't suppose he's really too interested. Or is he?'

'Mike, why are you being like this? Why are you being so flaming horrible? I'm sorry I was late, that I had you worried. I really am, but how could I tell him the truth? That I'd lived here with you for two years and then decided I wanted to be known as Mrs O'Farrell? What would he have thought of me?'

'Does he mean that much to you, Alice? Why didn't you tell me?'

She shrugged and made to turn away. 'I ... I suppose ...'

He caught her wrist. 'The truth, Alice!'

'I suppose because I never thought I'd see him again. That if I did he wouldn't remember the dirty ragged slummy with the scruffy half-dead kitten that he'd knocked over with his car at the Pier Head. The girl he'd given a guinea and a ten-shilling note to. More money than I'd ever had in my life. Money I used to come here. He ... he was part of the dream.'

He released her. 'I see.'

'He's a friend, Mike.'

'And a friend your own age, Alice. Much younger than your ... guardian – was that what you said?'

She nodded. 'I'm tired, Mike.'

With an effort he pulled himself together and managed a smile. 'We all are, Alice. Worn out with this Cotillion Ball nonsense. Oh, I know it's partly my fault for encouraging you. I'll tell Alexander to take your supper up to you, I'm going out.'

'Where are you going?' She was concerned. He looked upset although she knew he was trying to hide it.

'Out with some friends. If I'm going to have to put up with all those old bores tomorrow night, then I'm damned well going to enjoy myself tonight.' What he really meant was that he was going out to get drunk, to drown all his anger, jealousy, hurt and disappointment in a bottle of good Jameson's. This was no night for bourbon.

183

She heard all the noise and the shouting in the early hours when he finally got home and Alexander was trying to get him up the stairs to bed. She got up and looked sleepily over the banister rail.

'I wouldn't bother, Alexander. The pair of you will end up falling down the stairs. He won't hurt himself – drunks never do – but you might, so leave him.'

Alexander nodded and steered Mike in the direction of his study. She went back to her room, back to her hopes and dreams. She knew she'd have trouble trying to get back to sleep.

She slept late but it was lunch time when Mike finally emerged.

'I hope you're not going to get in that state tonight,' she snapped.

'Jesus, Mary and Joseph, don't start giving out! No one is going to show you up, Alice. You'll have your night of glory, your triumph and with *himself* watching you.' God, he felt awful. He was getting too old for wild drunken sprees. Where the hell was Alexander with that 'hair of the dog'? He turned towards his room, his head pounding. Alice stared at him as he stomped upstairs, puzzled by his behaviour. He seldom got so drunk and he seemed to have already taken an irrational dislike to David Williamson. Why? He wasn't in love with her himself. He'd said he wasn't. In fact, he'd said he would pity any man who *did* fall in love with her. No, he was just like, well, like the guardian she'd told David he was. She sighed heavily. Euganie would be here soon for the final rehearsal.

Mike was his usual affable, courteous self, thank God, Alice thought, when David Williamson arrived at seven o'clock. Her heart turned over at the sight of him, resplendent in the dress uniform of the merchant marine. She couldn't speak as he shook Mike's hand and then turned and took her own.

'I hardly know what to say, Alice! I can't find the words. You look—'

'Divine. Stunning. Magnificent, ' Mike interrupted smoothly. 'But then I'm an Irishman and we're renowned for the blarney.'

Alice looked up quickly and caught the sardonic look in Mike's eyes.

'You're right, sir. Any single one of them – no, all of them describe just how she looks.'

Before Alice could say a word, Mike handed her wrap to the younger man and called to Alexander to tell Jimmy to bring the car round to the front of the house.

'He's going to drive us there and come back later to fetch us. It'll be like a three-ringed circus down there. The road will be blocked, I shouldn't wonder.'

'I've never been to anything like this before. I asked around and found that it's a great honour to be invited to attend,' David said conversationally. He was still trying to equate this radiantly beautiful young woman with the girl on the dockside in Liverpool. She'd clearly had a great piece of luck, to be transported from dire poverty to what could only be described as opulent luxury.

'I'll tell you something,' Mike said affably. 'We don't usually move in such grand circles as a rule. We're "new" money, you see.'

'Really? I didn't think the class system existed here.'

'Ah, don't you believe it. It does here in this city at least. I'd say Charlestonians were worse in some ways. Weren't all their ancestors British? Isn't the place named after one of your kings? No, we're only invited because their star turn let them down.'

Alice was annoyed. It sounded awful put like that. As though her new friend Euganie Walton was a terrible snob and she herself was second best – which of course she was.

'Euganie's not like that!' she said coldly.

'No, but she's probably the only one who isn't. You won't find the likes of Mrs O'Hare and her friends where we're going. Ah, but you'll be all right, David. You're British and an officer and a gentleman.'

David looked mystified. He could sense the tension in the air. Maybe O'Farrell really resented the fact that his ward was being used as a sort of stopgap. Maybe he'd been snubbed at some time. He was Irish 'new' money: to a crowd of snooty colonials that probably meant he was viewed very much as an upstart.

It seemed as though everyone in Charleston was on Meeting Street tonight, Alice thought as excited anticipation mounted in her. The sidewalks were crowded and chauffeurs and carriage drivers cursed and swore as they tried to manoeuvre their vehicles along the street.

Outside the Charleston Club with its double circular staircase leading from the street to the Colonial doorway, and to the massive, dome-topped columns of the Scottish Presbyterian Church on the corner of Tradd Street, everything was at a complete standstill and chaos reigned. After five minutes of leaning forward and shouting questions and instructions to Jimmy, Mike had had enough.

'God Almighty, what a bloody mess! It's only across the street in the middle of the next block. We'll walk the rest of the way or we'll be stuck here until midnight. Jimmy, if you can get yourself out of this mess, go off home and don't bother coming back. We'll get a cab; it's bound to be as desperate as this later on. That's if it's cleared at all!'

The two stairways leading to the doors of the South Carolina Society's Hall were thronged with people. Slowly they ascended the flights of steps until they reached the second floor. Despite the crush, Alice could see that the huge room was pure Colonial in style.

She gasped. 'Oh, it's . . . it's . . .'

'Grand,' Mike finished for her. 'And stop looking like

a tinker's brat at a picnic,' he hissed. 'Haven't you as fine a home as any of this lot?'

Alice wasn't listening. She was overawed by her surroundings. One complete wall contained long windows and fireplaces sporting high mantels so that the whole room was filled with light and colour. Between the windows, placed on tables, were massive floral decorations, great banks of colour, mauve, lilac, blue, purple, indigo. There was trailing wisteria, with the contrasting dark green foliage of laurel and vine leaves, vibrant oranges, reds and the aureate splashes of yellow jasmine. As she drew closer she spotted intricate arrangements of flowers, ferns and twisted pieces of bleached white driftwood, worked into collages of ships and anchors, shells and fish, backed by spiky palm fronds symbolising Charleston, 'City of the Sea'.

At the far end of the room was a semicircular platform over which was a raised balcony supported by Colonial pillars festooned with ivy, vines and smilax. The balcony was also ablaze with colour, coleus, geraniums, oleander and roses of every hue. The centrepiece was a huge cornucopia – the horn of plenty – woven from bleached palmetto fronds, its mouth spilling forth a profusion of flowers.

'Oh, this is spectacular!' David Williamson, too, was overawed. He'd been to many beautiful places, sailed on the floating palaces that were the Cunard transatlantic liners, but this was magnificent.

Through the crowd Alice saw Euganie Walton with an older very severe-looking woman who was obviously her mother. Euganie wore a dress of silk organdie in a delicate shade of blue and her hair was held back by two diamond-studded clips. She caught sight of Mike and with some difficulty made her way over to the little group.

'Oh, Alice, you look gorgeous!'

'So do you.'

Introductions were made.

'Is it always such a crush?' Mike asked.

Euganie laughed. 'Yes, but it will soon sort itself out.'

'Where will I have to go to sing?'

'There.' Euganie pointed to a small stage flanked by potted palms which screened the black musicians. 'But not until the intermission. You can enjoy yourself first, Alice.' Euganie turned to David. 'One of my friends was telling me she had a tour of your ship, Mr Williamson. She said it's quite magnificent.'

'Maybe Mr Williamson will give you a conducted tour before they sail, Euganie,' Mike said smoothly.

'We sail in the morning, very early, I'm afraid.'

'Ah, well, never mind. I'm sure Euganie will be only too pleased to put your name at the top of the list on her dance card. Doesn't he look grand in that uniform and,' Mike glanced around, 'he's the only one actually *in* uniform. They'll all be dying of curiosity and you'll cause a stir.'

'Oh, Mr O'Farrell, you're shameless!' Euganie laughed.

Alice smiled at Euganie and then turned to Mike.

'Did you remember mine? Alexander said he'd given it to you.'

Mike withdrew it from his pocket. 'I have so. Alexander said that by now you'd be in such a state of nerves you'd go and lose it.'

'I see you still have that custom here.' David was amused. 'It went out of fashion after the war at home.'

'You should see what kind of dances they think are fashionable here,' Mike chuckled.

David laughed with him. 'Oh, I know what you mean, sir. The Charleston.'

The orchestra burst into life and Mike held out his arm to Alice. 'The first dance is mine. A privilege of age, I think.'

David turned towards Euganie and extended his arm.

188

The evening was so hectic, Alice thought. It was going so fast and she really wanted to savour every minute. She had danced with Mike and David but other young men – strangers – had also sought her out. She just wanted it to go on and on for ever but all too soon the intermission was announced.

It was Euganie's formidable mother who came to conduct her to the stage.

'Go on, Alice,' Mike encouraged her. 'This is your moment of triumph. Go on up there now and show them all what you can do. Show them you're better than any diva from New York.' His smile and words of support were genuine.

'Good luck, Alice,' David called as the stately dowager led her through the press of people.

Mrs Walton announced her and thanked her for so kindly stepping in for Miss Scarlatti at such very short notice. Alice smiled but she wasn't listening. She was going over the short speech, the first she had ever made, that she and Euganie had rehearsed. She knew she looked elegant; the admiring glances of the men and the often envious ones of the women assured her of that.

The great hall fell silent. Only the gentle rustling of evening gowns and the swishing of fans was heard for a second or two and then those sounds died away too. Oh, let them all wonder and whisper about where she'd sprung from and who her family were, Alice thought. She didn't care. This *was* the dream. She was living and breathing it.

Her voice carried clearly. 'Ladies and gentlemen, I can't hope to emulate Miss Scarlatti and I won't try. The pieces I've chosen are all well known and are not grand opera but I hope you will enjoy them.'

She turned slightly and indicated to the half-hidden orchestra that she was ready. She smiled over the heads of the crowd and began the 'Cradle Song', the easiest piece, one that everyone knew; it would give her confidence, Euganie had advised. After the first few bars, all trace of nervousness disappeared. Her clear soprano gave the piece new life, new movement, new concord. Her face was transformed with an ethereal glow, a beauty that came from the sheer joy of the force that possessed her.

Chapter Sixteen

It would be spring and then summer soon, Lizzie thought despondently as she trudged home from work. Already there were buds on the trees in the public parks and there had been a few mild days. She didn't really mind spring or autumn but the long hot days of summer were often hard to bear. She didn't know which was worse, winter or summer. You either froze or sweated. In summer the heat hung heavily over the rows of narrow streets. In the small overcrowded houses it was sweltering. Sometimes at night she felt as though the heavy air was pressing down on her chest, making breathing hard and sleep almost impossible. The back jiggers with their rubbish and putrid remains of vegetables and the privies in the back yards stank to high heaven and attracted flies by the dozen.

Rich people lived in houses with large windows in their bedrooms and on the ground floor, ones that opened out onto gardens with trees that provided shade. She'd seen them in Prince's and Newsham Parks, sash windows pushed up and crisp white net curtains which gave an illusion of coolness, moving slightly in the breeze.

At least these days Da wasn't so much trouble. He had money which she was sure came from Alice, the occasional few days' casual work which suited him, and there had been one or two short spells in Walton Jail. In fact he'd spent the last two Christmases there, the best Christmases they'd had in many a long year. She was sure that Constable Phillips had organised it. They'd had two parcels of food and five shillings from the Police Benevolent Fund. They were quite friendly now, she mused. She often saw him on his beat and he'd walk all or part of the way home with her. At first she'd been embarrassed, her eyes down, her head bent, ignoring the looks of censure and curiosity from friends and neighbours alike. Even Mam had mentioned it.

'There's nothing wrong with him, Mam, we just have a chat,' she explained to Nelly.

'I'll give you that, Lizzie, but you know what folk around here are like with the scuffers.'

She hadn't replied. She enjoyed their talks. They lifted the gloom and weariness at the end of the day. It was just general talk, local gossip, the weather, the problems of living in a city like Liverpool. Their strollings had ceased to be a cause of gossip. They drew amused glances now, at the slight, mousy girl in her cheap and often grubby clothes and the six-foot-five, barrel-chested, dark-haired policeman. She never let him carry anything for her, no matter how heavy the burden; it would somehow demean him. She knew from what he'd told her that if it was reported that he was escorting a young woman and carrying her bundles on a regular basis, he would be disciplined. It *would* demean him and the uniform he wore. So sometimes she had to struggle home from the bag wash, the washing in a bundle clutched to her chest, her arms aching, for she had never mastered the art of carrying the bundle on her head, the way most of the older women and the shawlies did.

As she trudged along, Lizzie spotted his familiar figure on the corner of Westmoreland Street, ostensibly keeping his eye on the pub of the same name. You couldn't miss him, he was so tall. Her expression brightened.

'Hello, Lizzie. Another hard day?'

192

She smiled up at him. 'No, it wasn't bad and it's payday tomorrow.'

'Aye, for me too.'

She just nodded, wishing her wage compared with his. They got good pay, did the scuffers, since the riots in 1919, but then they had a lot to put up with, not only from the 'civvies', as he called ordinary people, but from the 'higher ups' too. She'd thought he'd been pulling her leg when he'd told her of all the rules and regulations and the fines.

'The weather's a bit better now. Soon be spring.'

'Aye,' he agreed. 'I don't know where the time goes to.'

They'd reached the corner of Benledi Street.

'Lizzie, would you consider coming for a sail with me to New Brighton on Sunday?' he asked quietly.

She was so astounded that she could only gape at him.

'I don't get a Sunday off very often,' he went on, to fill her awkward silence.

'Well . . . I . . . yes,' she stammered. 'But . . . but . . . I ain't got no Sunday clothes.' Her cheeks burned with the shame and embarrassment of having to admit this.

'That doesn't matter, Lizzie. It's you I want to take on an outing, not a dressed up doll.'

'Our Alice's the pretty one, she always has been.'

'You underestimate yourself, Lizzie. To me you're a great looking girl.'

The smile that spread across her face erased the lines of care and deprivation. 'Am I?'

'Indeed you are, Lizzie.'

They agreed to meet at the Pier Head at two o'clock but she didn't tell her mam until the Saturday night.

'Do you think Maggie O'Hanlon would lend me a coat, Mam, for tomorrow afternoon?'

Nelly looked surprised. 'What for?'

'Well, I'm going to New Brighton for the afternoon and I've nothing decent at all.'

'Who's taking you?'

Lizzie fiddled with the edge of her frayed cuff. 'A feller.'

'What feller?'

'Jack, his name is.'

Nelly looked shrewdly at her daughter for a few minutes. 'It's Jack Phillips, that scuffer, isn't it?'

Lizzie nodded but to her surprise there was no exclamation of disapproval. Nelly strongly suspected that Tip's spells in Walton and the fact that these days he was far less violent were all due in some part to Jack Phillips. It was almost a year now since she'd had so much as a belt from Tip and that was a bloody miracle.

'Don't get your hopes up, luv. He's a decent enough feller but we're not his class of person at all.'

'It's just a bit of an outing, Mam.'

Nelly looked at her fondly. Her poor Lizzie. She'd been so broken-hearted when that big, daft Tommy Mac had been killed. He'd been her one chance to escape from number ten Benledi Street. Since then, well, Lizzie looked far older than her years and had had nothing in life to look forward to.

'Then go over and ask Maggie,' she said kindly, 'but don't tell her where you're going and who with. Their Fred's had a few run-ins with Constable Phillips and he's got the bruises to prove it.'

As soon as she'd got in from work on the Saturday she'd washed her hair but no matter how many times she combed it, it had no life, no shine, just hung limply around her pallid face. On Sunday, in desperation, she twisted it into a knot at the back of her head. It made her look even older and plainer but there was no help for it.

The coat she'd borrowed from Maggie was navy blue which didn't do anything to lighten her appearance, but it was new, bought from Blackler's, no less, with a windfall her da had had on a horse. It covered the shabby skirt and blouse and came down to Lizzie's ankles and for that she was thankful, for she had no stockings or shoes, just boots, the old-fashioned kind women used to wear, laced up but with a small heel. She had no hat. She looked at herself in the window of the tobacconist's shop on Scotland Road as she waited for the tram – Mam had let her have tuppence and hopefully Jack would pay the return fare. The image of herself gazing back from the shop window was depressing. The coat really didn't suit her as Maggie was much bigger than she was. Oh, she was so plain, and as dull as ditchwater and swamped by the huge garment, the sleeves of which she'd had to turn up twice.

Jack was waiting for her at the top of one of the covered walkways that led down to the floating landing stage. He looked so different, she thought, out of uniform. He wore a tweed jacket with leather patches at the elbows and well-pressed grey trousers. A grey knitted pullover covered an open-necked shirt and in place of his helmet he wore a flat tweed cap. That surprised her. Somehow she'd thought he'd have worn a bowler or a trilby.

He walked to meet her. 'That's a nice warm coat, Lizzie. You'll be glad of it, there's a real bite to the wind.'

'It's not mine. I borrowed it,' she admitted.

'Well, what does that matter?' he said kindly. 'I thought we might go up the tower and then for a bit of a walk along the front, then have a cup of tea and something to eat before coming back. Would that suit you?'

She looked up at him, her eyes full of excitement. 'Up the tower? Really?'

'Really. And tea.'

'I've been to New Brighton but I ... we ... never went up the tower.'

A frown creased his forehead and then he remembered that when she'd been young she'd been 'walking out' with Tommy Mac. That was what she meant by 'we'.

'Well, it'll be something new and we'll have a great day even if the sun doesn't shine.'

195

He bought the tickets and they climbed the staircase that led up to the open deck.

'We can come down into the saloon, if you get cold.'

'No, I want to see everything from up here.'

He watched her intently and with mild amusement tinged with pity as she exclaimed over seeing all the buildings on the waterfront and all the ships. She clung onto the rail with one hand and pointed as New Brighton tower, the fort and the lighthouse at Perch Rock drew closer. The ferry wasn't too crowded as the weather was still cold and he was glad of it. In the summer and on Bank Holidays people were crammed like sardines on every ferry, and on the beach of the small holiday resort you were lucky to get a few feet of sand to yourself. There were always kids running around, kicking up sand and nagging their parents for a penny to see the one-legged diver or the Punch and Judy show.

The wind has loosened the knot of Lizzie's hair and it blew untidily around her face but she didn't care. Eventually they sat down on one of the long wooden benches that were in reality life rafts.

'I don't often get a Sunday off and when I do I don't do much or go anywhere. This makes a nice change.'

'It's like a holiday for me.'

She looked years younger, he thought, with her hair loose, her eyes full of excitement and her cheeks tinged with pink by the wind. He judged her to be in her late twenties. He was thirty-seven, so it wasn't much of a gap. Not so wide that people would think he was just an old fool out with a young girl. He'd grown fond of her and, as Nelly had suspected, he was responsible for the cessation of violence in the O'Connor house. A year ago, on the way to Rose Hill Station after he'd arrested Tip O'Connor, who was drunk and decidedly disorderly, he'd described at great length what he would do to him if Tip ever laid a finger on any of his family again – a description

196

he'd repeated when Tip had sobered up a little. He knew the man was a bully and a coward but he made sure he saw Lizzie often enough to satisfy himself she hadn't been beaten, and enquired frequently after her mam.

There was still about twenty minutes before the ferry would tie up, so they sat and watched the shipping for a while, until he spoke.

'You know you could get a better job, Lizzie.'

'Who'd have me? I can read and write but I'm not clever. I've got no proper manners and I don't know how to . . . talk to people.'

'You could learn manners. You *are* clever and you talk to me. Your Alice had the nowse to get out and make a life for herself.'

'Our Alice was always different to me. It was something to do with her being able to sing, and besides she's younger.'

'There are other girls from Scotland Road who've done it, Lizzie,' he urged. She had no self-confidence. It had all been beaten out of her. 'Girls who've made a good life for themselves. Look at Maggie and Davie Higgins. They've got a whole building now for all the wedding dresses, veils and bridal things she sells. She doesn't sew them herself now, she just designs them and people come from all over, she's built such a fine reputation.'

'She used to live in Silvester Street, didn't she?'

He nodded. 'And there's Dee Chatterton who married Tommy Kerrigan and went off to Canada. They've got a fruit farm and I hear they're going great guns, expanding all the time. Abbie Kerrigan married Mike Burgess and he's a sergeant in the CID now and they live on Queen's Drive. They all came from Burlington Street. So you see you *can* change your life, Lizzie, if you have the determination. They were all hard up, the Kerrigans were as poor as church mice most of the time.'

'But they were never as badly off as us,' Lizzie pointed

out. 'At least their fathers had work or went looking for it and didn't spend their wages before they got home.'

'Sal Kerrigan could have told you something about that, Lizzie,' Jack insisted quietly. 'Her Pat couldn't pass a pub on the way home from work.'

Lizzie knew the Kerrigans vaguely. Sal was dead now and Pat was living in Ireland with Evvie and Keiran O'Brien. The two older lads had been killed in the war, along with Joan's husband. Monica had become a nun but then left the order. Lizzie didn't remember her very well.

'Your mam's not on her own for being beaten,' Jack went on. 'Do you remember that terrible business with Abe Harvey in Burlington Street? He didn't drink but he was a fanatical and a violent man.'

She remembered most of it, although it had been at the beginning of the war. His son Jerry, who was dying, had up and belted Abe with a poker and killed him. Jerry hadn't been hanged for it. He'd died just afterwards of consumption. A smile played around the corners of her mouth.

'What's the smile for?' He couldn't see anything in that particular case to amuse anyone.

'I was thinking of Hannah Harvey. They had more money than us but she was plain and quiet, like me.'

'Oh, aye. Hannah did best of all although she wouldn't look at it like that, not after having her husband shot and dying in her arms.'

It had been the talk of the entire neighbourhood, in fact most of the city, when she'd been wed. Timid little Hannah Harvey, the daughter of a labourer on the tugs, had become the Countess of Ashenden and lived in that huge house in the country with her little boy and dozens of servants. And apparently her husband had owned acres and acres of land and a famous and fabulous collection of jewels.

'Something like that only ever happens once in a blue

moon, Lizzie. It was just circumstances. She's stayed very quiet, never uses her title, never mixing with society, so I heard.'

Lizzie smiled again. 'They were all lucky, but can you see me in an office or a shop or running a big house? No, factory work's all I'm fit for, and I'm glad of it.'

'I don't believe that, Lizzie, but we'll agree to disagree, shall we?'

It was a wonderful day. You could see for miles from the tower and at the bottom of it was a huge ballroom. There were the amusements, a helter-skelter and a ferris wheel but she hadn't wanted to try them. They'd walked along the promenade and, because it was low tide, along the causeway that led to the old fort. Then they'd had fish and chips, bread and butter and tea and scones in a small but very nice cafe. It was the first time since Christmas that she'd had a full belly.

They didn't sit up on deck on the way home, it was too cold and almost dark. Downstairs the saloon was warm and smelled of engine oil. She fell asleep, her head resting on Jack's shoulder and he put his arm around her. Poor little lass, he thought tenderly, what kind of a future did she have? Maybe he'd been wrong to bring up all those other girls who'd done well for themselves. Maybe she'd remembered Tommy MacNamara. Maybe now she'd get depressed.

She still felt warm and sleepy on the tram but as they walked down Benledi Street the wind chased the drowsiness away, and Lizzie realised, with a touch of regret, that her cherished day out was coming to an end. Finally they reached number ten.

As she stood on the broken, uneven doorstep, Jack thought how small and vulnerable she looked. 'Next time I'm off on a Sunday, will we go on another outing, Lizzie? We could get a train to Chester.'

She was amazed. She'd thought no further than today. 'You want to take me on another outing?'

He nodded.

'Yes. Yes of course I'll come, Jack. It's been great today, it really has and I'm dead grateful.'

'I'm glad. You deserved a treat.' He raised his cap. 'Good night, Lizzie, I'll probably see you in the week, when I'm on my beat.'

She went inside and closed the door but Jack stood looking at the peeling paint and battered wood for a few minutes, deep in thought. He'd grown fond of her but if anything was to come of it, it would all have to be thought out and handled carefully. How would his mam take to Lizzie? How would Nelly manage without Lizzie's wage, and would Lizzie leave this hovel at all? He turned away. It was early days yet, he wasn't even sure of her feelings for him. She might not have any at all, except gratitude. But more and more he wanted to give her a good home; a safe, secure and comfortable life. One day.

Chapter Seventeen

Alice was silent all the way home in the car. She didn't listen to what Mike was saying and when he pressed her for an answer to a question she replied in monosyllables. Only now was it really beginning to dawn on her that she would probably never see David Williamson again.

The ball had been a great success. *She* had been a great success. When the last notes of the Easter Hymn had died away there had been a few seconds' total silence and then the applause had been deafening. To Alice's ears the sound seemed to shake the room. It was Mike who had stepped forward to hand her down from the platform. She'd positively glowed with radiance and pleasure, oblivious of the look of pride on his face.

After the intermission she was suddenly so popular that she had only had one dance with Mike and two dances with David – and how the minutes of those two dances had slipped by, minutes full of laughter, excitement and pure joy. She was like Cinderella in the fairy story. For this one night she was the toast of Charleston society and in those two dances she'd found her prince. But during the final dance he had spoken the words which now chilled her heart.

'You are certainly the belle of the ball tonight, Alice,' he'd stated, finding it more and more difficult to equate this girl with the one he'd seen, just once, in Liverpool.

She laughed, blushing with pleasure. 'I told you I could sing.'

'Yes, I seem to remember that you did, but never in a million years did I dream you had a voice like that. You should be at Covent Garden.'

'Where's that?'

'London. It's the home of opera. Or maybe Milan or Paris, Vienna – everywhere there's good music.'

'I'd be terrified. No, this is quite good enough for me. I've done enough travelling.'

He smiled down at her. 'I've never met anyone like you before, Alice. You are the most extraordinary person.'

Her eyes sparkled and exhilaration swept over her. Her heart felt as though it would burst and she wanted to sing once more. To sing all night and just for him.

'Who would ever have thought that the drab little sparrow could rise so high in the sky and sing like a lark.'

His words reminded her of India who, when she'd presented her for the first, and last, time had likened her to a bird, a nightingale.

'Have you been to all those places?' she asked.

'Not all, but I've been to quite a few countries. I'm an expert on the indigenous dock workers across the world!' He saw the puzzled look in her eyes. 'Take no notice of me, Alice, I was just trying to be funny. Now we stick to the Atlantic run, except of course when there are strikes at home.'

'Is there much trouble?' She hoped it wouldn't affect Mam and the kids. She'd go on sending the money; things were never as bad if you had a bit of money in your pocket.

He looked serious. 'Yes. The General Strike may have ended over a year ago but there's still a lot of unrest. People are resentful and there are still strikes.'

Alice seized on his words. 'So you might come here again?'

He looked at her a little wistfully. 'Alice, if there's another strike we'll be laid up, no more jaunting around these exotic tropical places. Then when it's over it'll be back on the Atlantic run again.'

She'd smiled, the dance had finished and she'd been whisked off by another young man she'd never met before that night. David's words hadn't really sunk in. Until now.

Jimmy had been waiting with the car. He'd been told by Alexander to ignore the earlier instruction. Have them come home in a common taxi cab when there was a fine motorcar, certainly not! They'd given David a lift back to the ship and Mike had shaken his hand and said if he was ever in this part of the world again he must come and visit them. There had been confidence in his smile. He read the newspapers. He knew what was going on back in Britain. He doubted they'd ever see David Williamson again.

David had taken Alice's hand. 'It's been a wonderful night. Maybe one day I'll see you on the stage of the Royal Opera House, Covent Garden, Alice. Do you remember what Charlie said?'

'Yes. He said one day you might pay to hear me sing.'

David had smiled at Mike. 'My younger brother. I thought he was being crass at the time but now I know he was being prophetic. Goodbye, Alice and thank you, both, for an evening I'll always remember.'

They'd watched him go. After he'd released her hand he'd walked swiftly up the gangway and then turned to give a quick wave before disappearing from sight.

'You're very quiet, Alice.' Mike's voice broke through her reverie. She'd hardly said a word and they were nearly home. He knew she was thinking of Williamson and he had to admit that the lad was pleasant, well-educated and well-mannered.

'I'm tired.'

'I expect you are. It's very tiring being the centre of attention.'

She turned and looked at him to see if he was teasing her. He wasn't.

'I mean it,' he said. 'It's exhausting. You've been in a state of nervous tension for days. But you were wonderful, Alice. You could see the looks of pure amazement slowly creeping over their faces. I wouldn't have missed it for the world. You weren't the paid entertainment as Sofia Scarlatti would have been. You were entertaining them because you wanted to and I think they realised that.'

He meant every word. He'd watched the faces of Charleston's society and the stunned looks had soon been replaced by genuine admiration. It had given him a glow of smug satisfaction, for they all thought that she was his wife and he'd almost burst with love and pride. It had taken a lot of guts for a virtually untrained girl to step into the shoes of Sofia Scarlatti, whose entire youth had apparently been spent at La Scala, Milan. Alice had been the star of the whole evening. Beautiful, confident, charming, talented. He'd been too busy with his own thoughts to turn and see how David Williamson was taking her performance, nor had he wanted to. He'd seen the expression in Alice's eyes whenever they alighted on the handsome young ship's officer. But it wasn't love. She was infatuated, that was all. She'd fallen in love with an image. She didn't know much about him at all and after tonight she'd probably not see him again and with any luck she'd forget him eventually.

As Alexander took their cloaks, Mike pulled a small box from his pocket and handed it to her.

'What's this for?'

'That's not very gracious, now, is it? Open it.'

She knew she should feel thankful, curious and excited, even exuberant but she felt empty and desolate. She opened the small red Morocco leather box. Inside was a gold pendant and chain. The pendant consisted of two letters. L and S entwined, and above them was a bird set with diamonds. She looked puzzled.

'Didn't you once tell me that you wanted to be known as the Liverpool Songbird?'

She smiled. 'I did. More than anything else in the world.'

'Now it's true. Well, almost. After tonight's performance, would you rather it was the Charleston Songbird? I could get the letters changed.'

She shook her head. 'No. This is beautiful. Thank you.' She closed the lid. 'I think I'll go up now. I really am tired.'

He nodded but his face was set in lines of disappointment. Every other gift he'd given her had been accepted with cries and shrieks of pleasure. 'I'll see you in the morning, Alice. Good night.' He turned away and headed for his study.

Alice went slowly up the stairs and when Ruth had helped her undress she sat down at her dressing table and began half-heartedly to brush her hair. The face of the girl who stared back at her was full of mute misery. Oh, she was sure he must love her. She'd not misread the look in his eyes. She'd not imagined the pressure of his arms round her waist, holding her closer than was deemed correct. She knew she'd been a great success but perversely it really didn't mean that much to her now. He was going away. In a few hours the *Aquitania*'s anchor would be raised. As she lay in her bed she would hear the three long blasts on the ship's whistle, the *Aquitania*'s farewell to Charleston and his, too, in a way. She couldn't let him go. She *had* to tell him how she felt. But how could she get to see him and to see him alone?

She looked down at the pendant Mike had just given her. No, she didn't want to be the Charleston Songbird. It was Liverpool or nothing. Liverpool! That's where he was going. They'd sail up to New York and then across the Atlantic to their home port. She felt a great surge of homesickness rush over her. Home for him probably meant a big house, his parents and Charlie. Home for her meant Benledi Street, Mam, Lizzie, Agnes, Mary, the boys Jimmy and Eddie. But, oh, how she longed to see them all again. She took the pendant from its box and fastened it round her neck. She gently fingered the letters. L and S. The Liverpool Songbird. Well, why not? The shadows of depression and despair melted away. She could easily get a job now. No one would turn her away or deny her audition and then . . . she would see David again. She'd see him as often as his ship came in. Their relationship would grow and he'd tell her he loved her and always would.

All other thoughts were banished from her mind as she stood up and began to rummage through her wardrobe, flinging clothes across the bed. From a cupboard she dragged out a trunk she'd noticed was stored there. It was full of clothes, men's clothes – Mike's father's, she assumed. She quickly emptied it. Her shoes went in first, then underwear, then dresses. She was so engrossed that she didn't hear the door open or notice Mike standing in the doorway.

'Alice, what are you doing?'

She got to her feet. 'Oh, Mike!' Her hand went to the pendant, almost defensively – 'I . . . I'm . . . packing. I . . . I want to go home.'

'This is all very sudden. You've never shown any inclination to go back. You know I would have paid for a visit.' Anger and bitterness filled his eyes. 'You have Charleston at your feet and you decide to go home! Jaysus, Alice! Don't lie to me. I'm not blind nor am I an eejit. You're going after him, David Williamson.'

'I'm not! I really do want to go home. I miss Mam so much.'

'Stop that bloody nonsense, Alice!'

She shrank back. She'd never seen him so furious before. In the depths of his dark eyes there were pinpoints of fire and the expression on his face frightened her. Now, for the first time, she saw him not as a benefactor or a friend she could laugh and joke with, but as a tall, strong, angry man. A man who could hurt her or who could force her to stay here. She hid her fear well.

'Oh, all right!' she said defiantly. 'Yes! Yes, I'm going after him. I. . .'

He could see the words forming on her lips but he didn't want to hear them. 'How do you know he wants you to follow him? Have you thought of that? How much do you really know about him? I'll tell you, Alice, not a bloody thing! He might well have a girl back there. He might even be married. You don't bloody know.'

'No! No, he's not married, there's no girl. I'm sure he would have said something.' For a moment her heart stopped. She felt sick. What if there *was* a girl?

'Why? We invited him out, to a rather grand evening as it turned out. He wasn't obliged to tell us his life story. All I got out of him was that he wanted to be a captain eventually.'

'Stop it! Stop it! I don't want to hear any more.' If she listened to Mike, she might begin to doubt herself and the rightness of her instincts. 'I want to go home!'

Mike felt as though his heart had been turned to stone. That ice water was running through his veins instead of blood. He wanted to take her in his arms and hold her tightly and keep her here. He wanted to kiss her and love her and erase all thoughts of Williamson from her mind. How could he let her go? How could he tell her that this house would be like a mausoleum without her? That his life would have little purpose or direction. And if he did tell her and beg her to stay, what answer would he get? That she didn't want him? That she could never love him? That maybe in time she'd even hate him if he tried

207

to keep her here. But surely he had to try.

'Alice, are you absolutely determined? Are you sure?' He'd fought a hard battle to keep the jealousy from his voice.

'I am! I know . . . I just know . . .' She spread her hands helplessly.

He turned away. He wasn't going to beg. He wasn't going to act like a fool – an old fool. His pride wouldn't let him. He had to retain some self-respect.

Alice was on the verge of tears. She didn't want to admit that there was even a slight possibility that Mike was right. She *knew* David wasn't married, but a girl?

'All right, Alice. Go. I've no claim on you.' The words were spoken in a harsh, brittle tone. Mike couldn't bring himself to put a single note of warmth in his voice.

'Can . . . can I . . .'

'Can you what?' He'd turned to face her, completely in control of himself again.

Alice looked at him with child-like pleading. 'Can I take all my clothes?'

'Sure, though there won't be many of them suited to a cold spring in Liverpool.'

She just hung her head. 'Mike, I . . . I . . . I'm sorry. You've been so good to me. I don't know how I would have ended up but for you.' Her hand went to the pendant. 'Can I . . . keep this? I don't want anything else.'

He nodded curtly and left the room. Alice began to pick up her clothes and fold them. She had saved some money, enough at least to get her home to Liverpool. She still had a horror of being penniless and so she had what she called her 'emergency' money.

She looked up sharply as the door opened. She hadn't expected Mike to return and was surprised and anxious to see him standing there.

Mike stared back at her. He'd gone straight to the safe where her jewels were kept. He'd had a mad impulse to pick them up and throw them one by one out of the window, but common sense prevailed. He'd taken a small bundle of dollar notes, one of many, and put them in his pocket. He'd shut the safe and sighed heavily as he'd turned toward the staircase.

'Take this. You'll need it,' he said quietly.

She looked down at the small bundle of green bank-notes he'd thrown on the bed.

'It's the same amount that I paid India to release you. She drives a hard bargain. Take it.'

Her cheeks burned with shame remembering just how she'd paid her passage to Charleston and how and where she'd met Mike. And now she was walking out on him. There looked to be a couple of hundred dollars in that bundle on the bed. 'Oh, Mike, I really am grateful.' There was a catch in her voice.

'I'll get Alexander to organise your packing and see to the luggage. There's no rush, Alice. There won't be any trains leaving tonight.'

'I'd thought I could go . . .'

'On the ship?' he finished for her. 'It's full. Not a single berth left. I heard him tell Euganie that. So, you'll have to go by train to New York. Oh, don't worry, Alice. You won't miss the boat. The train is far quicker.'

'Will I see you in the morning?'

He didn't answer. He left the room, slamming the door so hard that the portraits on the landing walls shook. Let them all think what they liked. He didn't bloody care.

Alexander looked around the room in disbelief. She *was* going. He hadn't believed it when he'd been summoned and told that Alice was leaving, that she was going back to England. Was it for a visit? he'd asked, so stunned he'd forgotten that it was not his place to question his employer. No, it was not, had been the curt reply. He'd wanted to ask what had happened, what had been said.

They'd all waited up, wanting to know how Alice had fared. They were all dog-tired but they'd been overjoyed when Jimmy had told them she'd been a huge success. But then there'd been a row or a fight of some kind. They'd all heard the raised voices and then the door slam and Mike's heavy tread on the stairs. Both Mr Mike and Alice had tempers.

'The first train is at six o'clock tomorrow morning,' he said sadly.

Alice nodded. 'When I've finished, could Jimmy take me down to the station?'

'You can't wait at the station until tomorrow morning.'

'This morning.' Alice nodded towards the clock. It was ten minutes past one.

'Well, you still can't go hanging around that place. Jimmy will wait with you, in the car.'

'No. That's not fair, Alexander. There must be a ladies' waiting room.'

'Why are you going?' Alexander felt that he could ask this now.

'I'm . . . I'm homesick.'

'You never told anyone that.'

'I didn't think I should. I didn't think it was "done" to tell the entire household everything.'

'Will you come back?'

'I don't know. Maybe, one day. You see, I promised Mam I'd go home when I was famous.'

Alexander shrugged. He supposed it was as good an excuse as any but he'd be sorry to see her go.

Jimmy brought the luggage down and put it in the hall. There was a miserable, depressing air hanging over the house, Alexander thought as he came downstairs. Everyone was upset to see Alice go, particularly Ruth and himself. Mr Mike was in his study, even though everyone else had now gone to bed. He could see the sliver of light under the door. He looked at the trunk and the cases and

210

then back to the strip of light. Oh, to hell with propriety now. Ruth, Ella and Florence had been in tears and he couldn't have his staff upset like this. It wasn't like the bad old days any more. He was paid a wage. He didn't have to keep his mouth shut. Mr Mike could sack him but he'd soon find another job and, anyway, the place wouldn't be the same without Alice. He did knock but there was no reply, so he opened the door and went in.

Mike was sitting slumped in the deeply buttoned leather armchair. The room was dark. Only the desk lamp was switched on. Alexander noticed that the cut-glass whisky decanter was half empty.

'Now what? Can't a man get a bit of peace in his own bloody house?'

Alexander decided that a coaxing approach wouldn't work. 'She's going and you're letting her go,' he said belligerently.

'So what? If she wants to go, let her.'

'We'll all be sorry.'

Mike's temper rose. He'd been drinking for an hour but he wasn't drunk. Far from it. Perversely, tonight it seemed that the more he drank the more sober he felt. 'I'm sure she'd like to know that. Now leave me alone. If she wants to make fool of herself—'

'She ain't just homesick then,' Alexander interrupted quickly.

'Don't you have eyes and ears all over the damned place? Don't you know as well as I do that she's going chasing after that bloody young Williamson?' Mike yelled. 'Young, that's the important word, Alexander. *Young.*'

Alexander gave up all pretence of ignorance. 'But I heard she only met him once before, back in Liverpool, and then just for a few minutes. She got hurt or something.'

'Of course she only met him once before! She doesn't bloody know him. She only thinks she does.'

'Then go and talk her out of it. Go and change her mind. She can't go chasing around the world.'

'She managed to find her way here – and anyway, it's none of your damned business.'

Alexander persisted. 'We're like a family. You said so yourself at Christmas.'

'I must have been drunk.'

'No, you weren't. Miss Alice is part of this house now. Part of the family. Go and talk to her.'

Mike wanted to yell that he would do no such thing. That he'd been humiliated enough for one night. Instead he shook his head firmly. 'No.'

'And that's definite?'

Mike lost his temper. 'Get out of here, Alexander!'

'Ruth, Ella and Florrie went back to bed crying their eyes out. I think—'

'Go to hell!' Mike shouted. He snatched up the decanter and hurled it at the marble fireplace.

It shattered into a thousand shards. 'Get out of here before I sack you! Before I sack the whole bloody lot of you!'

Alexander left sadly. His sadness was for Mike, for Alice and for all the staff, his family.

When the car was loaded Alice gave Alexander a quick hug before getting in. When she'd come downstairs she'd turned towards the study but Alexander had shaken his head warningly. So she walked out into the starlit night, looking sadly back at the house that had been her home for over two years. It had been more than a house, more than a home. It had been a new world. A new life.

She asked Jimmy to drive down to the harbour first, for reassurance. She got out and walked across the road and then breathed a sigh of relief. The ship was still there. Not quite so many lights blazed now, at least not from the portholes. People were asleep.

'Wait for me, I won't be long,' she told Jimmy before she hurriedly crossed the road and ran down towards the harbour. She'd just catch him. She'd tell him she would see him in New York. That she, too, was going back to Liverpool.

There was great activity on the dockside. The longshoremen were already getting ready to cast off the ropes that held the ship to its moorings. The anchor was almost up, she could hear the last clanking, grating sounds. No! She was too late. She scanned the boat deck, the only deck that seemed to be fully illuminated, apart from the bridge. She could see a few figures moving up there.

'David! David!' she yelled as loudly as she could and waved her arms frantically to attract attention.

There was no reply and everyone ignored her. They were all engrossed in their work. She jumped nervously when a voice from above bawled, 'Cast off aft!' a command echoed by the longshoremen. She watched with disappointment as the huge black hull moved slowly away from the harbour wall. She was just ten minutes too late. Even if they hadn't allowed her on board, she could have got a message to him. She went back to the car and told Jimmy to drive on.

She felt stiff, cold and emotionally drained by the time she boarded the Atlantic Coast Rail Company's train. The sun was just creeping up over the horizon. It would take thirty-six hours to get to New York, so she'd been told when she'd bought her ticket. There would be rest stops in Emporia, North Carolina, in Richmond, Virginia, Washington DC, Baltimore and Newark. But as the train pulled out, her weariness, her sadness at leaving left her. She was going home. Home to Liverpool and to Mam, and she was going in style too, but best of all she'd be going home with David Williamson. She'd have nearly five days of being close to him. He did get time off, he'd told her that. Oh, she couldn't wait to see the look on his

213

face when he saw her. He'd also told her that fraternising with the passengers was definitely frowned on but she didn't care about that. Rules were meant to be broken. She could hardly wait.

Chapter Eighteen

'I've seen yer before, miss, haven't I?'

As Alice passed her hand luggage to the white-gloved steward she smiled at him. 'Yes. I came aboard in Charleston and you went and found Mr Williamson for me.'

He grinned. 'And here yer are again.'

'Here I am. But this time I'm going home to Liverpool.'

'For good or just for a visit, like?' He knew he wasn't supposed to ask such personal questions, but he also knew she wouldn't mind. She was different. She was a Scouser, but obviously a wealthy one.

As she followed him down the warm companionway with its deeppile carpets and light oak-panelled bulkheads, she was aware of two familiar things. The faint smell of oil and the hum of the generators that sounded like a large cat purring. She wondered briefly whether Mog was enjoying her life on the *Castlemaine*. This all felt so familiar. This ship that was returning to Liverpool's heart, the River Mersey, she could now look on as being part and parcel of home.

'Will Mr Williamson be working?' she asked when the steward finally opened the door of her cabin and placed her bags on the bunk.

'Oh, yeah. Everyone turns to on sailing day, from the old man down to the bell boys. Never a minute to call yer own. Sometimes there's murder with the passengers, like, if they've been double-booked. The Purser nearly 'as a fit when that 'appens.'

She gave a fifty cent piece and he grinned again. 'I could get word to him, if yer like, but it won't be until we're out of the Hudson.'

'Would you do that for me?'

'Course I will, miss. Why don't yer go up on deck when we leave. Yer won't be able to see everything at its best, like, 'cos it's dark but it's great. Ellis Island, the Statue of Liberty – that's lit up – and then under the Verazzano Narrows Bridge – that's got lights on it too.'

'Thanks, I might just do that but I am tired. It's taken me thirty-six hours to get here by train.'

'It'd take a damned sight longer if yer were at 'ome, if yer get me meaning. They're all out on strike again.'

Alice took off her coat and hat and looked around. The cabin, or stateroom as he'd called it, was on the promenade deck and had every imaginable luxury. There was a separate sitting room with a green brocade-covered sofa and a walnut table and writing desk. The sleeping area was painted cream with gold and pale green mouldings on the doors. It was lit by electric wall lights that looked like gold sconces with candles in them. There was a proper bed complete with brass bedstead, not a bunk. In one corner was a marble washbasin with gold taps and hot and cold running water. A large oval mirror was mounted on one wall, over a walnut dressing table. The carpet was deep forest green. In a curtained-off section was a marble toilet that flushed. Beside the bed, on a table under the bell for the stewardess, was a telephone. She touched everything, marvelling at it all.

This *was* a first-class luxury cabin, she reminded herself. She was paying for all this. Twenty dollars, to be exact. It was sheer extravagance but she was going home in great style. She thought of the *Castlemaine* and its dark, cramped and smelly cabin, the terrors of the storm, and of Georgie

216

Tate. She wondered idly what he would think if he could see her now and if he would ever come to hear her sing – should she be booked to appear in Liverpool, that is.

A stewardess, a middle-aged, rather severe looking woman, dressed in a starched white uniform dress and cap, appeared and asked her if there was anything else she desired before she started Alice's unpacking. A pot of tea, perhaps? Alice didn't want to send the woman away nor did she really want to sit and watch her clothes being hung up and placed in drawers. She wouldn't know what to talk to her about or if you were supposed to talk at all. She said tea would be lovely.

After that she went up onto the boat deck as she'd been advised to do and as the ship moved slowly and majestically down the Hudson River, the white wake of her bow wave visible against the dark water, a rush of excitement held Alice in its grip. Oh, how much her life had changed. It was miraculous, that's what it was. She could never have dreamed that such good fortune, such luxury, such wealth could be hers.

There had been no time to write to Mam but she'd sent a telegram saying she was coming home on the *Aquitania* which would tie up at the landing stage on Friday at about noon. She hoped the brown envelope that would be delivered by a boy on a bicycle wouldn't upset Mam. People still had a horror of telegrams, after the awful years of the Great War. They'd all come down to meet her, Mam, Lizzie, Jimmy, Agnes, Eddie and little Mary. Oh, she longed to see them, hug them. She wanted to see their faces when they saw her dressed to the nines and paying for porters to carry her luggage and then they'd all go home in a taxi cab or maybe they'd go somewhere for a bit of a celebration. A meal, somewhere nice. Perhaps Reece's Restaurant.

'It's such a pity it's so dark.'

Alice jumped and then her face lit up. David Williamson

217

stood behind her. 'Oh, you didn't half give me a fright!'

'I didn't mean to. I was amazed when Morrison told me you were on board. I had to come and see for myself. I thought he'd got mixed up, or he'd been drinking. I've only just managed to get away.'

'I . . . I . . . decided to go home.'

'For a visit?'

She shook her head. 'No.'

'Was Mr O'Farrell upset? It's very sudden, after all.'

'I've been homesick for quite a while. I kept thinking about people, family, and after meeting you and the ball and everything, I just couldn't stay. He was upset and I suppose he's got a right to be, after everything he's done for me.'

'So, what will you do when you get home?'

Her eyes danced with excitement. 'Sing.' She laughed. 'I've got the training and the grooming now. It was one of the reasons why I went to America. But just one. The main reason was . . . was . . .' Suddenly the words wouldn't come out. She swallowed and tried again. 'I . . . I . . . went because . . .' Again her voice faltered, the words deserted her.

He took her hand. 'I really have to go now, Alice, or I'll get fired. I just had to make sure it *was* you.'

The physical contact with him sent her blood racing and her heart pounding. 'But I will see you again, soon?'

'Of course. We could take a stroll on deck tomorrow afternoon, if the weather's not too bad.'

Alice had a sudden vision of the cabin of the *Castlemaine* and herself lying on the floor wishing she were dead. 'Will it be very rough?'

'Not for a day or so at least.' He noticed the apprehension in her eyes. 'Don't worry, Alice, this ship was built for the North Atlantic. "Speed and Safety" is Cunard's motto. What's your cabin number? I'll get a message to you, a time and place.'

'It's B78, on the promenade deck.'

He turned away but then, seeming to remember something, he turned back. 'Alice, would you consider giving a performance here on board?'

She was startled. 'Me? Sing here?'

'Yes. I know it will be a great success and our passengers will be delighted with the diversion.' He stopped and frowned. 'I need a better – more appropriate – word than "diversion".'

'Entertainment?'

He smiled and her heart lurched again and she longed to reach out and touch his face, very gently.

'Entertainment sounds much better. You were magnificent in Charleston; you shouldn't hide your light under a bushel, as the saying goes.'

She nodded her agreement. Why not? She couldn't be any more nervous than she'd been at the ball. She just prayed she wouldn't be seasick again.

They met in the First-Class Lounge, an enormous room with a glass-domed ceiling, its ornately plastered coving depicting garlands of flowers tied with ribbon bows. The bulkheads were covered with burnished mahogany panelling. The carpet and the upholstery on the chairs and sofas was a shade of carnelian red. Two huge marble fireplaces graced each end of the room and beside each was a buffet.

There could be no displays of affection in such a public place. Such things were most certainly frowned on and often remarked on, too. She was beautiful, there was no doubt about that and she was a delight to be with.

'So, what do you do on here?' she asked, hoping to be able to understand and learn more about him.

'I'll simplify it, Alice. It's far too boring and technical to go into in great detail.' Her large, soft eyes were wide with interest and he warmed to her. 'Basically, I help to see that the engines keep running to turn the screws –

propellors – to "drive" the ship at different speeds. It's all valves and pressure gauges, terribly boring.'

'Oh, I'm not bored!' she replied but he could see the slight crease between her brows that denoted wandering concentration.

'I am!' he laughed. She was so easy to talk to and he was drawn to her. 'Tell me about yourself, before Charleston?'

Panic gripped her but she kept on smiling. 'That's not fair! I don't know *anything* about you, except that Charlie is your brother and you work here on this ship.'

'Well, I've got two younger sisters, one seventeen and one nearly nineteen. I live in Crosby, my father is a lawyer and I joined the Merchant Navy when I left Merchant Taylor's school. I've seen many different . . . exotic places and now it's your turn!' He leaned towards her. 'Where do you come from, Miss Alice O'Connor?'

She drew back and pulled a face. 'A terrible place, really "desperate" as Mike would say, but I don't want to think about that. I just want to sing.'

Somehow she'd managed to tell him very little of her background but she shared her hopes of appearing on the stage of Liverpool's theatres.

'Would you come and see me? You'd have to pay this time, I'm afraid.'

'Of course I will – and I know Charlie will. He started all this. I thought he was quite mad at the time, but he was right. You know, Alice, you'll be wasting your time staying in Liverpool. You should go to London.'

She tried to hide the stricken look in her eyes. 'I think I might be a bit nervous about that.' She didn't want to go anywhere where she'd have no chance of seeing him.

'Nervous? You'll have travelled the Atlantic twice. You've been to Charleston, New York and all those other places you mentioned.'

'They were only train stops, we didn't stay for long.'

'Alice, you shouldn't be apprehensive about anything. You're young, you're beautiful and you're very, very talented.' There was no mistaking the sincerity in his voice or his eyes.

She blushed furiously. He *must* feel something for her. He couldn't say such things and not have some affection, some love. It was just so awkward for him; maybe when they arrived in Liverpool she'd see more of him and then he'd be able to show her exactly how he felt about her. He must surely realise that it wasn't just homesickness that had prompted her rapid departure from Charleston.

She agreed to sing on Wednesday night, after dinner, in the Music Room on the boat deck, weather permitting. She'd sing the pieces she'd sung for Charleston society and then a couple of the more modern, popular songs. She'd also wear the white dress she'd worn for the ball.

Fortunately the weather held. It was breezy and there was quite a heavy swell, but conditions were nowhere near anything that could be termed rough or stormy. Given that there were other entertainments on offer, she was amazed at the number of passengers who gathered in the sumptuous Georgian-style room, with its pale green and yellow furnishings, and inlaid mahogany and rosewood panelling. A glass skylight, adorned with plaster cherubs holding garlands, made the room brighter and the diffused lighting offset the darkness of the wood panelling. There wasn't a stage of any kind, so she stood next to the gleaming grand piano. The resident pianist smiled at her.

'A good turn-out, Miss O'Connor.'

She bit her lip anxiously. 'I hope I don't make a fool of myself. It's my one dread.'

'No one as lovely as you could do that, and anyway, I'm sure they'd all forgive any gaffe,' he replied gallantly. He could see she was very nervous.

It was the Cotillion Ball all over again. In fact, she thought the response was better because after her introductory pieces everyone, including herself, seemed to relax. The evening lengthened as she sang requests. Champagne was sent to her for refreshment and it was after eleven when she finally managed to get away.

She was thrilled to see David waiting for her when she emerged into the companionway.

'You see, Alice, you had nothing to worry about – you were fantastic! They all loved you. I saw a few eyes being dabbed when you finished "The Londonderry Air".'

'I didn't see you. I didn't know you were there.'

'I was at the back; I crept in. I couldn't miss it, now could I? I look on you as my sort of protégée.'

She didn't really know what he meant but she wasn't going to ask. Instead she smiled at him.

'Will anyone be meeting you in Liverpool?'

'Yes, they'll all be there on the landing stage. I sent a telegram. It cost three dollars but I didn't mind.'

'Isn't it amazing that messages can be sent like that across the world?'

They had reached the Purser's Bureau and she was about to reply when a middle-aged man approached them.

'Please forgive me for intruding, Miss O'Connor, but I had to speak to you.'

She smiled politely but wished he hadn't interrupted. She wanted to be with David. To her dismay, David nodded.

'There's no need for you to apologise, sir. If you'll excuse me for fifteen minutes, there are a few things I have to attend to. I'll see you later, Alice.'

'Where?' There was a distinct note of pleading in her voice.

'First-Class Reading and Writing Room?'

She turned to the man, annoyance and suspicion in her eyes. 'Yes?'

'Miss O'Connor, it's a long time since I met anyone remotely like you.'

She managed a wry smile. How long was she going to have to stand here and listen to this old fool? When would he get to the point? *Was* there a point? He looked very ordinary, a bit on the drab side, grey hair and grey eyes. Of course, his evening clothes were impeccable.

'Shall we walk?'

Inwardly she sighed. Thank God David had said fifteen minutes.

'I'm returning from New York where I've had some business to attend to, although it wasn't a terribly successful trip.'

'Everyone's going to Liverpool.'

'Actually I'm not. Well, I'm not staying in Liverpool. I'm going straight to London on the boat train. I'm an agent, Miss O'Connor. A theatrical agent.'

A year ago she wouldn't have known what he meant; now she stopped and looked at him with interest. 'You mean you book people to appear on the stage?'

'Yes. I prefer to call them artistes but as I said, it's a long time since I met anyone like you. You are quite remarkable, Miss O'Connor.'

'Could you get me an audition?' She was eager now.

'I could get you any number of them.'

She beamed at him, her eyes sparkling. 'In Liverpool?'

'In Liverpool or Manchester, Leeds or Birmingham, but what I had in mind was auditions for the London musicals. You'd be wonderful in *Showboat* or *No, No, Nanette*. Every bit as good as Gina O'Donnell.'

She'd heard of these musical plays. 'But won't I need to know how to act?'

'You could learn, there are schools and academies.'

'In Liverpool?'

'I was thinking of London.'

They had reached the Writing and Reading Room and Alice sat down on a grey silk brocade sofa. 'I don't even know your name.'

'It's Victor. Victor Hardman. My agency is one of the best.'

'What would be the right thing for me to do?'

'Get enrolled at a theatrical school, audition for parts. I presume you'll have to earn a wage and I could get you work in some of the better class music halls.'

'And what do you get in return?'

'Ten per cent of all your earnings. I'm not trying to fleece you, Miss O'Connor. That's the standard rate. You'll get work, plenty of it. I can almost guarantee it.'

It was utterly fantastic. No one had ever offered her anything like this. No one had had this much faith in her, except perhaps Euganie Walton. She could be the star of a London musical! Little Alice O'Connor from Benledi Street. That thought lessened the euphoria. She couldn't leave Mam and the kids so soon. She couldn't say she was off to London when she'd only just set foot in the door.

'I want to sing in Liverpool first,' she said. 'It's an ambition. At the Empire or the Rotunda. I have my reasons and I haven't seen my family for a long time.'

'That's all right by me. I know both the managers, I'll write to them, and when we dock I'll have a messenger boy deliver the letters. But you will have to move to London if you want to be a real star. You'll have to live there. I can find you a place to live, a drama coach or a place in a drama class, and advance bookings. Shall we say in a month's time?'

She couldn't speak so she just nodded.

'And my percentage?'

She bit her lip. It was all too much. It had happened so quickly. There had been no time to think, to ponder. It was fate and for the first time she really began to believe that she had a talent, an exceptional talent. After all, Victor Hardman must have heard hundreds of singers. It must be true, what he was saying, that she had something better than most, a truly wonderful talent that would make her rich and famous. All she'd wanted to do was sing on the stage like Letty Lewis. That had been her original dream ever since the night she'd sneaked into the Rotunda. It had changed slightly after she'd met David Williamson. Then she'd wanted to sing on a theatre stage for him, just for him. She shook her head to try to clear her mind a little. It was crammed full of thoughts and ideas all jumping and jostling with each other. She'd never see David if she was in London and he was plying the Atlantic. She could stay in Liverpool and see him when his ship was in or she could go to London and become a star.

'Well, Alice O'Connor, what do you say?' Victor Hardman pressed, eager to secure this young woman and start her on the road to international success. Having her on his books would increase his bank balance, his credibility and his standing; after a frustrating trip in New York he was anxious for all three.

Alice swallowed hard, for the sides of her throat seemed to have stuck together. She looked around helplessly. 'Can I . . . can I think about it?' she managed to get out at last.

'Of course, but don't take too long. I'm not a very patient man and I've an ulcer that's beginning to play up. Probably too much rich food and drink on this ship.' He smiled ruefully and patted his stomach. He reached into his jacket pocket, withdrawing a pen, notepad and a business card.

'Here's my card, now let me take down your address.'

'Well, we might have moved but I suppose number ten Benledi Street will do for now. It's off Scotland Road. If we do move, I'll let you know.'

The agent's smile returned as David Williamson appeared. 'Ah, there you are, sir. I've just been setting out a glittering future for Miss O'Connor's inspection and, I hope, her acceptance.'

'What kind of future?' His tone was a little suspicious.

'Mr Hardman is an agent. He can get me work.' Alice looked up at David. Oh, how was she going to decide?

'I've offered her a career on the London stage. Top parts. Almost guaranteed success in shows like *Showboat*. You only get one real star in every generation and this young lady's it.'

'There will be a contract?' David was still wary. Alice was very young and unfamiliar with business deals, of that much he was certain.

'Drawn up by my lawyer. Miss O'Connor can have it checked out. It's all above board. No nasty surprises in the small print. I'll have it in the post to her as soon as I possibly can. Two copies. One for myself and one for her to keep.'

David relaxed and smiled at her. 'Alice, this is absolutely wonderful! Wasn't it timely that I persuaded you to sing tonight? Do you understand what it all means?'

Her heart sank like a stone and the pit of her stomach felt horribly cold. Oh, she knew very well what it all meant and he was urging her to accept it. The tears pricked her eyes but she fought them back.

'Alice, you can't turn down an opportunity like this.' He looked mildly concerned.

'No. No, I can't,' she answered, knowing that once again she'd be miles away from him. Did he in fact care for her at all? He *did*, she told herself firmly. He cared so much that he wouldn't stand in the way of her career. That's what she *must* keep thinking.

Chapter Nineteen

They had sat and talked for what seemed like hours, although he'd done most of the talking. There was such an ache in her heart as she'd listened to him enthuse about the opportunity she was being offered. It *was* the chance of a lifetime. She *must* take it. She was so *very, very* fortunate. She knew all that but she had just wanted to crawl away to her cabin: the fact that being a star would mean being in London and away from him never seemed to enter his head. At last he'd escorted her back and before he'd left her he'd taken both her hands and kissed her gently on the forehead. Both were the gestures of affection that a brother would make to a sister and she had cried herself to sleep.

The following morning she confirmed all the arrangements with Victor Hardman. First of all the Rotunda, then the Empire and then London. He'd also told her that she might not have to work the Halls for very long, maybe not at all. He wasn't certain but he'd heard a rumour that Gina O'Donnell was not well and was thinking of leaving *Days of Grace*.

But now it was Friday morning and, in the dismal grey light of the early March morning, the *Aquitania* made her way up the Mersey, majestically weaving her way between all the other ships in the river, who sounded their whistles or foghorns in greeting.

Below decks a sort of organised chaos reigned. People

were getting ready to disembark. Most of the luggage had been removed from outside cabin doors last night but there were still small cases, Gladstone bags, and the odd forgotten trunk in the companionways. Stewards and stewardesses moved quickly and with experience to help the exodus, all waiting to be paid off and get home themselves. They were almost all Liverpudlians and knew that there would be gatherings of relations waiting for them among the crowds who had come in their lunch hours, just to see the great ship tie up.

Alice had not slept well and had got up early, so early it had still been pitch dark. She'd had breakfast as they slowed down off Port Linus, on the coast of Anglesey, where the pilot had come aboard to take the ship up safely through the treacherous channels of the Mersey estuary.

At last through the fine, drizzly rain the familiar buildings of the waterfront slowly became visible and her heart began to make odd jerky movements as she clung to the rail. She was home! She could see the twin towers of the Liver Buildings with their Liver birds, the domed roof of the Mersey Docks and Harbour Board building, and between them the third of the trio, the soot-blackened but imposing Cunard building. Behind them she could just make out the Church of St Nicholas, the sailor's church. The docks were full of ships from the Elder Dempster Line, Booth Line, Lamport and Holt, Canadian Pacific, Shaw, Saville and Albion, and a dozen more companies, their liveries and house flags all so familiar, bright dabs of colour on a drab, cold Mersey morning.

She'd said goodbye to David last night. He was working now – everyone was. She was still confused about his feelings for her. She loved him, that was a certainty, but he'd been adamant about her going to London. He was so certain that it was the right thing for her. Clearly he wanted the best for her and surely that must mean something. Yet she seemed to be no closer to him emotionally now than when she'd met him in Charleston.

Determinedly, she put all thoughts of David from her mind. Her family, her *real* family, would be waiting down there among the crowds of people and the wagons, lorries, carts and cabs. Mam would have got them all scrubbed and dressed in decent clothes. Would they even now be straining their eyes, trying to make out where she was standing? Oh, Mam would be in tears – they all would, herself included.

The luggage boat had already departed for the stage and the tugs had taken the huge 45,000–ton ship in tow and had begun to manoeuvre her towards the landing stage.

The crowd was nearer now, it was possible to see individual people. How far down they looked. It was an incredible sight. Now people beside her began to wave and call out and were receiving similar greetings from ashore. Oh, she just wanted to get home now. To get off this ship that had changed her life so much. She started to wave too, her gaze scanning the upturned faces.

The hawsers were taken up and the ship secured. The gangways were lowered and Alice was almost weeping with disappointment. She couldn't see them! Not one of them. No one had come to meet her. She'd left this city with tears in her eyes. Now she'd returned and tears were stinging her eyes yet again. She waited for as long as she could in case they were late, but she knew the crew were eager to be paid off. She had to pull herself together, to fight down this bitter dashing of her hopes, she told herself as she directed the porter with her luggage towards a waiting taxi cab.

'Where to, miss?'

'Benledi Street,' Alice replied flatly.

He looked at her in astonishment. 'Are yer sure?'

'I'm sure!'

229

The porter and the cab driver exchanged glances.

'It's dead rough down there, miss,' the porter ventured.

'I know. It's where I come from. I lived there all my life except for the last two years.'

The cab driver took in the smart oatmeal wool coat with the deep fur collar and cuffs that she'd bought in New York, the amber-coloured cloche hat and the matching leather pumps. The hands that held the cream clutch bag were encased in soft cream kid gloves. He shrugged. 'Right, Benledi Street it is, you're payin'.' His face split into a wide grin. ''Ave yer come into a fortune then?'

Alice couldn't help but smile back, despite her distress. 'I suppose you could say that. I sing, on the stage.' She prayed that wouldn't turn out to be a lie. 'And I sang on the ship too.'

'Oh, worked yer passage then?'

'No, I paid for it. I did a special performance. It helps to make the time go quicker. You get fed up of seeing nothing for days on end but the sea.'

The man nodded before turning his attention to the traffic chaos on Mann Island. He had a brother who was a waiter on the *Sythia*. Nearly every family in this city had someone who went away to sea.

Nothing had changed much, Alice thought as they drove down Byrom Street and along Scotland Road. All the shops, the pubs and the churches looked exactly the same. Except that now there wasn't even the bit of greenery and tinsel that had been in evidence when she'd left.

Something must be wrong, she told herself. Maybe they hadn't received the telegram. That *must* be it. Or maybe Mam and Lizzie were out at work. They couldn't just take a day off to go and meet someone off a ship, not even a daughter or a sister. They'd get the sack. There were so many rational excuses and reasons. Why hadn't she thought about them last night when she'd been unable to sleep? But she'd been full of hope last night. Hope that they'd come to meet her. She'd been so confident that they would.

'What number do yer want, miss?' The driver's question broke into her thoughts and she realised that the cab had attracted a crowd of small, scruffy boys who were running alongside it, pointing and whistling.

'Number ten, please.'

'I'll take yer bags in for yer if yer like. This lot will have them nicked before yer can turn around. They should all be in school! Should 'ave the School Board round 'ere. That'd sort them out. Gerroff, you little bugger!' he bawled at one lad who had reached out to touch the leather case he'd just placed on the top step.

Alice got out and looked around as she stood on the pavement. Nothing had changed here either and the house looked ominously quiet.

'Are yer sure they're in?'

She shrugged. 'The door will be open, it's never locked. None of them ever are.'

He rolled his eyes expressively. 'Oh, aye, I know what yer mean. There's nothin' to pinch.'

She ignored his remark and delved into her purse for the money to pay him as he pushed open the door and transferred her things from the step to the hall. The hall was still devoid of lino or rugs, let alone the luxury of a long 'runner' of carpet that people who were better off had down their halls. Oh, this was a great homecoming. A flaming empty house. Tears were not far away again as she walked slowly down the passage and pushed open the kitchen door.

Nelly looked up from the range where she was trying to coax a fire from the rubbish the lads had gleaned from the gutters, before they'd gone to school.

'Mother of God! Alice! Alice, is that you, girl?'

Careless of her pale beige coat and hat, Alice flung

231

herself into Nelly's arms and began to sob, all the pent-up emotions bursting out. 'Oh, Mam! Mam! I missed you so much! I wanted you to be there. You never came to meet me!'

'Oh, Alice, luv, you're home. You're home now with yer mam. It's all right, luv. Hush now, queen,' Nelly soothed and Alice's sobs gradually grew quieter.

'Oh, Mam, why didn't you come to meet me?' Alice asked after wiping her eyes and blowing her nose on her handkerchief, unearthed from her discarded bag.

'Alice, we didn't know you were coming home. How could we?'

'I sent a telegram from New York. It cost a fortune.'

A look of understanding mingled with regret crossed Nelly's face. 'Our Agnes said someone had come with a letter. I never even opened it. I thought it was from the landlord. I chucked it on the fire.' She gazed up at her daughter in wonderment. 'Oh, never mind that now. You're home.'

Alice looked around. Everything was exactly the same. There was no sign of any new or added comforts. It was freezing cold and Mam looked even more worn out and thinner.

'I sent money, Mam. I sent it regularly each month. Money for food and coal and clothes. Where's it gone?'

Nelly looked back with sadness in her tired eyes. 'Do yer really *have* to ask that question, Alice? You know what he's like. I couldn't manage to save even a bit. The first lot came when he was here and after that, well, he went down to Victoria Street and told them that any further foreign mail was to be held there until he collected it. He went every month, regular as clockwork.'

Alice passed a hand over her forehead. Her head was beginning to ache. She should have known but she would never have credited him with so much sense – or rather cunning. Even if Mam had gone to the main post office in Victoria Street, they wouldn't have given her the letters even though they were addressed to 'Mrs' O'Connor. If 'Mr' O'Connor demanded them, he'd get them.

'Where's everyone?'

'Lizzie's at work, the kids are at school.'

'And Da?'

'It's Friday afternoon, Alice. You should remember what that means, luv.'

The nightmarish feeling that had come over her began to fade before the surge of rage that made her tremble. 'Oh, I know where he is and by God have I got something to say to him!'

'Alice, don't get upset. It's a waste of time, luv. I know. Tell me how you've been. Tell me about all the things you've done and the people you met. What was America like? Look at the style of you! I wouldn't have recognised you, luv, if I met you walking up the street.'

Alice was unmoved. 'There'll be time for all that later, Mam.' She opened her bag, pulled out her purse and extracted a white five-pound note. 'Go round to Holden's or Burgess's and get something for tea, a slap-up tea, Mam. Call at Martingale's and get them to deliver two hundredweight of coal, best anthracite, no rubbishy slack. We're all going to eat well, in a warm kitchen, and then we're all going to Sturla's for clothes and furniture!'

Nelly was staring at her open-mouthed. 'Oh, God, Alice, where did you get all this money?'

'I did nothing wrong, nothing I'm ashamed of. I've committed no mortal sins. I was lucky and I'm going to go on being lucky. I've got work, and we're never going to be cold, hungry, dirty and crawling with bugs ever again.' She turned towards the door.

Nelly caught her arm. 'Alice, where are yer going?'

'To find me da and when I do, Mam, well ...'

Nelly clapped a hand to her mouth and shook her head. Alice was no match for Tip, not when he had a belly full of ale, or whisky as it was now. That's what all the money Alice had sent had been spent on, she thought bitterly, that and gambling.

Alice was aware of all the curious and envious looks as she strode purposefully up Benledi Street. Well, let them all wonder and jangle as to where she had got the fine clothes. She didn't care. She was going to move her mother and the family out of the area as soon as possible. She'd find a nice house in a respectable area, but first she was going to sort out her da once and for all, and the fact that she was only five foot one didn't deter her. She knew how to use her brains now. Da's were addled with booze, not that he'd ever had that many in the first place.

As she walked along Scotland Road, ignoring the admiring glances and the whistles that came from pub doorways, she fumed. All this time she'd thought that the money she'd sent, Mike's money, was being used to give her family a decent standard of living. How could she have been so flaming stupid? Because she'd lived in luxury, because she'd lived with and moved among people who had scruples, she'd forgotten how bad things were at home. How devious, how cruel and unfeeling her da was.

As she approached The Widows she saw a policeman coming towards her. 'Officer!' she called.

It was Jack Phillips. 'Yes, miss?' His tone was respectful.

'Come with me, I want you to make an arrest.'

'An arrest? Who and for what?' He looked totally mystified.

'My father and for assault.'

Jack looked serious. 'Who has been assaulted?'

'Me. Well, not yet I haven't been, but I will be.'

'I don't understand, miss, and I'm not sure I can comply with your request.'

'Oh, to hell with all that! I'm going in there and I'm going to tell that old sod I want every penny of my money back. I sent money home from America, for my mam and the family and he ... he drank it!' She was shaking with temper, her words tripping over each other.

'Now I know who you are. It's been puzzling me, I never forget a face. You're Lizzie's sister, Alice. Alice O'Connor who went to America!' He paused. 'But I can't arrest someone for something he hasn't done yet.'

'How do you know our Lizzie?' Alice demanded, aghast. 'What's she done? I've only just got home and Mam didn't say anything.'

He grinned. She had certainly done well for herself and by the sound of things the fortunes of the O'Connor family were going to look up. She didn't have that beaten, gaunt look that Lizzie had when he'd first picked her up from the wet cobbles. Alice was a real beauty. Even with smart clothes Lizzie would still look homely beside her sister. 'She hasn't done anything. We have a bit of a chat now and then, that's all.' He didn't want to go into any detail about his as yet unannounced affection for Lizzie or the money he sometimes gave her, though not regularly. That wouldn't have done at all.

'Will you just follow me and stand by the door of the pub?'

'I suppose I could just be passing, but not lingering too long.'

'Then for God's sake keep behind me. I'll need protection. He'll belt me. Isn't protecting people supposed to be part of your job?'

He grinned. This one was in no way like Lizzie. She had guts to march into a pub full of hard-bitten men. He'd enjoy being a witness to this, there'd be a good chance that Tip O'Connor would go down for quite a long stretch. He'd make sure he kept four or five paces behind her.

She flung open the door but the pub was so fuggy with cigarette smoke that she stood just inside the room rubbing her smarting eyes. Gradually every head was turned towards her. Women never entered the saloon bar of a pub. They used the snugs and parlours and this one looked as though she shouldn't be here at all, not the way she was dressed.

Bernie Maguire was the first to recognise her. 'Bloody 'ell, it's little Alice O'Connor! 'Ere, Tip, it's your Alice!'

Alice turned on him 'You've got a bloody short memory, Bernie Maguire. One minute you're laying him out cold because he'd half killed me, the next you're propping up the same bloody bar!'

Tip turned and glared at her from small, bloodshot eyes.

Alice took a step towards him. 'So, Da, this is where the money went. Buying bevvies for half of Scottie Road! It was *my* money, Da! I sent it for Mam and the kids, not for you!'

'Don't yer talk like that ter me, girl!' he growled. She might never have been away. There was no word of greeting or surprise, let alone regret or remorse.

'I want it back. I want every bloody penny of it back, Da. So you can start by having a whip round from all your mates here!'

'Yer 'ardfaced little bitch! Don't yer bloody shame me in front of me mates. In front of the whole bloody neighbourhood!' Tip yelled.

Alice held her ground. From the corner of her eye she could just see the sleeve of a dark blue uniform jacket in the open doorway.

'I don't need to shame you, Da! You're a bloody disgrace to yourself! You're a no good, idle, vicious drunk and you always have been!' she yelled back, her cheeks burning, her eyes full of rage.

Tip lunged at her, catching her a glancing blow on the shoulder.

She stepped back. 'Go on, Da! Belt me, like you've always done, I don't care. I want that money back and I want it now!'

236

This time Tip's aim was better and the blow caught her on the side of her head. She staggered back, falling against Bernie Maguire. Some of the men began to mutter their disapproval, others nodded grimly. A man couldn't let a bit of a girl like that carry on the way she was doing and get away with it.

None of them had noticed Jack Phillips in the shadows. But as he moved quickly forward the customers of The Widows fell back – the policeman was well over six feet tall and built like a barn.

'I want him arrested for assaulting me and for stealing my money!'

A howl of rage erupted from Tip but no one went to help him as his arm was twisted up his back and handcuffs were snapped on. 'Tobias O'Connor, I'm arresting you for common assault and the fraudulent misappropriation of money. You have the right to remain silent . . .'

The crowd drew in a collective breath and Alice smiled grimly. 'You'll get at least five years' hard labour in Walton for that, Da!' she yelled as he was led away.

'Yer shouldn't 'ave done that, girl,' Bernie Maguire muttered.

Alice turned on him. 'He's a thief! He as good as stole that money from me. It was for Mam, not him. When did he ever give me anything except black eyes, bruises and cracked ribs? We all starved, froze, and got beaten up for years and you know it. Mother of God! You've belted him yourself often enough.' She turned away from him, her gaze sweeping over the assembly of grim-faced men. 'You're all the bloody same! You're all in here enjoying yourselves and what are your wives and kids doing? Taking in washing? Trying to sell bootlaces or matches? Begging in the streets, the way I did? You make me sick, the lot of you!'

'Watch yer mouth, girl,' the landlord warned quietly.

'I'll have the whole bloody lot of you arrested if anyone

so much as raises a hand to me or any of mine!'

'Jesus, Alice, you're just askin' for trouble! Go home, girl,' Bernie Maguire urged.

'I wouldn't stay here if you paid me – and people do pay me, to sing in theatres and at posh balls. I mixed with the best. I entertained the high and bloody mighty on the *Aquitania* but I'll never forget that I sang barefoot and in rags in the streets of this city while he was in here, drinking!'

She took a deep breath once she was outside. She could hear the raised voices from inside and she smiled. Well, she'd certainly given them a piece of her mind and they'd stood and taken it, something they would never have done from their own wives and daughters. But then their wives and daughters didn't have money behind them, or the self-confidence it brought.

A police sergeant had joined Jack Phillips. 'Are you the person accusing him?' he asked Alice.

'I am, and your officer saw him belt . . . hit me, and he took my money too.'

'You'll have to come to the station then, miss.'

'Look, I've just got home. I came in on the *Aquitania* and my mam needs some help. Can I come down later, please? He's not going to run off or complain, now is he?'

He pursed his lips but finally nodded. 'Don't be any longer than an hour.'

She flashed a smile at Jack and set off for Benledi Street. When she got home Nelly was still out so she decided to walk round to Holden's and meet her. Holden's was the nearest of the two corner shops whose proprietors had been good to them over the years. As she turned the corner, she nearly collided with her mother who was laden down with bags of shopping.

'You should have seen Ivy Holden's face when she saw the five-pound note! I told her that me dream's out, that you'd come home and you'd done well for yourself too.'

Nelly peered closely at her daughter. 'What's the matter with your face, Alice?'

'Da belted me in The Widows, so I had him arrested for assault. There was a policeman passing at the time, one who has chats with our Lizzie, so he told me.'

Nelly stared at her in horror. 'Oh, Jesus, Mary and Joseph! *You* had him arrested!'

Alice took her mother's arm. 'Mam, we'll all be better off with him in Walton. They'll make him work, and work flaming hard, and there won't be any whisky in there!'

'But Alice—'

'Mam, you've suffered for years. He's battered you, he's kept you short or, more often, given you no flaming money at all. He's no good. We're better off without him.'

'Oh, God, how long will he get? Will you have to go to court?'

'About five years, longer I hope, and yes, I'll have to go to Hatton Garden when they bring him up before the stipendiary magistrate. In fact I'll have to go down to Rose Hill in an hour. But stop worrying, Mam!'

'Alice, you shouldn't have done that. He *is* your da.'

'And I've rued it every single day of my life, except for these last two years. I just don't understand you, Mam. He had it coming to him and we're all going to have a better life. Especially you. We're going to move to a nice house with good furniture. We'll have proper beds with sheets and blankets and we'll have thick soft towels. You'll all have new clothes and you'll never have to worry about rent, or coal or anything else ever again. I've got work. I'm going to sing in the Empire and the Rotunda and then . . . then I'm going to London and I'll be a big star, Mam. But I'll tell you all about it – Charleston, the *Aquitania* – every single thing, when we've got a fire going and had something decent to eat.'

Nelly shook her head as Alice took one of the hemp bags, lent by Ivy Holden, and led her towards Benledi

Street. She couldn't take it in, she couldn't understand it all. Alice had just got home and yet now she was talking about going to London and being famous and rich. And she had changed. This wasn't her skinny, ragged little Alice. This girl had just had her father arrested in a pub full of his mates and neighbours.

They reached the front door and Alice pushed it open and smiled.

'We're going to have a proper home, Mam. Something you've never had in all the years you've lived here.'

Nelly felt the tears well up in her eyes. She squeezed Alice's hand and a slow, uncertain smile spread over her face.

Chapter Twenty

By the time Eddy and Mary got home from school, there was a meal on the table and a fire roaring up the chimney.

They stared at their sister, open-mouthed.

'Is that our Alice?' Eddy asked incredulously.

'Yes, it's me, lad, all the way from America,' she laughed. He seemed to have grown taller but he still looked pale and undernourished. Then she hugged Mary and swung her round in delight.

'You're ten now! Ten!'

'Alice, where did you get them clothes? They must 'ave cost a fortune.' Eddy reverently stroked the fur cuffs of her coat that had been flung over the back of the armchair.

'Oh, don't you worry, you'll be dressed up to kill by this time tomorrow. All of you. There'll be no more police hand-outs. Now come on, get stuck in.'

They needed no second telling. Nelly tried to exercise some control and stop them cramming the food into their mouths with their hands, snatching pieces of bread and butter like wild animals. They'd never tasted butter before. She moved quickly round the table slapping hands and clipping ears.

'God, Mam, you'd need an army general to put some manners on this lot,' Alice sighed, 'but I suppose there's not been much on the table, has there?'

Nelly shook her head.

'Well, all that's over now and Mam, will you please sit down and eat.'

'I'll have a bit later on.' Nelly watched with satisfaction as the food disappeared.

'No you won't, Mam. That's what you've always done. You starved yourself to feed us. Now sit down and tuck in while there's still something left to tuck into.'

Her mother shook her head. 'Old habits die hard, Alice.'

'Is our Jimmy working, Mam?' she asked, when Nelly had finally sat down.

'Not really. Nothing steady, like. He gets a few days, now and then.'

'Where is he now?'

'Shovelling coal into sacks, down at the docks somewhere. Lots of lads do it. It doesn't pay much, a few coppers, but it's better than nowt.'

While the children ate, quarrelling over such luxuries as cakes and biscuits, with Nelly constantly admonishing them, Alice was deep in thought. She'd forgotten what living in number ten Benledi Street was like – the total absence of the bare necessities, never mind anything approaching comfort, the fact that there were no cleaning materials of any kind, dishes, pans or utensils. You've got a short memory, girl, Alice thought to herself grimly. There were still no beds either. The house smelled of damp, unwashed bodies and half-dry old woollen jumpers that hung on a rack and pulley near the ceiling. She couldn't stay here. She would *not* sleep on a bug-infested mattress. She'd have to go to a hotel for a few days. The Stork in Queen Square wasn't bad. And she couldn't take them to Sturla's, the local department store, in their present condition. They were filthy, their clothes grubby, creased and torn. No, they'd have to have a bath and probably their hair needed delousing. God, how did I ever live like this? she asked herself. Coming home had

242

suddenly turned into a humbling experience.

Nelly leaned back, replete, and surveyed the table. Not a crumb was left. It was a good job Alice had saved something for Lizzie, Agnes and Jimmy. She got to her feet.

'What are you going to do now, Mam?'

'Clear this lot away.'

'Oh no you're not! We're going to take all these chipped mugs, enamelled plates, the old stew pan and kettle and the other few bits in the scullery and chuck them out. In fact we're going to chuck everything out into the yard.' She turned to her brothers and sister. 'Right, you lot, down to Burrows Gardens Baths. Buy some paraffin and Durback soap on the way. Soak your hair with the paraffin then give it a good wash with the Durback. That should shift the nits. And then we're going to Great Homer Street and you're all getting rigged out. You too, Mam.' Alice took her purse from her bag and delved into it. She'd changed her money from dollars to pounds on the ship.

'What about Lizzie, Agnes and Jimmy?' Nelly asked.

'We'll be back by the time they get in. My clothes should fit the girls if there's no time to get them new ones tonight and we'll just have to guess Jimmy's size. Do they stay open late, Mam?'

'Until eight on Fridays.'

'Good. I'll buy beds and bedding too and a decent tea service and new pans. They can deliver them – I should think they'll be delighted to. It'll be a big order and all in cash!'

'Are you coming with us to the baths or will we come back here?' Nelly asked, still slightly dazed.

'I'll wait for the others. You come back here for me.'

Alice started to clear the kitchen. She kept three chipped enamel plates for Lizzie, Agnes and Jimmy's supper and also three badly discoloured mugs for their tea. The pitifully small and battered collection of things that Nelly

243

had managed to acquire and keep she dumped in the back yard which was already full of rubbish. Then she went upstairs. Nothing had changed much. The damp patches were still on the walls, but they'd grown bigger. The black mould still surrounded the ill-fitting window frame that was so rotten it would be easy to push it out altogether. The old straw-stuffed mattresses, covered in their dirty ticking and piles of rags that served as bedclothes, were still on the floor. Tears pricked her eyes as she thought of the sheer luxury she'd lived in for the past two years. Well, she couldn't move this lot by herself, so she'd wait until they all came back from Sturla's and they'd chuck them into the yard too. She felt no qualms about having her da arrested. Not when she looked around these rooms.

She heard the front door open and turned to make her way down the stairs, which in itself was perilous, most of the boards having been used for firewood. Lizzie was talking to someone and the other voice was that of a man.

As she came into the hall, Lizzie stopped dead. 'Holy Mother of God! Is that you, Alice?'

Alice jumped down the last two steps and flung her arms round her sister. 'Oh, Lizzie! Lizzie! I've missed you so much, I really have.' She could feel every one of her sister's ribs, and the bones of her shoulders dug into her.

'Alice! Alice, it's . . . it's . . . great! God, look at you!' Lizzie stood back, still holding Alice's hands, while she surveyed her sister's outfit.

Over Lizzie's shoulder, Alice saw the huge figure of Jack Phillips. He was smiling.

'I'll come down to the station soon, I promise.'

'It'll wait for a while,' he answered.

'Why have you got to go to the police station?' Lizzie asked anxiously.

'Because this afternoon I had Da arrested. He belted me and he'd used all the money I sent for Mam. Constable Phillips here marched him down to the nick.'

Lizzie turned and looked at Jack for confirmation.

He nodded.

'I hope he rots in Walton for ever!' Alice declared. 'Come on and get your supper. Where's our Agnes? Is there any sign of Jimmy yet?'

'Oh, Agnes gets in a bit later, she's got further to walk. Our Jimmy's got a few days' coal shovelling.'

'I know, Mam told me.'

'He'll work until he drops and he'll be filthy when he does get in.'

As if to prove her point, the back door opened and Jimmy stood there covered from head to foot in coal dust, his shoulders sagging with weariness.

'Don't touch our Alice, the state of you!' Lizzie cried.

'God Almighty, Alice! Alice, it *is* you!'

'Just sit down and get that down you.' Alice ruffled the short, badly cut hair and instantly a small cloud of black dust wafted over her hand. 'Then you can go down to Burrows Gardens Baths like everyone else. When they get back we're going to Sturla's to buy half the shop. I've chucked everything out.' She grinned and then turned to Jack Phillips. 'Do you think you could give me a hand with the stuff upstairs? There's not much but it's bound to be alive with bugs. They'll all have proper beds and bedding tonight.'

'But won't the bugs get into all the new stuff too?' Lizzie enquired, tucking into a plate full of steak and kidney with mashed potatoes and gravy, all cooked in pans borrowed from Mary O'Hanlon and Jinny Thomas.

'No. We're not staying here, we're moving.' Alice looked up at Jack Phillips. 'Do you think you could find out if there are any houses, in a better street than this, to rent immediately?'

'There's a house at the bottom of our street, Media Street, that's empty and has been for two weeks.'

'Do you know the landlord?'

'Very well. I can ask him tonight, when I finish my shift.'

Lizzie looked at her sister, so confident and in control. 'Alice, Mam might not want to leave here,' she said carefully. 'She might not want to go away from all her friends, all the neighbours who've been so good to us. They've not had much themselves but they've kept us out of the workhouse for years.'

'Lizzie, it's not miles away!'

'It's not far, just off Kirkdale Road,' Jack agreed quietly. Alice flashed him a grateful smile.

Lizzie, too, smiled at him. 'We'll be neighbours then.'

Alice noted the look on both their faces and felt pleased. It seemed as though Lizzie had found someone special at last and he didn't seem to mind the state of the house or Lizzie's old and faded clothes.

'Where did you get all the money from, Alice?' Lizzie asked.

'I worked for it, at first. Then the club was closed down. They have a stupid law over there, called Prohibition. No one's allowed to drink, at least not in clubs and bars. They don't have pubs.'

'It's not so flaming stupid, they could do with one like that here,' Lizzie said grimly.

The front door slammed and Alice took the second plate from the oven in the range.

Agnes stood in the doorway, silent, unable to believe her eyes.

'It's me, Agnes. I've come home. Haven't you grown up!'

'I'm sixteen now. Oh, Alice!'

There was yet another tearfully joyous reunion and while Agnes ate, Lizzie explained all Alice's plans. Jack and Alice were moving the mattresses into the yard and Jack said they should burn the lot, they were a health hazard.

'The whole house is a health hazard,' Alice agreed. 'They should burn the whole street to the ground.'

'I know, but they won't. Will you come with me to the station now that we've cleared upstairs?'

Alice sighed. 'I will and it'll be a pleasure. In fact it'll be pure joy to see him go down.' She remembered Mike telling her how he'd felt when he'd arrived on the doorstep of the house on Rutledge Street. Well, she couldn't belt the living daylights out of her da, it was physically imposs-ible, but this was the next best thing. She turned to Lizzie. 'Look, while I go down to Rose Hill, you and Agnes get a wash and wait for Mam. Tell her I won't be long.'

Alice picked up her coat and followed Jack Phillips out. As they walked along Scotland Road, she questioned him. 'It's strange you being friends with our Lizzie,' she ventured.

'I knocked her over, one dark winter's night. I picked her up and took her home.' He shrugged. 'Ever since, we've been friends. I take her out on trips now and then. She deserves a bit of pleasure.'

Alice looked up at him. 'Just now and then?'

Jack grinned. 'Well, as often as I can. Incidentally, I had a bit of a word with your da about a year ago.'

Her eyes grew hard. 'I could kill him, I could, and with my own two hands!'

'No, you couldn't. Look what he did to you today. Your face will be black and blue tomorrow and anyway he's not worth it.'

'I don't care about my face. It's nothing to what Mam and the rest of us had to put up with. That's why I left. He half-killed me and he once threw our poor little Mary out into the street. Bernie Maguire belted hell out of him both times, but give Bernie a couple of glasses of the hard stuff and his memory goes. You saw that this afternoon. But Mam says Da's not laid a finger on anyone for a year now. Your "bit of a word" seems to have worked.'

Jack smiled. 'Maybe. Anyway, you look as though you've done well for yourself.'

'I have. I didn't at first. I was down to my last few cents. Then I got a job, singing in a nightclub – I think they might have them in London. And I got ... er ... lodgings in a house the like of which you'd never believe. I got lucky. There was a gentleman who helped me. He was very kind.' She looked up at him. 'He was older than me, very rich, but he came from the Dublin slums originally. He understood me and what I'd been through. Because I could sing we got asked to parties, soirées, and I sang in the intermission at one of the grandest balls in Charleston. I sang on the ship, too, on the way home, and now I've got an agent. When I get this lot sorted out I'm going to have to go and see the managers of both the Roundy and the Empire.'

Jack nodded. 'You always had a beautiful voice, Alice. All you needed was a chance and you got it.'

They'd arrived at the red-brick building and he held the door open for her.

'Oh, at last! The pair of you have decided to come in.' The desk sergeant was openly sarcastic and none too pleased.

Alice glared at him, not in the least intimidated. 'I had things to attend to. Things more important than my da.'

'Right then, let's get it all down on paper. Phillips, I'll take her statement, you do your own. Madam, do you want to see meladdo downstairs? He's swearing and yelling like a trooper.'

'I never want to see him again – except perhaps in court. I sent fifteen pounds a month home, for two years. It was expressly for my mother. I sent it in letters addressed to her, not him, but after the first one he went to Victoria Street and told them in future he'd collect them. He's managed to get through three hundred and

248

sixty pounds. He misappropriated it. They never saw a penny of it.'

After the formalities, she went out and hailed a passing taxi. She knew it was extravagant, it wasn't far to walk, but she was running out of time.

They were all waiting, and Lizzie and Agnes had managed to give themselves a good wash down in the scullery with a bar of mild Fairy soap Nelly had bought.

It didn't take long to get to Great Homer Street. 'Right, we've got an hour. Mam, you see to the beds, bedding, towels and furniture. I'm going to find the floorwalker and explain everything. If necessary I'll speak to the manager himself.'

Nelly took her arm. 'Alice, luv, there's no need to go mad, we don't need too many things. There's the future to think of.'

'Mam, the future is taken care of. I've got money and I'll earn more, so stop worrying.'

Nelly was still cautious. 'It's just that . . .'

'I know, Mam, it's like being a kid let loose in a toy shop, that's the way I felt. Go on, pick what you want.'

The floorwalker respectfully accompanied Nelly as she selected her purchases while the manager himself accompanied Alice. She'd been living abroad, she was in the entertainment business, she told him confidently. When she'd arrived home this morning on the *Aquitania* – first class of course, she stressed – she'd found her family in dire straits due to the selfish malevolence of her father. She would be buying furniture, beds, linen, household goods and clothes for them all. She would be most grateful if he could store most of the furniture for her as in the next few days they would be moving house, but would it be at all possible to have some delivered tonight? She was dreadfully sorry it was so late. Of course, everything would be paid for in cash.

The manager, an avaricious gleam in his eye, said he'd

recall the driver from home, or drive the van himself if necessary. And they were not to rush choosing things, time meant nothing, nothing at all.

She flashed him a brilliant smile. 'That's very good of you, but we don't want to inconvenience you too much. I'm hoping to appear at both the Rotunda and the Empire before I go to London at the end of the month. If I do, there will be complimentary tickets for yourself and your wife.' Good God, she thought as her little speech came to an end, is this really *me* speaking like this? So confidently, even with a touch of arrogance and to a man who two years ago would have had her ejected if she'd set foot in the place.

The van driver came back and with the help of the manager and the floorwalker loaded most of the things into the van. Staggering underneath a pile of boxes, Nelly, Lizzie, Agnes and the kids waited for Alice to pay the manager and thank him again.

She counted out the large white banknotes then held out a gloved hand. It had cost her one hundred and fifty pounds, a small fortune, but it brought her close to tears when she saw all their faces glowing with pleasure and excitement.

The manager beamed. 'Miss O'Connor, it's been a pleasure, a real pleasure to have your patronage. I hope you'll come back if there's anything you've overlooked.'

'Of course, and I won't forget the tickets.'

Jack Phillips joined them in Benledi Street straight after work and helped them get the beds up. Nelly shook out the crisp white sheets and tucked them neatly round the new mattresses. Then she covered them with the soft blankets, fluffed up the pillows and finished off with the heavy cotton bedspreads patterned in different colours. Most of the clothes were left unpacked, as there were no wardrobes.

'How many bedrooms does this house in Media Street

have?' Alice asked, as she rummaged in a box full of straw for the new tea set.

'Three. There's a parlour, a kitchen, a scullery and—'

'A yard and a privy, like this, I suppose,' Alice cut in.

'Yes, but bigger and in far better condition. There's a coal bunker in the yard and a wash house.'

Nelly looked up. 'Oh, I never got a mangle or a dolly tub or a washboard!'

'Mam, for God's sake don't start worrying over the washing yet. The boys can have one room, Mary and Agnes can have another, and you and our Lizzie can have the third.'

'What about you?'

'I'll be staying at the Stork, Mam, at least to sleep. It's nearer for the Empire and . . . and at the end of the month I'm going to have to go to London.' She put on a falsely cheerful smile. 'But let's not think about that now. We all deserve a cup of tea, it's been a tiring night.'

When Jack had gone, promising to do what he could about the house, and the younger kids had gone to bed, wearing pyjamas and nightdresses for the first time in their lives, Alice urged Nelly to go to bed too.

'Mam, you're worn out. Go on up, please. Get a good night's sleep, you've no more worries.'

When Nelly had gone, Alice, Lizzie and Agnes sat in front of the range in the dismal kitchen, the glowing embers of the fire and the one gas jet on the wall giving a poor illusion of comfort.

'Will you really be going to London, Alice?' Agnes asked. She was pale and thin, her light brown hair making her look like a younger version of Lizzie.

'Yes. I'll have to sing in the music halls before I can get a part in a real show and I'll live in digs. Victor Hardman is going to arrange it all. What are you going to do, Agnes?'

Agnes shrugged her thin shoulders. 'Carry on working

251

in the match factory, I suppose, until I can find something a bit better. I've always wanted to do shop work but no one would even look at me the way I was dressed.'

'Jack told me you can do anything if you really want to,' Lizzie said. 'He reminded me about Abbie Kerrigan, Dee Chatterton, Maggie Higgins and Hannah Harvey.'

'I'll bet you've got as much money as Her Ladyship now,' Agnes said, awestruck. Alice thought of Hannah Harvey. You really couldn't get much higher in society than the Countess of Ashenden and Hannah was the only really rich person she knew much about; then she remembered Mike. She smiled and shook her head. 'No, but I know someone who has. Mike O'Farrell – he became my guardian, and then my husband.'

'Your husband!' Agnes almost shrieked the words.

'No. Not really my husband. It was just to stop any gossip and we got invited to more places being a "respectable couple".' She didn't want to dwell on her departure from the house on Rutledge Street so she changed the subject. 'What about you, Lizzie? That Jack Phillips seems fond of you.'

'I think he is but I don't know for sure. He's been so good to me – to all of us, Alice.'

'If he asked you, would you marry him?' Alice asked quietly.

'I don't know. He lives with his mam, and . . . she might not take to me.'

'So what? It's him you'd be marrying, not her. Besides, she might be glad of someone to look after her in her old age.'

'Oh, I don't know, Alice. It's been such a—'

'Long, tiring day,' Alice finished for her. 'For us all. Go on to bed, the pair of you. I'm going to get a taxi to the Stork.'

She hugged them both, clinging on to Lizzie. 'Oh, Lizzie,' she whispered, 'I'm so happy I came home. I got

252

the chance of a new life when I went away and now I want you all to look on tomorrow as the beginning of your new lives.'

'It will be, Alice, and now, if Jack asks, I will marry him. You see, before, I couldn't leave Mam. Agnes and me were the only wage earners and Agnes doesn't get much. Mam did a bit of office cleaning, when she could get it, but she's worn out, Alice.'

'I know, Lizzie. I haven't forgotten what life was like in this house and I never will. But we're all going up in the world now and I'll be so happy if you do get married. You deserve to be happy, you've had a rotten life so far.'

'Go on and get to the hotel or they'll be shut,' Lizzie urged with tears of pleasure in her eyes.

Chapter Twenty-One

To Alice's frustration, the departure from Benledi Street was delayed as the landlord of the house in Media Street was away on business for a few days. Alice fretted but Lizzie told her to stop it.

'It's only a few days, Alice, for God's sake,' she scolded.

'But I wanted everyone out of here before I do my first show. Victor's arranged everything, every detail. Mr Gregson at the Rotunda is expecting me to call to see him soon.'

'Well, if you don't go and see those blokes soon, there'll be no show. At least not one with you in it.'

She was right, Alice mused as she walked along Scotland Road towards the Rotunda.

When she reached it, it was closed but she remembered the back entrance, the stage door.

The same old man was in his little box, reading the *Daily Post*.

'Is Mr Gregson in?' she asked.

He looked up annoyed, then his expression changed when he took in her appearance. 'Yes. Who wants 'im?'

'Miss Alice O'Connor. He'll be expecting me.'

She waited impatiently until he came back and then ushered her along the corridor and into a small office.

Gregson greeted her effusively. 'Miss O'Connor, Alice, I'm delighted to meet you. I was getting a little worried in case you'd changed your mind. Victor wrote and told me how talented you are. When I telephoned him in London he couldn't have been more enthusiastic or confident. Will you audition for me?'

'Of course.'

She followed him down the labyrinth of corridors until they finally arrived on the stage. The atmosphere was strange. Very quiet, very hushed, almost like a church, she thought.

'What kind of a repertoire do you have, Miss O'Connor? Victor and I didn't really discuss it in detail.'

'Everything from "Beautiful Dreamer", "'Bye, 'Bye Blackbird" to the Easter Hymn from Mascagni's *Cavalleria Rusticana*.'

'Well, we won't need that one. Have you a favourite piece?'

'I have,' she smiled, 'but I don't think you'd be interested. Shall we try "Whispering" and then "Always"?'

He nodded his agreement. They were popular songs.

From somewhere in the dark nether regions of the wings a man appeared and sat at the piano. Gregson disappeared down the steps that led to the seats in the front stalls.

She looked up. She could see nothing. There were no lights burning in the auditorium, just a couple on the stage itself. She went through the two numbers with ease, then, just to support her earlier statement and without the accompaniment of the piano, she sang 'The Last Rose of Summer'. In the silent theatre and without any instrumental backing it seemed almost celestial.

Gregson virtually ran up the steps. 'Vic said you were good, but I never thought you were *that* good. Can you start next weekend? One of our regulars has let us down. Friday, Saturday and Sunday?'

'For how many weeks?'

'That depends. Vic said you wanted to do the Empire

as well and then I believe you're off to London.'

'I'll do two weekends here and I have to go and meet the manager at the Empire. With luck I'll do two weekends there, and then as I promised Victor Hardman I'll have to go to London.'

Gregson rubbed his hands together, thinking of the increase in profits from the box office. 'I'll get the posters done today and advertise in the *Echo*.'

'You may not need to advertise. I should think there'll be half the neighbourhood here once word gets round that one of their own's on. I was born and brought up off Scottie Road. In Benledi Street.'

He looked at her in amazement. She wore a fine wool crepe suit in forest green, trimmed with jade green. Her hat was jade green velour with a huge dark green bow on one side. She wore silk stockings and dark green leather pumps with a T bar across the instep. Her bag and gloves, both leather, both dark green, completed the outfit.

'Would it be possible to have some complimentary tickets for my family?' she asked.

'How many would you like?'

'Is sixteen too many? Best seats?'

'Just for Friday then.'

She smiled. 'Shall we work out a proper programme now or would you like me to do it and send it in to you?'

'We'll work it out now. Will you need to rehearse?'

'On Wednesday and Thursday, in the morning.'

As she followed him back to his office, her heart began to beat faster as she remembered the night she'd crept in and seen Letty Lewis.

It was as though he read her mind. 'How would you like to be introduced – billed?'

She smiled broadly. 'As the Liverpool Songbird.'

They moved house on Tuesday. Alice was relieved to have had Tip's trial over, and him safely in Walton Gaol, before the family started their new life in Media Street. She had ordered a van in good time to take all the new furnishings and clothes.

Mary O'Hanlon, Jinny Thomas and Ethel Maguire, Nelly's closest neighbours and friends over the years, came to see them off.

'God love yer, Nelly, but yer deserve all this.' Mary O'Hanlon took Nelly's hand and squeezed it.

'Yer do, girl,' Ethel sniffed, 'and we'll all miss yer. There's no good us sayin' we'll have happy memories of the good times, 'cos there bloody well weren't any.'

'Oh, give it a rest, Ethel, you'll 'ave *me* in tears next. I've lived here all me married life.' Mary's voice was full of emotion.

'Well, yer not going ter live over the water or out in the wilds, are yer? It's only down the road a bit an' I wish our Peggy would up an 'ave our Joe nicked. I've 'ad almost as many clouts as you 'ave, Nell.' Jinny smiled grimly, trying to lighten the atmosphere.

'Will I get our Lizzie's feller to give him a talking to, if you know what I mean, Jinny?'

'It wouldn't do no good, Nelly.' Small-boned, with rounded shoulders, Jinny had a slight hump on her back from being constantly hunched against the weather, and from hard work. 'God, I wish they'd take "obey" and "until death do us part" out of the bloody wedding vows. There's been no "better", it's all been flaming "worse". Is that scuffer really your Lizzie's feller?'

'I think so, although neither of them have said anything,' Nelly replied.

'And your Alice is on the Roundy Friday, Saturday and Sunday. God, I'd love ter see her, Nelly,' Mary sighed, folding her arms under her ample chest.

'Get the sixpence off your Maggie, she's working, and it's the chance of a lifetime. I'm going ter gerra loan off our Peggy,' Jinny announced.

258

'Wait until the news gets around, Nelly, the whole of Scottie Road will be there, up in the gods of course! Your Alice. God, everyone will beg, steal and borrow just to see her. The pawn shops will be bustin'! Your little Alice up there on the stage!' Mary shook her head in wonderment.

'I still can't get over it myself. These last days have been like . . . like a dream.'

'Then keep on dreamin', Nelly, girl. There's not many around here who even have dreams, never mind see them come true.'

'Mam, the taxi's waiting and our Eddy is actin' up!' Agnes called, resplendent in one of her new outfits. From her new cotton knickers edged with a bit of lace, to her smart blue cardigan suit, silk stockings and navy shoes and hat, she felt every inch a lady.

Mary nudged Ethel with her elbow. 'Don't those two girls look different with their hair cut short? Our Maggie's been wanting to get hers done and I've 'ad murder with 'er time an' again. Now I've seen those two and what's more she'll see them, I might as well save me breath. I 'ave ter say it takes years off your Lizzie, Nelly.'

'Mam! He's kicking the toes out of 'is new boots!'

Nelly sighed. 'Some things never change, do they?'

Before she could move, Alice came out of the house and slammed the door shut behind her.

'Well, that's it. Goodbye number ten Benledi Street – and good riddance!' She frowned as she saw the pushing and shoving that was going on between Eddy and Jimmy. She moved smartly and clipped her youngest brother over the ear.

'You behave yourself, Jimmy O'Connor! I'm having no messing about from you! Get in that taxi cab with Mary and Agnes and leave our Eddy alone or you'll get another belt around the ear and that's a promise!'

'Ah, eh! It was 'im that started it! It's not fair!'

259

'Well, she's not changed much either, 'as she, Nell?' Ethel chuckled. 'Always the one with the backchat, always the one ter stand up to 'er da. She's always had guts, 'as your Alice. She gets them from you. Well, good luck to 'er!'

'Come on, Mam, everyone's ready.' Alice hugged all three women briefly, heedless of their grubby, greasy pinafores. 'There's no amount of money can buy what you've done for us and given us over the years. Mam's not far away, you come and visit whenever you like. And if anyone starts knocking you about, tell our Lizzie and she'll get Jack Phillips to have a bit of a word. It worked wonders with my da.'

Nelly echoed Alice's sentiments as she hugged them in turn, wiping away a tear. Mary sniffed and both Jinny and Ethel were clearly fighting with their emotions.

'I'll have some tickets sent down for you – all of you!' Alice called as the cab pulled away from the kerb with the usual following of small, grubby, shouting kids.

The three women watched the cab turn the corner.

'Do yer think she'll be 'appy in Media Street, Ethel?'

Ethel raised her eyes skywards, pursing her lips and shaking her head. 'Jaysus, Mary, it's not the bloody moon she's gone to! I'd swap places any day of the week. All that furniture and more being kept in Sturla's. Every comfort, no worries except what yer going to 'ave fer tea an' should yer wash the antimacassars on the sofa in the parlour today or tomorrow. I've got young Vi and Vinny Murphy and the baby livin' in my parlour. Well, it's no use standing 'ere jangling while the front step's as black as the hobs of hell an' he's still snoring in 'is pit, the idle, useless git!'

Chaos still seemed to reign the next day in the new house as there was so much to unpack and arrange. Alice arrived at half past eight, to see the kids got to school and that everything was being sorted out before she went for rehearsal. She found Nelly sitting upright on the brown hide sofa in the parlour. In addition to the sofa there were two armchairs, a plant stand with its glossy-leaved aspidistra in a brass pot, a sideboard that Alice planned to adorn with a lovely set of crystal comprising a fruit bowl, a biscuit barrel and cheese dish, and a glass-fronted cabinet, as yet bare, as were the mantel shelf and the walls which were waiting for the pictures and bric-a-brac Nelly had chosen.

'Mam, what are you doing in here? Are you feeling all right?'

Nelly turned to her. 'A parlour, Alice! Me with a parlour and it full of furniture. It'll be too grand to use, Alice. I'd be frit to death of the kids smashing something.'

Alice took her hand. 'You'll get used to it all, Mam. Mrs O'Hanlon and Jinny Thomas and Ethel Maguire will be calling in to see you. You can have your cups of tea in here.'

Nelly was horrified. 'What! Use that good china that's going to go in that cabinet – when we find it.'

'Oh, Mam, it was bought to be used, not just admired.'

'They won't expect it, Alice. They'd be terrified of breaking it. No, I'll use the other stuff.'

Alice smiled at her. 'At least you've got a choice now, Mam. Will we have a cup of tea before I go to rehearsal?'

Nelly got up. 'You know half the neighbourhood will be there, luv, on the night.'

'I know, so I'd better do my best and wear my party frock!' Alice laughed.

They decided that she would sing an Irish medley, the area being predominantly Irish Catholic. She chose 'The Rose of Tralee', 'The Londonderry Air' and 'I'll Take You Home Again, Kathleen' for her first spot. Her second would be livelier, a selection of the songs she'd sung and heard in America. She'd thought long and hard about the

Irish selection; the first two had been such favourites of Mike's. She knew they'd go down well with the audience, but would she be all right? Would she break down? She'd been so busy that she'd hardly had time to think about either Mike or David. David was away, that much she knew, having scanned the shipping pages in the *Journal of Commerce*. But perhaps it would be best in a way. If he were to come to see her at all she'd prefer it to be at the Empire; that really was Liverpool's premier theatre.

She'd decided to wear the green chiffon dress she'd worn for Maura O'Hare's soirée, and was just fastening the band of green ribbon decorated with diamanté stones when Mrs Harris, the dresser, came in.

'It's not time yet, is it?'

'No, luv. But there's a lad out there asking for you. A bit scruffy, he is, but he said he sailed with you on the *Castlemaine* and he's got a present for you.'

She leaped to her feet. 'Georgie Tate! It's got to be Georgie Tate! Oh, bring him in, Mrs H, bring him in.'

He'd hardly changed but she could tell he'd tried to look his best for tonight. He stood awkwardly in the doorway, clutching a cardboard box.

'Georgie! Oh, come here and give me a hug! I never thought I'd ever see you again.'

He put the box on the floor as she threw her arms round him.

'You've made it, Alice. I told yer it'd be all right in America.'

'It nearly wasn't, but yes, it's all turned out great.' She smiled at his awed expression. 'Are you still sailing on the *Castlemaine*?'

He nodded. 'But I got a bit of promotion, like.'

'You're not the cabin boy now?'

'No. I learned how to fire the donkey boiler and when old 'Arry died, they gave me 'is job.'

'So you've got on yourself then?'

262

'But not as well as you 'ave, Alice.' He remembered the box and picking it up pushed it into her arms. 'It's for you.'

She opened the lid and a radiant smile lit up her face. 'Oh, Georgie! Isn't it beautiful!' Nestling in the box on some straw was a tiny black and white kitten.

'It's one of the last litter old Mog had.'

She stroked its downy little head. 'Had?'

'We found her dead one morning in the corner of the galley she always slept in. But she'd had a busy life, and she went peacefully.'

'Oh, Georgie, Mog was my lucky charm and I often thought of her.'

'I know, that's why I brought her son for yer.'

'Mrs Harris will look after him until the show's over. I'm going to call him Georgie to remind me of you.'

He went bright red from the tips of his ears to his forehead. 'Would you . . . would you sing me mam's song, Alice? Please?'

A slight crease appeared between her eyebrows. The programme was set; still, she couldn't disappoint him. She had promised. She smiled. 'Of course I will. I'll sing it first – just for you.'

They both heard her five-minute call and the sharp rap on the dressing-room door.

'You'd best get to your seat quickly, or we'll both be late. And thank you, Georgie.' She hugged him again.

She had a quick word with the stage manager, who nodded, and then went to consult the conductor of the orchestra.

She could only see the first two or three rows, the lights were so bright. The rest of the theatre seemed to be in total darkness, but she knew they were there – all of them. When she was announced, when Mr Gregson said, 'Ladies and gentlemen, it's my pleasure to introduce to you Miss Alice O'Connor, the Liverpool Songbird,' her heart leaped and she nervously fingered the gold pendant Mike had bought her.

Gregson's words drew a great response. She walked to the front of the stage where the microphone was placed.

'Ladies and gentlemen, there's an addition to the programme. A request. A promise I made two years ago to a Liverpool lad who befriended me.'

Nelly and Lizzie, in the front row of the dress circle, exchanged puzzled glances.

Alice carried on, 'It was his mother's favourite. So, for Georgie Tate who taught it to me, "If You Were The Only Girl In The World".'

She stepped back and nodded to the conductor.

As she sang, the memories came flooding back. The nights she'd sat with Georgie on the deck of the *Castlemaine* when he'd taught her this song and others. Then she'd been dirty, ignorant, but full of hope.

The applause was loud in her ears and she threw her arms wide with joy as the opening bars of 'The Rose of Tralee' were played.

She forced herself not to think of Mike, David, Nelly or any of her family as she went through the medley. At the end when she gave a little bow there was a tremendous roar from the upper circles, the gods. The noise was deafening as everyone stood and clapped and cheered and whistled. Her heart felt as though it was going to burst and tears of pure joy trickled down her cheeks. This wasn't the Plantation, or the Charleston Cotillion Ball, or even the *Aquitania*, it was the Roundy, and it was the best. The best ever because this was her home and these were 'her' people. She knew out there sat Mam, Lizzie, Jack and all the rest of the family. And there'd be the O'Hanlons, the Thomases, the Maguires. Now she was truly the Liverpool Songbird.

There were shouts of 'Encore!' from the better seats and 'More! More, Alice, girl! More!' from up in the gods.

She looked at Gregson in the wings and he nodded; the supporting acts weren't all that good; if she wanted to go on all night it was fine by him.

Only when the orchestra struck up did the applause die down and complete silence fall.

These are for you, Mam. For all the times you went without so I could eat. For every bruise and black eye and cut you took for our sake, she thought. She also knew she'd have to exert an iron control over her emotions.

She looked up at the dress circle. 'This is a very special song for me. It's old-fashioned but it was taught to me by someone I love very dearly, my mam.'

She took a very deep breath as Signor Bransini had taught her to do.

Just a song at twilight,
When the lights are low
Where the flickering shadows
Gently come and go . . .

Her voice soared through the theatre. Sweet, clear and full of emotion. Only once did she falter and her vision was blurred by tears, but it only seemed to add feeling and sincerity.

In the front circle Nelly's tears flowed freely. Lizzie dabbed her eyes with Jack's handkerchief and even Agnes was sniffing to hold back the tears. The three younger children were mesmerised and sat totally still.

They wouldn't let her go. Every time she bowed and ran towards the wings, Gregson led her out again. She sang every song she knew, including the three she'd sung at the ball in Charleston. The Easter Hymn she sang without accompaniment, for the orchestra had no score for it. The audience didn't understand the foreign words, but everyone sat enthralled. Without any conscious effort their spirits seemed to rise like Alice's voice.

It's like . . . like something that should be sung in church, Nelly thought and said a quiet prayer to the Blessed Virgin for the great gift that had been bestowed on her Alice. Just to listen to her erased all the years of terrible hardship and shame. Everyone – and they were all hard up – had pitied the poor O'Connors, but no more. Not after tonight.

Alice was exhausted and emotionally drained when she finally got back to her dressing room. Gregson had had to bring down the curtain in the end.

Mrs Harris was waiting, her face aglow with pleasure and there was respect in her eyes. 'I've never heard anything like that, Alice. Never, in all the years I've been here. Talk about bringing the house down. You're too good for places like this. It's opera you were born for.'

Alice shook her head. 'No, I wouldn't like that. It would be much too grand for the likes of me. I'll be more than happy with stage musicals.' She struggled to control her overflowing emotions. 'He had to bring the curtain down. I couldn't do any more. I just couldn't, but it all means so much, so very much. You see, I used to sing outside here. I sang to the queue for pennies. Begging, in rags and often barefoot.' She brushed away a tear with the back of her white-gloved hand.

'These came for you.' The dresser handed her a huge bouquet of pink roses. There was a card attached to them.

'I only just heard and there's not a seat to be had all weekend, but good luck. I told you I'd pay to see you and I will. At the Empire. Sincerely, Charlie Williamson.'

She sat down, her face buried in the bouquet; more memories came flooding back. The dockside, the blaring of the car horn, the startled whinny of the horse, her scream as Mog jumped from her arms and cowered beneath the huge hooves, and then the shiny chrome radiator of the car. The smell of engine oil, the humming sound, the face, full of concern, bending over her as she

266

regained consciousness. David's face. And then the doctor and Charlie and those words. Those words that had inspired her and taken her across the world following her dreams, her ambitions, impossible though they had seemed then. But the dream had come true and she knew, she just *knew* that David loved her. It was only fate, in the guise of timing, that kept them apart.

There wasn't time to dwell on her thoughts, the small room was quickly filled with her family and Mr Kay, the manager from Sturla's, and his wife. She felt as high as a kite and hugged them all, even Mr and Mrs Kay who were virtual strangers.

'Oh, Alice, Mam was so cut up when you sang just for her!' Lizzie's face was glowing with pride, her eyes moist. 'We all were. It's a good job I don't wear rouge and powder otherwise it'd look such a mess.'

'Oh, Lizzie, I didn't mean to make you cry, but I nearly broke down myself.'

'I know, we could tell, and then Mam began to sob, but quietly.'

Jack had elbowed his way in, towering over everyone, as usual. 'Alice, I've ordered two taxis. I think your mam's a bit over-wrought,' he added.

Nelly was sitting on a chair, very still, very quiet, as though detached from everything that was going on around her.

Alice was all concern. 'Mam? Mam, are you feeling faint?'

Nelly came out of her trance-like state. 'No. No, luv, I'm fine. It just got a bit hot and crowded.' She clutched Alice's hand tightly. 'It's a gift from God, Alice. I never realised it until tonight. I've never heard you sing like that before.'

'I had voice training, Mam. For over a year I had singing lessons.'

'But that last one, Alice, I couldn't understand it but it

sounded as though it should be sung in church. That's when I knew. That's when I thought, it's a gift from God.'

'I know, Mam, but I'll never forget who it was who first taught me to sing – you. Now come on, let's get everyone home, we're all worn out.'

She helped Nelly to her feet and Lizzie took her arm. Alice detached the note from the flowers and thrust them into Nelly's arms.

'Not the last roses of summer, Mam, the first. From now on you'll always have roses. Every week.'

Chapter Twenty-Two

The following Monday, the trio of Nelly's old friends called for a bit of a jangle and a good look round. Alice had gone to see Arthur Jackson, the manager at the Empire.

Nelly opened her door, wiping her wet hands on her all-enveloping pinafore.

'Mary! Ethel! Jinny! Come in. It's great to see you.' She ushered them into the hall with its cream paintwork and the runner of good Axminster down the hall and up the stairs, where it was secured by brass rods. On the wall was a picture of Our Lady, Queen of Peace.

'Glory be to God, Nelly! You've even got carpet on the stairs!'

'That was our Alice's idea. I told her lino is much easier, it just needs a quick mop over, but no, she wouldn't 'ave it. I make them all come in the back way.' Then, knowing her neighbours well, Nelly asked if they'd like to do the 'grand tour', as she put it.

Mary O'Hanlon made no show of refusing the offer. 'Well, that's what we've come for, an' ter see you of course.'

'Aye, only the fact that it was Sunday yisterday and all the kids were 'ome, we'd 'ave come sooner,' Ethel added.

'Well, I'll show you round and then we'll have a cuppa.' Nelly beamed as she flung open a door. 'Right, this is me parlour.'

They all gaped.

'It . . . it's like a palace, Nell! Cut glass, roses, and, oh, a china cabinet – I'd put our Maggie on Lime Street for one of them!' Mary inspected the cabinet closely while Nelly tutted at the very idea, although she knew Mary was not serious.

'Velveteen curtains! *Velveteen!* And a carpet, no rag rugs!' Jinny was just as impressed.

They exclaimed and marvelled at everything, especially the new gas cooker in the kitchen.

'No more ashes to rake out, no more blackleading or taking a chance on how hot the oven gets. Eh, many's the bit of meat I've ruined in that bloody oven of mine. An' yer know how often we 'ave meat. Once in a month of Sundays. Isn't it a bloody miracle. How does it work? Do yer just turn these knobs an' out comes the gas?'

'Well, to tell you the truth, Mary, I'm a bit wary of it still,' Nelly confided sheepishly. 'Our Lizzie and Agnes think it's great though, but I'm terrified we'll all get blown sky high or someone will leave the gas on and we'll be found dead in our beds.'

'Oh, you'll get used to it in time, Nelly. Would yer look at that, Jinny! Tiles all round the sink and draining board.'

They all trooped upstairs to marvel and exclaim over the furnished bedrooms, the bedside rugs, the quality of the linen. Then it was down into the kitchen for tea. None of them wanted to sit in the parlour so they settled themselves round the kitchen table.

'She's spent a fortune, Nelly.'

'Aye, over a hundred pounds, and she pays the bills. The rent, the coal, the gas, the electric, she's even talking about having a phone put in! A phone, I ask yer! I don't know anyone else who has one so what use would it be?'

They all nodded their agreement.

'Where is Alice?' Ethel asked.

'At the Empire, seeing about the weekend after next.'

'You've got to admit it, Nelly, she was really great. She brought the 'ouse down every single night, so I heard.'

'They wanted her to stay on, offered her extra money.'

'And they put the admission price up too,' Ethel added grimly.

'But she's promised this Victor person to go to London.'

Mary nodded her thanks as Nelly refilled her cup and passed her the sugar bowl. Mary put three heaped teaspoons in. Sugar was a luxury. 'What exactly does he do, this feller?'

'He's very important in London, so she said. He's going to get her into a stage show but she'll have to do a few of the music halls first, just to earn some money for her keep and get some stage experience. He'll find her decent "digs", as she calls them. You know, lodgings. He says she'll do even better in London.' Nelly shook her head sadly. 'I've only just got her home and she's off again.'

'An' what does this feller get out of all this? Blokes like that don't do things out of the goodness of their hearts.'

'He takes ten per cent of everything she earns. She says that's normal too, she's got a proper contract, all legal, like. It came by post. Well, the post feller knew we'd moved here so he brought it here special like. She sent one back an' kept the other one.'

'Do yer trust this Victor chap, Nelly?'

'I don't know. I've never met him. She does and so far she's had nothing but good luck.'

'Aye, well, I hope it keeps fine for her. I wouldn't fancy living in London meself. All that traffic an' all them people. Did yer know they 'ave trains that run under the ground? In tunnels! Wouldn't that put the fear of God up yer!'

'Well, we've got trains that run up in the air, the docker's umbrella. The *overhead* railway. Will you have a biscuit?' Nelly offered the plate around. 'Jesus, Mary and Joseph, listen to me. "Have a biscuit?" I've never been

271

able to afford even the broken ones they sell off cheap.'

'Do yer think you'll like it 'ere? What are the neighbours like?' Jinny asked, dipping a gingernut into her tea.

'Well, her next door sort of smiled at me yesterday. And the one from number six said "Nice ter see yer, Mrs O'Connor. I went ter see your Alice." But I've seen no one else. Our Lizzie's feller lives just at the top of the street.'

'Wouldn't yer think his ma would come down an' introduce 'erself?'

'I don't think she's like that. Our Lizzie will have her hands full with that owld one, I can see it comin'.'

Suddenly Nelly remembered her washing, half done and out on the line that stretched across the back yard and half still in the copper in the wash house. 'Me washin'!' she said, struggling to her feet.

Jinny grinned broadly. 'Oh, to 'ell with the flamin' washing. I've left mine to steep in the dolly tub.'

'And I'll go down the bag wash this afternoon. We wanted to come and see yer, Nell. The flamin' washing can wait. Anyway, by the time it's dry it's covered in smuts. Makes yer wonder why yer even bother sometimes. All that rubbin' and scrubbin' when half the time it don't look any better.'

'You'll get talked about, not having it out on the line yard by dinner time,' Mary stated with a sniff.

'Oh, to 'ell with them all an' all that flamin' nonsense! 'Er at number twenty never does 'ers until Tuesday, sometimes Wednesday, the lazy mare! They'll all be just "droppin' in" ter see yer soon, you mark my words, Nelly O'Connor. Yer could charge a ha'penny a time.' Ethel laughed. 'You're already the talk of the neighbourhood, what with moving here and your Alice and your Lizzie an' her scuffer.'

It was nearly an hour later when they left and Nelly washed up the cups and went back to her washing. She hoped they would come again, she thought as she pegged out the clothes. Aye, and she wouldn't mind a few more callers too, for she felt lonely and isolated with the kids at school, Agnes and Lizzie at work and Alice out most of the day and going back to that hotel at night. She wouldn't have Alice home much longer either. A leaden feeling came over her and she felt a headache starting.

Alice's fame had spread through the city. Every seat in the house was booked for every performance and the management of the Empire, which faced the magnificent neoclassical façade of St George's Hall with its statues, lions and cenotaph, were delighted with her.

She was introduced to everyone. The stage hands, the conductor and members of the orchestra, and her dresser, Miss Fairchild, who was considerably younger than Mrs Harris but just as enthusiastic.

'It's great to have someone local be such a success,' she gushed as she arranged a row of bottles, small boxes and brushes on the dressing table.

'I'm not the only one. Half the stars on the stage and the wireless come from Liverpool,' Alice said, shaking out her stage dresses.

Miss Fairchild stopped her, ignoring Alice's sigh. 'I know, but they all went to London,' the dresser reminded her.

'And I'm afraid I'll be going too very soon.'

'More's the pity. Now what will you be wearing?'

'The white chiffon.' Alice paused. 'I don't want to upset you or anything, but I can see to myself.'

'No you can't. You'll need someone to do up buttons, see that your hair and make-up are right and that there are no visitors.'

Alice sighed again. If this was how it was then she'd just have to accept it. She hated anyone fiddling with her hair and she wasn't impressed by having her face painted like a doll. She loathed being ordered around by fussy women. But it was all part and parcel of her life now.

Friday night was a repeat of her success at the Rotunda. She was on stage for the first half of the performance and when she got back to her dressing room she was breathless, her eyes sparkling, her cheeks tinged pink with exuberance. The room was full of flowers.

'Where did all these come from?'

'Admirers.'

'Men?'

Miss Fairchild smiled wryly. 'Men, stage door Johnnies. Have you never heard of them?'

'No. What do they want?'

'To take you out to supper and . . .' She left the sentence unfinished but Alice knew what she meant. It was like The Star of India but the price here was only some flowers and a meal.

'Alf on the stage door said two of them are *very* persistent,' Miss Fairchild confided conspiratorially.

'Who are they? Did they give a name?'

'Apparently both the same name, brothers. Charlie and David Williamson.'

Alice was instantly on her feet and heading for the door.

'Where are you going?'

'It's David! David and Charlie! I've *got* to see them!'

'Well, you're not going rushing out there, it's not done. I'll go and tell Alf to let them in.'

It was only a few minutes but it seemed like an hour, as Alice paced the floor nervously. Three times she checked her appearance in the mirror and on the third occasion rubbed off her lipstick and some of the rouge. She hated stage make-up but it was necessary because of the brilliance of the lighting.

'Here we are, Alice, as promised, although we had to

274

fight our way through a mob.' David was laughing. Like everyone else in the theatre, he'd been thrilled with her performance, even though he'd heard her sing before.

He kissed her lightly on the cheek. 'Each time I hear you sing, you get better and better.'

'I wouldn't have recognised you,' Charlie grinned. 'Now if you'd looked like this two years ago, I'd have stayed with you in that grubby little cafe for ever.'

Charlie was just as charming as his brother, she thought. 'We've come to take you to supper, at the Adelphi.'

She stopped herself from shrieking out, 'At the Adelphi!' It was Liverpool's finest hotel where all the wealthy and titled people stayed.

Miss Fairchild was already holding her cape and evening bag, and it was Charlie who took them from her and put the rich velvet wrap round Alice's shoulders.

'We've already booked, so there's no rush,' he said as they left the theatre and walked the short distance along Lime Street to the hotel.

The sumptuous foyer and reception rooms didn't draw gasps and cries of admiration from Alice. She was used to luxury now. The house on Rutledge Street and the *Aquitania* had made opulence common place. She barely glanced at her surroundings as they were ushered into a fine grill restaurant to a table laid with a crisp white damask cloth, real silver cutlery and crystal glasses, and a small arrangement of flowers as a centrepiece.

David removed her cloak and passed it to a waiter. The maître d' was very respectful.

'Well, to start we'll have a couple of bottles of Bollinger, please. This is a celebration.' David smiled at Alice. 'And then we'll peruse the menu for a while.'

The man nodded and walked away, snapping his fingers to attract the attention of the wine waiter.

'You'll take London by storm, Alice,' Charlie enthused. She blushed slightly. 'Oh, I don't know. I've no real stage experience. I'll need to learn to act.'

'Oh, don't worry about that. When Gina O'Donnell first starred in *Showboat*, she had no acting experience, so I heard. I follow the stage careers of beautiful ladies. It's sort of a hobby. I go to London as often as I can.'

David looked at him pointedly. 'That's why we're not often home at the same time. It's something Mother gets upset about.'

'Well, you're away more often than I am,' Charlie shot back.

'Don't start becoming tedious, it's Alice's celebration. I've followed her career. I'm her biggest fan. Anyway, who is this Gina O'Donnell?'

Alice just sat watching David. He'd said he was her biggest fan, that he'd followed her career. She felt as though she was on a cloud.

'She's Irish, she came to Liverpool in nineteen twenty-two with her sisters. She's very beautiful, gorgeous red hair and so . . . so bubbly. She's got a temper to go with her hair, I believe.'

'Then she won't want me for competition, will she?' Alice pointed out.

'She's in *Days of Grace* now but I also heard she's not been well lately. There are rumours that she's going home to get married.' Charlie laughed as the cork from the first bottle of champagne popped.

'I don't know where you get all this gossip from but let's forget her, this is Alice's night,' David insisted.

They both raised their glasses to her. 'Here's to you, Alice, may you conquer the world!' Charlie said expansively.

'And I echo that. It's just a pity we sail again tomorrow, but I wouldn't have missed tonight for the world.'

As David casually imparted his news Alice felt the excitement of the evening evaporate and the wine suddenly had a bitter taste.

She went to see him off. She drove down to the landing stage and stood, as she'd done two years ago, and watched the *Aquitania* until she was just a dot in the distance. She'd gone on board and they'd had ten minutes together. With the ship due to sail, it was all he could spare.

'You were really wonderful last night, Alice,' he said warmly.

'Thanks, I enjoyed my supper too. Charlie's so funny sometimes.'

'And sometimes he goes too far.'

She laughed, unsure of herself. 'I . . . I'll be in London soon. Will you come and see me?'

'When I get some decent leave, I will, but you'll no doubt see Charlie before me. He does escape there as often as he can. He seems fascinated by the place – the theatre in particular – but don't let him monopolise you, Alice, he can be a bit overpowering at times.'

She protested. 'Oh, he's not.'

He took her hand. 'I'll have to go now, Alice, I'm sorry. I always seem to be rushing away from you, but the sea is my life, my career, you do understand?'

She'd managed a smile. 'Of course I do. I have to go to London for *my* career.' But the tone of her voice had had little conviction in it.

She did see Charlie. He called at the theatre on the Saturday night, took her to supper at the Adelphi again and asked if she would like to go to Southport for lunch on Sunday. There were some very good hotels and restaurants and the Marine Drive was quite beautiful. She agreed, for he was a link with David and he was fun to be with. 'It's being stuck in a gloomy, dismal office all day that makes me desperate to get out and about. An office full of old bores. Oh, they're all very polite and distinguished, but so boring!' He went on to tell her a bit more about his job as an accountant, which he obviously disliked. 'When I escape I tend to go mad – just a bit!'

277

'You don't look in the least like an accountant,' Alice said. 'I mean I've never met one but I imagine them to be old and dull and, well, boring.'

'I know, but Father wanted me to do something "professional". The law is unbelievably boring and medicine is so grisly and gruesome that I opted for accountancy. It pays well.' He now had the highly polished, marooncoloured little Jowett sports car he'd coveted for so long.

'And will David be a captain one day?'

'The master of a ship, Alice,' he corrected her. 'One day, but it seems to take years to get there. It appears to be a matter of waiting for dead men's shoes and they all seem to live until they're about eighty.'

She shuddered. 'That's a horrible expression.'

'But true. Can we go out again this week?'

'I'm sorry, but I really must make arrangements to go to London.'

'But I will see you before then?'

'We'll see,' she laughed.

On Tuesday, to her surprise, Victor Hardman paid her a visit at Media Street. Alice introduced him to her mother and showed him into the parlour.

'Will I make some tea, Alice?' Nelly whispered.

'Yes please, Mam.'

He sat in an armchair, while she sat on the sofa facing him. In the centre of the sideboard was a vase full of pale pink roses and their perfume hung heavily on the air.

'I was getting myself organised,' she said defensively before he could ask why she hadn't been in touch, apart from to return the contracts.

'No doubt you were. If you hadn't turned up at the Empire or the Rotunda on the nights I booked they would have been on the phone to me, so I knew nothing had gone wrong there.'

'I played the six nights at the Rotunda and six nights at the Empire and I had to get the family sorted out.'

He glanced around and she uttered a prayer of thanks that he'd not had to come knocking on the door of Benledi Street. 'And they both wanted me to stay. They both offered me more money. Even a percentage of the box office takings, a very small one. I did the whole first half of the show each night and to packed houses.'

'It's no more than I would have expected. This is your city. Your home town. But down to business. I've arranged for digs in a house in Bloomsbury. The lady is a widow and needs the money but she'll only take decent people. Mrs Winters, her name is. I've also arranged for you to appear at the Falstaff, the Queens, the Bedford in Camden Town and Collin's in Islington. That should cover your expenses. You'll have to get some stage dresses made or bought.'

Alice looked worried. She had dug deeply into the money Mike had given her. 'How much will I have to spend on them?'

'About five or six guineas. No need to have anything very expensive.'

'They're expensive enough!' Mike had bought all her clothes and she now wondered just how much they had cost, especially the evening gowns.

'And I've managed, with a lot of greasing of palms, to get you the lead in *Days of Grace*, starting in four weeks' time.'

'*Days of Grace*? But ... but what about acting? What about ... Miss O'Donnell?' she asked, her heart racing.

'Gina never had much in the way of drama lessons; she was a natural, like you.'

'But won't she be annoyed, upset?'

'Gina's going home to Ireland. She's marrying her agent, Edward Vinetti. At the moment her understudy is playing the lead.'

'Why is she giving it all up? She's only young. I did hear she wasn't well, but—'

Victor stood up. 'She's going home because she's dying, Alice. She's got consumption.'

Alice was stunned. How terrible. Oh, how unfair life was. She'd never even seen a picture of Gina O'Donnell, but she'd heard she was young, beautiful and talented. Then she shivered, remembering Charlie's words about 'dead men's shoes'.

'How often will I be able to come home?'

'What do you want to come home for? I'm offering you a fantastic career on a gold plate and all you can do is ask about coming home.'

'I'm not being ungrateful. I have my reasons.'

He saw, or he thought he did. 'You want to see the family from time to time.'

She nodded. 'And someone else, too.'

He studied her face. Her eyes had become misty as though she was reliving a beautiful dream. Then it dawned on him. 'Ah, the young man on the ship?'

She nodded again. It had been wonderful that night at the Adelphi, but now it looked as if it would be months before she saw him again and he'd stressed that the sea was his life. Nor had he declared himself. The little gestures he made, just holding her hand or kissing her cheek or forehead, couldn't be called passionate by any stretch of the imagination.

'Are you in love with him, Alice?'

The question, asked so directly, took her by surprise but eventually she nodded.

'And does he love you?'

'I . . . I don't know. He's never said.'

'Alice, you have to be a special kind of girl to marry a sailor, no matter what his rank is. You'd spend half your married life on your own. You'd have to bring up any children on your own and I just can't see you doing that.

And even if you married him, you'd have to choose between him and your career, and I don't want you to have to make that choice. Nor is it money I'm thinking of. You have a great gift, Alice, and you're very young. It would be nothing short of criminal to give up such a career. Don't waste what you have, don't deprive hundreds – thousands of people of the opportunity to see and hear you. To bring a little pleasure into their lives, even if it is only for a few hours.'

Nelly came in with the tea and Alice thanked her. Seeing the look on both their faces, Nelly decided not to linger. She closed the door quietly behind her.

'Fame doesn't last for ever,' Alice countered.

'No, it doesn't. There are always younger girls coming along. What kind of a family does he come from?'

'Posh. His father's a barrister. His brother's an accountant. I don't know what his sisters do, if they do anything at all, that is.'

'In that case you'd have to give up your career if you married him. Married middle-class women just don't go out to work. Especially not to appear on the stage in public. At private, select events, yes.'

Maura O'Hare's soirées and the like, she thought.

He finished his tea and got up. 'I'll meet you off the train at Euston Station on Sunday morning. I believe the sleeper gets in about seven o'clock.'

She nodded. She knew she should feel thrilled. Over the moon, or 'me dream's out', as Mam always said, but she felt miserable and confused as she closed the front door after him.

Nelly came into the hall. 'He's gone then?'

'He's gone, Mam, and I've got to get the overnight sleeper train to London on Saturday night. He's got it all arranged. A place to live, some work and then I'm to have the main part in *Days of Grace*. Mr Hardman's managed to swing it for me.'

'Then why are you looking so unhappy, luv?'

'Because I don't know when I'll be able to come home again to see ... everyone.'

'Alice, you can't waste your life, your gift.'

'I know, Mam, but it's going to be so hard to go away again, and this time I feel I have even less choice than I did the first time I left.'

Chapter Twenty-Three

Alice was miserable and apprehensive as she walked up the platform towards the barrier in Euston Station. Everyone had cried when they'd seen her off. She'd been near to tears herself. Four weeks she'd had at home, that was all, and it might be months before she got home again. She hadn't felt like this when she'd gone to America. So much had happened now; she'd changed so much.

Victor Hardman was there to meet her and to drive her to her digs in the quiet, respectable road in Bloomsbury. She glanced despondently out of the window, knowing she must pull herself together and soon.

Mrs Winters, her landlady, was a small plump woman, dressed in dark clothes, obviously still mourning her husband. Alice wondered how long he'd been dead, but she didn't want to ask. She showed her up to quite a big room with a bay window. The curtains, carpet and bedspread were of good quality and the furniture, although old, had been well cared for.

'It's lovely, thank you,' she replied to the woman's enquiry as to the suitability of the room.

'Then I'll expect to see you in my office in Islington tomorrow, Alice,' Victor Hardman said. 'We've a busy few days ahead.'

She nodded and after they'd both gone she sat on the bed and kicked off her shoes. She'd never felt so lonely in her entire life before. She lay down on the bed and gave in to the depression she'd been fighting all day. 'Oh, David! David! I'll never see you again, I just know it!' she sobbed into the pillow.

She didn't have much time to think after that miserable afternoon and night. There were people to meet, theatres to visit and shopping to do for stage dresses. The two outfits she bought were promptly taken back to the shop as they were totally unsuitable, Victor told her. He went with her on the next trip and she bought two of the flashiest, over-trimmed dresses she'd ever seen. Once she'd have thought them gorgeous, but not now. She hated them. Nor was she very impressed with the theatres. They were shabby compared to those in Liverpool.

'What kind of people come to these shows?' she asked. Although many poorer and modestly paid people went to the Rotunda, so too did richer people who arrived in cars and taxis, wearing evening dress.

'If you mean are they similar to the first-class passengers on the *Aquitania*, then no. They're working-class people who want to have a good night out. They only get one day off a week, most of them.'

She nodded. 'Then they'll get it.'

'I was beginning to think you were becoming a snob.'

'A snob? Me? I come from the slums of Liverpool. I've only just moved the family into that house in Media Street. It cost me a small fortune too. I need the money.'

'You'll get it when you start in *Days of Grace*.'

Her first performance was at the Bedford in Camden Town. It had been agreed that she would sing mainly the rather old-fashioned songs, and she was told that the audience would join in, in fact she should encourage them to do so. They loved a good sing-song. Then she would do a couple of her jazzy numbers.

She had to use a communal dressing room; she'd had one to herself at both the Rotunda and the Empire and she couldn't help feeling she was going down in the world,

284

not up. There were no dressers either, so she did her own hair, applied her own make-up and fastened her own dress, the bright red one with all the red and black fringing. She loathed it. The room was noisy and hot, for there were other girls and women in various stages of undress. Suddenly she caught sight of a woman with blonde hair piled in curls on top of her head, in what was now a very old-fashioned style. Her dress was old-fashioned too and looked slightly faded and worn. With a tremor of shock she recognised the woman. It was Letty Lewis. She made her way across the room and as she drew nearer she could see how heavy the singer's make-up was. It only served to emphasise the lines at the corners of her eyes and mouth.

'Miss Lewis?'

'I'm Letty Lewis, luv. Do I know you? I ain't seen you around before. New to the game?'

'No, not new, but this is my first time in London.'

'What's your name?'

'Alice. Alice O'Connor. I'm from Liverpool.'

The woman smiled and the lines on her face deepened. 'Oh, I had some really good times up there. They're really appreciative, not like the crowd you get in some parts. They're not bad in here.'

Alice ignored the churning of her stomach. 'I saw you once. I wasn't in the audience. I crept round the back. I couldn't afford the price of a ticket. You sang "Beautiful Dreamer".'

'Did I? Lord luv a duck, I can't remember what I sang last week, let alone all those years ago.'

'Two and a half years ago it was, that's all.'

'Then you've come up in the world and fast.'

Alice smiled. 'I was lucky, but you were my inspiration. I was singing in the street outside and a lady was good enough to give me a threepenny bit. She said all I needed was some training and grooming. I didn't even know what she meant. Then I saw you and I knew I wanted to be like you. That's how it all started. That and something a man once said to me.'

'Never believe a thing a feller tells you, Alice. Then you won't get hurt. But was I really your inspiration?' The smile and interest were genuine.

'You were. I went to America. I did well, very well. Then I came home to Liverpool and did well there too.'

'You need luck in this game, and plenty of it. You should have stayed in America, that's where the big money is.'

Alice shook her head sadly. 'I couldn't. There were reasons.'

Letty shrugged. 'Isn't that your name they're calling?'

'Oh, God, yes!' Alice pushed her way through to the door and then ran along the corridor.

Letty Lewis followed her. There was a juggling act on after Alice, then a magician, then herself. She'd go and listen to the girl, Letty decided, see how good she was.

They were a noisy audience, Alice thought, but she finally got the silence she needed after the first verse of 'Always'.

Watching from the wings, Letty Lewis turned to Tommy Clarke, the stage manager. 'She's too damned good for this place. That's *real* talent.'

'I know. She's in line for *Days of Grace*, the lead, too.'

'Well, good luck to her. I hope she makes the most of it because it doesn't last long. An' it's bloody hard on the way down.'

'If she's got any sense she'll marry a feller who can keep her in luxury.'

'Do they ever have any sense?' the older woman cackled. 'I didn't at her age.' And with that she turned her wise, experienced gaze to the sparkling young girl in front of her.

She'd done her spots at the other theatres and her spirits

felt lighter. At the end of every performance the applause had been deafening. Every manager wanted her to stay – they knew that with the stage musicals and the cinemas, the days of the music halls were numbered and they were desperate to make as much money as they could while the audiences were there. But the day finally came when Alice went with Victor to do her first rehearsal of her first stage show, the long-awaited *Days of Grace*. The cast seemed friendly enough, particularly Lucy Venables who had been understudying.

'Am I relieved you've come to take over. I know I can never live up to Miss O'Donnell's standard and so do the audiences. Bookings have been falling off and that's no good for anyone! The first thing they do is drop our wages and they're not much to start with,' she grinned.

'I would have come sooner,' said Alice, almost apologetically, 'but Mr Hardman had made firm, longstanding bookings for me and he says he never cancels because it's not good for his reputation. It's not good for business or my career either.'

Lucy nodded, and started to explain some of the intricacies of Alice's part.

It was a hard, exhausting day. Not only did Alice have to sing, she had to speak and act as well, something she'd never done before. Her movements were jerky, her lines stilted even though she'd learned them over the past weeks until she was word perfect.

'Oh, God. I was awful!' she said to Lucy when she came off.

'Not with the songs though, you've a great voice and, don't worry, the rest will come. Just wait until you have to wear that bloody awful costume and the even worse wig! I've tripped over that damned frock more times than I can remember.'

Alice found out at the end of the week, when there was a dress rehearsal in the morning, specially for her, that what Lucy had said about the dress and wig was true.

There was no one she knew in the audience to see her debut, except Victor Hardman, but that didn't bother her now. She would have hated David to see her in this awful get-up and with her face painted like a doll. To her surprise she got a standing ovation as she took her final bow.

She received rave reviews and bookings picked up. Every night there were bouquets and cards and invitations. She wished she could send all the roses home to Nelly but she made sure they all went to hospitals and churches. She had opened an account with Cunningham's the florists on Scotland Road and a bouquet of roses was to be delivered to Nelly each week. She wrote once a week too, telling of all her good fortune and sheer awe at being called a 'star' in the newspapers and sending Nelly the clippings. She knew that this was what her mam would want to hear, not the fact that there was still something missing in her life, that it really wasn't all glamour and fun.

'Don't you ever go out with any of these men?' Lucy asked, flicking through the invitations. 'Some of them are very well off and there's one here who's got a title.'

'No. I go with Victor for a quiet supper then back to Bloomsbury. If he can't make it, I go on my own. They know me now and give me a nice secluded booth in a corner, so I can have my meal in peace.'

'I don't understand you, Alice. Did you have to leave someone in Liverpool?'

'Not really, he left me.' She paused then said quickly, 'But not in the way you think. He's an officer on the *Aquitania*.'

'Not much of a romance then, is it? You down here, him trailing back and forth across the Atlantic.'

'No, it's not. But I had to choose.' Her voice was filled with longing, but deep down she realised what she'd just said wasn't true. She hadn't had anything to choose between. She didn't even know if he loved her. She'd seen more of Charlie than of him.

'Why don't you come on out with us?' Lucy invited her. 'Me and a couple of the girls are going for a bit of supper and a drink to a place round the corner.'

She agreed but it didn't do much to lift the depression that was beginning to plague her. She kept telling herself how lucky she was. There were girls in the chorus who would kill to live the life they thought she lived, but it didn't work. She was miserable and homesick, something she'd never been in Charleston. She'd written to Mike once, just to let him know she'd arrived home safely and that her career looked very promising. She'd had one letter back. Brief but to the point. He'd thanked her for her letter and wished her success and he'd signed it, 'Sincerely'. Sometimes she looked back on those days with Mike as the happiest she'd known. Had she treated him fairly? She felt a twinge of guilt. Oh, but Mike was a man of the world. And once he got used to it, his world wouldn't be all that different without her in it, of that she was sure ...

A week later she was wakened by Mrs Winters knocking on her bedroom door. Alice dragged on a robe and opened the door, rubbing the sleep from her eyes.

'It's a telegram for you, Alice.' Mrs Winters held out the small, buff-coloured envelope but her eyes were on the girl's face. No one liked telegrams, they were usually harbingers of bad news.

Alice opened it, her eyes wide now, scanning the lines. It was very short, but to the point.

'ALICE. MAM VERY ILL. COME HOME. LIZZIE.'

'Oh, Mam!' She threw the paper on the floor and ran her fingers through her hair.

'What is it, Alice?'

289

'It's Mam, she's very ill. I've got to go home. Now! Right now, this very minute.'

Mrs Winters was instantly efficient. 'I'll bring you up some tea and toast. Get dressed, pack a small case and I'll let Victor know. Lucy will stand in for you. Then I'll call you a taxi. Come on, Alice. By the time you get home she may have rallied. It might be something like influenza that she'll get over. Your sister didn't say what was actually wrong, now did she?'

The rest of the day passed in a blur of being pushed into cabs and onto trains. As she waited at Crewe for her connection, she walked up and down the platform ceaselessly, her mind in turmoil. She exhausted herself and fell asleep on the last leg of the journey, waking only when the train stopped with a jolt in Lime Street.

She ran down the platform, threw her case into the first taxi she saw, gave the driver the address and then fell back against the seat. She begged the cab driver to hurry.

'If I go any faster, luv, we'll overturn going round one of these corners. It's not a bloody race track – there's still a lot of horse-drawn wagons and there's no shiftin' them.'

It was dark and she seemed to have been travelling all day. When she arrived she thrust a ten-shilling note into the driver's hand and didn't wait for her change.

Agnes opened the door to her insistent knocking. Alice caught her and hugged her briefly. 'Oh, Holy Mother of God, what's the matter? What's she got? Why didn't someone tell me she was ill?'

'Because we didn't know. She'd been down to see Mrs O'Hanlon and when she got back she said she didn't feel well. "I'm just tired. It's old age creeping on," she said. Then she collapsed. Alice, it's pneumonia and it's bad.'

'Pneumonia! She's never had a bad chest! Not ever, not even in Benledi Street with all the cold and dampness and never having enough to eat.'

'The doctor said it wasn't anything to do with getting

290

cold or living in a damp place. He said it was vi . . .' Agnes struggled with the unfamiliar word, 'viral pneumonia.'

'Is that better or worse than the other kind?'

'I don't know. He said she should go to hospital, but you know Mam. She's terrified of hospitals, just the way she was about the workhouse.'

Alice ran upstairs and opened the door of the bedroom Nelly shared with Lizzie. Before she could cry out, Lizzie placed a finger on her lips and moved towards her.

'Don't start crying or carrying on, Alice. You'll only upset her,' Lizzie whispered.

Alice fought to control herself. 'How long has she been . . . like this?'

'She collapsed yesterday. We thought she'd just been doing too much. Mrs O'Hanlon's got rid of her lodgers and Mam went down to help her clean up after them. She said the lodger's room was like a pigsty and that Mrs O'Hanlon couldn't offer it to anyone else in that state. Our Agnes and me got her to bed but then she began to gasp and fight for her breath, so I sent for the doctor. She won't go to hospital, so he's left her some medicine but he said . . . he said she was exhausted. That she didn't have a strong constitution, so she had no strength to fight it.'

Alice swallowed hard and went and knelt on the floor beside the bed. Nelly was propped up with pillows but she looked small and suddenly frail and her breathing was very laboured.

'I'm here, Mam, it's Alice. I've come home.'

Nelly's eyes opened slowly and she tried to smile.

Alice took a thin hand, roughened by years and years of work. 'They've given me a few days to come home and see you. I'll go back when you're better.' She was trying hard to keep her voice steady.

Nelly became agitated and Alice got up and smoothed the prematurely greying hair away from her forehead.

'Hush now, Mam. Don't get upset.'

Nelly's words were slow. 'Alice, don't stay too ... too long.'

'Mam, in a few days you'll be up and about, then I'll go back.' She was fighting to control the tears and trying to keep her voice from cracking with anguish.

'No. Don't ... don't waste ... the gift.' Nelly was struggling hard now.

'You know I won't, Mam.'

Nelly closed her eyes. 'The ... Lord giveth ... and He taketh away, Alice.'

Alice could barely make out the words. She bit her lip and laid her cheek next to Nelly's, the tears pouring down her face and wetting the pillowcase.

Lizzie gently put her arm round Alice's shoulders and drew her away.

'Let her rest. I've sent for Father Mulcahey.'

Alike seized on this slim hope. 'Sometimes the sacrament makes them better. You know it does, Lizzie. Ma Wentworth from Athol Street had it three times. Oh, Lizzie, she can't go! She can't! She hasn't even had a year's comfort and security in this house. Surely God won't take her now, not yet, not until ...' She dissolved into quiet sobs and Lizzie clung to her.

'God is good, but if her time's come ...' Lizzie murmured. She had little faith that the sacrament of extreme unction would cure her mam. She'd sat here all day, watching Nelly getting worse.

She took Alice's hand and they both knelt beside the bed and Lizzie produced her rosary beads. She had already covered a small table with a clean cloth. Two candles, blessed, stood in small china holders. There was a bowl of Holy Water, a cupful of clean water in another bowl. A clean white handkerchief was also laid out, as was a saucer containing bread crumbs.

The parish priest arrived just as a taxi drew up outside

the house. He nodded to the man who got out and silently paid the driver: Father Mulcahey was carrying the Eucharist and could therefore converse with no one.

Again it was Agnes who opened the door. She beckoned the priest inside and stared up at the stranger.

'Yes?'

'Does Alice O'Connor live here?'

'Yes, but you can't see her now. Me mam's dead poorly.'

'I thought someone was, seeing the priest, but may I come in? I've travelled a long way and I'd like to see Alice before . . . before I go back to America.'

Agnes gnawed her lip, torn by indecision. America *was* a long way.

'All right, come on in. You can wait in the parlour and I'll tell her you're here, but if she won't see you, you'll 'ave to go.'

He nodded. 'That's fair enough. It's O'Farrell. Michael O'Farrell.'

Chapter Twenty-Four

As he looked around the room he realised what she'd spent his money on. That was just like her. She loved her mother dearly, he knew that. Just as he'd loved his own whom he'd seen lowered into the earth at Glasnevin Cemetery only a few days ago. That was why he'd come back. He hadn't come because of Alice, but once in Liverpool the urge to see her had been too strong for him to overcome. He'd got a cab and gone to Benledi Street only to be told she'd moved to this house. Benledi Street, and in particular number ten, had reminded him forcefully of his own childhood and youth. He'd looked at the peeling paint, the rotten wood, the cracked and broken steps and the dirty, fly-blown windows. The house was empty but it wouldn't be for much longer, there was a family moving in the day after, a family of eight who had been living in a cellar, so the woman next door had informed him.

His passage was booked on the *Berengaria* sailing to New York. He was going back to America tomorrow. But would he go? Now it looked as though Alice was about to lose her mother too. The priest hadn't been called for a simple ailment.

There was a knock on the front door, and since Mike was the nearest, he answered it.

A small, rotund man with glasses, well dressed and carrying a black bag, stood on the step. 'How is she now?' the doctor asked.

'I'm sorry, sir, I've only just arrived. I've no idea.'

Agnes appeared from the kitchen and ushered the doctor upstairs and Mike went back to his solitary musings in the parlour. He sat on the sofa and dropped his head in his hands. He knew how Alice must be feeling. He understood.

His mother's body had been taken to the church where it had remained until the funeral Mass the following day. It was an Irish custom. He'd sat in the chill, silent church all night with her. Just the four candles, one at each corner of the bier, and the flickering red light from the sanctuary lamp pierced the darkness. During those long dark hours he'd found it impossible to pray. If God was so good, as they were constantly being told by the clergy, then why did He allow such poverty and hardship to flourish? Oh, the Church came up with half-baked answers. No mere man should challenge God's reasons. All would be revealed on the Last Day. In the meantime one should believe blindly and without questioning.

That didn't wash with him and hadn't done for a long time. Who actually decided which person, which family, should suffer? Maybe he shouldn't be blaming God at all. Maybe it was all the fault of society. Of greedy, callous, cheating men. The survival of the fittest.

He remembered his boyhood in the Coombe. The biting, stinging cold rain and sleet driving in from the sea, sweeping up the Liffey. His threadbare clothes, his often bare feet numb with cold. The gnawing pains of hunger. The humiliation when he'd had to beg. The desperation when he'd turned to stealing. And the lies he'd told his mother about where he'd got the money or the bits of food.

He remembered standing at the foot of the statue of Daniel O'Connell at the bottom of the street that now bore the name of the man who had won Catholic emancipation for Ireland. He'd taken Kitty and Dee, young as they were, their little faces pinched and white, in the hope that people would take pity on them and be generous. It had been Christmas, although exactly which Christmas he couldn't remember. Only that the people rushing to do the last of their shopping had no time or money to give to the three ragged urchins, three out of a whole army of starving men, women and children that wandered the cold streets of Dublin.

He heard footsteps on the stairs and looked up hopefully. The front door was opened, then shut, and he heard a car pull away from the kerb. The doctor had gone. Obviously there was nothing else he could do. He hesitated to smoke, they might not like it. Instead he leaned his head against the back of the sofa and closed his eyes. He remembered the first time he'd come to Liverpool, all those years ago, following his father to America. He could almost feel the dust and the heat and the long miles he'd travelled on the American freight trains. His da's face when he'd confronted him. And his face when he'd died, twisted into a sneer by the stroke. Did he still hate him? There was only one answer to that question. Yes, and he always would. There seemed to be no sign of Alice's father. Maybe he, too, was dead. And Alice? Oh, how he missed her.

After she'd gone, there had seemed no point in anything. The house was like a morgue. He'd been bad-tempered, sullen and had been drinking heavily until Alexander had threatened that the entire staff would leave if he didn't pull himself together. In a highly indignant and irate manner his butler had told of the barefaced lies he'd had to tell people that there had been a very private domestic occurrence in Dublin that had upset his employer, hence the heavy drinking and sullen attitude and depressed moods. Mike smiled wryly to himself. Only Alexander could get away with that. So he'd made an effort. Thrown himself into his work, increased his fortune

297

and, when people asked about '*Mrs O'Farrell*', he'd told them that – like the angel from heaven that Alice surely was – she'd gone to Dublin to help nurse and comfort his poor mother who was not in the best of health. He himself was very distraught about the 'drastic domestic occurrence' that had upset him too, and about which he couldn't utter a single word, on his mother's life, it was so private. And, as to how long his mother would need Alice, sure it was almost impossible to know, wasn't it? And with that he would change the subject. But there was little pleasure in life. He had no time to enjoy his money, he wouldn't allow himself the time. Over the months the pain had begun to ease.

He had no idea if she and David Williamson were engaged. Or even worse, married. He had asked the cab driver if he'd heard of her. The man had. He'd been effusive in his praise. He'd been to see her and she was the best. She was one of their own, too. The Liverpool Songbird, she was called, and they were dead proud of her. Mike had smiled at that, remembering the pendant he'd given her. He'd sold all the other jewels after she'd gone and Ruth had removed every trace of her from that bedroom. It was now virtually sealed, the furniture covered with dustsheets, the shutters always tightly closed.

He got up and walked into the hall and knocked gently on the kitchen door.

Agnes opened it, clutching Georgie the cat for comfort, her eyes red and puffy. 'Go on upstairs to your mammy, girl, I'll watch the others.'

She passed the cat to Mary and then fled past him and he looked at the solemn, frightened faces of the three children in the room.

'Who're you?' Jimmy asked belligerently.

Obviously he took after his father, Mike thought ruefully. The other two were very quiet and still. 'I'm Mr O'Farrell, a friend of Alice's.'

'You're Irish,' the lad said.

'I am so, but I live in America. That's how I met Alice. Will I tell you about how I got there on the ship and then riding the freight trains and the desperate things I did?' He saw the first spark of interest in their eyes. At least he could be of some help, keep them interested, keep their thoughts away from upstairs where their mammy lay dying.

When he heard the ponderous footsteps coming down the stairs, he knew they belonged to the priest and that Nelly O'Connor had breathed her last. He went into the hall as a sobbing Agnes fled past him into the kitchen.

'She's gone then, Father?'

The priest nodded.

'God have mercy on her soul.'

'She'd had a hard life. It had weakened her, but God was good, she had every comfort in her last days.'

Mike felt his temper rising. Again the bloody pathetic empty platitudes. 'If she'd had them earlier, Father, she might not have died. If someone had done something about the beatings and the deprivation, the constant worry of just keeping alive and keeping her children alive, the shame of not having even a ha'penny to put on the collection plate. Just think of all those pennies, sixpences, shillings and maybe the odd florin or two that could have kept her, her family and many other families supplied with a loaf of bread and maybe a few fishes.' Mike's voice was harsh, the sarcasm heavy and intentional.

The priest was not used to being spoken to like this. 'You're an Irishman? A Catholic or . . .?' The voice had a sharp edge to it.

'I'm not an Orangeman if that's what you can't bring yourself to say. I'm a Dubliner and I was brought up a Catholic. I've just buried my own mother, God rest her and God bless her memory. She, too, had a hard life when I was young. Our parish priest always used to remind us of the Beatitudes, particularly "Blessed are the poor". I never did see any reason, understanding or compassion in that, Father. Especially as our particular fellow lived in comfort and had a full belly. I wonder, when Christ said those words, did He mean that the clergy were to be exempt?'

The other man looked horrified. 'That's blasphemy!'

'Is it, or is it just a question?'

'You've lost your faith. You've fallen from a state of grace.'

'I fell a long time ago, Father. Will I show you the scars? Or just the door?' He was in no mood to have moral issues, blasphemy or lack of faith heaped down on his head. By his accent the priest was a Mayo man. Maybe that explained everything. They were dour and devout to the point of martyrdom in the west.

As he closed the door he turned and saw Alice standing at the top of the staircase. 'Oh, Alice, I'm sorry.' He held out his arms and she flew down the stairs. There was no cry of recognition, no question as to why he was here. It was as if she'd been expecting him.

'Oh, Mike! Mike, she's dead! I can't believe she's gone! At the . . . the end she just opened her eyes and tried to smile at me. She . . . she couldn't speak. Oh, Mam! Mam!'

He held her tightly as she sobbed, the pain of his own loss twisting the knife in the wound.

Lizzie came slowly down. 'You're Mr O'Farrell?'

He nodded.

'I'm going down the street for my . . . friend. I won't be long.'

Mike nodded and drew Alice into the parlour and sat her down on the sofa, his arms still round her.

'I was in London. They never told me! Our Lizzie should have sent for me sooner,' she sobbed.

'Don't put the blame on her, Alice. She doesn't deserve it.'

She looked up at him, realising for the first time that it *was* actually him. 'What . . . how . . .?'

'I came home for a funeral too. My mother was buried three days ago. I had a few days with her and I'll always be thankful for that. You had a few hours, Alice. You didn't arrive too late. Take comfort from that.'

She was a little calmer now. 'I'm sorry. How . . . what did your mother die of?'

'A massive heart attack. She'd had a couple of strokes, the last one two weeks ago. That's why Kitty wired me.'

'I . . . I *am* sorry.'

'She had twenty years of good, comfortable living, Alice. Loved by her daughters and grandchildren, respected by her neighbours, and her faith never deserted her. She went to Mass every day, and I know she made charitable donations to her old neighbours. I comfort myself with that.'

'Mam . . . Mam only had a few months and I was so selfish. I could have stayed in Liverpool, everyone begged me to, but no, I had to go to London to become a bloody "star".'

'Don't blame yourself. A talent like yours should never be suppressed.' He smiled. 'Are you a star?'

She nodded. 'I suppose so. I met an agent on the ship coming home. I'm the lead in *Days of Grace*.'

He didn't want to mention David Williamson but he couldn't stop himself. 'And what happened to your young engineering officer? Do you still see him?'

'No. I did when I first came home, but not since I've been in London.'

The knowledge should have cheered him but it didn't. He hated to see her so smitten with grief and his own grief was still raw. He'd taken a photograph of his mother and her rosary beads as simple tokens to remind him, although both his sisters had urged him to take more.

The door opened and a giant of a man entered, immediately making the room seem smaller.

'I'm Jack Phillips, Lizzie's friend. I'm also a police constable.'

Mike nodded. He should have guessed by the man's size and bearing. 'Mike O'Farrell, a friend of Alice's from Charleston.'

'I've told Lizzie to put the kettle on and to get the younger kids to bed. I've also sent for the two women who do the laying out. Tomorrow I'll get in touch with the Co-op Funeral Directors.'

Alice managed to smile gratefully at Jack. She couldn't think about arrangements. 'Will you stay?' she said, turning to Mike.

'My passage is booked on the *Berengaria* to sail tomorrow, but to hell with it. I'll not leave you in this state, Alice.'

'I'll sleep here tonight. I'll share with Mary and Lizzie. They . . . they'll want Mam's room to lay her out.'

'Then I'll go to a hotel. Jack, can you recommend one, a decent one?'

'There's no need for that, Mike. We've got a spare room.'

'Thanks. I'll give you a hand to arrange things,' Mike offered.

Jack nodded. Neither Alice nor Lizzie were in any fit state to cope with the formalities and he'd be glad of some help. He couldn't take time off. It wasn't his mother or a very close relative who had died.

Mike found it strange at first. Two old women came and laid out the mortal remains of Nelly O'Connor. Then white sheets were hung round the walls. A candle was placed at each corner of the bed and a crucifix hung on the wall behind it. A small, cheap Holy Water font was hung on the wall near the door. All this was done by a trio of silent, grieving women who, he was told, were Nelly's friends from the old street. How customs varied,

302

he thought. How much easier for her to be taken to the church, but that would have been inconvenient for the worshippers as obviously the funeral wouldn't be for a couple of days.

It was late when he and Jack left the house and walked down the road to Jack's home. Jack introduced Mike to his mother who went upstairs to make up the bed in the spare room. Jack indicated that Mike should sit down. He glanced around at the comfortable, homely living room. There was no real luxury but everything was clean and well cared for.

'Will you take a drink with me, Jack, for your hospitality?'

'I will,' Jack said, smiling gratefully. 'I have to say this, Mike, she had a terrible life did poor Nelly O'Connor. God alone knows what she ever saw in Tip in the first place, but she stuck it out. At least her last days were spent in comfort – thanks to Alice – and not in dirt and poverty and with only a pauper's grave.'

'I'll pay the funeral expenses. I told Alice she'd have the best. My mother had a hard life too. We had nothing but she always said that she wanted to go out with some style, God willing. Well, Mrs O'Connor will go in style, too.'

'That's very generous of you.'

'Will there be a wake? Is it the custom here?'

'For some, but I don't think they'd want one. They're too upset and I don't hold with them myself. They usually end up in a drunken brawl. Grief, guilt, overwrought nerves and drink don't mix very well. Old scores and slights are mentioned and then one thing leads to another and we get called in. It's not very dignified.'

'With that bit I'd agree. It's our custom in Ireland to take the body to the church to lie overnight.'

'On its own?'

'Usually, yes. Sometimes a nun will keep a vigil, but I

303

stayed with my mother. I felt I owed her that much, I'd been away so long.'

'Will you be able to get another sailing?'

'That's no problem. Cunard run a very fast, efficient and regular service.' He paused and looked straight at Jack. 'Maybe I'll get the *Aquitania*.'

'I know about him,' Jack said quietly. 'Lizzie told me.' Mike nodded.

'He's pleasant enough, I suppose,' Jack went on. 'Never met him, of course, but I've seen his father, in the Crown Court. He's a big noise barrister.'

Mike nodded again and they let the matter drop. 'And what of himself? Has he been warned off or did he just disappear?'

'He's in jail. Walton. He got six years for assault and fraudulent misappropriation of money. Alice put him there.'

'Alice?'

'Aye. The day she arrived home and saw the state the family were still living in, she marched into the saloon bar of The Widows, packed with hardbitten men, and cursed him up hill and down dale. And she didn't mince her words to the others either. Of course Tip belted her, so I arrested him. She's got guts, has Alice. She got up in the dock and told everyone how he'd beaten her and the entire family for years. That he'd spent every penny of the money she'd sent specifically for her mam and addressed to her mam. He denied it. He yelled across the court that she was a liar. She yelled back that she'd call the post office clerk as a witness and where did everyone think he got so much money from when he never did a stroke of work?'

'Jaysus! I know she's got a temper but she must have been breathing fire. So, that's where all my money went. To finance a drunken wife beater.'

'Your money?'

Mike nodded. 'She insisted on working – singing – until the place was closed and after that . . .' he shrugged. He looked squarely at Jack Phillips. Jack was about his own age and he liked the fellow. He was obviously a man of principle. Mike felt so alone now, despite his sisters and their families. He'd loved his mother and now he ached for Alice's love and what was he going back to? Nothing. A big silent house and a few business acquaintances. He wanted to talk of his love and his grief; maybe it would help. He sighed and decided that Jack Phillips was a man to be trusted with those two emotions which were tearing him apart.

The glasses were refilled time and again as Mike told Jack his life story and of his love for Alice. Jack, in return, confessed his love for Lizzie, and the fact that he'd told Tip O'Connor that he'd break every bone in his body if he laid a finger on any of them. They were in similar positions, they told each other. They were both in love with younger women although Jack had no competition.

'You'll be able to marry her, Jack, after a suitable period of mourning.'

'Who'll see to the rest of the family? Agnes is only sixteen.'

'You think Alice will go back to London?'

'Yes. She's got some kind of a contract. If she breaks it she could be sued in court.'

Mike nodded. He'd be willing to pay any amount to free her and take her home with him. But where was home? Oh, he'd inherited the house, made his own money to add to his father's and made his mark in Charleston but there was no one there at all who mattered. And what about Dublin? The homeland was always close to an Irishman's heart, his own included, but Dublin was a changed city and with his mother dead he hadn't the heart for it.

* * *

305

There was a brief shopping expedition for mourning clothes. Lizzie and Alice made the purchases between them, while Jack and Mike made all the arrangements and completed the formalities. Nelly would go to St Anthony's, her old parish, where she'd worshipped until her death. It was the one thing she'd insisted on after she'd moved house. Every Sunday they'd all gone to nine o'clock Mass in the church beside a pub called the Throstle's Nest. On this, her last visit, there would be a full Requiem Mass and the hearse would be drawn by two black horses, with black plumes on their bridles. The rest of the family would go in two open carriages, the weather still being fine, and the whole procession would be led by the official mourners employed by the Co-op Funeral Directors. Normally, except for very grand funerals, the bereaved walked behind the hearse and there were no official mourners. But this was to be a very grand affair, Mike had spared no expense. Nelly O'Connor and his mother had one thing in common: the most expensive funerals that both Liverpool and Dublin had seen in a long time.

Alice, supported by Mike, went in the first carriage with Jack and Lizzie; Agnes and the others followed in the second one. They were all surprised and touched to see a line of people the whole length of Scotland Road. Men doffed their caps and hats, women crossed themselves, a few of the old shawlies dipped a bit of a curtsy, as though the cortège was that of royalty. Oh, Mam would have loved this, Alice thought, glad that the heavy black veil that covered her hat and extended to her shoulders hid her face and her red, swollen eyes.

'She never 'ad much in this life, God 'elp 'er, but she's going out like a queen,' Mary O'Hanlon sniffed as she and Ethel and Jinny sat in their pew watching the mourners file into the church.

Ethel wiped her eyes. 'God forgive me for saying this,

306

an' in His holy house too, but I hope that swine rots in prison!'

'Amen to that, Ethel,' Jinny said grimly. 'An' God forgive us both for cursing a man in His holy church.'

'She's got money now, has Alice. Did you see the fine gentleman, Mr O'Farrell, from America?'

Jinny nodded. 'He's only just buried his own ma, God rest her an' God bless the mark afterwards.'

'And that Jack Phillips will sort that old devil when he gets out of clink.'

'She'll marry 'im, yer know, Ethel,' Mary said.

'Lizzie will?'

Mary O'Hanlon nodded and wiped her eyes again as Father Mulcahey began the *De Profundus*.

'Out of the depths I have cried to thee, O Lord,

'Lord hear my voice.

'Let Thy ears be attentive of the voice of my Supplication. If Thou, O Lord, shalt observe iniquities; Lord who shall endure it?'

Most of the congregation didn't fully understand all of the words, or too much of their sentiment, but they made the responses at the end of the prayer.

'And let perpetual light shine upon her. Amen.'

Alice tried to keep back the tears but her body shook with her sobs. She'd never see her mam again. She knew, she believed, that Mam would be in heaven. She'd had her hell and her purgatory, too, here on earth, all the years she'd put up with Da, because long ago she'd made vows to 'love and to cherish, for better or for worse'. Alice hadn't informed the Governor of Walton of Nellie's death; she hadn't even thought about her father. There was a great ache, an emptiness in her heart, in her whole body.

She and Lizzie held each other's hands tightly when they went up for Communion. They had to pass the coffin, covered with roses and white Madonna lilies, and they

307

both stopped, and laid a hand on it.

'Goodbye, Mam,' Lizzie said softly while Alice choked with emotion.

Only the closest neighbours and Jack's mam went back to the house for the buffet Mike had ordered from Reece's. There were bottles of a good Madeira wine and a couple of bottles of Jameson's too, but no one lingered too long. Lizzie urged Mary, Ethel and Jinny to take all the remaining food and wine home with them.

'Oh, God luv yer, Lizzie, but we couldn't. It'd be like taking from the dead,' Mary said.

'It'll be no such thing. I'll get it packed into baskets and you take it home, ladies, otherwise it'll be out and into the bin with it,' Mike retorted.

'Ah, you're a good, generous man, Mr O'Farrell.'

Alice managed a smile before the tears again threatened to overwhelm her.

Chapter Twenty-Five

It *was* the *Aquitania* that Mike was due to sail home on, and he was hoping that Alice would want to come and see him off. He'd thought that Williamson might have called at least to express his condolences to Alice. There had been enough obituaries in the papers and surely he read the newspapers, but there had been no sign of him. There hadn't even been a card. So much for his affection for Alice.

They said their farewells in the house in Media Street and Mike felt the same longing, the same desire, the same frustration... yet his pride wouldn't allow him to declare his love for fear of ridicule, like the night she'd left Charleston.

'So, you'll go back to London, Alice?' He tried to make his voice light.

'I've got a contract and besides, I have to work, otherwise I won't be able to stop thinking of ... Mam.'

'I could buy you out of the contract, if you want out.'

'And what would I do then, Mike? Mope around here?'

'You could come back to Charleston.' He held his breath, every nerve in his body on edge, every muscle tensed.

'No, but thanks, for everything. I really mean that. I couldn't have coped without you, but I can't go back to Charleston.'

He hid his bitter disappointment well. 'You know you

only need to send a cable, Alice, if you need help.'

She nodded and then there was a pause before she spoke again.

'Mike if . . . if ever you come back to see your sisters, will you come and see me?'

'I will, that's a promise, but it might be a long time. You might be married to a duke or someone like that, by then.' He attempted a smile but it died before it reached his eyes.

She smiled. 'No. Though a girl from round the corner did marry an earl, but he was crippled in the war and she was widowed in a horrible way. He died in her arms. No, I don't want to be like Hannah Harvey, or the Countess of Ashenden as she is now.'

He hugged her and kissed her on the cheek, while his whole being longed to hold on to her for ever, to carry her off in his arms to Charleston or Dublin or anywhere where she'd forget David Williamson.

When he left Liverpool, the weather was fair but he knew it probably wouldn't last. They picked up passengers in Cobh in County Cork and passed the old Head of Kinsale and were out into the Atlantic Ocean before he encountered David Williamson passing through the First-Class Smoking Room.

'Ah, Mr Williamson. Haven't I had my eyes peeled since we sailed just looking for you.'

'Mr O'Farrell! I had no idea you were aboard. How are you? Have you been home on business or was it pleasure?' His attitude was polite and pleasant.

'I came home to bury my mother,' Mike said flatly.

'I'm so sorry. Please accept my condolences.' Williamson's manner had now changed to one of grave respect and Mike wondered if he'd been trained to handle such a variety of situations. Was there some sort of course they all went on to enable them to cope, to use the right words for every occasion?

'Condolences accepted. Have you seen Alice?'

'No, she's in London. She's doing very well, from what Charlie tells me and from what I read in the papers. Charlie's going down to see her next month, I believe.'

Mike's expression changed. 'If you read the papers and hear so much from your brother then you'll know that Alice is in Liverpool and has been for the past four days! Her mother died.' Suddenly all Mike's anger erupted. 'You're a self-centred, thoughtless bastard, Williamson! All the politeness and concern is only skin deep. You know how she feels about you.'

David was shocked both by Mike's news and the personal attack on his character. 'I don't understand, sir. How *does* Alice feel or think?'

'If you made the effort to see her you'd find out, wouldn't you? She followed you to America, although why she bothered I don't bloody well know,' Mike snapped and walked away before he lost his temper entirely and punched that sanctimonious, patronising little upstart in the face.

David stared after him, astounded by his words and attitude. Alice had told him she'd gone to America fired by ambition and he could see no reason to disbelieve her. Maybe O'Farrell was jealous. Maybe he'd fallen in love with his ward and asked Alice to marry him. Had Alice turned him down? Perhaps that's why she had left Charleston so hurriedly, and why O'Farrell was behaving so oddly. David Williamson shrugged his shoulders and went on to see to his next task.

It wasn't a good crossing, it being the end of September, although the Atlantic was the most treacherous of oceans and storms were frequent even in summer. There were very few people in the dining rooms for meals, and the sounds of breaking china and glass accompanied their eating.

311

Mike had never suffered from seasickness and as he stood in the First-Class Writing Room watching, through the long floor-length windows, the heaving grey mass of water that seemed to match his mood, his thoughts were on the future. His future.

What was there to keep him in Charleston? Why hadn't he gone home years ago? Why shouldn't he sell up and go back to Dublin? Dublin *was* home and he knew every inch of it and each inch had its memories. He'd buy a house, maybe not in the city itself. Maybe in Dalkey or Sandycove or even Dunlaoghaire. He'd find things to occupy himself with. His sisters had friends and his nieces and nephews were growing up. Why live out a solitary existence in Charleston where he had few friends and no family? That patronising, ambitious little snot of a junior officer didn't love Alice at all and when she finally found out, as she surely would in time, she'd need someone to help pick up the pieces. Why not himself? Maybe she'd even come to love him – just a little.

As the bow of the ship plunged down into another trough and thousands of gallons of foaming water crashed down on her, Mike hung onto the bar across the window and came to his decision. He'd go back to Charleston and sell up. Wind up the business or find a buyer for it. That wouldn't be hard and he'd get a good price. Then he'd come home to the most beautiful country on God's good earth, as he'd described it to Alice the first time he'd met her. He would wait. With age came patience, and only a narrow strip of water would separate them then, a channel it took only eight hours to cross instead of an ocean that took nearly five days, and that on a fast ship like this one.

At the beginning of October Alice went back to London.

'I don't care what you say, Lizzie, I'm having a phone put in. If there had been one earlier . . .'

'Alice, stop blaming yourself. It was all so quick.' Lizzie

changed the subject. 'Where will I be able to phone you?'

'At Victor's office or at the theatre. Mrs Winters doesn't have a phone. I'll write the numbers down.'

They all went to see her off at Lime Street and she hugged every one of them in turn.

'Agnes, you'll have to help Lizzie, it's not going to be easy for her.'

Agnes had already realised this but gave her assent anyway.

'Now you three, particularly you, Jimmy, no nonsense. Mam will be watching you.'

'From up there?' Mary pointed to the glass-domed roof of the station.

'From up there, luv. She'll be watching over you. If you work hard at school then when you're fourteen, maybe we'll send you to a school to learn to use a typewriter.' Mary was bright and showed all the signs of becoming a beauty. Alice's eyes met those of Lizzie; they were thinking along the same lines. No more dirty, badly paid, monotonous factory jobs. Agnes was now employed in Bunny's on the corner of Church Street and Whitechapel. Jimmy was apprenticed to a plumber, so he'd have a trade in his fingers and would always find work. Eddy and Mary were still at school.

There was no one to meet Alice at Euston, so she got a taxi to Bloomsbury.

Mrs Winters welcomed her warmly. 'The show must go on, Alice, and time is a great healer. I missed Mr Winters terribly for years.'

'How long has he been gone?' It was the question she'd always wanted to ask but never had.

'Almost eight years now. But not a day goes by without my thinking of him. But life must go on – like the show.'

When Alice arrived back at the theatre, everyone was glad to see her, especially Lucy.

'It'll be great to get back in the chorus. I just don't

have, well, that special something. I've no confidence in myself and none in the role and it shows.'

'It'll be good in some ways to get back to work.'

'It'll take your mind off things, Alice, and you should go out more, you really should.'

'Maybe I will, soon.'

It wasn't long before Charlie Williamson turned up in her dressing room with a huge bouquet.

'I told you I'd see you soon.'

She smiled at him. He obviously didn't know about Nelly. 'I've been home, Mam died. I've only been back here a week.'

He looked concerned and guilty. 'Oh, Alice, I'm so sorry, I really am. So, you'll need cheering up a bit. I've booked supper at the Savoy.'

'Will you give me fifteen minutes to change?'

'I'll wait outside. I parked the car nearby as there's a nip in the air already.'

She'd never been to the Savoy Grill before. It was very impressive, far more opulent than the Adelphi, but it didn't compare with the First-Class Dining Room of the *Aquitania*.

'Mike O'Farrell came to see me,' she said by way of conversation after their orders had been taken.

'He travelled all the way from Charleston?' Charlie asked, amazed.

'Not especially to see me. He, too, had just buried his mother and he said he couldn't be in Liverpool and not call to see me. I don't know what I would have done without him. He took care of everything, from all the formalities to the buffet, and he insisted on paying for it all too.'

'Well, he is your guardian, after all.'

She didn't reply. She thought she detected a note of petulance in his voice.

'Is David home? He did promise to come and see me when he got some decent leave.'

'I can't keep up with all his comings and goings. He has Maisie demented with the washing. Mother told her to send it out to the laundry with everything else, but she won't. It won't be back in time, is the stock reply.'

So, they had a maid, Alice thought but without much surprise.

'He did have a week's leave, but he spent nearly all of it studying for yet another ticket.'

She felt disappointed and it must have shown in her face, for Charlie leaned towards her. 'It's his career, Alice. He enjoys it and he's ambitious.'

'I know,' she answered in a small voice as the hors d'oeuvres were served and the wine poured.

'But *I'm* not in the least ambitious. I'll be happy to toddle along contentedly earning my salary in obscurity for years. I *could* become ambitious though, given the right incentive.'

Alice looked at him in surprise. She sipped her wine slowly. She'd had nothing to eat since lunchtime and she didn't want to make a fool of herself or say things she would later regret.

'All I ever wanted, Charlie, was to sing on the stage. After the day you knocked me down and took me aboard the ship, my great ambition was for David to hear me sing on stage. I suppose in my stupid naive way that's why I followed him to America.'

'Did you? You never told me that before. I thought Mr O'Farrell had sent for you.'

She shook her head. 'No, it was all part of a dream, Charlie. I wanted to go to New York but I didn't have the fare for a decent ship. I got a tramp and ended up in Charleston. It was quite by accident that I met Mike O'Farrell.' She thought it prudent not to disclose the fact that Mike wasn't her guardian. There would have to be

315

endless explanations and she didn't want that. 'He's been very good to me.'

'Yes, David said he was very protective of you.'

'What else did David say?' She just wanted to talk about David.

'That you were stunning. That you had them all at your feet. That it was a great honour to be invited to that very, very exclusive ball.' He paused. 'Alice, I wouldn't expect to see David very often if I were you.'

She looked up, puzzled, the fork halfway to her mouth. 'Why not?'

Charlie shrugged carelessly, not wanting to make trouble. 'As I said, the sea is his career and it takes years to reach the top.'

She could understand that. She'd had ambitions too. Fate had been kind to her and she'd got the breaks early, but it wasn't like that for everyone.

'Does he ever write home when he's away?' she asked, pushing the petits pois round her plate. She really wasn't very hungry.

Charlie laughed. 'Now that's a huge bone of contention at home. Mother says he should. Father says it's a waste of time and energy because by the time he posted the letter in New York and it was processed, it would come back on the *Mauretania* or the *Berengaria* – they're the Royal Mail ships – and he'd already be home. And he's not very good with letters. Oh, he'll send a cable if it's someone's birthday, or there's been a change of port or a long delay, but that's all.'

As Alice listened, she wondered why Charlie seemed to be putting his brother down. He did it jokingly, but the jibes were there just the same.

On the way home, wrapped in her satin quilted evening coat with a long, floating chiffon scarf swathed round her head and shoulders, she wondered whether Charlie was trying to warn her about something. Was he telling her,

316

in a roundabout way, something Victor had stressed, that it was a special type of girl who married a seafarer? David had told her himself that the sea was his life, so she shouldn't expect him to be running around after her and driving to London and back when he had important examinations to study for. But surely he could find time to write or phone when he was at home. He had said he was her biggest fan.

It was when they reached her digs that it suddenly dawned on her. Maybe Charlie didn't want her to see David because he was falling for her himself. After all, he drove frequently to London. There were always flowers, champagne and supper in the best places for her.

He got out of the car and held the door open for her.

'Thanks for the meal, Charlie, it was really something special. It's very good of you to drive all this way to see me. It *is* a long way.'

He smiled. 'I'll come down every week, if you would like me to, Alice.'

'No. No, really, Charlie. I do get very tired and I'm ... I'm not over Mam yet.'

Instantly he became solicitous. 'Oh, I'd forgotten. Forgive me for being so crass, Alice, but I will come down again soon.'

'At the end of next month maybe?' She tried not to sound off-putting or dismissive. She did like him, he was good company, but she certainly didn't love him and never would. He was just a friend.

Chapter Twenty-Six

Alice stood in Victor Hardman's office and looked out of the window at the traffic in the street below. November was a miserable month. Gloomy and often foggy. Fog so thick you could hardly see a hand in front of you. Fog that made breathing hard for many people. She remembered the long, bitter winters in Benledi Street. Now she had good clothes to keep out the cold, a warm home, nourishing food, and she travelled in comfort.

It seemed a lifetime since she'd dragged herself home from a day's work to a cold damp house where there was no food and no fire and she had been forced to go out and sing in the streets. She wondered if, as they grew up, Jimmy, Eddy, and Mary would remember those days of terrible hardship. She and Lizzie and Agnes would always remember. A smile played around her mouth as she thought of her sister. She was glad that Lizzie had found Jack Phillips. It was an odd match. But he had a good steady job, a nice home and he'd treat her well.

For the first time in months she thought of her father. He still had a long time to serve in jail and it was a harsh routine in Walton. If he survived, when he came out he'd go looking for them all. Well, Mam had gone, she herself had gone, and Lizzie would be gone soon, if she had read the signs right. Jimmy would be nineteen, Eddy sixteen and Mary fifteen, and all Agnes had to do was send for Jack Phillips if Da landed on the doorstep one day.

Victor finished his conversation and replaced the receiver sharply. He wasn't having a good morning and his ulcer was playing up. He leaned back in his chair. 'So, what's the matter with you, miss? Not happy with the idea of the new part? *No, No, Nanette* has been running for over two years, and it's a very successful show, Alice.'

'I know, I went to see it – Charlie took me. I wanted to see what it was like and I didn't want to go on my own.'

'You don't need to make excuses, Alice. You can go where you like and with who, or is it whom, you like.' A thought suddenly occurred to him. She seemed quite taken with this Charlie. Was she going to tell him she was getting married? 'Isn't he the brother of your young mariner?'

'Yes, but Charlie is just a friend. He cheers me up, that's all.'

'So, what's the matter with you now?'

She turned again towards the window, not wanting to face him. 'I don't want to star in *No, No, Nanette* or in any other show.'

He sat up abruptly. 'Why the hell not? Do you want more money? Is that it?' he snapped. It all came down to this in the end, usually. Oh, they pouted and sulked and used every trick and excuse in the book, but money was always the root of the problem.

'No, I don't want any more money. I'm not greedy, you know how I live.'

'Yes, very modestly for someone in your position and at your age. You're one of the thriftiest stars I know. You hardly spend a penny on yourself, except for your clothes, and you don't have trunks full of them either, considering the public image you have to live up to.'

'I can remember what living in poverty was like. Real poverty. It's something that stays with you.' She saved hard. Quite what she was saving for she didn't know yet. But the fear of being reduced again to the way she'd lived in Benledi Street never really left her.

She turned to face him. 'I want to go home. Well, go back north, away from London.'

He stared at her, unable to speak for a few seconds. 'What the hell for? You told me yourself you've come from the gutter, from singing in the streets, to become one of the highest paid entertainers in this part of the business and with a regiment of fawning supporters. It's a dream come true and now you want to throw it all away? Jesus, Alice!' He thumped the desk, making the inkstand and the phone rattle.

'I don't want supporters – fans. It *is* a dream come true, or it was. It was all for Mam, and now she's gone, so what's the point?'

He stood up and walked to the window to face her, gripping her wrist and searching her face for some inkling of an explanation. 'It's that bloody seafaring fool, isn't it?'

She snatched her hand away. 'He's not a fool!'

'He is, because he doesn't appreciate just what you've achieved. Or maybe he does and he's jealous. He never comes down here to see you or take you to supper, does he?'

She couldn't argue with that. 'If I go back north, there'll be more chance of seeing him, I don't deny that, but . . .'

'But what? Has it ever occurred to you that he really has no romantic interest in you?'

She turned on him furiously. 'He has! He told me he'd followed my career! If you remember, it was him who asked me to sing on the ship.'

'Thinking, no doubt, about his own prospects. It would be seen by his superiors as showing initiative. A feather in his cap.'

'He said he was my biggest fan!'

'Then why does he never come to London? Or is this "romance" being conducted by proxy, via his brother Charlie?'

321

She was smarting with the humiliation. 'There isn't time for him to be traipsing up and down to London. They dock one day, disembark the passengers, clean the ship up, bunker up, load up with fresh stores and are away again in two days.'

'Oh, for God's sake Alice, don't take me for a fool. He must get leave. No company expects its employees to work like that month after month without a break, especially its officers. And from what I remember they employ an army of cleaners and tradesmen to clean up and repair any damage, and another army of dockers to do the bunkering.'

'He's studying!' she snapped back. 'Anyway, I'm sick of London. Sick of all the "fawning" as you call it.'

He sat down again at his desk. 'So, what will you do up north?'

'They still have plenty of good theatres. When I first met you, you said you could get me jobs in Manchester, Birmingham, Leeds.'

'Alice, have you thought of how it's going to look? People will say you're sliding, coming down in the world, a has-been.'

'I don't care what they think or say, I—'

'Then you should, Alice, because without them you've no bloody job at all!' he yelled at her, finally losing his temper.

'I want to go home!' she yelled back.

He threw his hands in the air in a gesture of resignation. 'All right! All right! Pack your bags and go home. I'll get you what jobs I can, but touring is no life, Alice. No life at all and you still won't see much of lover boy.'

'I'll manage.'

'It's your life, your career, Alice, but you're wasting it.'

They were an echo of Nelly's words and she shivered, but she'd had enough. She felt miserable and lonely. She'd made no real friends. Occasionally she'd go out with Lucy

322

and the others, but not very often. She also knew that because of this they thought she was a snob.

'Can I ask a favour?'

He'd gone back to his paperwork as though he'd forgotten about her. 'Now what?'

'Can I use your telephone?'

He gathered up a sheaf of papers and stood up. 'Help yourself. I'm going out for some fresh air.'

She felt better as she dialled the number. Now at least the confrontation was over, along with the shouting.

It was Mary who answered.

'What are you doing off school?'

'I'm sick. I've got a bad cough and our Lizzie said I was to stay in bed today. Mrs O'Hanlon's coming up later with me dinner.'

Alice caught her breath and immediately thought the worst. A bad cough. Oh, God, not consumption, she prayed. 'Isn't Lizzie coming home at dinner time?'

'No, she's meeting her Jack.'

Alice sighed. 'Well, when she gets in, will you tell her I'm coming home. Tomorrow. Tell her there's nothing wrong. I'll explain it all tomorrow.'

Down the wire she could hear Mary coughing and spluttering until she finally got over the spasm.

'Mary, don't you get out of that bed again. If the phone rings, ignore it!'

As she replaced the receiver she bit her lip. Maybe it was just as well that she was going home. She hadn't liked the sound of that cough at all.

She packed her belongings and gave Mrs Winters a message for Charlie, should he come calling for her.

'I'm sorry to see you go, Alice,' Mrs Winters said as they waited for the taxi, 'and leave such a good career, but it's your business. It's your life.'

On impulse Alice hugged her briefly. 'Thank you for everything.'

That evening, when the train finally arrived at Lime Street Station, Lizzie and Jack were waiting at the barrier. Lizzie looked worried.

'Alice! What's wrong?'

'Nothing.'

Jack took her case. 'Is this all?'

'The rest is being sent on. Come on, we'll get a taxi.'

'We'll get the tram and like it,' Lizzie said firmly and Jack led them across the road to wait at the tram stop.

'Is Mary any better today? I've been worried sick about her since yesterday.'

'I had the doctor out to her and it's just a chest cold. He left some linctus – which is murder to get down her – but she's better today. She can stay off school the rest of the week.'

'Oh, thank God. I had visions of, well . . .'

'She hasn't got *consumption*.' Lizzie whispered the word for it carried a social stigma and there were quite a few people waiting in the queue.

'Where were you yesterday dinner time anyway?' Alice queried once they had settled themselves on the tram for the short journey.

'I met Jack. I'll tell you when we get home.' Lizzie looked over her shoulder and smiled at Jack who was standing on the platform chatting to the conductor. He knew a lot of them and the drivers too.

They got off at Kirkdale Road and walked the short distance to Media Street.

'Our Agnes will have given them their tea and cleared up by now,' Lizzie stated as they knocked on the front door.

Jimmy opened it, scrubbed clean and in his Sunday clothes.

'Where are you going, meladdo, all done up like a dog's dinner?' Lizzie demanded.

'I'm going to Frankie's, then we're going to the Astoria.'

'Well, don't you be late in and don't go getting into trouble. I don't like that Frankie Kennedy, he's a bad influence on you.'

Eddy and Mary were sitting at the kitchen table, with Georgie stretched out in front of the fire, his fur sleek, purring softly. Eddy was engrossed in a book and Mary was learning, by rote from an atlas, the capital cities of the countries of the Empire. It surprised Alice to see them so quiet and industrious.

'Did you bribe them or threaten to murder them?' she asked.

'Jack had a long talk with them all about what to do with their lives and how if you worked hard at school, you'd get a good job and therefore have a better life.' Lizzie smiled again at Jack. He took a real interest in all of them and could explain and coax far better than she could. He should have been a teacher, she'd told him, he had infinite patience and yet that air of authority needed to keep a class of unruly hooligans in order. He'd replied that there just hadn't been the money for anything like that and besides, he'd fought in the Great War and needed to earn a living when he left the army.

Lizzie made a pot of tea and beckoned Alice into the parlour. Jack followed.

'All right, our Alice, what's up? Why have you come home?'

'Because I'm fed up with London. It's just bed to work. It's not what I expected. I've no real friends and everyone I care about is up here.'

Lizzie looked appalled. 'You mean you've given up your career? You've given up singing?'

'No. I'm going to sing up here, in the north. Victor will find me work. There are plenty of good theatres here, better than some down there.'

Lizzie digested this in silence. Maybe it was just as well. 'Will you live here?'

'No, there's no room. I'm going to ask Charlie Williamson to find me a house, on the Wirral or near Chester. I thought about it on the train.'

'Oh,' was all Lizzie said.

'You don't sound very interested.'

'I am, it's just that, well, I've been dying to tell you *my* news. Jack and me are getting married after Christmas, that's where we were yesterday, buying the ring.' Lizzie stretched out her left hand, on the third finger of which was a small diamond solitaire.

All Alice's irritability left her and she jumped up and hugged Lizzie. 'Oh, Lizzie! Lizzie! I'm so happy for you! And you, Jack! Oh, bend down, I can't reach up to give you a kiss!'

Laughingly Jack obliged and Alice congratulated them again.

'You'll be going to live up the road then?' she asked when they'd settled themselves down again.

'Yes. Jack's mam wasn't too sure at first, but now we get on just fine.'

Alice wondered at this. Mam had always said two women in one kitchen didn't go. Not for very long, anyway.

'Our Agnes is nearly seventeen and the kids are all much better behaved now and I'm just down the road, if they need me.'

'Have you set an actual date yet?'

'Saturday, the first of February, at St Anthony's. Jack's got to get a dispensation from Father Godfrey because it's not his parish.'

'Will Father Mulcahey marry you?'

'No. He's retiring. It's a Father Rimmer. You will be my bridesmaid, Alice?'

'Of course,' she answered, but she suddenly and inexplicably felt sad.

* * *

The following day she phoned Charlie and made arrangements to see him at the weekend. In the meantime, he said he would make enquiries with estate agents.

They all had their evening meal together. Jack was on duty but he'd be calling in later, Lizzie said.

Alice had been thinking about things. She'd mulled the idea over and over in her head all day.

'Lizzie, I've been thinking.'

'What about?' Lizzie asked, pouring the gravy over Jimmy's meal. If he did it himself there wouldn't be enough to go round and she'd have to make more. He had an appetite like a horse.

'Well, you're getting married and going to live with Mrs Phillips.' She thought she saw Agnes raise her eyes to the ceiling and then pull a face, but she wasn't sure. 'This house is only rented so I'm going to buy a house. I've saved every penny since I went to London.'

'You! Buy a house? God Almighty, Alice!'

'What's wrong with that?'

'Nothing, it's just that, well, people like us don't *buy* houses.'

'People like us have come up in the world.'

'You might have, Alice, but I'll be happy enough with Jack in a rented house. I don't want anything grand.'

Alice ignored the note of censure in her sister's voice.

'It won't be "grand". I'm not thinking of a flaming palace like Hannah Harvey lives in, but there will be more rooms than this house so what I was thinking was that you and Jack can live here and the rest of you can come and live with me, in a nice house in the country.'

There was total silence as they all looked at her across the kitchen table. A silence filled with shock. It was Jimmy who broke it.

'In the country! I don't want to be stuck in the country, there's nothing to do! Frankie Kennedy said they went to Ireland once to a place in the country and it was awful.

There was nothing to do except go to church. That was the big event of the day.'

'And how am I going to get to work? I'll never see any of my friends!' Agnes was equally indignant.

'We'd have miles and miles to go to school,' Eddy complained.

'And you won't be there all the time, Alice,' Mary added.

Alice had been unprepared for this wall of opposition and complaint. She'd been sure they would all jump at the chance.

'But it'll be much better for you. Away from all the muck and the fog and the germs. Clean fresh air, good country food.'

Jimmy was openly mutinous. 'Well, I'm not going, Alice.'

'And neither am I,' Agnes stated flatly. 'We've been happy here, Alice, and besides, Mam . . . well, Mam died here. It would be like . . . sort of like leaving her on her own.'

Alice got up. 'Oh, suit yourselves! I was only thinking of you! This isn't exactly what you'd call a world away from Scottie Road, is it?' She stormed out and ran up the stairs to the bedroom she was sharing with Lizzie. The one Mam had shared with Lizzie.

She sat down on the bed. Oh, they were so ungrateful! They all had short memories. It was to put food in their mouths that she'd walked the streets of this city, singing. And since she'd left Liverpool she'd worked so hard, saved when she could have easily spent all her money on clothes and jewels or running around London nightclubs. All she'd wanted to do was give them a better, healthier life. Lizzie obviously wouldn't leave, she'd be happy here, but the others could have so much more, if they wanted it.

She looked across the room and caught sight of herself in the mirror on the wall. She wasn't a girl any longer, she was a woman, but had she become too grand for them? Were her expectations of them too high? And what was that Agnes had said? It would be like leaving Mam on her own. It was ridiculous but she too seemed to feel her mother's presence in the room. She dropped her eyes, afraid that over her shoulder in the mirror she would see Nelly's face. She'd changed, but surely for the better. But was she now too sophisticated for them? Had she grown too far away from them and their simple expectations of life? She suddenly remembered how she'd always sworn that whatever she did, however far she rose in her profession, she would still be the same inside. But she wasn't. She looked up and across at the mirror. A woman stared back. An attractive woman with large brown eyes and softly waving tawny-coloured hair. What had happened to little Alice O'Connor from Benledi Street? Had that girl gone altogether? Had she climbed so high that she'd grown too far away from her family and her humble roots, of which she'd always been so proud?

When Lizzie came into the room, there were tears on Alice's cheeks.

Lizzie took her hand. 'I know you meant well and I told them that, but they're city kids, we all are. You'll probably enjoy it, I suppose it will be a sort of escape for you, but they'd hate it, Alice.'

'I know, Lizzie, and I'm sorry. I seem to have lost sight of what I really want, what I really am.' She pressed a hand to her heart. 'Here. Go and tell them I'm sorry and that I'm not upset or annoyed with them.'

'But you're still going to go ahead with the house? You won't stay here?'

Alice shook her head. 'No, I'll be in and out like a fiddler's elbow. I'll just disrupt things, and besides . . .'

'What?'

'I can feel Mam here, Lizzie, and I . . . I don't think she approves of me any longer.'

329

Lizzie was scornful. 'Oh, that's just plain daft, Alice! Mam would never, ever haunt you, if that's what you're trying to say. She loved us, she couldn't have been a better mother, not married to the likes of Da and taking all those beatings. For God's sake, Alice, don't be so flaming morbid!'

Alice managed a smile. 'You were always the one with plain common sense, Lizzie.'

'And wouldn't I need it with a sister like you!' The words were accompanied by a smile and a laugh.

Chapter Twenty-Seven

Christmas was a very busy time for Alice. She was booked to appear for a week in Manchester, then a week in Leeds and then, after the holidays, a week at the Empire.

She seemed to find herself most of the time on trains and in taxis, and some of the digs left much to be desired. Sometimes Charlie drove her to the theatre. He had been very good about helping her to find a new home, and they'd looked at houses near Chester and on the Wirral. She had almost made up her mind about a picture post-card cottage with a thatched roof, low beamed ceilings and a lovely front garden in Saltney Ferry, near Chester. It certainly wasn't a palace but there was plenty of room should any of her brothers and sisters decide to change their minds, or come to stay for a bit of a break.

Charlie had arranged for a man from the village to do the garden and any odd jobs, and his wife would come in and clean while Alice was away. She'd also see that there was plenty of food in the pantry for Alice's return.

Lizzie and Jack had gone to see the cottage and after admiring everything, tried again to point out the disadvantages of Alice buying it, not least of which was the fact that she would be running two households.

'You'll need furniture and carpets and curtains and all the other things like pots and pans and sheets and towels, like when we moved to Media Street, and you know how much all that cost.'

Alice knew she had a point, but she was determined to get away from the small rows of closely packed terraced house and dank, dirty courts. At least her new home had a bathroom, for one of the bedrooms had been converted. A proper bathroom was something the house in Media Street didn't have. But she did go home for Christmas itself, loaded down with presents and food, the cottage still being only partly furnished.

She, Lizzie and Agnes sat up late on Christmas Eve, reminiscing about other, less happier, Christmases.

'Oh, we're just making ourselves miserable, let's talk about something else,' Alice said after Lizzie had related the events of the Christmas after Alice had gone to America.

'The wedding plans?' Agnes suggested.

'Yes, it's not too far away now, Lizzie,' Alice replied and they all talked on into the early hours of Christmas morning, all hoping the new decade would prove to be better than the last.

Two days after New Year, Alice opened at the Empire. Her 'spot' was for the last half-hour of the show which gave her plenty of time to dress.

Miss Fairchild was delighted to see her back. 'I'm so glad you decided to come home,' she beamed as she buttoned up Alice's dress.

'London seemed to have lost its excitement, its glamour for me. It's just too big. I used to do the show, perhaps have supper with Victor, then go back to Bloomsbury. In the mornings or sometimes in the afternoon, if there wasn't a matinée, I'd rehearse.'

'Not much of a life.'

'No.'

As Miss Fairchild brushed Alice's hair and then covered it with one of the new fashionable, silver mesh, close-fitting caps, there was a knock on the dressing-room door.

'It's not time yet. We've fifteen minutes,' Miss Fairchild called out.

'I know. But there's someone here to see Miss O'Connor,' Alf shouted back from the corridor outside.

Alice sighed. 'Charlie again.'

'Don't you want to see him?'

'He's been so good to me, so helpful, that I just can't send him away.'

'Of course you can. It's just before your performance. We could say you've a bad headache, or an upset stomach caused by nerves.'

'No. Let him in.'

Miss Fairchild shouted Alice's instructions and the door opened.

Alice gave a cry of delight, her heart leapt and she jumped up from the stool in front of the dressing table and its mirror surrounded with lights. 'David! David! I never expected to see you!' Her eyes were shining with happiness.

'Well, I've got a week's leave and plenty of studying to do but I thought, to hell with it.'

Charlie appeared behind him. 'You mean I twisted your arm until you said "Oh, to hell with it!" '

'You look wonderful, Alice. You seem different, so . . . sophisticated now.'

She smiled wryly.

'What made you come back?' he asked.

'Oh, I was homesick and fed up with London.'

'The homesickness I can understand, but why throw away your career?'

'I haven't. I've just moved it up north. They'll be having the stage musicals at theatres here soon. It's not the other side of the moon.'

'Supper again?' Charlie asked and she nodded, delightedly.

Miss Fairchild interrupted. 'I'm going to have to ask

you two gentlemen to leave now, we've only got five minutes.'

They left but when Alice went on stage her heart too was singing. Oh, he was still the same. He hadn't changed one bit. She'd made the right decision to come back, to buy a house in Saltney Ferry. His visit was proof of it. He'd come to see her, even though he was still studying so hard. She'd dismissed Charlie's remark about twisting David's arm from her mind. She put everything into her performance, for she was singing for him and in some songs directly to him. She couldn't see either of them, but when she sang 'Always' her voice was full of emotion.

This time supper was in a small but very smart restaurant in Bold Street. 'I thought it might be a bit quieter than the Adelphi,' Charlie said. 'It's got a secluded, exclusive atmosphere.'

All through the meal Alice's eyes never left David's face and she looked as though someone had switched on a light inside her.

Charlie and David did most of the talking, keeping up a laughing banter, but Alice felt uncomfortable with the thought that on Charlie's part some of the remarks might be serious. She and David didn't have a minute alone together, Charlie saw to that, she thought with some annoyance, except when he excused himself for five minutes. 'Call of nature, I'm afraid,' he'd whispered. It wasn't strictly true, but it would give David time to tell Alice about his plans.

'Have you settled into your new home now, Alice?' David asked, as Charlie left.

'Well, not really, I've been so busy, but by February I should have some time to get everything sorted out properly. Things tend to go a bit flat in February and March, as people don't want to leave their firesides.'

'I know it's very belated, but I was sorry to hear about your mother.'

She nodded. 'I still miss her.'

A silence hung between them.

'Alice—'

'I'm—' They both spoke at once.

'You tell me what you were going to say,' she urged.

He fiddled with his wine glass. 'Company policy has changed. Bookings tail off in January and February. The weather most of the time is atrocious and fewer people make the Atlantic crossing, so they can manage with just the *Berengaria* and the *Mauretania*, so we're off cruising again. To the islands of the West Indies.'

Her heart dropped like a lump of lead and she felt sick with disappointment. He was going away again for two months.

'We'll be calling at Charleston again. I had a wonderful time there, thanks to you, Alice, and Mr O'Farrell.'

She thought his tone changed when he spoke of Mike.

'Alice, you know that the sea is my life,' he said earnestly.

She gazed across the table at him. 'I know. Just like singing is mine. Not totally my life though.'

He nodded but didn't seem able to respond.

'So?' Alice questioned when the silence became unbearable. 'You were talking about your life.'

'I . . . well, I was just, er, remarking on what the sea meant to me.' He turned as he saw his brother re-enter the room.

Charlie returned to the table. At least, he thought, she didn't seem too upset at David's news.

'Yes.' She didn't want to think about it now so she changed the subject. 'My sister's getting married on the first of February.'

'Lizzie?' Charlie asked with interest.

She nodded. 'She's marrying her policeman, they'll live with his mother.'

335

David smiled at her. 'So, you'll be a bridesmaid then.'

'Yes, me and Agnes and Mary. The lads are complaining already about the suits and stiff collars they'll have to wear. She doesn't want a great fuss, but she's waited a long time for her happiness and I think she does deserve a grand do.'

'You don't look very pleased about it, Alice,' Charlie remarked.

'It's just that I don't want to upstage Lizzie. I don't want to spoil her day. So many people know me now, I don't want them to turn up just to see me.'

David refilled her glass. 'That's very considerate and kind of you, Alice. And who is the best man?'

'I don't know, they haven't said. Probably one of Jack's mates from work.' She smiled at him. 'Will you come and see me again before your leave is up?'

He looked uncomfortable, even a little awkward, Alice thought.

'I'll try, but there's so much to do and I do have some prior engagements.'

She was disappointed, wondering what the 'prior engagements' were.

'But you'll have Charlie to squire you around all the northern cities.'

'If she'll let me, that is.' Charlie sounded petulant.

David laughed. 'You know I rely on you to tell me how Alice's career is going.'

Charlie said nothing and Alice sensed a certain coolness between them.

'I'll go for the car,' Charlie said. They'd borrowed Mr Williamson's Minerva for the evening as there were only two seats in Charlie's Jowett sports car.

Two days later Alice went back to Media Street, at Lizzie's request.

'Honestly, Alice, it's bad enough trying to organise this

336

wedding without having my chief bridesmaid always missing.'

'Lizzie, you know what it's been like for me.'

'Oh, I'm not going to argue, Alice. Now about your dress and headdress.'

'Haven't you sorted that out yet? What would you like me to wear? It's *your* day, Lizzie, not mine or Agnes's or Mary's. We all take second place to you.'

'I was going to have you in that pretty shade of green, *eau de nil*, until Jack's mam and Mary O'Hanlon had a fit and said it was unlucky.'

'That's just superstitious nonsense.'

'Well, I'm not taking any chances. I thought pink. A deep pink or maybe magenta. That would brighten up a grey February day.'

It was not one of Alice's favourite colours but she said nothing.

'With circlets of pink and white wax flowers. Maggie Higgins sells them at her Gowns by Margo.'

Even worse, Alice thought, but then checked herself. Lizzie just had different taste, she liked different things, that was all. If everyone had the same taste, life would be very boring.

'And what about your dress, have you got it yet?'

Lizzie blushed. 'Yes. I got that and the veil and head-dress from Maggie's too.'

'From Gowns by Margo?'

Lizzie nodded. 'I can never think of her as anything other than Maggie Higgins from Silvester Street. But she has a good price range and she designs them all herself. And she's honest. I know if I chose a dress that cost pots of money but made me look like a May horse, she'd tell me.'

'She would too, that one. She always had a tongue so sharp it's a wonder she's not cut herself with it!'

'It's white taffeta, cut very plain with just a bit of lace

set into the bodice and two tiny bows of blue ribbon at the wrist. That's her trademark. I'm having a headband, or "bandeaux" as she calls it, with just a few small white wax roses at the front and a long veil.'

'It sounds gorgeous, Lizzie, and you'll look like a dream.' Alice meant what she said. Sometimes, she reflected, things turned out for the best. If Tommy Mac had survived there would have been no dress from Gowns by Margo.

'I wish I could get the same enthusiasm out of our Jimmy and Eddy. All they do is moan and complain, saying their mates will skit them.'

'Oh, take no notice, Lizzie. All men hate weddings and dressing up.'

'Jack has ordered carriages. Won't that be something?'

'Is he wearing his uniform?'

'Yes, so I suppose he'll at least be warmer than me. Maggie advised me to wear a flannel petticoat underneath. She said it won't show.'

'Who's going to give you away?'

Lizzie's mouth was set in a hard line. 'Well, it certainly won't be Da, thank God. No, Mr O'Hanlon is giving me away. He's going to borrow a suit from his brother.'

'I hope he behaves, Lizzie. He's almost as bad as Da with a few drinks down him. He'd cause an argument in an empty house!'

'Mary's threatened him. She told me she said if he puts one foot wrong, he'll be carted off to Rose Hill 'cos half the police force will be there as guests. They won't, but he's not to know that.'

Alice laughed. 'And who's the best man?'

'I don't know yet.'

'God, Lizzie, it's only four weeks away! Surely he can find one of his mates?'

'Oh, it will all be sorted out, Alice,' Lizzie said, refusing to meet her sister's eyes. Jack had kept in touch with Mike

O'Farrell and had written asking if it was at all possible, if Mike was over in Dublin buying a house, would he stand for him? He didn't want Mike to come especially, just if he was in this part of the world. If he wasn't, then Tom Burns, his sergeant, would be his best man.

Jack and Lizzie had discussed it often, before Jack finally wrote to Mike.

'It's a way of bringing them together, Lizzie,' he'd argued.

'So was Mam's death and his ma's death. I would have thought that with all the sadness and shock it would have brought them closer, but it didn't.'

'Everyone was upset, Lizzie. No one was thinking about love and happiness.'

'But now because we're getting married you think she'll be more receptive?'

'You never know, they did part friends.'

'Our Alice has a temper, Jack, and she can be so contrary at times. I don't think she'll take kindly to our meddling.'

'Let's just wait and see,' he'd replied and so the letter had been written. So far there had been no reply from Mike, and Lizzie knew they were running out of time.

A telegram arrived the following week in the form of a cable from the *Mauretania*.

'DELIGHTED TO OBLIGE. WAS ON MY WAY HOME ANYWAY. MIKE.'

'We're going to have to tell her,' Lizzie said.

'I know.'

Lizzie put her arms round him – she barely came up to his chest. 'You're matchmaking, Jack Phillips!'

He grinned down at her. 'So? He loves her and I thought that if they got together, especially for a wedding . . .'

'Oh, I hope she doesn't realise what you're up to and throw a tantrum and refuse to be chief bridesmaid.'

'She won't, and anyway, even if she does, there's Agnes and Mary.' Like Alice, Jack didn't want Lizzie's day over-shadowed by her sister's fame.

'When is the *Mauretania* due in?'

'I don't know but I'll find out. He may want to go to Dublin for a few days first, take the overnight ferry on the same day the *Maurie* docks, which might be a better plan all round.'

Mike had been surprised and touched when Jack's letter had arrived. He had been in the process of packing up. He'd sold his business for a fat profit and also the house and most of its contents. He had no intention of buying a house the size of this one, so what furniture he'd decided to keep would be shipped over later. He'd finalised the details, by letter, with a solicitor in Dublin and was now the owner of a detached, Victorian villa in Dunlaoghaire whose two long piers reached out like arms to encircle the harbour where the mail boat arrived and departed each day.

Both Kitty and Dee had urged him to move into their mother's house, which was standing empty and would be nearer for visiting, but he'd refused. It was his mother's house. He wanted somewhere new, outside the city, but still in County Dublin and near enough for a drive into town.

He read Jack's letter again. Of course Alice would be a bridesmaid. How would he cope with that? He'd heard from Jack that she'd come home but that she still didn't see much of Williamson. Charlie, yes, but the other one seemed to be away all the time. Alice had told them he'd be sailing around the warm waters of the West Indies for two months. Mike had taken hope from that piece of information. Maybe there was still a chance, especially at a wedding. 'You're a crafty sod, Jack Phillips, that you are,' he'd said to himself, smiling.

'I can't see much to smile about,' Alexander had remarked acidly. He'd stayed on to supervise the packing. The rest of the staff had gone, with tears and a good bonus in their pay packets.

Alexander had impeccable, glowing references and had been offered three places already. Mike had given him a gold hunter watch and chain with a tiger's eye fob, plus a gold cigarette case, inscribed, and six months' wages. Alexander had been more than just a butler, and leaving him was like leaving a friend.

Jack met Mike at the landing stage on a bitterly cold Tuesday morning. They'd had to anchor in the Sloyne until a large enough place on the landing stage had become available. The *Berengaria* had saluted her sister ship as she'd passed, en route to New York, with the three traditional blasts on her steam whistle. 'And God be with the lot of you,' Mike had muttered.

He shook Jack's hand warmly. 'Jesus, Mary and Joseph, I hope it's not going to be like this on Saturday.'

'A bad crossing, was it?'

Mike hailed a taxi. 'It was bloody desperate. We went through three blizzards in a day. I think there were only half a dozen of us in the dining room each day, but never mind all that, how are you in yourself, Jack?'

'Fine. Everything is under control. What about you?'

'Great altogether, although those two rossies beyond in Dublin are not too happy that I won't live on their doorsteps. Kitty is moving into the old house, she's got six kids. Dee had more sense, she's only got three. I think she puts bromide in Fergal's tea and I'll bet she doesn't own up to that in confession,' Mike laughed. 'How's Alice?'

'She's fine. She's promised Lizzie she'll sing. Do a solo piece, probably "Ave Maria".'

'When's she coming up to Liverpool?' He sounded non-

341

chalant, or hoped he did. But he was longing to see her. To laugh and smile with her, to take her hand, to kiss her cheek – as a friend would in greeting, except that he wanted to kiss her lips and hold her like a lover.

'She's supposed to be coming home on Wednesday night,' Jack informed him.

'Tomorrow.' He would see her again tomorrow. He felt his pulse quicken. Maybe at a wedding she might just soften towards him. Maybe.

Alice arrived home on Wednesday night, just after the evening meal had been cleared away. She wore a dark blue velour coat with a thick silver fox fur collar which was turned up round her ears, while her navy hat was pulled well down.

'You picked a wonderful time of year to get married, Lizzie, it's freezing! We'll all catch our deaths! Is it tomorrow we've to go to Maggie Higgins's for the final fitting?'

Lizzie nodded.

'Where's Jack tonight, on duty?'

'No, it's been a rest day today.'

'I wish I had rest days.'

'I thought you had plenty of time to yourself. I thought you enjoyed the peace of the country.'

'I do, it's just that I'm never there much. I seem to spend my life on trains.'

'You travel first class.'

'It's still a train though, isn't it?'

Lizzie took a deep breath. She'd have to tell her soon, otherwise Jack would land on the doorstep with his best man in tow. 'Alice, I've got to tell you something.' Lizzie looked down to hide her excitement and plucked at the edges of her cuffs, as though removing bits of imaginary fluff.

'Holy Mother of God. You're not expecting, are you?' Alice cried.

'No, I'm not! Would I have a white dress and veil and a Nuptial Mass if I was? It . . . it's about Jack's best man.'

'What about him? I thought you'd sorted all that out. Who has he asked?'

Lizzie grinned. 'It's Mike O'Farrell. He's sold up and bought a house in Ireland. They . . . they should be here any minute now.'

Alice jumped up. 'Mike? Mike has come over to be best man?'

Lizzie nodded. 'They've kept in touch since Mam died.'

Alice wasn't sure how she felt. Glad, sorry, surprised. 'Why didn't you tell me, Lizzie?'

'Because . . . well, I wanted it to be a surprise.'

Alice pressed her hands to her cheeks. 'Well, it's certainly a surprise.'

'And we didn't know for certain that he could make it until three days ago. He sent a cable from the ship.'

Before Alice could reply she heard the front door open and then voices, Jack's and the one with the gentle lilt that she remembered so well, and then he was there in the room beside her and she smiled at him. A warm, genuine smile.

'They've told you, I see,' he laughed.

Alice stretched out her hands in greeting. 'About two minutes ago.'

Mike took them in his. 'You get lovelier with time, Alice. I was trying to work out how old you are now.'

'That's not very gallant of you, is it? At least you're honest. I'm twenty-two.'

'Ah, then you're still only a babe in arms,' he joked, still holding her hands. He fought down the urge to take her in his arms and kiss her.

'And you're still full of the blarney, Mike, but it's good to see you. I'm still a bit dazed, they could have told me sooner but it was *supposed* to be a surprise.'

'They're a pair of eejits – made for each other!' he

laughed, searching her face for something, some sign of affection, but although she was still smiling at him there was no special light, no special glow of love in her brown eyes.

Lizzie and Jack exchanged glances and both men sat down.

'Lizzie tells me you've bought a house in Dublin. That you sold up.'

'I did, so. Ah, what was the point of it all, Alice? I'd never particularly liked that Charleston house, however magnificent it was. It was *his* and when he died it was convenient for me to stay on. But then I decided to come home. I've got a house in County Dublin, not the city itself. It's out at Dunlaoghaire, by the sea.'

'What will you do?' Alice asked.

They'd slipped easily back into their old ways. Just like a couple, Lizzie thought, watching them closely.

'You mean apart from being persecuted by my sisters? Oh, there's so much to do and see. It's a changed city in many ways. The beautiful Georgian buildings may have been built by Englishmen, but it's *our* city now. There are museums, libraries, art galleries and statues by the dozen. I can stand all day on the quays. There's always someone who'll talk to you, tell you their life history if you've the time and inclination to listen. And all Irishmen like a good chat about the horses. I heard two of them on the Ha'penny Bridge last time I was home. "Did you get anything on that horse you had in Leopardstown?" says one. "Ah, no, aren't they still out looking for the contrary animal with flash lamps!" It was great altogether,' he laughed. Then he became serious. 'Maybe I'll set up some sort of trust, for the poor, particularly kids, but not one administered by the clergy, there are too many penalty clauses attached. If you've not behaved, missed Mass, been a troublemaker, then there's nothing down for you.'

'Surely not.' Alice was frowning.

'It happened in nineteen eleven in the lock-outs. If you were in Larkin's union, then you starved. The union ran out of money and support from the Liverpool branch. There was no strike pay. But I'd rather trust the union with my money than the clergy, any day.'

The look that passed between Mike and Alice was one of understanding. Of bitter memories recalled and shared.

'So, you see, I'll barely have a minute to myself.'

'You'll not stand for election as a TD for Dail Eireann?' Jack asked.

'No, Jack, I've no interest in politics. I've no strong views either way about the Taoiseach's policies.'

Lizzie suggested that the men went into the parlour and she'd bring them some tea; she and Alice had some details to discuss.

'Are you pleased to see him, Alice?' Lizzie asked when she returned to the kitchen.

'Yes, I am, but I . . . I feel guilty, Lizzie. He was so good to me and I just ran out on him.'

'Well, you're older and wiser now. He thinks a lot of you.'

'I know, he always made sure I was all right.' She misconstrued Lizzie's words.

'Maybe a lot more than you think.'

'No, Lizzie, he's always been a friend, a very good and generous friend.'

Lizzie stood up. 'The way David and Charlie Williamson are?'

'No. Charlie, maybe. But David . . .' Alice's expression softened.

'Oh, for God's sake, Alice, grow up! Face it. You never see him – a few meetings here and there. You don't even know him very well. He's all part of your dream, an impossible dream. Forget him!'

Alice also got to her feet, surprised and annoyed by

345

Lizzie's vehemence. 'Well, all the rest of the dream has come true, Lizzie, hasn't it?'

'Yes, and you're still not happy, are you? When the dream becomes reality it's not a dream any more; it dies, Alice. Oh, I'm going to say good night to Jack, I'm worn out.'

Alice sat for a long time after Lizzie had gone to bed. She could hear the two men talking in the parlour but she couldn't make out the words, nor did she want to. Lizzie was trying to make her face the reality about David and most of what her sister had said was true. She seldom saw him, but that didn't mean she didn't love him or that he didn't care for her. If they were married she would still see little of him; it was something she'd have to accept – gracefully. Then she remembered Victor's words about the women of middle-class families. She sighed heavily. She was no longer an ignorant, dirty, scruffy waif, but even if she married David, she'd never be middle-class, she'd always be a working-class girl from Benledi Street.

Chapter Twenty-Eight

Saturday dawned cold but clear. There had been a heavy frost overnight and all the windowpanes were covered by delicate traceries of ice that looked like lacework. Alice had the boys light fires in all the rooms, even the bedrooms.

'At least we'll be warm when we leave the house,' she commented. 'And, thank God, it's not snowing, raining or blowing a force-ten gale,' she added as she helped Lizzie with her veil and bandeaux.

'How is Agnes managing?' Lizzie asked.

'Fine. She's got those two hooligans well under control and our Mary's no trouble. Our Jimmy was complaining about his collar being too stiff and too tight, but she told him he was lucky you didn't have him in top hat and tails, that you'd seriously thought about it. You should have seen the look on his face! All three of them are moaning about not being able to have any breakfast.'

'Well, I'm not having everyone in church nudging each other and wondering why they're not going to Communion.'

'Our Agnes told them that too. She said they should be thankful you're so considerate. The wedding could have been at eleven o'clock or even later instead of at ten and they'd all be famished and near to fainting by then. Mind you, I'm a bit hungry myself.'

'Holy Mother, I couldn't eat a thing, I'm so nervous!'

347

Alice was already dressed in the magenta taffeta dress that had a sash round the hips, which ended in a large stiff bow. The circlet of wax flowers was already fixed firmly onto her head. She thought she looked awful but at least people wouldn't spend too much time gaping at her. Until she sang, that was. She'd decided on Schubert's arrangement of 'Ave Maria'. She stood back to admire her handiwork and smiled. 'Oh, Lizzie, you look a dream! Mam would have loved to see you.'

'She can, Alice. I believe she *can*.'

Alice nodded. Lizzie had always been plain, but in her wedding finery, her face lit up with love and excitement, she was transformed. Alice helped her downstairs.

Mr O'Hanlon stood awkwardly in front of the fire in the kitchen. He knew Mary would make his life a misery if he spoiled Lizzie's day and made a show of her before the entire congregation and the fine gentleman from America. Especially as she'd be dressed up to the nines for once in her life, mainly in clothes borrowed from neighbours. He'd made a show of her for most of their married life, she'd said acidly, but today was different. Let no one have any complaint about Ignatius – known to all as Iggy – O'Hanlon's behaviour.

The two boys looked bored already, Alice noticed.

'Eddy, go out into the scullery and get the flowers. Did they send pins for the buttonholes?' she asked her sister.

Agnes nodded. She was worn out already from trying to keep her siblings under control and clean. Like Alice, she wasn't very impressed with her dress.

'And don't you dare open your mouth about these awful frocks, Agnes, or I'll kill you! It's *her* day.'

Agnes nodded and fervently hoped that Tommy Healy from further down the street wouldn't come to the same conclusion she and Alice had reached.

Eddie brought in the flowers and placed them on the table.

'Now go and stand at the front door and let us know when the carriages arrive.' Alice was pinning on Mr O'Hanlon's buttonhole.

'They left Jack's house ages ago so they should be here soon,' Agnes informed them.

She was right, for no sooner had Eddy got to the door than he came pounding back down the hall. 'They're here! They're here!'

Jimmy muttered something about what his mates would think of them in their daft outfits, a sentiment fully agreed with by Iggy O'Hanlon who ushered him, Eddy, Mary, Agnes and Alice to the door.

'It's going ter be a birrof a crush,' he remarked.

'Not if everyone keeps still.' Alice's gaze was fixed firmly on her brothers.

Jimmy mumbled something under his breath and Eddy looked sullen as they climbed in. Half the street had come out to see Lizzie, and the women stood in groups, arms folded, chatting, admiring or criticising, while their children ran up and down, shouting and yelling with the excitement of the occasion.

Lizzie had a bit of trouble with her long veil but was finally installed. She beamed with happiness at her neighbours, and didn't feel the least bit cold. What she did feel was nervous. Very nervous.

The aisle of St Anthony's had never looked so long, she thought as she tucked her arm into Iggy O'Hanlon's while Alice and Agnes arranged the train of her dress and the veil. The two boys, to their great relief, had been sent on up to the front pews where Mary, Ethel and Jinny (all in borrowed finery) had pride of place.

The church was full. There were even people standing at the back and up the side aisles. It wasn't often there was a wedding of such grand proportions. Three bridesmaids, two open carriages of the type you saw royalty using, and the flowers in the church must have cost a fortune. They'd also heard that the best man had come all the way from America. Imagine that. And the bride's sister was Alice O'Connor, a big star in the theatres in London. The information was whispered around the church.

The organ burst into life and Alice kept her eyes down, not looking left or right. She wanted people to look at Lizzie, not her.

Mike looked very handsome in morning dress – pinstriped trousers, white shirt, pale grey tie and black jacket without tails. Jack, too, looked fine, resplendent in his dress uniform, the buttons and badges highly polished, his helmet placed on the seat of the pew.

Throughout the Mass, Alice tried to concentrate. Lizzie was happy, she was radiant with joy. But she herself felt strangely out of place although this was her church, she'd been baptised here, and these were her people. As she stepped out and walked to the altar rail, turning to face the congregation, she caught Mike's gaze. He smiled at her, a smile of encouragement and pride that reminded her of Maura O'Hare's soirée and the Cotillion Ball.

Her voice rose clearly and sweetly and the congregation was reverently hushed. There was not a single cough, sniff or shuffling of feet.

Mike bent his head and closed his eyes, giving the appearance of being deep in prayer. In fact his heart was being torn in two. She looked so beautiful, despite the unfortunate dress, and it was so long since he'd heard her sing. He must have been mad to have come, but he'd been drawn inexorably, like a moth to the flame and he was burning up with desire and despair. He prayed to God, something he seldom did, to give him the strength to overcome his pride, or at least be able to hide the emotions that were tearing him apart. Surely, surely she must feel moved by the ceremony. Could she not see, or at least have some inkling of the love he felt for her?

Jack had pressed him to speak of his love. How could she know how he felt if he didn't tell her? he'd reasoned. But the demon pride still wouldn't allow him to expose his feelings to her. Besides, what if by some miracle she agreed and they got married, what about her career? He couldn't take that away from her. It was what drove her on, it was what had made her pull herself up from the gutter to become the star she was born to be.

But as the last silvery notes died in the silent church, he was remembering what Jack had urged on him.

The rest of the day went well, the photographs, the meal laid on at the Stork Hotel and the happy couple duly dispatched for three days' honeymoon at the small but very select Cleveland Guest House in Southport.

Mike had ordered cabs to take the family and Mary, Ethel and Jinny home. After a day with only one glass of champagne that he thought tasted worse than lemonade, and Mary giving him looks like daggers that would kill you stone dead, Iggy O'Hanlon headed for the nearest pub.

'Just you remember your Vinny wants that suit back termorrer!' Mary called after him from the window of the cab.

'Well, at least he looked the gear an' behaved 'imself,' Ethel remarked.

'Aye, 'e can stop out all night now for all I care.' Mary leaned back against the leather seat. 'God, but I'll be glad to get these shoes offen me. They're our Maggie's an' they're too flamin' small!'

'Lizzie looked very well, I thought,' Mike said.

Alice wore her navy coat with the fur trim over her dress, for the winter afternoon was already fading and the temperature was dropping. 'She looked beautiful. Not like our old Lizzie at all.'

'Does it not make you think of other weddings?'

'What other weddings? Don't tell me our Agnes is going

351

to elope with that Tommy Healy. What bit of gossip have you heard that I haven't?' she laughed.

'Nothing, I swear to God.'

She looked up at him, her eyes questioning. 'Then what weddings?'

He managed a smile. 'Ah, take no notice of me, I have this terrible habit of rameishing on. I suppose it's back to work for you now?'

She nodded. 'Manchester, the opera house, although it's not opera I'll be performing. And what about you?'

'Oh, I'll get the ten o'clock boat to Dublin tomorrow. I've got so many things to do. I've hardly unpacked and I'll have those two sisters of mine in on top of me wanting to arrange things and organise me.' He tried to sound offhand. He was glad he hadn't taken Jack's advice. She had obviously not had a single thought all day about a wedding of her own, unless it was to David Williamson and that didn't bear thinking about.

March was wild and wet and Alice had begun to feel the strain of her hectic lifestyle, so she asked Victor to find her an understudy for her three days in Blackpool.

'I'm worn out, I feel awful and I know I'm not giving my best performances.'

He agreed. He reminded her that he'd warned her that touring was hell.

Things had settled down well in Media Street, she thought, staring out of her lounge window at the sodden fields beyond her garden fence, fields that were becoming dark and obscure as evening approached. Georgie, who had grown from a kitten into a sleek, well-fed cat, was stretched out in front of the fire. So far Lizzie hadn't had a row with her mother-in-law and Agnes seemed to be coping very well at home, far better than anyone had thought possible. Lizzie had told her that they'd had a couple of letters from Mike and when the weather got better he was going off to do a tour of the country – his country, most of which he'd never seen.

She felt miserable and lonely. Everyone seemed to have busy, interesting lives, except herself. The rain dripped persistently down the windows. What was it that Lizzie had said to her? 'When the dream becomes reality it dies.' Lately she'd begun to think there was a lot of truth in that statement.

Already it was nearly time for dinner, but she couldn't be bothered to cook something. She didn't feel hungry. She'd begun to wonder why she had bought this cottage in the middle of nowhere. She knew no one and she hardly ever saw the Laidlaws, the couple Charlie had hired as gardener and cleaner and who looked after Georgie when she was away. She didn't want to spend any more time alone. She'd ring Charlie.

At last someone answered the phone and went off to find him. As she waited she could hear laughter and music in the background. There was obviously something going on there too.

'Alice. How are you?' Charlie asked and she could tell from his voice that he'd been drinking.

'As miserable as sin. I was wondering if you could come down and see me, but obviously you've got company.'

'Well, there is a bit of a do going on but they won't miss me.'

'No. No, Charlie, I can tell you're enjoying yourself and it's a horrible night to have to drive so far and then back home again. I'm all right, really I am, just at a bit of a loose end.' She forced some cheerfulness into her voice.

'I'll come down tomorrow, early. We'll have the day together. Go for lunch and maybe a stroll around Chester, then get some dinner. How does that sound?'

'Great. I'll see you tomorrow then. Enjoy the rest of the evening.' She replaced the receiver before he had a chance to start apologising.

She looked at the clock on the mantelpiece. It was much too early to go to bed; she'd listen to the wireless then have an early night. She scooped up the cat and sat in an armchair and closed her eyes. Georgie settled himself and began to purr. It was a miserable night and she was just feeling sorry for herself. Depressed because she was tired. She'd be fine in the morning.

It was still wild and windy the following morning, but the rain had stopped, there were a few breaks in the cloud and the sun struggled to shine through. She dressed with care. A close-fitting knitted suit in pale beige under her new chocolate-brown coat. Her hat was beige, trimmed with brown satin ribbon, and as a last touch of elegance she wound a long cream silk scarf round her neck, letting the ends fall over her shoulders and down her back.

Charlie arrived at ten o'clock, looking none the worse for wear.

'Alice! As gorgeous as ever!' He kissed her on the cheek, feeling more confident than he'd felt for a long time. *She'd* phoned *him*; usually it was the other way round. She did look smashing and they were going to spend the whole day together.

They laughed and joked all the way to Chester and Alice felt so much better. The sun was shining now, the clouds had disappeared, but the wind was still strong and she had to hang on to her hat.

He parked the car outside the Grosvenor Hotel and ushered her inside, guiding her into the grill restaurant.

'Just to make up for my tardiness last night, we'll have champagne.'

'At lunchtime?'

'Why not? Some people have it for breakfast.'

She wrinkled her nose with distaste. 'I think I'd sooner have tea. What was going on anyway last night when I phoned?'

'Oh, Captain Walmsley and his family were over for dinner. He and Father have been friends for years, they went to school together. Mother and Mrs Walmsley are great friends too. They've got a son in the Royal Navy, he's away, but Cecelia, Eunice and Victoria were all there, and David, of course.'

Her eyes lit up. 'David's home?'

'Well, he'd have to be, wouldn't he? I mean, the dinner was for him and Cecelia.'

She stared at him and a sickening feeling washed over her. 'Why?'

'Their engagement, of course.'

The room began to rotate slowly. No! He couldn't do this to her! She loved him. She'd loved him for years, since the day he'd picked her up in his arms and carried her aboard the *Aquitania*. There was a rushing noise in her ears. 'I . . . I . . .'

Charlie thought she was going to faint, all the colour had drained from her face. 'Alice, you didn't realise?'

'How . . . how could I?' The room was still rotating and all sound seemed to be blocked out, all but the strange rushing noise.

'I thought he'd told you. It's been on the cards for years. She's the ideal wife for him. She's been used to having her father away so much. She'll cope admirably, she has her own interests and circle of friends. Her father is the captain of the *Samaria*, so he'll help David all he can with his career. At the rate he's going he could be one of the youngest masters in the entire line.'

'I . . . I . . . thought . . . he . . .' She couldn't go on, the words were choking her.

'He's fond of you, Alice, and he really does admire you tremendously because you've done so well. He's always saying he's your biggest fan.'

The tears were blinding her now and she hung her head. 'I thought he loved me.'

355

'Oh, Alice, I'm sorry, so sorry! But you've still got me. You know I worship you.' He reached across the table and tried to take her hand but she snatched it away.

'It was just a dream. A mad, impossible dream. And ... and everyone warned me.' She wasn't aware that she'd spoken the words aloud. 'I've been chasing a dream. All these years I've been fooling myself!'

'No, Alice. You've got the best part of the dream. Your career.'

She stared at him blankly. 'But ... but it was all for ... him. Don't you see, it was all for him.'

'He does admire you, Alice.'

Admire. Admire. Admire. The word beat inside her head and she felt so small, so humiliated, so ashamed. 'Because I came from the gutter? He picked me up, remember? I'm not good enough, that's the real reason. I came from the slums, my da's in jail and I put him there!'

She got up, looking around wildly and knocking a glass of champagne over but she didn't notice. 'I want to go home! I ... I ... can't stay here!' She ran from the dining room, unaware of the shocked and surprised looks of the other diners.

Charlie grabbed her bag, threw a five-pound note on the table, almost snatched her coat from the waiter who had approached, and ran after her.

By the time he reached the street she was already sitting in the car, huddled down in the seat, sobbing. He felt such a heel. He'd really thought she knew or had guessed, that it was himself she was really interested in.

'I want to go home,' she sobbed.

'Oh, Alice, darling, I'm so sorry. Please, sweetheart, put your coat on. You've had a terrible shock and it's freezing cold.' He tried to tuck it round her but she pulled away from him.

The commissionaire came over and asked if he needed

any assistance. Was the young lady ill? Charlie thanked him but refused the offer, thinking he'd better get out of here fast before they became the centre of an incident.

He swung the crank handle once and the engine turned over. He threw the handle into the back, leaped in beside Alice and put his foot down on the accelerator.

He heard her scream, then choke, and turned to look at her.

He was horrified. 'Oh, Christ Almighty!' he cried, slamming his foot down hard on the brake. One of the long flowing ends of her scarf had become caught up in the spokes of the wheel and she was being strangled! He began to yell for help and to tear the scarf loose. The commissionaire, who was an ex-army man, rushed to his aid. Within seconds and by sheer brute force they had wrenched the scarf clear and loosened it from round her throat but her face was a pale mauve colour, her eyes were closed and she was fighting for breath.

'For God's sake, get a doctor!' Charlie yelled at the man.

'A doctor will be no good, sir, it's hospital she needs and quick. Take her to the Countess of Chester's Hospital. You can't miss it!' the man yelled after the rapidly disappearing car. It had only taken a few seconds, one turn of the wheel, but it had almost cost the poor woman her life, he thought as he dispersed the small group of people who had gathered and went back to his post.

Chapter Twenty-Nine

Charlie sat in the waiting room with his head in his hands. He was close to despair and wanted no one to see the tears in his eyes. He'd nearly killed her. Why the hell hadn't he checked that that damned scarf wasn't trailing? It was all his fault. He should have driven down last night. She'd have been at home. Safely at home. He could have explained properly, calmed her down, reassured her.

There had been a time when he'd thought David *had* fallen for her, but when he'd deliberately picked an argument with him to find out, David had told him that what he felt for Alice was admiration. He did feel a certain amount of affection for her, nostalgic affection for the waif who, against all odds, had become a star, but she wasn't going to form any part of his life, that belonged to the sea. Cecelia knew that, so he'd assumed that Alice knew it too. But she hadn't.

'Mr Williamson?'

Charlie looked up at the grim-faced woman dressed in dark blue with the stiffly starched apron and cuffs, a starched and intricately pleated cap covering her hair.

He stood up. 'Can I see her, please? How ... how is she?'

'She's comfortable.' The tone was crisp.

Charlie's taut nerves snapped. 'What the hell is that supposed to mean?'

'Mr Williamson! Control yourself. I will *not* stand for such language!'

'I'm sorry, Sister, please forgive me, but I'm so worried.'

'She is just that. Comfortable. She's been very lucky indeed. She won't see you, I'm afraid. Has she relatives? Mother, father?'

'No, neither. Her sister and brother-in-law are her closest relatives. He's a policeman,' he added, thinking it might be useful.

'Right then, and how do we contact them?'

Charlie tried hard to concentrate, to collect his thoughts, to remember. There was a phone at the house in Media Street but they'd all be out, Agnes and Jimmy at work and Eddy and Mary at school. There was no phone at Jack's house. 'I think the local police station is Rose Hill, Liverpool. If Constable Phillips isn't there, then maybe someone could go to his home. It's in Media Street, Liverpool, but I don't know what number.'

'Thank you. And now I think the best thing for you to do is go home.' Sister's eyes were steely; she had no time at all for this irresponsible generation who tore around the country in their flashy motorcars.

Charlie nodded miserably. If Alice wouldn't see him, there was no use in staying. 'But she *is* all right?' He looked pleadingly for confirmation.

Sister nodded.

'I'll phone later on, or perhaps tomorrow.'

In reply he got a curt nod before the woman turned and walked away.

Alice lay in the hospital bed dazed, slightly dizzy and weak. When she'd arrived they'd put a mask over her face which had made breathing easier, but her throat felt as though scalding hot water had been poured down it and her neck hurt. They'd been very good to her, although she didn't remember being driven here, she must have passed out. After the doctor had gone, Sister had asked her if she wanted to see the young man who was waiting outside. She'd shaken her head vehemently.

They'd given her some medicine and she drifted in and out of sleep for the rest of the day. Then when she'd woken properly it was dark, the lights had been switched on and Lizzie and Jack were there. A sob made her catch her breath but she reached out and Lizzie took her hand and held it tightly.

'Oh, Alice! Alice! You gave us a terrible fright! It's taken hours to get here and all the way I've been in such a state.'

Tears welled up in Alice's eyes.

'I'm going to go through every bloody book I can lay my hands on to see if there's anything I can charge that bloody lunatic with!' Jack's expression was grim.

Alice shook her head. It really wasn't Charlie's fault. She'd been so upset, she'd rushed out – but she didn't want to think about that now. She didn't want to think about either Charlie or David Williamson.

Lizzie stayed holding her hand tightly while Jack went in search of the doctor and the ward sister.

The fact that he was in uniform seemed, to a certain degree, to impress them both.

'I'd like to know exactly how my sister-in-law is, sir, if you don't mind.'

The doctor frowned. 'She's very, very lucky, that's how she is. She could have broken her neck. She has a very badly bruised larynx, in fact the whole throat is bruised and swollen and there's a slight strain. That's due to the force with which the head was jerked suddenly and violently backwards.'

Jack looked concerned. 'When can she come home?'

'Tomorrow, I think. She's had a sedative for the shock and should sleep tonight. There's nothing more we can do, it's just a matter of time. Time will reduce the swelling and the bruising but she mustn't even try to speak for at least five days.'

'Thank you, sir.'

The doctor turned away and Jack addressed Sister. 'I'll arrange transport, ma'am.'

'I'd telephone first, but I'd say she should be discharged at about noon.'

Jack thanked her and went back to relay the information to Lizzie and Alice.

After Lizzie and Jack had gone, Alice lay awake staring blankly at the blind that covered the window on the far side of the ward. Tomorrow she could go home, but where was home? Her cottage in Saltney Ferry or the house in Media Street?

If she went to Media Street, would she get any rest with everyone in and out at all times of the day and night and with Mary, Ethel and Jinny calling in too? On the other hand she'd have company, she wouldn't have much time to brood. If she went to the cottage she'd have all the time in the world to rest, but she would spend all day thinking, thinking about things she wanted to forget. Eventually she fell asleep, the dilemma unresolved.

She felt better the following day. Less dazed, less shocked, although her throat still felt as though it was on fire. She was instructed to drink as much as possible, although nothing that contained citrus like orange juice, and tea was only to be drunk when it was tepid. She must eat only soup, blancmange, semolina pudding and the like, but she didn't feel like eating anything. She just wanted to go home.

Jack and Lizzie arrived at noon. Jack had managed to persuade the inspector at Seel Street, the police garage, to lend them a car for a few hours. It was an emergency, he'd explained. Once he'd mentioned Alice's name there was no problem. The inspector's wife was a great fan.

'Alice, luv, do you want to go to the cottage? I'll stay

362

with you for as long as you need me. Or do you want to come home, to Liverpool, to Media Street? I'll only be up the road and our Agnes is very capable. They're all out of the house for most of the day and I'll keep any visitors away until you feel up to seeing them. The cottage?'

Alice shook her head. No, it wasn't really home. It had never had that special feeling; she hadn't really spent much time there at all and now she never wanted to go back. Someone could go and pick up her things and Georgie and then she'd sell it. Home was where her family were.

Lizzie looked relieved. She had talked to Jack about it all and they'd agreed that Lizzie would stay with Alice at the cottage but she hadn't really relished spending all her time stuck out in the country.

Jack was given a list of instructions by Sister while Lizzie helped Alice dress, then he guided them outside to the parked car.

'Where did you get the car, Jack?'

He helped both Alice and Lizzie in. 'I borrowed it from the police garage. Oh, it's all right, it's on loan for a few hours. I'll drive you home and then take it back.'

After she had sipped the concoction the hospital had given her, Alice went straight to bed.

'Our Agnes has warned them she'll murder them all if they come in banging doors and clattering up and down the stairs, so you try and sleep,' Lizzie told her. 'And I've told Mary O'Hanlon, Ethel Maguire and Jinny Thomas that you are not to have any visitors for a week. Those were the hospital's instructions. I've also told Agnes and the others that if that Charlie Williamson phones, to tell him to clear off – politely.'

By the end of the week Alice felt better. At least, she was over the shock, the pain in her neck had eased and her throat was not so sore. She'd said a few words to

Lizzie, telling her briefly what had happened. It had been awfully hard to stop herself speaking. Even more so because she wanted to pour out to Lizzie all the pain and heartache. How hurt and miserable she was.

Their old neighbours came, en masse, after church on Sunday and expressed their concern and sympathy.

'We've all said an extra decade of the rosary every night for yer, Alice, luv,' Mary informed her. 'An' they've said prayers in the school too.'

'An' I went to Benediction yisterday an' all,' Ethel announced. 'I told my lot they could all fend for themselves for an hour. "Get yer idle, useless da ter make yer tea," I said. Well, yer should 'ave seen the gob on 'im! Off down the pub like a shot he was!' Ethel shrugged. 'But yer comin' on great now, Alice. So your Lizzie tells us.'

'You were dead lucky, Alice. I reckon it was yer mam watchin' over yer,' Jinny said sagely and with deep conviction.

Alice thanked them but when they'd gone she burst into tears.

'Alice! Alice, stop it! You're not supposed to get upset!' Lizzie put her arms round her sister and held her close. 'Why the hell did Jinny Thomas have to go and say something like that?'

Alice leaned her cheek against Lizzie's shoulder. 'Oh, Lizzie, I miss her so much.'

'I know, we all do. I'll tell you one thing though, if she'd been here, this wouldn't have happened. She'd have given that Charlie a right tongue-lashing and told him to clear off at the start.'

'It wasn't his fault, Lizzie.'

'Of course it was!'

Alice was quieter now. 'No, I ran out of the Grosvenor without my coat, hat or anything. I . . . I was too upset, I didn't know what I was doing.'

'Alice, hush, you mustn't talk too much yet. Not until you've seen the specialist next week.'

'He told me that . . . that . . . David has got engaged. He's going to . . . to . . . marry someone else. Her father's a captain.'

Lizzie didn't reply. She wanted to say that it really didn't come as a surprise to her. David Williamson had shown no romantic interest in Alice at all and she'd told Alice so. It was all a fantasy Alice had built up in her mind.

'Oh, Lizzie, I hate them! I hate them all. The whole bloody family!'

Lizzie smiled at her. 'That's better. That's more like the Alice I know. And I agree. They wouldn't let you over their doorstep, Alice, no matter how well-dressed or how famous you were. That Charlie never took you home, did he? You'll get over it. I did. It was awful after poor Tommy was killed, I had nothing to live for, but life had to go on. Mam needed me.'

Alice managed a weak smile. Lizzie was right. She had been walking out with Tommy Mac and she'd known he loved her. It must have been much harder for Lizzie.

As she walked back up the street towards home, Lizzie was relieved. Alice seemed to be over the worst. She'd survive, and without the bloody Williamsons. This was her home and she was surrounded by people of her own class who really cared about her.

Alice's appointment with Mr West at Rodney Street, the Harley Street of Liverpool, was at ten o'clock the following Friday and Lizzie went with her.

They were shown into a magnificent Georgian house and into a room with deep sash windows, highly polished floor, Arabian rugs, antique furniture and deep, comfortable chairs. The receptionist was very pleasant, explaining that Mr West was running a little late but that they wouldn't have long to wait.

Alice felt quite calm now. Her throat was still a little sore if she talked too much but she'd had enough time to think over what Lizzie had said. The affection she'd thought David Williamson had for her *had* been a fantasy. He'd been bound up in her dreams for years. The pathetic, idiotic idea that she loved him had been born the day he'd carried her aboard the ship and had stirred her emotions, emotions that had grown and become deep-rooted in her mind. It still hurt her terribly to think about him and she seemed to see his face everywhere, but Lizzie told her firmly to put him out of her mind. Now she must concentrate on her career. Hadn't there been some talk of her making a gramophone record?

'Miss O'Connor, would you follow me, please?' The receptionist's voice broke her reverie.

Lizzie gave her a smile and a nod of encouragement and settled down to wait.

Mr West was a tall, thin, distinguished-looking man with silver-grey hair, a goatee beard and gold-rimmed spectacles. He was studying notes in a brown folder when she was ushered in.

He smiled. 'Please sit down, Miss O'Connor.'

Alice sat while he referred to the notes again and then gently felt her throat. He asked her to swallow hard several times, then to repeat a rhyme and read a paragraph from a book.

He nodded. 'Good. You're progressing, Miss O'Connor. The swelling and the bruising have almost gone.'

'When will I be able to sing again, Mr West?'

He looked at her with mild astonishment. 'Sing?'

'Yes. It's my career. I . . . I . . . was quite well known in London. I starred in musical stage shows.'

He looked at the notes in the folder again and then looked directly into her eyes. 'Miss O'Connor, it would be very cruel and unprofessional of me to lie to you, but you will never sing again. The vocal cords have been too badly damaged. You do realise that you were being strangled and could have died? You were very lucky.'

She stared at him, stunned, not fully understanding the importance of his words. 'I'll ... I'll ... never ...'

He shook his head and then pressed a button on the wall.

The receptionist appeared.

'Would you bring Miss O'Connor's sister in, please?'

The colour drained from Lizzie's face when she saw Alice. Alice was sitting like a statue, so still, so pale and in what appeared to be a state of deep shock.

'I'm Mrs Phillips, sir. Her sister.'

'I'm terribly sorry but I have had to give your sister some very bad news. I had no idea that she was on the stage.'

'What is it?' Lizzie asked in a hoarse whisper, her eyes never leaving Alice's face.

'She'll never be able to sing professionally again. Maybe in years to come a verse or two at a family get-together, but not on the stage. Her voice would go completely and the damage would be irreparable.'

Lizzie's hand went to her mouth to stifle the cry. Oh, Holy Mother of God! She'd thought that Alice was going to be fine, that she'd be given the all-clear to return in a month or so to her profession and she'd forget David and Charlie Williamson.

Mr West suggested that when they got home Lizzie should call their local doctor who would administer a sedative for the shock. He was extremely sorry to have had to impart such bad news, but it had been necessary, unfortunately.

Lizzie thanked him and led Alice out and hailed a taxi. All the way home Alice didn't say a word and her hands were as cold as ice.

Lizzie stoked up the fire in the parlour and was about to phone their doctor when Alice stopped her.

'No, Lizzie. I don't want to be drugged. I don't want to live in a half-dazed world.'

Lizzie immediately went to her side and held her closely. 'Alice, it'll be for the best.'

'No it won't! Oh, Lizzie, I promised Mam I wouldn't waste my gift, and now I have!' The tears were spilling down her cheeks. 'She . . . she said to me just before she died, "The Lord giveth and the Lord taketh away." I . . . I . . . had everything I'd ever wanted, Lizzie, except for *him* and that wouldn't have worked out. I know that now. But I wasn't satisfied. I wasted it. I threw it all away because I'd forgotten who I was and where I came from.'

'Alice, stop that, it's nonsense! I won't have you talking like that. Mam was proud of you and she'd have understood.'

'No, Lizzie, she wouldn't. She knew me too well, she was warning me. It was pride, and vanity, and wanting something I couldn't have, and now . . . now there's nothing.'

Lizzie drew away and gently pushed Alice down onto the sofa and took her hands. 'You *do* have someone, something, left out of all this mess, Alice.'

'What? Who?'

'Mike. Mike O'Farrell, and he loves you, Alice. He always has done. He told Jack.'

Alice shook her head. 'No, Lizzie, he was just fond of me.'

'It was – is – more than just fondness, Alice! For God's sake, don't be so blind and stupid again! Why do you think he left America and came back to Ireland? It was to be nearer to you if you ever needed him.'

Alice stared at her uncomprehendingly.

'It's the truth, Alice. You can ask Jack. Mike's loved you since the day he first met you.'

'Then why . . .?'

'Because he's a proud man, Alice. He's older than you

368

and you once told him if you'd had a choice of fathers, you'd have picked him. How do you think he felt then and would feel later on if he told you he loved you? And not like a father loves a daughter. Or should do,' she added grimly, thinking of their own father in Walton Gaol. 'He's afraid of rejection, of you thinking him an old fool. He'd marry you tomorrow, Alice. For God's sake don't throw away your hopes, your life, the way I did before I met Jack! Don't just give up, Alice!'

'I didn't know, Lizzie. I just didn't know. I walked out on him. I ... I ... can't go to him now, like this, with nothing.'

'Alice, you can't sing but that won't matter to him. You're alive, you're young, you're beautiful. He loves you. He won't want anything more.'

Alice dropped her head. 'No, Lizzie, I can't. I just can't expect him to pick up the pieces. To take ... second best.'

Lizzie stood up and, shaking her head, left Alice on her own. She knew what she was going to do.

Alice sat rigidly still. She couldn't take it in. She was still reeling from the shock of her visit to Mr West and now Lizzie was telling her that Mike loved her. That he'd always loved her.

She thought back to her years in Charleston. He'd taken her away from India's. He'd saved her from becoming a whore. He'd given her everything because he'd loved her and he'd asked nothing in return. She remembered his smiles of encouragement and pride but behind those smiles had been love. A love that had endured everything. He'd stood back and watched her at the ball with David Williamson. He'd smiled and been polite when all the time his heart must have been torn with jealousy. And that night she'd left him. Then at Lizzie's wedding he'd asked her if it made her think of other marriages and she'd been flippant. Oh, he'd hidden his feelings well, very well.

As she laid her head on her arms and began to sob,

deep inside were the first stirrings of realisation and love. An awareness of the fool she'd been. She'd had to lose everything before she could realise what really mattered. That Mike loved her and she loved him. Not a wild fantasy love but a quiet enduring love, and now it was too late, she could never go to Mike like this, when that great gift, her talent, had gone.

As the days passed, Alice became listless and depressed. She was tired of being brutally honest with herself, looking deep inside herself, searching for the girl she used to be and longing for the time, those few short weeks, when with Mam they'd moved here to this house. She'd been happy then, really happy, but she'd also been happy in Charleston. Confident and glad to be known as Mrs O'Farrell, the young, beautiful and talented wife of the wealthy Mike O'Farrell. She knew she'd been envied by so many of the people they'd mixed with. But all that had happened before the *Aquitania* had docked on that fateful day.

Her heart was aching with misery and loneliness, despite being surrounded by family. Most mornings it was hard to get up but soon she would really have to make an effort to pull herself together, but she was so weary, so very weary.

'Are you going to stay in that dressing gown all day, Alice? It's ten o'clock.' Lizzie's voice was sharp.

Alice had her head in her hands and didn't look up or answer.

'There's a package arrived for you.'

'A package?'

At last Lizzie saw some interest, some animation in her sister's eyes as she handed over the small brown paper parcel. 'It came by registered post to our house.'

Alice stared at it. There were foreign stamps on it. Irish stamps.

370

'Well, open it. I'm dying to see what's in it.'

Alice tore off the paper to reveal a velvet-covered box and a folded piece of notepaper. She opened the box slowly. Inside was a brooch. A very beautiful brooch in the form of a peacock. Its tail was spread wide like a fan and was studded with diamonds, emeralds, rubies and sapphires; its body was gold and blue enamel.

'Oh, Alice, it's gorgeous! It's a peacock! Jack and I saw them in the botanic gardens on our honeymoon. They were beautiful.'

'They are, but . . . but they can't sing, Lizzie. They can only make a horrible screeching noise.' She laid the box down on the table and turned the folded piece of paper over in her shaking hands. Had Mike heard? Was he being cruel? Was this his way of trying to hurt her? If it was, it was all she deserved for the years of pain and anguish she'd caused him.

'You read it, Lizzie. I . . . I can't.'

Lizzie opened the note.

'What does he say?'

'It's not a letter, Alice. It's a song, or a few lines of one.'

'Read it!' Alice's voice was strident. She wanted to know how he felt; she wanted to know the worst.

But come ye back, when summer's in the meadow,
Or when the valley's hushed and white with snow,
For I'll be here, in sunshine or in shadow . . .

Lizzie fell silent; there were no more words, there was nothing else to read. She gently lifted Alice's chin and looked into the brown eyes that were swimming with tears. 'For God's sake go to him, Alice. Forget your pride, go to him!'

371

Epilogue

The pale sunlight of that early spring morning sparkled on the grey-green water of the bay and washed over the harbour at Dunlaoghaire and the mail boat that had just docked.

As the passengers began to disembark, he scrutinised their faces, but it was the sunlight sparkling on the stones of the brooch she wore on the lapel of her coat that finally caught his eye. Then it fell on the tears on her cheeks as she ran to him and he caught her and held her in his arms.

'Oh, Mike, I've been so stupid! I . . . I . . . never realised. I never realised that it was you I loved.'

He held her away from him and smiled into her eyes. A smile full of love and happiness. 'That doesn't matter. You're home now, alanna. We're both home.'

He kissed her gently on the lips and she clung to him.

'For better or for worse, in sickness and in health, till death do us part, Alice. Mrs Alice O'Farrell. And this time it will be legal and sanctioned by God and man.'

The Liverpool Matchgirl

by

Lyn Andrews

Liverpool, 1901. The Tempest family is all but destitute, barely able to put food on the table. When Florrie falls ill with pneumonia and Arthur is imprisoned after a drunken fight, their thirteen-year-old daughter Lizzie finds herself parentless, desperate and alone.

Despite her young age, Lizzie has spirit and determination. In a stroke of luck, she gets a job in the match factory, and foreman George Rutherford takes her under his wing. A new home with the Rutherfords promises a safe haven, but the years ahead will be far from trouble-free. And when Lizzie gives her heart, how can she be sure she has chosen a better man than her own father?

Available now from

HEADLINE

Liverpool Sisters

by

Lyn Andrews

It is 1907 in bustling Liverpool. Thanks to their father's success, sisters Livvie and Amy Goodwin are moving to leafy Everton. But tragedy strikes when their adored mother Edith dies in childbirth. The girls are still missing Edith every day when Thomas introduces their new stepmother-to-be – a woman just a few years older than Livvie.

Thomas is an old-fashioned man, who expects to make the important decisions in his daughters' lives. He plans for Livvie to marry a wealthy neighbour's son – not Frank Hadley, the kind and handsome factory manager Livvie is attracted to. Livvie's relationship with Frank is a dangerous enough secret, but her interest in the Suffragettes could drive Thomas to the edge.

For the Goodwin girls, the happy future they once took for granted is far from certain . . .

Available now from

Headline

Heart and Home

by

Lyn Andrews

Cathie Kinrade is all too used to hardship. Growing up on the
Isle of Man in the 1930s, she sees her da set sail daily on
dangerous seas while her mam struggles to put food on the
table. Cathie has little hope for her own future, until a chance
encounter changes her fortunes for ever.

Fiercely determined, Cathie leaves for Liverpool, a bustling
modern city full of possibility. With a lively job as a shop girl
in a grand department store, and a firm friend in kind-hearted
Julia, Cathie has found her niche.

But the discovery of an explosive secret could put everything at
risk. And when love comes calling, Cathie's new friends fear
that she may be set to trust the wrong man with her heart . . .

Available now from

HEADLINE

Lyn Andrews

'An outstanding storyteller' *Woman's Weekly*

Now you can buy any of these bestselling books from your bookshop or direct from Lyn's publisher.

To order simply call this number: **01235 827 702**
Or visit our website: **www.headline.co.uk**